THE JANE SEYMOUR CONSPIRACY

The Marquess House Saga
Book Four

Alexandra Walsh

SAPERE
BOOKS

THE JANE
SEYMOUR
CONSPIRACY

Published by Sapere Books.

24 Trafalgar Road, Ilkley, LS29 8HH,
United Kingdom

saperebooks.com

ISBN: 978-1-80055-487-0

To Imad, my other brother
Love you loads

DRAMATIS PERSONAE

Marquess House

The Woodville Rivers Family:

Dr Perdita Elizabeth Woodville Rivers, now Mackensie, Marquess of Pembroke

Piper Eleanor Woodville Rivers (Piper Davidson), Viscountess Severn

Mary Fitzroy — Grandmother of Perdita and Piper. (Deceased)

Hector Woodville — Mary's husband. Father of Louisa. (Deceased)

Louisa Woodville — Daughter of Mary Fitzroy. Mother of Perdita and Piper. (Deceased)

James Rivers — Father of Perdita and Piper. Husband of Louisa. (Deceased)

Cecily Fitzroy — Mary's sister, mother of Randolph Connors

Lettice Hawkland — Ancestor of Perdita and Piper

Lady Pamela Johnson — Long lost family member

Brad Johnson — Lady Pamela's husband

The Mackensie Family:

Dr Christopher 'Kit' Mackensie — Perdita's husband. Works for both his family's company, Jerusalem, and is being to trained to take over from his father, Alistair, running Marquess House

Alistair Mackensie — Father of Kit, Stuart and Megan. Husband of Susan. Owner of Jerusalem and integral to the running of Marquess House

Susan Mackensie — Mother of Kit, Stuart and Megan. Wife of Alistair. Integral to the running of Marquess House

Stuart Mackensie — Middle Mackensie child. Works for Jerusalem

Megan De León — Eldest Mackensie child. Runs Jerusalem from the family home in Andorra

Pablo De León — Megan's husband. Works for the Andorran government

Joseph De León — Megan and Pablo's son

The Black Family:

Callum Black — Piper's partner. Younger son of Deborah Black

Dr Deborah Black — Mother of Elliot and Callum. Chief Librarian and Archivist at Castle Jerusalem

Elliot Black — Eldest son of Deborah Black. Pilot of the Jerusalem planes

Samantha Carver (Sam) — Wife of Elliot Black. Pilot of the Jerusalem planes

The Marquess House Team:

Jenny Procter — Chief Librarian and Archivist at Marquess House. Distant cousin of Alistair Mackensie

Stephanie Mullins — Jenny's new assistant

Cora Freeman — Kit's new assistant

Sir Stephen Haberfield — Head of MI1 Elite

Gary Ashley — Haberfield's assistant. Responsible for Marquess House's protection

Warren Dexter — Perdita's ex-fiancé. Works for MI1 Elite

Sarah Eve — Head of Catering and Events at Marquess House. Godmother of Perdita and Piper

Alan Eve — Sarah's husband. Former Head of Security, now semi-retired

Billy Eve — Eldest son of Sarah and Alan. In charge of building maintenance and architecture at Marquess House

Larry Eve — Younger son of Sarah and Alan. Head of Security, referring to his father while he learns the job

Mark Llewellyn — Head of The Dairy.

Briony Llewellyn — Runs the Louisa Woodville Trust, the animal sanctuary based at Home Farm, the childhood home of Perdita and Piper

Nicola Weaver — Historian and member of Nympha

The Connors Family:

Randolph Connors — Son of Mary Fitzroy's sister, Cecily Connors

Lady Marianne Connors, *née* O'Rourke — Estranged wife of Randolph Connors and mother of Xavier Connors

Xavier Connors — Son of Randolph and Marianne Connors. Second cousin to Perdita and Piper. Father of Ruby and Pearl Connors

Amber Connors, *née* Prust — Xavier's wife. Mother of Ruby and Pearl Connors

Ruby Connors — Elder twin. Daughter of Xavier and Amber Connors

Pearl Connors — Younger twin by half an hour. Daughter of Xavier and Amber Connors

The Tudor Court

Henry VIII — King. Famous for his tangled love life

Jane Seymour — Third wife of Henry VIII. Mother of Edward VI. Daughter of Sir John and Lady Margery Seymour. Died twelve days after Edward's birth

Anne Boleyn — Henry VIII's second wife, mother of Elizabeth I. Daughter of Thomas Boleyn and Elizabeth Howard.

Executed for treason

Katherine of Aragon — Henry VIII's first wife, mother of Mary I. Daughter of Isabella I of Castile and Ferdinand II of Aragon. Died at Kimbolton Castle in Cambridgeshire

Prince Arthur — Elder brother of Henry VIII, first husband of Katherine of Aragon

Princess Mary — Daughter of Henry VIII and Katherine of Aragon

Lady Margaret Douglas — Niece of Henry VIII. Daughter of his elder sister, Margaret Tudor

The Seymour Family:

Sir John Seymour — Father of Jane Seymour

Lady Margery (Wentworth) Seymour — Mother of Jane Seymour

Sir Edward Seymour — Eldest son of John and Margery Seymour

Catherine Filliol — First wife of Edward Seymour. Had an affair with her father-in-law, John Seymour

Anne Stanhope — Second wife of Edward Seymour

Sir Henry Seymour — Second son of John and Margery Seymour

Barbara Wolfe — Wife of Henry Seymour

Sir Thomas Seymour — Third son of John and Margery Seymour

Elizabeth Seymour — Daughter of John and Margery Seymour. Married three times: Sir Anthony Ughtred, Gregory Cromwell, 1st Baron Cromwell and John Paulet, 2nd Marquess of Winchester

Dorothy Seymour — Daughter of John and Margery Seymour. Married twice: Clement Smith of Little Baddow, Essex and Thomas Leventhorpe of Shingle Hall, Herts

John Seymour, the Younger — Son of John and Margery Seymour. Died young

Anthony Seymour — Son of John and Margery Seymour. Died during the Sweat in 1528

Margery Seymour — Daughter of John and Margery Seymour. Died during the Sweat in 1528

Mrs Doddy — Jane's former nursemaid

The Boleyn Family:

Thomas Boleyn, Earl of Wiltshire — Anne Boleyn's father. Disputed Earl of Ormond

Elizabeth (Howard) Boleyn — Mother of Thomas, Henry, Mary, Anne and George Boleyn. Sister of Thomas Howard, Duke of Norfolk

Thomas Boleyn Jnr — Eldest son of Thomas and Elizabeth Boleyn. Died either as a child, in his early twenties or early thirties. He divides opinion

Henry Boleyn — Second Boleyn son. Died either as a child, in his early twenties or early thirties. He divides opinion

Mary Boleyn — Elder sister of Anne Boleyn. Mother of two of Henry VIII's illegitimate children

William Carey — Mary Boleyn's husband

Kathryn Carey — Mary Boleyn's daughter

Henry Carey — Mary Boleyn's son

George Boleyn, Viscount Rochford — Youngest Boleyn brother. Trainee diplomat. Executed for treason

Jane (Parker) Boleyn, Viscountess Rochford — George Boleyn's wife

Elizabeth Wood, Lady Boleyn — Aunt by marriage to Anne Boleyn. Married to James Boleyn, younger brother of Anne's father, Thomas

James Butler, 9th Earl of Ormond — Suggested as a husband for Anne Boleyn. The betrothment was annulled when Henry VIII fell in love with Anne

Lady Joan Fitzgerald — Married: First: James Butler, 9th Earl of Ormond. Second: Sir Francis Bryan

Piers Butler, 8th Earl of Ormond — Father of James Butler

The Bryan Family:

Sir Francis Bryan — Cousin of Jane Seymour, Anne Boleyn and Mary Boleyn. Friend of Henry VIII. Known as The Vicar of Hell

Lady Elizabeth (Bryan) Carew — Sister of Sir Francis Bryan. Wife of Nicholas Carew. Daughter of Margaret Bourchier and Thomas Bryan

Sir Nicholas Carew — Husband of Elizabeth Bryan. Brother-in-law of Sir Francis Bryan

Mary (Fiennes) Norris (d. 1531) — Cousin of Elizabeth Carew through their mothers: Margaret Bourchier and Anne Bourchier. Wife of Sir Henry Norris

Sir Henry Norris — English courtier, friend of the king and Groom of the Stool. executed alongside Anne Boleyn

Philippa Spice — Long-time mistress of Sir Francis Bryan. Mother of his illegitimate son, Henry Spice

Jasper Bryan — Son of Sir Francis Bryan

Lois Bryan — Daughter of Sir Francis Bryan

The Blount Family:

Elizabeth (Bessie) Blount — Mother of Henry Fitzroy and Elizabeth Tailboys (illegitimate children of Henry VIII). Daughter of Sir John Blount and Lady Katherine Pershall

Henry Fitzroy — Acknowledged illegitimate son of Henry VIII. Duke of Richmond and Somerset. The most powerful nobleman at court after the king

Gilbert Tailboys, 1st Baron Tailboys of Kyme — Bessie Blount's first husband

Edward Clinton, 1st Earl of Lincoln — Bessie Blount's second husband

Louis Blount — Brother of Bessie Blount

Alphonso Blount — Brother of Bessie Blount

Margaret (Meg) Blount — Sister of Bessie Blount

William Blount, Baron Mountjoy — Master of the Royal Mint

Courtiers and Other Characters:

Joanna Dingley — Mother of Ethelreda Malte (illegitimate daughter of Henry VIII). Laundress in the palace

Lady Mary Berkeley — Mother of John Perrot (illegitimate son of Henry VIII). Daughter of Susan Fitzalan and James Berkeley

Sir Thomas Perrot — Husband of Lady Mary Berkeley

Lady Jane (Pollard) Stukeley — Mother of Thomas Stukeley (illegitimate son of Henry VIII). Wife of Sir Hugh Stukeley

Sir Hugh Stukeley — Husband of Jane Pollard. Knight of the Body to Henry VIII

Audrey Dingley (fictional) — Maid and friend to Jane Seymour. Sister of Joanna Dingley

Thomas Howard, Duke of Norfolk — Soldier. Close friend of the King

Mary Howard — Daughter of Thomas Howard. Wife of Henry Fitzroy

Madge Shelton — Cousin of Anne Boleyn. Lady-in-waiting to Anne. Mistress of Henry VIII

Thomas Cromwell — Right-hand man of Henry VIII

Cardinal Thomas Wolsey — Senior cleric and adviser to Henry VIII

John Fisher, Bishop of Rochester — Supporter of Katherine of Aragon and Elizabeth Barton

Lady Jane Dormer — Friend and lady-in-waiting to Katherine of Aragon

Eliza Darrell — Lady-in-waiting to Katherine of Aragon

Blanche Twyford — Lady-in-waiting to Katherine of Aragon

Lady Katheryn Parr — Lady-in-waiting to Katherine of Aragon

Lady Elizabeth Guildford — Lady-in-waiting to Katherine of Aragon

Elizabeth Barton, the Holy Maid of Kent — Prophetess and nun

Thomas Cobb — Elizabeth Barton's patron

Sister Adwenna (fictional) — Mother Superior of the Convent of Llyn Cel

Mark Smeaton — Musician. Executed for treason and adultery with Anne Boleyn.

PROLOGUE: THE TOWER OF LONDON, MAY 1536

"Who's there?"

The shadows deepened around her, but she did not move, refusing to be lulled into a trap. Waiting, watching, but no shapes materialised out of the darkness, the whisper of another's breath did not reach her ears. As her eyes became accustomed to the darkness, edges of furniture drifted into visibility, the differing patches of shadow forming into carpets, small tables, chairs, a footstool. A log broke apart on the smouldering remains of the fire, sending sparks up the chimney and making her gasp. Her eyes flickered around the room; the momentary burst of flame illuminating corners where danger might lurk, but from what she could see from her hidden alcove, she appeared to be alone.

Moving on silent feet, she edged towards the nearest tapestry. Placing her palm on the glittering threads, she pushed it back against the wall, waiting to see if it resisted, if the shape of a spy was revealed, but there was nothing. Flitting through the shadows, she repeated this manoeuvre on each hanging, not realising she was holding her breath until she released it upon discovering no one was concealed within the arras.

The cup stood on the long side table, waiting, ready, beside a decanter of sweet wine. Remembering her instructions, she reached into her pocket, removing the twist of paper. Forcing herself to remain calm, to control the tremor in her hands, she loosened the edge and tipped half of the white powder into the goblet. Returning the secured twist to the lining of her sleeve, she rotated the glass, coating the interior with the dust-like substance. Counting to ten, as she had been instructed, she hurried to the fireplace and emptied the residue of dust into the cooling embers. It flared brightly for a second, then vanished. The goblet looked untouched and, with great care, she replaced it on the waiting tray before melting back into the shadows and through the hidden door in the alcove.

A few steps into the passageway, a candle flared, and she shielded her eyes, dazzled by the unexpected light.

"Is it done?"

"Yes," she replied, her heart pounding with nerves, adrenalin pumping through her body now her task was complete.

"All we can do is wait," the other woman whispered. "We must return you to your chamber, my lady; no one must suspect you ever left."

Hurrying through the winding passage, she shivered; wanting revenge was one thing but carrying it out was quite another. When she reached the brightly-lit warmth of her own chamber, she dismissed her women and knelt at her prie-dieu to pray, wondering what lives she had saved that day.

PART ONE: MARQUESS HOUSE, 2021

CHAPTER ONE

Emerald green light spilled through the stained-glass window as the water closed over the head of Dr Perdita Rivers.

"Perds, wait!"

Dark hair swirling around her like a mermaid, she ignored the voice, diving deeper, swimming the length of the pool before surfacing in a rush of water that caused her husband, Kit Mackensie, to jump back in order to avoid a soaking.

"Morning," she said with a grin, treading water. "Did you want me?"

Kit considered her for a moment, then began to unbutton his shirt. He stripped to his swimming trunks and dived in beside her.

"Race you," he said, and set off, his front crawl slicing through the water with barely a ripple.

"Not fair," shouted Perdita, chasing him, gaining stroke by stroke until they reached the end of the pool together, laughing.

"You should have woken me," said Kit as they continued their swim at a more relaxed pace.

"I didn't have the heart," she replied. "It's been such a busy few weeks and you were fast asleep; it seemed unfair to disturb you."

"With Dad being unwell, it has been quite stressful," he admitted. "Although, I bumped into Mum on the way down here and she told me she's booked an emergency dentist's appointment for him. She's already enlisted help in case he needs to be manhandled into the car and driven there."

Perdita laughed. Kit's father, Alistair Mackensie, was in charge of running everything behind the scenes at Marquess House and was the bravest man she had ever met, except, it seemed, in the face of visiting the dentist when he was suffering from toothache. "At last," she said. "He's been in agony for weeks."

"We all have our weaknesses," said Kit with a wink. "I think the only reason he's agreed to go is because Mum gave him an ultimatum last night. She threatened to go back to Andorra without him. He daren't refuse but Mum has asked if we can have our weekly catch-up an hour earlier? She doesn't want Dad to have any excuse to wriggle out of his appointment."

"Of course," said Perdita. "Let me do a few more lengths, then I'll head back."

Kit kissed her, then hauled himself out of the pool. "I'm going to grab some breakfast," he said. "See you later."

He disappeared into the changing rooms while Perdita ducked under the water again, waving as Kit left the grotto a few minutes later. After twenty lengths of the pool, she swam towards the wide circular end, a design feature her twin sister Piper had suggested, creating a lagoon in the shallower end of the swimming pool. It was bathed in twinkling early morning sunshine and, lying back in the water, she admired the shimmering pinpricks of light on the walls as the sun rose on the spring day. The quartz in the stonework caught the natural sparks of light reflected in the tiny fragments of mirror scattered throughout the exquisite mural of mermaids that flowed around the walls.

The grotto had been an unexpected discovery three years earlier and since then it had been transformed from a forgotten Victorian curiosity to a space used and enjoyed by everyone within the walls of Marquess House. From the moment Perdita and Piper had uncovered the room with its mermaid-strewn walls and abandoned pool, they had been determined to bring it back to its former glory. For Piper, the reconstruction of the mural had been a labour of love and both twins spent a great deal of time in the delicate and magical space.

Aware time was ticking on, Perdita walked up the shallow steps, swathing herself in a large towel. She wondered how everyone would take her announcement at the upcoming meeting. Mentally crossing her fingers that they would understand, she hurried back to her room to change.

"Next is the breakdown of the petty cash..." began Alistair, and Perdita exchanged an amused glance with Kit. Having discussed this topic with him the previous evening, Perdita allowed her mind to wander as Alistair and Kit finalised the details.

They were in Alistair's office. It was now four years since she had first sat here, listening as he explained that she and Piper had inherited Marquess House, the estate that had belonged to their estranged grandmother, the historian and philanthropist, Mary Fitzroy. Alistair had explained that she and Piper were the main beneficiaries of Mary's will and, apart from a few personal bequests, they had inherited everything — her manor house, an extensive research centre and a vast fortune. They were now worth in excess of £300 million between them.

It had taken the twins a while to come to terms with their inheritance. They could not understand why their grandmother had shunned them in life — abandoning them after their mother's death when they were seven years old — yet had embraced them in death. Determined to unravel this mystery, Perdita had resigned from her university job and moved into Marquess House.

Once ensconced, she had searched her grandmother's books for clues and, to her astonishment, had discovered a trail of information left by Mary for her to find. With the help of Alistair's son, Kit, Perdita had uncovered more than she had imagined. Not only had she discovered the truth about her mother's death and the real reason Mary had stepped away from them, she also revealed an incredible but provable alternate version of Tudor history.

Perdita and Piper were now settled in Marquess House and beginning to feel more in control of their lives, their vast inheritance and the legacy bequeathed to them by their grandmother. Perdita was making full use of the research centre and extensive archive, while Piper had taken on responsibility for the art collections and the vibrant artists' studios they rented to up-and-coming talent. Kit had begun to shoulder more of his father's responsibilities, as Alistair was hinting he might like to retire within the next few years. While Piper had finally admitted to her relationship with Callum Black, Kit's best friend since childhood.

There was another change, too. On the mantelpiece in Alistair's office, the photograph of a baby boy was positioned where Alistair could see it from his desk. The previous year, Kit's elder sister, Megan, had given birth to a son, Joseph. Perdita allowed her gaze to linger on her nephew before Alistair broke into her thoughts.

"The next thing on the agenda is the storage facility in Bath," he said, wincing with pain as he turned to Piper who had added the item.

Kit threw Perdita a conspiratorial look and they suppressed their grins. Piper giggled. Alistair ignored them.

"As you know, I've been going through the art collection," said Piper, "partly because it's a long time since a full inventory has been taken, but also to try and find some interesting pieces for The Mary Fitzroy Heritage Centre. The items on show at present are superb but we have such a vast collection and so much is in storage, it seemed a good idea to rotate the exhibits as often as we can manage."

The Mary Fitzroy Heritage Centre was a project both twins had been involved with from the moment Perdita had discovered the architectural plans their grandmother had commissioned six months before her death. Mary's intention had been to convert an old tumbledown farmhouse and outbuildings that lay on the far edges of the Marquess House land into a purpose-built museum and research centre. She had felt that the vast amounts of history in the Pembrokeshire area were often neglected by scholars and she wanted to change what she thought was a huge oversight.

The museum had been open for over a year and had been a huge success. Exhibitions had included histories of local families, many of whom had loaned artefacts and paintings, while a new Victorian wing had recently opened, complete with a miniature theatre as part of one of the exhibits.

"Great idea, Pipes," said Perdita. "Is this why you've been exploring the paperwork about the storage facility?"

"Yes, but, Alistair, I was wondering why Mary kept everything so far away? There must be decent storage facilities nearby. I've discovered her collections are split between warehouses in Bath, Newcastle, London, Manchester and Glasgow."

"The Bath warehouse was owned by the son of one of the former members of staff here," explained Alistair. "He was about ten years older than me and he began the business with a small loan from the Marquess House Trust. Mary always supported these enterprises but it was also for security purposes. Spreading the collection between numerous facilities meant if anything happened to one section, there were plenty of others as back-up. However, the items you're referring to are mostly the larger pieces: paintings, sculpture, furniture. The documents, particularly those which are delicate or of a sensitive nature are, as you know, divided between the Marquess House and Jerusalem vaults, as is our collection."

"Ah," said Piper, "that would explain it. However, there is something I'd like to check. One of the vaults is listed as 'Private: Mary Fitzroy' but there's no inventory and when I spoke to the manager, he said they have no records either. Do you know what might be stored there?"

"It's unusual," agreed Alistair, "perhaps it was a private vault…"

"Mum's stuff?" the twins asked together.

Alistair gave them a sympathetic smile. "Your mother's belongings were divided up between your grandmother and your father. Her jewellery collection is listed within the Marquess House inventory."

"What else would Granny have placed in storage?" asked Perdita.

Alistair considered her question. "I really have no idea," he said. "Your grandmother was meticulous about her collections. I would suspect that rather than this being a huge mystery, it's a clerical error and the details are filed incorrectly. Would you like me to have someone look into it?"

"No," replied Piper, "I was planning to visit the various collections. Bath is the nearest and it's a beautiful city; I haven't been there for ages. As the undocumented vault is there it makes sense to go."

A knock on the door interrupted Piper, and Mark Llewellyn, the head of conservation, put his head around the door.

"Am I too early?" he asked.

Perdita waved him inside. "No, come in. Sorry Pipes; didn't mean to interrupt."

"I'd finished anyway. Depending on my workload, I plan to visit Bath soon to discover what's in this unmarked section of the storage area. I suspect it'll be nothing but as I'm trying to create a full inventory, it's important to check."

Mark had dragged up a chair and sat at an angle to the twins, a tablet balanced on his lap.

"And the final item on the list is the cleaning of the chapel," said Alistair, "which is the reason you are here, Mark?"

Mark grinned.

"Exactly," said Perdita. "We all know the chapel is cleaned regularly but the intense clean is an annual event. This year, Mark asked if we could extend it. I'll let him explain."

"It struck me there is no complete record of the friezes, carvings and decorations that feature throughout the house," Mark began. "This includes the many stained-glass windows, as well as the original features. The floor in the Great Hall is recorded in detail but, if everyone is in agreement, I'd like to put together a team to document and study the rest of the internal decoration. The mermaid frieze is unique, as are the other carvings; with the cleaning of the chapel about to begin and with the new scaffold towers, it seemed the ideal place to start. We could do a full inventory of the chapel and see if there are hidden secrets before moving on to the rest of the house."

"Fine with me," said Piper. "I've done a number of sketches and paintings of various aspects of the house and chapel, too. I'd be happy to contribute them and do a few more if you think it would be of use?"

"Piper, that would be wonderful," enthused Mark. "I also need to check the central ceiling boss."

"Is there a problem with it?" asked Alistair.

"Possibly," said Perdita. "I was in the chapel a few days ago and I took a few pictures. As you know the central boss is a Tudor rose surrounded by the mermaid who features on the walls around the rest of the house. When I zoomed in, there appeared to be a hairline crack running across the centre of the rose."

Mark passed the image which he had enlarged on his tablet to Alistair, who examined it before showing it to Kit and Piper.

"It may be a flaw in the paint," said Mark, "but we do need to check it, and this seems the perfect opportunity."

As Alistair brought the meeting to a close, the door adjoining Susan Mackensie's office to Alistair's opened. "This is your ten-minute warning, dear," she said, failing to suppress a laugh.

"It saddens me that none of you are dealing with my plight with the correct deference or showing any sympathy," said Alistair, as he closed down his computer and began shuffling away his files.

"We've been more than sympathetic for nearly two weeks," laughed Kit. "You are your own worst enemy. I'll clear up here; you go with Mum. Good luck."

Alistair left the room grumbling, while Kit locked away the more sensitive files. Mark also left, promising to email them when he had put his team together for this new project.

"Before you two leave," said Perdita, "there is one quick thing I was going to say."

"What's up, Perds?" asked Piper. Kit dropped into his father's chair.

"I've decided on my new research project."

"Which is?" asked Piper.

"While Mark and I were in the chapel the other day we began discussing the unusual iconography on the chapel ceiling." Ceiling bosses ran the length of the chapel, some decorated with flowers and mermaids, while others featured delicately carved painted faces. "It was then Mark and I thought it would be an opportune time to make a record of it with up-to-date photographs. No one has done a structural inventory of the ceiling for six years, so it's long overdue. Anne Boleyn is depicted in the fourth ceiling boss in the chapel, which is why I'm going to explore Marquess House for information on Anne Boleyn to try and discover why…"

"Are you insane?" interrupted Piper, her voice sharp with fury and fear. "With all of history spread before you, why must you delve straight back into the era we've been told to stay away from in no uncertain terms? Can't you do as Granny Mary did and change your area of interest?"

Perdita was ready for this. She and Piper had been warned to stop meddling in Tudor history by a secret branch of the government called MI1 Elite, and had almost lost their lives in their attempts to expose the secrets they had uncovered. Taking a deep breath, she spoke in her calmest voice, "Anne Boleyn has a connection to this house and I don't think it was simply because it was part of her dowry when she became Marquess of Pembroke. There's something else hidden here and I want to discover the truth."

"But Perds, why?" said Piper, her green eyes flashing with fury. "We nearly died; Kit was on his knees with a gun to his head. Why would you want to put any of us through that again?"

The image made Perdita shudder; it was one which still surfaced in her nightmares. "Kit?" She turned to her husband.

"I have to admit I'm struggling to understand your motivations," he said.

"Aren't you curious to know what really happened to Anne Boleyn? Why she's the fourth face in the chapel?"

"Yes," he admitted, "I suppose, but it seems unnecessarily dangerous. Dad and I made endless agreements to keep you both safe. Are you sure this doesn't contravene them?"

Anger was spiking through Perdita; she did not question them in the choices they made about work, and it infuriated her that both Kit and Piper felt they had any authority over her decisions.

Piper saw her expression and sighed. "Nothing I can say will dissuade you?" she asked.

"No, not this time, Pipes."

"Or me?" asked Kit.

Perdita shook her head.

Piper reached over and hugged her. "In that case, if you email me Anne Boleyn's dates, I'll keep my eyes peeled in case I come across anything in the right timeframe when I'm looking at the inventory of the art collection."

"Thank you," Perdita said.

Piper shrugged. "We stick together, no matter what," she said. "Even if I think you're deranged."

"No matter what," Perdita echoed. "Kit?"

"I'm sorry if I sounded judgemental about your decision; you have my full support."

"Really?"

"You're impossible Perdita Elizabeth Woodville Mackensie," said Kit, "but I wouldn't have you any other way."

"Actually, I'm Dr Perdita Rivers, Marquess of Pembroke."

Piper rolled her eyes making Perdita grin, then she picked up her shoulder bag, the burst of irritation between them already forgotten.

"See you for lunch?" Perdita asked as Kit prepared to return to his own office.

"Yes, when I saw Sarah earlier, she said she might set it up on the terrace if it's warm enough." Sarah Eve was godmother to Perdita and Piper and her whole family worked at Marquess House. She was head of catering and events at Marquess House, her husband, Alan, had been head of security but was now semi-retired and that role had been passed on to their son, Larry, and their younger son, Billy, was in charge of building maintenance and architecture.

"I'll let Cal know," called Piper, heading off for her studio in the vast courtyard in the old stable yard. "See you later."

Perdita glanced at her watch and turned towards the corridor leading towards the research centre where she had arranged to meet Jenny Procter, the chief archivist and head librarian, a smile of excitement creeping across her face.

CHAPTER TWO

"Hi," called Perdita as she breezed into her office in The Dairy where Jenny Procter was laying out the items Perdita had requested. Books nestled on protective cushions and, to Perdita's delight, the boxes of original research for her grandmother's books about Anne Boleyn stood side-by-side on a table to one side of the office.

"Hello lovey," called Jenny.

The Dairy was a custom-built restoration, authentication and storage facility within Marquess House which had been funded by her grandmother and Jerusalem, the vast business owned by the Mackensie family. It housed a dedicated team of conservators and other experts required for the authentication of historical artefacts, as well as a state-of-the-art restoration facility. The high-security vaults used by both companies to store their more delicate or valuable items were in this facility where access was limited.

Mary had often worked in a suite of climate-controlled offices near the restoration area when she was studying original documents. Perdita had adopted this practice too, although she had updated her grandmother's grey and blue colour-scheme to a pale green and white with new furniture and a bigger L-shaped desk, adding a huge artwork painted by Piper.

As Perdita dumped her computer bag on her office chair, Jenny said, "Anne Boleyn," her blue eyes twinkling.

"Yes, the fourth ceiling boss in the chapel, not to mention the second wife of Henry VIII, mother of Queen Elizabeth I, most famous for being beheaded on trumped-up charges of adultery and incest."

"The very same," said Jenny. "As you requested, I've collated Mary's bibliography from her two books featuring Anne and, where the primary sources are in our vaults, I've set them up in the meeting room adjoining your office. There were too many to lay out in here. However, I do think you're re-treading old ground as far as Anne Boleyn is concerned."

"Really?" Perdita tried and failed to keep the disappointment from her voice.

"Sorry love," said Jenny, "but Mary rather exhausted the information we have and there doesn't seem to be anything awry, nor do we have anything new. The primary sources in our collections, both Marquess House and Jerusalem, corroborate the accepted version of history."

"What a shame," said Perdita. "I was hoping there might be things Mary left out because her books do follow the traditional line. I wanted to re-read Granny's notes. It's always intrigued me that four women accompanied Anne to the scaffold, four loyal companions who were by her side until the end and yet, their names have been lost from history. It's a wonderful mystery."

Jenny laughed. "If anyone can solve it, love, it's you. I'll leave you to explore; give me a call if you need anything else. Your grandmother's books are on your desk, as requested."

Perdita called goodbye, a wave of excitement tingling through her. Reaching for the pile of leather-bound books, she extracted the two she required — *The Anne Boleyn Question* and *The Missing Heirs of Henry VIII*. Running her hand over the covers, she remembered the first time she had read them. It had been a surprise to discover her grandmother had used this particular set of her published works as diaries, making personal notes throughout; marginalia which had given Perdita an insight into the world and the mind of the grandmother she had never known. Kit, she recalled, had interrupted partway through her discovery on that fateful day.

She smiled as she relived the conversation, at that point unsure where Kit fitted into the structure of Marquess House. He had arrived, crashing through the door, carrying a tray of pastries and coffee, his curly hair wild and his blue eyes brimming with laughter. As he demolished an entire croissant in two bites she had asked,

"*What do you actually do here, Kit? Are you a solicitor like your dad?*"

"*Yes and no. I am a solicitor but I work for our family business, Jerusalem. The legal stuff is only one side of it. We fund archaeological digs all around the world, as well as rescuing and restoring important antiquities and documents. If they're of national interest, we either lend or donate the items to the government of their country of origin, depending on the political climate at the time. Megan runs the organisation from Andorra. She covers Africa and Asia. Stuart looks after the Americas, the Caribbean and a few other places. I do Europe, Scandinavia, Australia and New Zealand.*"

In those early days, her attraction to him had been something she had denied. The connection between them had been undeniable though.

Perdita opened *The Anne Boleyn Question* at the central section where there was a collection of plates showing various buildings connected with Anne Boleyn. Details of letters, stained-glass windows, plaques and portraits of Anne Boleyn were listed, including images of the striking 'B' pendant, which was prominent in many of the paintings of her.

As an expert in jewellery and its symbolism, Perdita had long ago investigated the history of Anne Boleyn's famous gem. Anne had owned an 'A' necklace, as well as the famous pearl rope from which the golden 'B' had hung. She had also possessed a brooch made up of her initials: AB. All three pieces of jewellery had vanished and the consensus among historians was that the pieces had been broken up and melted down after Anne's fall from grace. However, Perdita was intrigued that the young princess Elizabeth appeared to be wearing the 'A' necklace in the famous family portrait hanging at Hampton Court.

The image was one which caused much debate as it was wholly inaccurate in its representation of Henry VIII and his family. The main flaw was the central image showing Jane Seymour alongside the king, with Edward VI as a youth of six or seven. As Jane had died twelve days after Edward's birth, this was an impossible grouping. On either side of the trio were Princess Mary, daughter of Katherine of Aragon, and Princess Elizabeth, the daughter of Anne Boleyn, wearing the tiny 'A' necklace. Perdita used a magnifying glass to study the reproduction of this image before returning to the beginning of the book.

Turning to the first chapter, 'The Boleyn Women', Perdita was soon engrossed in Mary's tale of Anne Boleyn. Her grandmother's prose was readable, energetic and bulging with information. Mary treated the facts like a narrative, drawing Perdita into the sixteenth century and Boleyn family history. As she read, she reached the place she had been searching for, the explanation of the blood connection between three of Henry VIII's wives. Pausing, Perdita reached for an A3 pad and, removing a sheet of paper, she began to draw a basic outline of Anne Boleyn's family tree, which linked in Catherine Howard and Jane Seymour, wives five and three, respectively.

Anne's parents were Thomas Boleyn and Elizabeth Howard, and Perdita added Sir William Boleyn and Lady Margaret Butler, Thomas's parents, before drawing a line above

Elizabeth and writing Thomas Howard, 2nd Duke of Norfolk and his first wife, Elizabeth Tilney.

Returning to the family trees in her grandmother's book, Perdita saw that Thomas Boleyn was one of six children. Elizabeth's family was vast, comprising seven brothers and a sister, as well as a half-brother and two half-sisters from her mother's first marriage to Humphrey Bourchier. Her father's second marriage to Agnes Tilney provided Elizabeth with eleven more half-siblings. Reaching for another piece of paper she wrote them down with their dates of birth and, where appropriate, spouses. At this stage, she decided to desist from adding offspring as it would prove too distracting.

Instead, she drew lines downwards from Thomas Boleyn and Elizabeth Howard, adding the year 1498, the date scholars believed they married, before filling in the names of their known children: Thomas, Henry, Mary, Anne and George. A letter stated Elizabeth had given her husband a child every year until 1505 and there was also a memorial plaque dated to 1520 for Thomas and Henry, dividing opinions as to whether these two children died in infancy or as young men. Perdita made a note to explore it more fully, wondering if there would be anything in their archive that might provide illumination into the missing Boleyn sons.

Perdita knew two of Henry VIII's queens were first cousins: Anne Boleyn and Catherine Howard. Anne's mother, Elizabeth, and Catherine's father, Edmund, had been brother and sister, but Perdita had been less sure concerning the blood link to Jane Seymour. Another family tree showed the connection.

Elizabeth Tilney, the mother of Elizabeth Howard, had a half-sister, Anne Saye. They shared the same mother, Elizabeth Cheney, who had married first Sir Frederick Tilney, then Sir

John Saye. While Elizabeth Tilney went on to make a spectacular marriage to Thomas Howard, Anne Saye married Sir Henry Wentworth. It was their daughter, Margery Wentworth, who would go on to marry Sir John Seymour and give birth to Jane, Henry's third queen, making Jane the second cousin of Anne Boleyn and Catherine Howard.

Walking back into the boardroom where the research was laid out, Perdita opened the boxes containing the research from *The Anne Boleyn Question* and felt the usual tingle of excitement connected with examining ancient documents. When she had first moved into Marquess House, she and Kit had explored the boxes of research left by Mary and discovered a secret revealing the level to which history had been altered. Lifting the lid on the Anne Boleyn box, Perdita wondered what it might reveal. Reaching for the first folder, she turned the pages of neat handwriting, interested to see if there were clues within, hints that her grandmother had missed.

Delving further, she pulled out folder after folder, each labelled and with a brief summary and index at the beginning. Laying each one side-by-side on the long table, she felt as though she were in search of treasure. However, a few hours later, it was clear, as Jenny had suggested, there was nothing out of the ordinary.

"Last one," sighed Perdita, wondering if this was a wild goose chase when to her surprise, she saw the final folder was labelled "Jane Seymour".

"What have we here?" she murmured. "Why is there research about Jane Seymour?"

Even as she posed the question, sense caught up with her curiosity and she realised any writer discussing Anne Boleyn needed to research Jane Seymour as the two women's tenure at court overlapped. She returned to her desk in order to study the contents of the folder in more detail.

The research inside followed the same pattern as the others, beginning with a short index.

1 Jane Seymour — family tree

2 Links to Anne Boleyn

3 Early years

4 Lady-in-waiting to Katherine of Aragon

5 Lady-in-waiting to Anne Boleyn

6 Scandal at Wulfhall

7 Excerpt of letter — unknown recipient or sender — ref: JS? — illegitimate children?

Perdita stared at it in surprise. Illegitimate children connected with Jane Seymour seemed impossible. Jane was known as the quiet, mousy, dull wife. The shy creature, the perfect Tudor spouse, the contrast to Anne Boleyn's wildness. Though that had always felt a strange contradiction. The descriptions of Jane's demureness was in opposition to the descriptions of her behaviour. The suggestion of shyness and chastity did not tally with the idea of a lady-in-waiting who was prepared to perch on her sovereign's knee when the queen was pregnant, a tale that made up the narrative of Anne's fall from grace. Not to mention preparing her wedding chest while her rival was in the Tower of London facing her death. Now, here was a letter suggesting that Jane Seymour was thought to have had two illegitimate children.

Perdita rifled through the pages to extract the letter. The original was not in the folder, instead there was a photograph and a transcript which Perdita read with eagerness:

My Dear Cousin, it is with sadness I received your letter, we shall miss you at court this festive season. Preparations begin and the revels will be sumptuous once again. To cheer you in your sick bed, here is a diversion. A young lady has returned to court, accompanied by her ambitious brother. She is pious, devoted and, perhaps, a little dull. Yet, rumours follow her like shadows. It appears the king is devoted to this lady, even while the queen carries his child. Most intriguing is the king's refusal to believe the tales about Jane and her cousin, Sir Francis B. They have been close friends for many years, denying anything other than a bond of kinship despite the gossip of her supposed offspring, hidden many miles from here in a far-flung manor. My husband suspects the Seymours intend to trap the king as there are rumours that he tires of the queen…

"December 1535," Perdita murmured. "Anne Boleyn was executed on 19 May 1536 and the rumour was that Henry was casting eyes at Jane for a while before he removed Anne, so this falls into the correct time period, but who is Sir Francis B and what on earth is this about children?"

Excitement buzzed through Perdita, distracting her from her quest for secrets about Anne Boleyn. Was there a scandal about Jane Seymour that had been suppressed? Or, as was so often the case, did this letter refer to a different woman who bore the same name? It was a recurring problem when studying the Tudors. Checking the provenance of the letter, Perdita saw it was from the Marquess House archive listed as part of the private collection of Lettice Hawkland. To her frustration there was no information pertaining to where Lettice had procured it. Reading to the end of the description she noted that it had been authenticated by Mary and the document was from the sixteenth century.

"This is astonishing," muttered Perdita to herself, returning to the transcript. "I've never heard rumours like this about

Jane Seymour. It was always Anne Boleyn who was seen as the temptress, but, if this is to be believed, Jane was even wilder than Anne."

Perdita reread the letter, puzzling over the text before reaching for her grandmother's books to see if these comments had been included in any of her published work. Scouring the indices, she cross-checked every reference to Jane Seymour but, to her frustration, there was nothing concerning the letter. Perdita was so distracted by this unexpected piece of information, she barely looked up when there was a knock at the door.

"I was beginning to wonder if I'd been stood up."

"Kit, what's the time?"

"You're not late," he laughed, walking over to her and kissing her, before perching on the corner of her desk. "I finished a call and decided to run away before another one came through. Do you still fancy lunch or are you busy?"

Perdita saved her notes, then stood up. "I'm never too busy for lunch with you," she said.

Hands entwined, they made their way to the terrace where Sarah was serving a vast buffet lunch.

"I'm sorry if you thought I was being unsupportive earlier," Kit said. "It was concern for your safety, nothing more."

"Thank you," Perdita replied, as they made their way through the Lady Isabel Room to the terrace. "It means a lot to hear you say that."

"You're the most important person in my life; I want you to be happy and know you're loved."

As he bent to kiss her, a piercing whistle interrupted them. Piper was seated at the long trestle table that Sarah and her catering team had set up with Callum Black beside her.

"Oy, Lovebirds," Callum shouted, causing the smattering of people to laugh, "get a room!"

Kit raised a hand in greeting, while Perdita grinned.

"It's all legal and above aboard," said Perdita, flashing her wedding and engagement rings under his nose.

For the next hour, they discussed various aspects of their current projects. Perdita glanced over at Piper, who was once more like her old self, sparkling with happiness and confidence, the twin who was more comfortable in the limelight. Perdita was aware a great deal of this was due to her sister's relationship with Callum. Despite a shaky start, the two had become close friends before their feelings had spilled over into something more.

Stuart Mackensie, Kit's older brother, joined them. "This is very civilised," he said, waving his hand around to take in the happy hum. "It's been so long since I lived at Marquess House, I'd forgotten about all these traditions."

Kit grinned. "You'll never want to leave now you've remembered."

"Would it be a problem?" Stuart asked, looking from Perdita to Piper.

"You living here?" asked Piper.

Stuart nodded.

"Of course not," replied Perdita. "We keep telling you, this is your home too."

Stuart had been living in New York but a few months ago, he had arrived unexpectedly and asked if he could stay. "I was about to book a flight back to New York," he had explained, "and for the first time ever, it felt like the wrong thing to do."

"Why?" Kit had asked in surprise.

"It felt too far from home," he replied. "I figured it would be as easy to work from the UK as the US; after all you manage it, Kit, and Meg does it from Andorra."

"But you're an international man of mystery," Piper had teased. "Well, that's how Kit and Cal always describe you."

"True," he had grinned, "but perhaps even dashing international men of mystery suffer from homesickness."

Surprised but delighted, Perdita and Piper had suggested he take over Kit's old suite of rooms which had been redecorated when he had moved in with Perdita.

"It'll be good to have you around," Kit had said. "You've been away too long."

Since then, Stuart had divided his time between Marquess House and a penthouse apartment he had bought on London's Southbank. Three years earlier, he had been very involved with the funding and organisation of raising a wreck in the waters off the coast of Dale, a nearby village. One of his most time-consuming tasks was working closely with the team leader of the project and former work colleague of Perdita's, Dr Olaf Dade, as the wreck was painstakingly restored. Its permanent home was at The Mary Fitzroy Heritage Centre and as each stage of the project was completed, a little more of the restored wreck was opened to the public.

Stuart was halfway through telling them about the latest restoration stage when Alistair and Susan arrived. "Mum, Dad, what's the prognosis? Will you live?" he asked.

"An abscess from a broken filling," said Susan.

"I have antibiotics and when the swelling has gone down, I'll need to have the filling replaced," said Alistair.

"You've been very brave," said Perdita, her face solemn, even while her eyes danced with laughter.

"Thank you for managing not to laugh when you said that, my dear," said Alistair, a glimmer of his old humour resurfacing. "Kit, it is at your mother's insistence that I take the rest of the week off."

"Actually, it was my insistence," replied Kit. "You need a break."

When they had departed, Perdita pushed her plate away and looked at her watch.

Beside her, Kit glanced at his phone. "I'd better go, I'm expecting a call from Meg."

"Before you go," said Piper, "I thought I might visit Bath next week to look at this mysterious vault."

"No problem," said Kit, "I'll ask Cora to sort out a hotel nearby. Is it for one or two?"

When Kit had begun to take on more of Alistair's responsibilities, it had been decided he would need an assistant. Cora Freeman had been recommended. Her security-level clearance was the highest possible and her background in the armed forces meant, should it be necessary, she could double as a bodyguard for Kit, Perdita or Piper. When they had met Cora, Perdita had found it difficult to believe someone so slight could prove any sort of threat, but they had warmed to her immediately and Cora had been happy to relocate to Pembrokeshire. She had moved into a cottage on the estate three months earlier and now Perdita wondered how they had ever coped without her.

"For one, unless you wanted to come, Perds?" said Piper.

"Not really, although, if you find anything interesting — like documents — I can always join you. I can be with you in a few hours."

"Never let anything come between you and an unread document," laughed Piper.

"Nothing," Perdita replied. "What do you think might be in there?"

"Probably paintings or even years of old admin and paperwork," Piper replied, "but I'd like to know, and if it means we can free up some space, it would be useful for when we're rotating the paintings at the museum."

"How long will you be gone?"

"Two nights at most. The catalogue for this collection is meticulous. The real reason is to check this mysterious unmarked room."

As Piper disappeared back towards her studio, Perdita wandered back to The Dairy, a feeling of anticipation tingling through her at the idea of a secret room. Despite Piper's pragmatic view, Perdita could not help but hope her twin was about to make an unexpected and exciting discovery.

CHAPTER THREE

The chapel was draped in dust sheets, a thick drugget protected the floor, and all around were people in white protective suits, photographing, cataloguing, cleaning and restoring the intricate ceiling. Scaffolding towers were situated at points down the aisle, joined by a robust structure of walkways, making it possible to traverse from one end of the chapel to the other, enabling a close-up study and appreciation of the carvings and symbols above.

Perdita stood in the doorway, adjusting her own cotton covering and mask, her eyes seeking out Mark Llewellyn.

A crouched figure stood up on the central tower and waved to her. "Are you coming up?" Mark called.

"Of course. You didn't think I'd miss the big reveal, did you?"

Mark pointed to the stairway that led to the first tower and Perdita hurried up, pausing in wonder when she reached the top.

"Have you managed to persuade Kit to come up here yet?" Perdita asked as she reached Mark.

"No, even with the staircase and walkway he declined," said Mark.

Despite his love of high-octane sports, Perdita found it strange that her husband was scared of heights. "Poor Kit," she said. "He's missing a treat."

"There's no point him being up here with his eyes shut," replied Mark.

"Let's examine this hairline crack," said Perdita, her protectiveness of her husband making her change the subject.

From the moment they had discovered this potential defect, Perdita had been eager to see it up close for herself. The many carvings around the house had offered Perdita clues during her earlier research and she had written this up for Mark but this ceiling boss was something entirely new for her. Adjusting one of the arc lights on the walkway, Mark illuminated the carved Tudor rose that marked the central point of the chapel. This spectacular piece of carving was the central hub around which the pattern of the ceiling flowed.

"It's beautiful," said Perdita. "When it was first painted it must have been staggering; the Tudors did love their vivid colours."

"Tudor décor was a riot of colour. It was the Victorians who toned it all down," agreed Mark. "Look, can you see the line going across the centre. My first thought was that it was a crack in the paint as it seemed unlikely a solid piece of wood like this would split, especially in such a perfect line."

Perdita peered at the hairline crack, her eyes tracing it from one side of the rose to the other. "It's across the centre…" she began and turned to Mark. Even with his protective mask she could see by his eyes that he was grinning. "What?" she said. "You've made a discovery?"

"Look at the sides, right up here." He shone a laser pen, directing Perdita's eyes.

For a moment, she could not work out what he was showing her, then she gave a small "Oh" of surprise. "Is that a hinge?" she gasped.

"We think so," he nodded. "There's a lot of cleaning to do but we don't think this is a crack; our new hypothesis suggests this Tudor rose has a secret hidden within it and the central line is an opening."

"Mark, this is incredible," said Perdita. "Have you ever come across anything like this before?"

"No, but this isn't my area of expertise. My guess would be there is a stone boss marking the central point of the chapel and this carved wooden cover was added either at the time of building or later."

"Will you be able to open it today?" asked Perdita, enthusiasm overcoming pragmatism.

Mark laughed. "It would be wonderful but, no," he replied. "We need to document it properly before we can even begin to think about opening it. When we do, I promise you and Piper can have a front-row seat. Kit, too, if we can persuade him up here."

"Thanks Mark," grinned Perdita. "Have you discovered anything else unusual?"

"Not yet, but we've barely begun. This chapel is a work of art so no doubt there are a few more secrets to uncover. Do you want daily or weekly updates?"

"Weekly, unless of course you find something spectacular."

With a wave, Perdita wandered away from Mark, making her way down the staircase and into the heart of the chapel. Looking towards the altar, she noticed Mark had placed barriers around it, protecting it and keeping the area sacred. Perdita felt a small flutter of relief. There were burials in that part of the chapel and she had not liked the idea of them being walked over.

In the chapel porch, Perdita pulled off her protective outer layer and headed back towards The Dairy to continue her research. Despite her and Jenny's best efforts, they had discovered nothing else in the Marquess House archive pertaining to Jane Seymour. Over in Andorra at Castle Jerusalem, Callum's mother, Dr Deborah Black, who held the equivalent position to Jenny at Marquess House, had also completed a thorough search in both the Jerusalem and Marquess House storage archives but had found no documents.

Perdita wondered if the very absence of material was suspicious. When she had suggested this to Kit the previous evening, he had considered her question for a while before replying, "Part of me wants to think so, but like you, I'm beginning to wonder if we're seeing mysteries even when there aren't any."

"Perhaps the reason there is nothing about Jane Seymour is because no one involved with either organisation has ever done any research into her, therefore, there are no references? Although, why would Gran have a folder marked Jane Seymour?"

"Remember, though, Perds," he had pointed out, "your grandmother stopped writing about the Tudors around that time."

Perdita knew Kit had been avoiding reminding her that this was the time when her mother had died and the family estrangement had begun.

"Perhaps she put it all in a box and forgot about it," he had continued.

"You're right."

"When you asked Jenny for your grandmother's research into her books, it had been in deep storage in Andorra for years. It was Mary who had requested to see it not long before she died and we know that was because she wanted to update her information on Catherine Howard. If there had been anything interesting or relevant about Jane Seymour, she probably would have added to the folder you found."

"True, it's probably background for her Anne Boleyn book," Perdita had agreed, but despite logic telling her Kit's assessment of the situation was correct, her instinct was to keep searching.

Returning to her desk in The Dairy, Perdita glanced at her watch. Piper had set out for Bath early that morning in order to assess the collection in the storage facility. Almost as though she had summoned her sister, Perdita's phone pinged with a text from Piper and a photo of the storage facility.

Perdita sent a message back and settled down to work. She had gathered as many biographies of Jane Seymour as possible, which were disappointingly few. To try and flesh out Jane's movements, Perdita had asked Stephanie Mullins, Jenny's new assistant, to begin working her way through the many Anne Boleyn biographies to track Jane Seymour. Jenny had also suggested they do the same with biographies of Katherine of Aragon, Henry VIII and Jane's son, Edward VI.

"Jane is there," Perdita had said, "but she's in the shadows and we need to bring her forward into the light."

Opening her computer, Perdita pulled up her notes, continuing to convert the information she was collating into one of her vast timelines so she could see the exact chronology of Jane's life. Laying it out this way, however, was causing Perdita some consternation because, not only were there huge chunks of Jane's life unaccounted for, but also the information available was often contradictory. Perdita was curious to discover why this was the case and, in particular, where Jane could have been during these missing years.

A few hours later, there was a knock on the door and Kit arrived.

"Hello you," she said.

"Hello," he smiled. "How are you getting on?"

"Interesting," she replied.

"I know that expression," he laughed. "Do you want to tell me or is it too soon in your working theory?"

Perdita grinned. "It would be helpful."

"The dream team, back together," said Kit, settling into the chair opposite Perdita. "What have you discovered?"

"It may be nothing…" she began.

"But you don't think so," interrupted Kit.

Perdita shook her head. "Instinct tells me there is something off here," she said, "and you don't really notice the contradictions until you begin to lay them out in chronological order."

"Would you like me to make notes?"

"Maybe later, but we're not at that stage yet," she said. "Do you mind if I talk it through with you?"

"Talk away; it's the best way to find the anomalies."

Perdita ran her hands through her hair, searching her notes, then she began, "As you know, Jane Seymour was the third wife of Henry VIII, remembered as being the mother of Henry's only legitimate son, Edward VI. Jane died under two weeks after Edward's birth and is always presented as Henry's favourite wife because of the two-year gap between her death and his next marriage…"

"Which was to Anne of Cleves," interrupted Kit. "The two-year gap wasn't because the king was heartbroken though, it was because no foreign power was willing to risk the lives of any of their female relatives by marrying her to an axe-wielding maniac."

"Quite right," agreed Perdita. "Even Jane's appearance at court causes a question. Jane's main biographer claims she arrived at any point between 1527 and 1529."

"Which is quite broad," said Kit.

"Exactly. If Jane first went to court in 1527, she would have been nineteen years old when she was sworn into Katherine of Aragon's court, where her second cousins, Anne and Mary Boleyn, were adding their own elegance and sophistication to proceedings. Henry has already had an affair with Mary Boleyn, resulting in one, possibly two, children, Kathryn and Henry Carey, using the surname of Mary Boleyn's husband, William Carey."

"And were Henry and Anne involved at this point?"

"Yes, at this stage Henry was besotted with Anne, which was part of the reason he refused to acknowledge Mary's children as his own. If he claimed them, it would mean his pursuit of Anne was on even more dubious ground because in the eyes of the church she would have been seen as his sister because of his relationship with Mary. Considering he was trying to divorce Katherine of Aragon because she had been married to his brother…"

"Hypocrite is the word that springs to mind," said Kit.

"However, another of Jane's biographers suggests Jane Seymour arrived at court to serve Anne Boleyn on the earlier date of 1527. But at this point, Anne Boleyn is listed as one of the women in Katherine of Aragon's court. Anne doesn't begin to establish her own rival faction until mid-1528, when she is given a rich chamber in the gallery of the tiltyard at Greenwich. Anne's influence has been growing but this is one of the first outward signs of her increasing dominance. Jane Seymour, however, continues to be listed among Katherine's women. When the Sweat hits London in 1528, Henry sets out with Katherine in order to avoid the illness, while Anne returns to Hever Castle, her family home, where both she and her father become ill but survive."

"Where's Jane?"

"There are no records of her whereabouts until later in the year; however, the assumption is that Jane remained in Katherine's service," said Perdita. "The king is desperate to divorce, but the Catholic church disallows it, claiming his marriage is legal and binding. By December 1528, the king is becoming impatient. Anne is back at court with her own lodgings but Jane Seymour is again listed with Katherine of Aragon."

"Are you saying there were two courts of women?" asked Kit.

"Yes, there was the queen's pious Bible-reading court and Anne's racier group, where all the dancing, fun and flirting took place."

"Poor Jane Seymour; do you think she was with Katherine by choice?"

"It's what her biographer suggests but it doesn't feel right to me," said Perdita. "The King's Great Matter — as he called his divorce — drags on until 14 July 1531, when Henry and Anne quietly ride away from Windsor Castle, heading for the manor of Woodstock. This was the last time Katherine of Aragon saw Henry. He had finally made the move and left her. Again, it's assumed Jane remained with Katherine, until in November 1531, Queen Katherine of Aragon was forced to leave Henry's court and moved into a household of her own at The More in Hertfordshire. It had once been owned by Cardinal Wolsey but by then was apparently a bleak and cheerless place designed to break Katherine's spirit."

"Henry was a real charmer, wasn't he?" said Kit.

"A gent in every sense," replied Perdita. "Although, Katherine had a household of approximately two hundred people, so she wasn't exactly roughing it. What's interesting is that Jane Seymour, who until then had been one of Katherine's ladies-in-waiting, is absent from the household records. In February 1533, Katherine's household was moved to the even more remote Ampthill in Bedfordshire and still no mention of Jane. There are few surviving records from Jane's family home, so she may have returned there but I suspect not and she isn't listed in Anne's court either.

"A few months later in August 1533, Katherine was moved again, this time to Buckden where she had a reduced household of ten ladies, a physician, an apothecary and her confessor. Even Jane's main biographer admits it's unlikely that Jane was part of this household. Many historians claim that this is when Jane must have joined Anne's court, particularly as in the New Year's gifts of 1 January 1534, one of the queen's ladies who receives a gift from the king is a 'Mrs Seymour'. It's assumed this was Jane; however, if it is, then why are there no more mentions of her until two years later in 1536 when she suddenly catches the eye of the king. Historians suggest the 'Mrs Seymour' mentioned was actually Anne Stanhope, the new wife of Jane's eldest brother, Edward Seymour."

"So where was Jane?" asked Kit.

"From the records available, no one knows," replied Perdita. Before she could continue, her phone buzzed and Piper appeared on the screen.

"Perds," she said, a grin unfurling on her face. "You're never going to believe what I've found?"

"A Picasso?" laughed Perdita, beckoning Kit over.

"No, an untouched archive; boxes and shelves and drawers of documents, papers, letters," she said rotating around the room, showing Perdita the treasure within, "and this…" Piper's phone moved over a wooden box with metal fastenings. Opening it with great care, she folded back the cloth protection to reveal a bound manuscript. Perdita gasped as Piper zoomed in on the cover. The leather had darkened with age but traces of gold leaf glimmered in the light from Piper's phone. At its centre was a pentagram, each point ending in a star accompanied by a small cup. Within this was a Tudor rose with five crowned roses splaying out, aligned with the points. This was surrounded by swirling patterns and Mediaeval beasts and, across the top, the words: *The Pentagram Manuscript*.

"I think you might need to see this for yourself," said Piper.

Perdita was already reaching for the internal telephone to organise a task force to head to Bath.

CHAPTER FOUR

"This is astonishing," said Perdita as she followed Piper into the room.

Beside her, Mark and Jenny gasped in surprise. Perdita had tried to gauge the size of the archive Piper had discovered in the storage facility from the phone call but none of them had anticipated this many documents.

"Why though?" said Jenny, walking around the well-ordered room. "Why did Mary hide it all?"

Mark was already talking into his Dictaphone, detailing his first impressions.

"And you discovered this, Piper, when you were going through the catalogues of the other collections?" said Jenny in wonder.

"It was listed as 'Private'," said Piper. "There were no records with the catalogues and the manager here had no knowledge of what was inside. When he looked into it more carefully, he discovered this was a climate-controlled room and, as it was off the main facility storing the art collection, he had always assumed it was the overspill. He's kept it at the same temperature and humidity as everywhere else."

"Did his staff never check it?" asked Mark, appalled at such dereliction of duty.

"It was checked once a month but as there was no inventory, it didn't always appear on the paperwork," said Piper. "No one has visited these facilities for years; Granny and Alistair reviewed the information every year but there was no need to come in person."

"It seems Granny did her utmost to keep it hidden," finished Perdita.

"This collection is vast," said Jenny. "What on earth would have made her want to hide so much information?"

"Granny hid this three months after Mum died," said Piper. "She was suffering from grief. Perhaps it was her way of trying to move on?"

All the deaths and heartache caused by the family secrets hovered in the air, tangible, immoveable and for a moment, Perdita wondered if they were betraying her grandmother by uncovering this archive. If Mary had gone to such lengths to hide these documents, perhaps they should remain in their dark tomb. However, before she could speak, Mark's voice, hoarse with excitement, called her name.

"Perds, quick!"

He was standing to one side of the room beside a small square table, underneath which were two drawers and on top, the vast wooden box. Perdita's breath caught in her throat as the ghosts of the past disappeared with a whispering sigh and the intoxicating pull of the documents drew her in with their siren song.

"This is the one?" asked Perdita.

Piper, who was already moving towards Mark, grinned. "Yes, once I'd seen what was inside and realised the potential value of these documents, I came out and locked it back up again until the cavalry arrived."

Mark was handing out cotton gloves.

"Not wearing the full protective suit, Mark?" asked Piper, her tone innocent.

"No," he replied with dignity. "I know Kit and Cal think I wear it for fun but it's a very serious piece of equipment."

Stepping away from the box, he beckoned Perdita and Piper forward.

Perdita took several deep breaths, commanding her hands to stop shaking, her mind travelling back through all the documents she had studied since inheriting Marquess House, each one revealing a new secret, another layer of deception peeled away in order to present a different view of history, a more correct version than the one peddled in the books of academia. Would this document prove to be another piece in the strange puzzle revealing itself to her across time?

Beside her, Perdita could hear Mark holding his breath. Jenny was gripping Piper's arm as though she might faint without the support, and all eyes were on her as Perdita opened the ancient cedar box and pulled back the thick hessian cover to reveal the leather-bound manuscript.

"It's stunning," murmured Jenny, leaning forward.

"Is that gold leaf?" whispered Mark as they gazed at the unusual pentagram pattern.

"This is incredible," Perdita said. "The condition is far beyond anything I expected."

"No one has touched it for years, it's no wonder it's so well preserved," said Jenny. "Do you think it's genuine, Mark?"

Perdita stepped back and Mark peered at the cover.

"Until we've tested it, I can't tell," he said. "Mary has either hidden it here because it's a fake and she wished to remove it from circulation or it's here because it's incredibly valuable. Whichever it is, I won't know until I'm back at The Dairy."

"May I?" asked Perdita, indicating she wanted to open the manuscript.

"Of course; it won't damage it," said Mark.

Perdita opened the cover and, turning the pages with care, she gasped at the stunning illumination of five women in a stylised forest. The roses and cups from the cover were replicated around the margins and in the distance through a path in the trees was a castle with a flag depicting the pentagram from which the manuscript had gained its name.

"These are poems," said Perdita a few moments later. "Five lines each, not quite iambic pentameter. They're written in English, listen:

"Dark branches part, a path revealed as we five ride
A quest upon the final words of one so dear.
The lady, Morgan, sweet, kind, revered
Her death we now revenge with tears
Our oaths once taken, do our loyalties bind
Each one a noble grace does bear,
Our hearts are true, as we do venture
Far and wide, with one voice do cheer
Five ladies, we, of high renown,
Of noble blood and lines, our sons we hope to find…"

"Ladies?" said Jenny. "These poems are about five women?"

Perdita continued to scan the poems, photographing sections of the pages until after a few minutes, she looked up, her grey-green eyes alight with wonder. "The names," she said, showing Mark the pictures, "look at the names."

"Enid, Morgan, Nimue, Igraine and Gwenddydd…" read Mark. "These are women from the Arthurian legends."

"Do you think it's anything to do with the Arthurian ceiling in the tower at Marquess House?" asked Piper, who had spent a considerable amount of time replicating many of the images.

"Perhaps," said Perdita but she had another quarry in her sights. Turning back to the pages, scouring the images, she searched each tiny etching until at last she exclaimed, "A date!" and Mark leapt forward with such enthusiasm Perdita almost lost her balance as she moved out of his way.

"1533," he whispered, staring at the manuscript as though it were a holy relic. "Perds, if this is real, this could be the find of the century."

"If we're allowed to tell anyone about it," muttered Piper.

"In 1533, Anne Boleyn was pregnant with Elizabeth I," continued Perdita. "Katherine of Aragon had been banished from court and Jane Seymour was missing from the records."

"Jane Seymour?" said Jenny.

"We can't rule her out, Jen," said Perdita. "Granny's file contained the most extraordinary letter which was possibly about Jane."

"Do you realise, Perds," continued Mark, not listening to Perdita and Jenny's conversation, "if this is genuine, it could have been the inspiration for The Devonshire Manuscript?"

"What's The Devonshire Manuscript?" asked Piper.

"It's a series of poems written by a selection of ladies-in-waiting at Anne Boleyn's court," said Perdita. "The original is in the British Library and is bound in its original stamped-leather binding. It contains 184 poems, most of which are written in a style known as the courtly love tradition. The most interesting thing is that the manuscript has been written in nineteen to twenty different styles of handwriting, making it a huge collaboration."

"Do you have the names of any of the women involved?" asked Piper.

"At least two were written by Mary Shelton, who was Anne Boleyn's cousin," said Perdita. "Lady Margaret Douglas, the king's niece; her then fiancé, Thomas Howard, the younger half-brother of the Duke of Norfolk and Mary Howard, the Duke of Norfolk's daughter, who was married to Henry VIII's illegitimate son, Henry Fitzroy. Writing poems and creating stories was a pleasurable, as well as a competitive way of passing time for the ladies of the court. Anne Boleyn was known for encouraging these forms of entertainment."

"This is written in a similar style," said Mark, who was bending over the text. "If the 1533 date is correct, it's possible this was written at the same time, perhaps as a form of competition. Look, is that another date — 1537, I think."

"Which puts it firmly in the eras of both Anne Boleyn and Jane Seymour, as Anne died in 1536 and Jane in October 1537," said Jenny.

"Are there transcripts anywhere?" asked Perdita.

"Try the drawers," Piper suggested.

Perdita wrenched open the top one and pulled out one of her grandmother's familiar manila folders. Under this were two bound documents. Jenny held out her hands and clearing a space on a nearby shelf, she began to sort through the papers inside. In the second drawer there were several old-fashioned school exercise books.

A warm smile spread over Jenny's face. "My goodness, they bring back memories," she said. "Mary always used them when she was working out new ideas."

"Anything useful?" asked Piper, joining Jenny.

"Yes," she said, her voice full of excitement. "There's a bound, handwritten transcript, with a date — 1798 — as well as a typed version, which I assume is a transcript of the handwritten version. There's a summary at the beginning of the typed document, which from the style of type and ink I would guess to be late 1940s to early 1950s. Mary may have typed this herself."

She passed it to Perdita, who read aloud, "*An example of poems written in the courtly love tradition. The tale is largely in English and, if the dates are correct, could have been the inspiration behind Edmund Spenser's later epic poem,* The Faerie Queen, *an allegorical work in praise of Queen Elizabeth. It may also have been a partner to* The Devonshire Manuscript. The Pentagram Manuscript *is a poem following a young woman and her female companions as they quest for the sacred pentagram in order to be imbued with strong and healthy sons in the marriage bed. These sons are then described by their mothers as they perform heroic deeds, saving the land from a tyrannical king. Arthurian influences abound, drawing on the courtly love traditions of the Henrician court."*

There was silence as Perdita stared around at the others. "This is incredible," she said. "Do you think it's genuine?"

"There are very strict protocols for fakes in both Marquess House and Jerusalem," Jenny said. "Even before we had today's level of technology for authentication available, Mary was meticulous about removing any document she felt might not be genuine from the public domain…"

"But this *is* removed…" interrupted Piper.

"Not like this," said Jenny. "We have a storage area within the Jerusalem vaults and all the fakes are listed. If we have irrefutable proof they have been illegally made, then they are destroyed, no matter how beautiful. If Mary had thought this wasn't real, she would have given it to Alistair and Jerusalem. The fact she hid it suggests to me it is genuine and, whatever is inside it, scared Mary so much she wanted to bury it somewhere far away."

There was an uneasy silence.

"Do you think there are more secrets in this manuscript?" asked Perdita, her heart beginning to pound again.

"Without doubt and, all of this," said Jenny, sweeping her hand around to encompass the rest of the archive, "is somehow connected to it or to the other work Mary was doing at the time of your mother's death."

Perdita looked at Piper, who was staring around, her face pale.

"Are you suggesting all of this is information that Mary felt would be dangerous if the Secret Service discovered it existed?" asked Piper.

"This would be my hypothesis," Jenny said.

"In that case," said Piper, "I think we should box it all up and take it home to be properly catalogued and transcribed. What do you think, Perds?"

Perdita stared at Piper in surprise. "I thought you'd be the one suggesting we close the door and leave it all well alone," she said.

"Now we know we're connected to this secret, I want to understand as much as possible. It might be important," she hesitated and Perdita noticed Piper's hand flutter protectively in front of her, "later on," she finished.

"Jenny, Mark, this is your area of expertise," said Perdita, eyeing her sister with curiosity. "What do you think?"

"Piper's ordered a lorry to transport the paintings and it'll be climate controlled so it wouldn't be difficult to box this up and move it at the same time," said Mark.

"We'll have to allocate storage at Marquess House, which might take a few days to organise," added Jenny, "but there's no reason why we can't relocate the entire archive over the course of a week, maybe ten days."

Perdita beamed. "In the meantime," she said, picking up the bound typed transcript, "I'd like to read this to see exactly what we're dealing with."

PART TWO: LONDON, 1528

CHAPTER ONE

With relief, Jane Seymour curtseyed before bidding farewell to
her mother, Margery, and hurrying, fleet-footed, in the wake of
her second cousin, Mary Boleyn. Each step took her further
from the stultifying atmosphere of her family and their home
of Wulfhall to the heady freedom of the court. Even as she
rounded the corner, her mother's voice continued to issue
instructions and dire warnings but as the door shut behind her,
blocking the inner sanctum from the outer chambers, Jane
drew a deep breath and swallowed in relief. Mary threw a look
over her shoulder and grinned as she led the way towards the
sleeping quarters for the Maids of Honour.

"My mother was the same," Mary said, "when I set off for
France, she continued calling instructions as Father and I rode
away."

"You were a child though," said Jane, staring at her older,
sophisticated cousin in awe. "I'm nineteen years old."

"True, but to your mother, you will always be a child. Never
mind, Jane, I have heard she will be returning to Wulfhall later,
your freedom from parental restraint beckons," laughed Mary
as she threw open the door to the bedchamber that would
belong to Jane. "Ah, here's Anne."

A tall, slender, dark-haired woman was straightening the
embroidered counterpane on the four-poster bed while
instructing Jane's maid, Audrey Dingley, as she unpacked. The
maid smiled at Jane, who grinned back. Jane's eldest brother,
Edward Seymour, a rising star in the Henrician court and
Jane's champion in securing her a position with the queen, had
explained that Audrey was the sister of one of the laundresses,

and, according to Jane's father, had been given the position as Jane's maid as a royal favour. Jane did not understand the reasoning behind this but Edward assured her it was a compliment.

Despite this, Jane could not understand why either the king or queen would trouble themselves with the appointment of such menials, but who was she to complain? Audrey was young and helpful, a huge improvement on the fearsome creature, Mrs Doddy, who had overseen her and her sisters at Wulfhall. The woman had dogged their footsteps, halting any fun before it could begin. When Mrs Doddy had declined the offer made by Jane's mother, Margery, to accompany her to court, Jane had danced around her bedroom, delighted to be free of another layer of restriction.

Staring around her well-appointed but small room in wonder, Jane took in every detail. A fireplace dominated one wall, while panelled, carved wood covered the others. On the floor was a rug with swirling patterns and in one corner a washstand. Two chairs were arranged by the fire and beyond these a small table. A four-poster bed occupied a great deal of the remaining space, with a truckle bed at its foot for Audrey's use. Jane could not believe this would be for her, alone. Having always shared with her sisters Elizabeth, Dorothy and Margery, this space felt like a luxury beyond belief.

"Jane," said Anne, her smile wide as she walked forward to greet her, "how lovely to see you at court, at last. You must have been dying of boredom down in Wiltshire."

"Although, Wulfhall is known for its interesting trysts," said Mary, her finely plucked blonde eyebrows raised in amusement.

Jane blushed. Her brother had warned her about this but she had not expected the snide comments to begin upon her arrival. It had been seven years earlier when the tale of her father's affair with his daughter-in-law, Catherine Filliol, had filled the corridors of the court with scandalised whispers. Jane could not understand why it continued to cause such wry amusement among the extended family.

Her brother, Edward, had since disowned both his sons by his first marriage, while Catherine had been sent to a convent and the marriage annulled. Jane hesitated; her mother had given strict instructions never to comment on her father's transgression, but Margery was not here and Jane was bored with the pitying looks thrown at her whenever the topic arose. Raising her head and drawing herself up to her full height, she smiled, trying to mimic Mary's sophisticated amusement.

"Alas," she sighed, forcing laughter to bubble through her words, pushing aside the pain and humiliation John Seymour's actions had wrought with his sordid affair, "things have been very dull since Father's, er —" she hesitated with exaggerated deliberation as though selecting her words to find the most amusing — "liaison. Mother has kept us all on a tight rein."

"You're at court now, Jane, a maid of honour, life is about to become far more exciting," Anne laughed, before dismissing Audrey with a nod of her head. "Now, my dear, come here and let Mary and me look at you before you meet the queen."

"I'm going to meet her today?" Jane asked, with a thrill of mingled fear and excitement.

"Of course," said Mary, who was sorting through Jane's gowns and accessories, "as soon as we've made you decent. Your dress will suffice but your sleeves are grubby from your journey, as well as being far too workaday. Here, Jane, these are better."

Mary held up Jane's most expensive sleeves, the pair she thought would be suitable for elegant banquets. The dark blue velvet was embroidered with silver thread and tiny seed pearls, yet when she observed Mary and Anne's dresses, she realised they were encrusted with gems and golden thread, making her own feel drab. Mary and Anne's dresses were far more lavish than anything Jane had imagined wearing during the day, while around their necks were creamy ropes of pearls each suspending matching letter 'B' pendants. Three magnificent pearls hung from the base of the letter, dancing against each other and creating a musical accompaniment to the women's elegant movements.

"It's a shame we don't have a 'J' to lend you," said Mary, catching Jane's glance at her necklace. "Father gave us these as well as our initials, 'A' and 'M', he was going to have one made for Jane Parker, too, now she's married to George but it hasn't arrived yet or we could have persuaded her to lend it to you."

While they were talking, Jane found herself being tugged and twirled as they swapped her sleeves, removed her hood, smoothed back her hair and repositioned the wide gable style preferred by the queen, Katherine of Aragon, allowing a hint of her pale blonde hair to show. Anne disappeared through a side door, returning a moment later with a rope of pearls and matching earrings, which she draped around Jane's neck, while Mary attached the heavy dops to her ears.

"Much better," said Mary as the Boleyn sisters moved around Jane who was in equal measures, bemused, irritated at being treated like a country cousin and delighted at the attention she was receiving from Mary and Anne, whom she had always admired.

"Agreed," said Anne. "Are you ready to meet the queen, Jane?"

Without waiting for an answer, Anne swept from the room.

"Don't mind her," said Mary, squeezing Jane's hand as they followed, "she behaves as though she's queen of England already."

Jane did not know whether to laugh or whether this joke about the queen could be misconstrued as treason. Wiping her hands, wet with nerves, on her skirt, she decided a smile would be the easiest response.

As they glided along the corridor, the light of its flickering torches pushing against the gathering gloom of the winter afternoon, Jane listened as Mary reminded her of the etiquette of meeting the queen for the first time. Her mother, Margery, had been drilling these lessons into her for months and Jane regretted the fact she had not listened, instead allowing her mind to wander during these lectures, daydreaming about all the fun she would have when she was at court.

"This meeting will be informal," said Mary. "At this time of the day, there are often men from the king's court in the queen's rooms; in fact, the king himself might be there. He should have returned from hunting."

"The king?" whispered Jane.

"There's nothing to worry about," laughed Mary. "He won't bite. In fact, I doubt he'll even notice you."

"Of course," said Jane. "Why would he be interested in a lowly maid of honour?"

"Sweet Jane, the king is interested in all members of the court, from the kitchen boys to the highest duke in the land, it is one of his few saving graces. No, my dear, the reason he will not see you is because Anne will be in the room. He doesn't see anyone when Anne is shining like the sun."

"But you and the king…"

"All done," said Mary, her tone brisk. "My duty has been completed and my husband and I have been rewarded." Jane could hear relief, rather than bitterness in Mary's golden tones. "The king has a son and a daughter carrying the Carey name, a second royal family, to join the ranks of Henry Fitzroy, his son by Bessie Blount, should it ever be necessary. However, as Anne has taken his fancy, he can't acknowledge our offspring for fear of consanguinity — our close relationship might hinder his plans for a match between he and Anne."

"Are you saying Anne and the king are…?"

"Not at this stage, it remains flirtation."

"Does the queen know?"

"Queen Katherine ignores it, knowing that this too shall pass," Mary said, then smiled as she opened an ornately carved door, beckoning Jane into the brilliant colour of the queen's room.

A wave of noise crashed over her, jewels flashed, music played and laughter sparkled through the air. Gaping at the crowded room, Jane shuddered to a halt, staring around at the splendour, until a gentle push from her cousin propelled her forward.

"Wait by the fire while I see if the queen is free," said Mary.

Jane murmured a few indistinct words, unsure herself what she had intended to say, before edging towards Anne who was already seated beside the leaping flames. A Bible lay open, but ignored, in her lap, as she chatted with a tall man, their laughter pealing like bells through the room.

Shuffling nearer to her cousin, Jane positioned herself beside a window and, in an attempt to gather her racing thoughts, she stared out at the winter afternoon, finding peace in the fading view of the extensive gardens. The sky was turning from indigo to purple as the winter palette of greys, whites and muted greens drained into the twilight. Pinpricks of diamond-starlight glimmered like promises in the gathering night. With her composure returned, Jane withdrew her gaze from the disappearing garden and turning her glance within, tried to take in the explosion of glamour that was the court.

Light burst from golden candles in elaborate candelabras positioned on tables and plinths around the room. The scent of woodsmoke caught in her throat, accompanied by the heavy perfumes and oils anointing the skin of the courtiers. Gems flashed on sleeves, in ears and around throats, while silver and gold twinkled through the air like sylphs. Heavy tapestries glimmered in the candlelight, the metallic thread sparkling, giving an eerie sense of movement to the figures stitched within the great Biblical scenes. Wooden panelling carved with heraldic beasts and adorned with the pomegranate symbol of the queen were warm and welcoming, drawing the gathered crowd in with a sense of knowing intimacy.

From one corner came the sound of the lute adding a layer of excitement and revelry as two women and two men tried to sing a round, with more enthusiasm than success, causing laughter. Everywhere Jane turned, there was colour, life and animated conversation, yet despite the glittering bonhomie, she sensed a flutter of unease beneath the light-heartedness.

Staring around in wonder, Jane was mesmerised. Her expectation of the queen's court had been one of quiet Bible study, pious learnings and devotions. Any hopes of fun she had entertained would have been when she was away from the queen's chambers, joining her brothers, Edward, Henry and Thomas and her many cousins; to hunt, to dance. In these assumptions, she had been wrong. Within these walls were the leaders of court fashion, the witty, the sophisticated and the dangerous. A feeling of infinite possibility and anticipation rose. This was joy indeed; it was life, passion, excitement and she was at its heart.

A woman moved and a man, who had been hidden from view gave a deep chuckle, his handsome face alight with mischief as he made a comment. Jane's breath caught in her throat. *He was here.* Dropping her eyes, heat coursed through her and she cursed her flaming cheeks. Drawing in deep, calming breaths, controlling the roiling jealousy in her stomach as he placed a hand on the woman's arm, his touch familiar, she fought to compose her features, attempting to emulate the knowing smile of her cousin, Anne Boleyn.

Wondering if she dared to steal another look, she raised her eyes in one smooth sweep and, as she did, he glanced in her direction. For a moment, his face stilled, becoming as impassive and unreadable as a mask, before he registered surprise, followed by delight. Excusing himself from the woman, he turned, pushing his way through the crowd but before he could reach her side, Mary returned.

"The queen will see you now, Jane. Remember, despite what you may see around the court, modesty and a demure countenance are the key to success when you are under the queen's eye. This is a courtesy introduction, tomorrow after Prime, you will be formally inducted by the queen."

"What does that involve?" asked Jane, flustered by her encounter, yet determined to make a favourable impression on the queen.

"Nothing dramatic, the queen will discuss your beliefs and explain how she likes her ladies to conduct themselves in her presence."

Jane dropped her gaze, trying to bite back her disappointment as she wondered what restrictions would be placed on her behaviour. Swallowing her irritation at this immediate curtailment of her freedom, she could hear her mother's voice inside her head issuing dire warnings should Jane disobey, insisting the queen's rules were to be adhered to, no matter what the cost. *"It won't be like home where your father and I have been lenient, understanding and forgiving parents. The queen has high standards, young lady, you must not disgrace us or the family name..."* Jane had resisted asking whether it was possible to lower the Seymour name any further but had desisted because her father had been in the room and, for all his faults, she did love him.

Pushing her mother's dire warnings aside, Jane followed Mary to the far end of the room where Katherine of Aragon sat on a wide, padded chair, her friend, Lady Jane Dormer at her side. Jane forced her face into a shy smile. Mary sank into a deep curtsey and Jane, a few paces behind, held out her skirts and lowered herself beside her cousin.

The queen paused in her embroidering of the blackwork collars on the shirt of fine lawn she was stitching for the king. Jane's foot had turned awkwardly as she lowered herself and she hoped the queen would not leave them in the obeisance for long, it would be inopportune if she were to lose her balance and stumble.

"Your Majesty, this is Jane Seymour," said Mary. "She is our second cousin, the daughter of Sir John and Lady Margery Seymour and the sister of Sir Edward Seymour."

"Arise, my dear, you are most welcome," came the queen's quiet voice. Jane was surprised, she had expected Katherine's Spanish accent to be more pronounced but it was subtle, an echo, hinting at a lost past. "Your brother, Sir Edward

Seymour and your cousin, Sir Francis Bryan were both abundant in your praise when they requested a position for you within my court."

"Thank you, Your Majesty," said Jane, her eyes lowered.

"It was with a glad heart I heard you are a devout reader of the scriptures. Your brother claims you would often eschew dance lessons in favour of Bible study," continued the queen.

For a split-second Jane was about to laugh and utter a contradiction — she loved to dance, far preferring it to the monotony of reciting the Litany and learning her catechism — but a glance at the queen made her realise this was a serious comment. Confused, she gave another shy smile and replied in a low voice, "Yes, Your Majesty, the word of the Lord is such a comfort."

"Your wisdom is beyond your years, my dear. I wish you well while you are in my court. You shall attend Prime tomorrow."

The dismissal was gentle but firm, the direction to go to the religious service at daybreak was not something she could refuse. Mary bobbed another curtsey, which Jane imitated before they edged away, leaving the queen to resume her murmured conversation with her favourite lady-in-waiting. Following Mary through the crowd, Jane wondered why her brother had painted her as devout. Far more used to the teasing of a large family, she assumed Edward had made this jest in order to amuse himself at her expense. Forcing her to rise early and attend Prime was so far removed from her preference to sleep as late she was able would no doubt be his idea of an amusing jape to welcome to her court.

"Will I really have to attend Prime?" Jane whispered to Mary as her cousin led her across the room towards the other maids.

"Yes, if the queen has requested your presence," replied Mary, then with a glimmer of amusement. "Although surely someone as devout as yourself would welcome it."

"But…" Jane began wondering if she had missed something. Why was everyone behaving as though she were bordering on taking the veil?

"You must go tomorrow," said Mary, "however, the queen doesn't expect you to attend every morning, twice a week should suffice. In the meantime, let me introduce you to a few people."

Jane smiled as Mary walked towards a group of women who were playing the card game, Primero. Their names passed in a flash, as Mary pointed from one elegant courtier to another,

"Lady Jane Stukeley, Margaret Blount and Lady Mary Norris." The women nodded a greeting but Mary swept her away pointing out other members of the court, ranging in age from their early teens to dowagers. "I thought your cousin, Lady Elizabeth Carew, would be here by now. She joined her husband, Sir Nicholas, on the hunt today. There's our brother, George, with Sir Francis Bryan, another cousin we share."

Threading her way through the crowd, Mary led Jane to the two men who were speaking in low, intense voices.

"Sir Francis Bryan, what an honour," said Mary, curtseying to the taller of the two men. Jane bobbed beside her, rising to meet his intense gaze, its potency undiminished by the fact he wore an eye patch.

A jousting accident had caused the injury, yet the eye patch, embroidered to match his dark green and russet doublet, did nothing to mar his intense good looks. Francis towered over her, his dark brown moustache and beard were trimmed and curled in the latest fashionable style, while the casual manner in which he wore his well-tailored clothes added to his aura of intense glamour.

"I believe it was your intervention, along with her brother, Sir Edward, which won Jane's place in the queen's court," continued Mary.

"Lady Carey, Miss Seymour, this is a pleasure indeed," Francis said, taking Jane's hand and bowing over it. As their fingers met Jane felt her heart quicken.

"George, my dear, you remember our cousin, Jane Seymour?" continued Mary, turning to her younger brother.

"Hello Cousin Jane," interrupted George Boleyn, his voice brimming with a confidence bordering on arrogance. "You're here at last. Francis and Edward have been speaking about nothing else for the past few days."

"How was the hunt?" asked Mary, accepting a glass of spiced wine from a page before passing one to Jane.

"It was most satisfactory," replied George, downing the remains of his own goblet and taking another. "Francis tells me you're a keen hunter, Jane. We shall have to take you out."

"It would be marvellous," Jane agreed. "There is nothing quite so invigorating as a good ride across a winter field."

George snorted with schoolboy laughter and Jane shot him the scorching look of contempt she reserved for her own younger brothers. Francis frowned at George, wrinkling his nose in distaste before turning his back on him, blocking him from the conversation.

"Ignore him, Jane, we are not all sniggering buffoons," he said. "The hunting here will suit you very well, my dear, I shall ensure you have a decent mount."

"Why, thank you, Sir Francis," she replied, aware he continued to hold her hand.

His sandalwood scent was wrapping itself around her like a lover and she breathed him in. This was all she had dreamed about for months. Ever since his letter had arrived suggesting she join him at court, his words tantalising.

"…*we can be out from under your parents' watchful eyes. Think of it, my love, to stroll in the grounds of Hampton Court, to hunt, to dance, to write our poems, to be together. Would this not be a joy?*"

"We must ensure her time here is full of amusement," said Mary and George let out another guffaw.

Francis was about to respond when, in the distance, came the sound of marching boots. A sense of anticipation swept through the room as all eyes turned towards the double doors of the chamber. Jane stepped behind Francis unnerved by the crackling tension as the marching grew louder, cutting through the chatter and laughter. Jane looked towards the queen who had placed aside her embroidery and was licking her dry lips, her face pink with a desperate urgency when the doors were flung open and the king filled the doorway.

Jane gasped. Henry VIII was magnificent; a giant of a man who exuded a fierce, animal-like magnetism, an energy of such intensity it felt tangible. Jewels dripped from his elaborate tunic, his stockinged legs rippled with muscles and his vibrant red hair and beard glowed like the setting sun. Around her, people fell away and, in a heartbeat, Jane, too, dropped into a deep obeisance. The room felt airless as Henry's eager, sparkling brown eyes swept from face to face.

"Rise, rise," he called, his voice jovial. "This seems a merry gathering. Why, Francis, you have returned, come with me, we have much to discuss…"

Stepping back, merging into the crowd, Jane watched as Francis was swept away by the king.

Henry threw a polite nod to his wife, before searching the crowd, his eyes finding Anne Boleyn seated by the fire. She did not look up and Jane watched, fascinated. While everyone else in the room seemed determined to try and catch the king's eye, to smile with sycophantic grace, Anne ignored him. Dragging Francis behind him, the king, looking as nervous as a young bridegroom, approached her.

"Anne...?" she heard him say, his voice low, tentative.

Anne rolled her eyes, sighing, as though to speak to the king was a terrible inconvenience. He reached inside his doublet and withdrew a small velvet pouch. Anne gave him a scornful look before upending the gift to reveal a pair of perfectly matched emerald earrings. Jane's eyes widened; they were known as the stone of successful love, a meaning which must have been apparent to Anne because with a smile as radiant as the morning, she held them out to Henry to attach to her ears.

His deft fingers fastened the earrings, his hand resting on her shoulder when he was finished. Anne gave a shy smile at odds with the piercing look with which she met the king's eyes. Raising her hand, Anne allowed Henry to lead her to a private alcove away from the prying eyes of the rest of the room. Francis was seated beside the king and moments later, Anne beckoned for her siblings, Mary and George, to join them. A board was produced and a rowdy game of draughts began, with Anne smiling up at the king with devotion. Unable to resist, Jane turned to look at the queen. Katherine's eyes were like blank glass, her hands were clenched into tight fists, ripping the delicate lawn fabric to shreds.

"Come, Jane, this is no time to gawp," said a quiet voice. Lady Elizabeth Carew, the sister of Sir Francis Bryan was beside her. "My apologies that I was unavailable when you arrived, there were matters to which I had to attend. Come, sit with us, it might be safer than aligning yourself with your Boleyn cousins."

Following Elizabeth to a table near the window, Jane gazed around at the room, her eyes resting on Anne and the besotted king laughing at her witticisms. She wondered how it might feel to command the heart of the king of England.

CHAPTER TWO

"Good night, Your Majesty."

Jane curtsied with the other women before backing out of the door, leaving the queen with Lady Jane Dormer. Following Mary Zouche, Lady Elizabeth Guildford and Lady Katheryn Parr, Jane glided into the receiving room.

"Good evening, ladies," said Lady Guildford, the most senior of the women. "We shall retire. The queen will attend Matins in the early hours of the morning; would any of you wish to join her?"

Jane felt the older woman's eyes bore into her but her gaze remained lowered.

"Miss Seymour?"

"Lady Guildford, my plan this evening is to study my scriptures in quiet contemplation before keeping a night-long vigil to our beloved Virgin Mother, hoping to find an answer to the queen's pain. It is with great anticipation I view this task; however, if you would prefer me to attend…"

"No, my dear, I will hear of no such thing," interrupted Lady Guildford. "One of the others shall accompany the queen; may your contemplations bring you peace of mind and answers for Her Majesty."

With her head lowered, Jane bobbed a curtsey and glided from the room on silent feet. The guards outside Katherine's door moved aside as she passed and with measured footsteps, she made her way down the torchlit corridor. As she turned the corner, she glanced back at the guards, who had watched her retreat then disappear from view. Throwing back her shoulders, a grin unfurled across her face as she thought of the evening ahead. Resisting the urge to gather her skirts in her hand and run, she sped up as much as she dared, arriving in her chamber a few moments later.

Her maid, Audrey, was waiting.

"Everything's ready, madam," she said, helping Jane to remove her heavy gable hood.

Jane sat at the small table, where a mirror gleamed in the candlelight. Audrey released Jane's blonde hair from its heavy coil and began brushing it with firm strokes. Opening a small wooden casket, Jane assembled her brushes and with seasoned strokes applied tiny red dots of crushed cinnabar on her cheeks, blending them in until her skin glowed with a warm blush. Another small brush tidied her eyebrows before she dipped it into a pot of powdered fig stem which she swept over her pale eyelashes to give them a hint of colour. On her lips she painted a pale pink shimmer made from rose petals and beeswax before sitting back to admire her handiwork.

"No more prudish Miss Seymour," she murmured and Audrey laughed.

The two young women were close in age and, over the months, had become friends. Jane had been fascinated to discover the reason for Audrey's elevated position as a lady's maid to one of the queen's women was because the king was close to her sister, Joanna Dingley.

"It's a secret," Audrey had whispered one evening when Jane had smuggled a jug of wine back to her room. The two young women were sitting in Jane's bed drinking, their tales becoming wilder as they became further intoxicated. "My sister has a child, a daughter, named Ethelreda and the king is her father."

"This is shocking," Jane had giggled. "Is your sister very pretty?"

"She's beautiful; all blonde hair and curls and sparkling eyes."

The following day, Audrey had sworn Jane to secrecy, promising to use her sister's camomile rinse to bring out the brightness in Jane's hair.

"You don't need to bribe me," Jane had laughed. "I won't tell anyone."

After years of keeping the secrets of her father's indiscretions and her mother's sorrow, the Seymour children were adept at obscuring the truth. Audrey had been true to her word and the two young women had formed an even closer friendship as they began to swap tips on make-up, hair and fashion. Having been used to three younger sisters, none of whom shared her interests in such things, Jane was delighted to have made a friend who could help and advise her. In return, Jane was teaching Audrey to read.

Jane was aware she was not a natural beauty but with the help of a few cosmetics, her pale skin and large eyes could appear brighter and rosier, giving her confidence, which boosted her appearance beyond all powders and paints. As Audrey brushed out Jane's long, straight hair, Jane noticed golden lights gleaming and smiled. Her hair would lighten in the summer but during the winter she felt it was drab, tending towards ash tones rather than the gold she preferred. Audrey's potion, however, seemed to have worked its magic.

"Here's your new French hood," said Audrey, attaching the dark green velvet band across Jane's head. With deft fingers, she swept the rest of Jane's hair into the long cowl and stood back to admire the effect.

A far larger portion of Jane's blonde hair was visible than when she wore the more severe gable hoods, preferred by the queen. Jane inspected this new, racier, more daring version of herself in the mirror and grinned. Despite what she may have told Lady Guildford, Jane was not planning to spend the night in quiet contemplation, she was attending a party with the younger courtiers and had no intention of wearing anything other than the latest fashions. Unlacing her plain green sleeves, she waited while Audrey attached a new pair made of emerald silk embroidered with red thread and adorned with a smattering of dark red carnelians. Discarding her leather boots, she pushed her feet into embroidered satin slippers before peering at herself again in the small looking-glass on her table.

"Will I do?" she asked, searching for reassurance rather than praise.

"Jane, you look beautiful," replied Audrey truthfully. "He won't be able to keep his eyes off you."

The two women shared a complicit grin and Jane laughed, "Which was my objective."

"Here's your cloak," said Audrey. "I'll wait up for you and if anyone asks, I'll refuse to open the door, saying you mustn't be disturbed as you're praying for help for the queen."

Hugging her friend, despite knowing this was a lack of propriety, Jane opened her chamber door, checked there was no one around and disappeared into the shadowy corridor. Heading further into the palace, towards the rooms occupied by Henry's leading courtiers, Jane paused at the end of the corridor where it branched into two. She peered first to the left, then the right, trying to remember the directions given to her by Francis earlier in the afternoon.

She hesitated; had he said left? Yes, he had, she was sure of it. Padding down the draughty passageway, she faltered when she heard voices ahead. Stepping into the shadows, she held her breath as the queen and a number of women processed by candlelight towards her private chapel. Damn, he had said left for the queen's chapel, right for Lord and Lady Stukeley's rooms. Retracing her steps, Jane slipped along the corridor until she reached another bend and to her relief, she saw Sir Nicholas Carew chatting to Francis beside the doors to the Stukeley apartments. Shaking out her skirts and straightening her hood, she walked towards them, smiling.

"Jane, you made it," said Francis, kissing her hand. "I was worried the queen might drag you off to pray."

"She thinks I'm keeping an all-night vigil to the Virgin Mary," Jane replied.

"More like an all-night homage to wine and song," replied Nicholas as the three entered the room. "Joan, Hugh, the lovely Miss Seymour has arrived."

"Jane, what a pleasure," said Lady Stukeley, smiling a welcome, beckoning Jane into the room. "Francis is never happy unless you are in the room."

Francis laughed and Jane blushed. A goblet of wine was thrust into her hand, before Francis grasped the other and led the way through the crowd. Musicians played, a group danced a galliard and all around them people laughed, drank and ate. In one corner, Jane saw Lady Elizabeth Carew and Lady Mary Norris, the wife of another of the king's close friends, Sir Henry Norris, who held the title The Groom of the Stool and was one of the wealthiest men at court.

Nicholas went ahead of them and joined his wife, Lady Elizabeth. Francis followed and Jane was welcomed into the fold; space was made on the wide padded seats and greetings of welcome called. While Jane did not enjoy deceiving the queen, she had no desire to spend her evenings in contemplative Bible study with the older ladies of the court. At present, with her brother away, she had no chaperone and her parents' instructions had been clear, she was not to attend parties such as these alone. Jane worked on the premise that if they did not know, it could not harm them. Word would instead reach them that she was devout and pious, they would assume Queen Katherine was having a calming influence on her wild ways. As Francis slid his arm around her waist, she knew this could not be further from the truth.

Outside the wind howled and rain lashed at the windows. Jane leaned into Francis, enjoying his nearness, relaxed and happy with her friends and extended family as they gossiped about the king. The past three months at court had been a revelation for Jane. Finally allowed to be responsible for herself, to make decisions and without the worried tones of her mother following her wherever she walked, her confidence had grown and she had blossomed.

Being close to Francis, seeing the approval and love in his eyes whenever they were together, had made her understand how it felt to trust someone, to love them, to know they were a part of your soul. Although she and Francis had been discreet, they had snatched moments alone as often as they were able in between his work with the king and her duties to the queen. The awe Jane had felt the first day at court had receded and she was becoming a well-liked member of Queen Katherine's court.

While religion was not important to Jane, her excellent memory made it easy for her to remember huge passages of Biblical text taught by her former nursemaid, the strict and humourless Mrs Doddy. Her ability to recite these tracts was earning her a spurious reputation of piety and theological knowledge, when in truth, the mystery of the Holy Spirit was not one she had ever wished to solve. Jane, who was equally as able to recite the poems of Thomas Wyatt, William Dunbar, John Skelton, even Geoffrey Chaucer, although she found his work old-fashioned, or any of the ballads that were popular, found her new-found façade of religious devoutness highly amusing.

Every day, Jane watched as Anne Boleyn was pushed further into the king's arms by the scheming men in her family, while the queen was diminished. At present, Katherine was praying for deliverance from Anne and the return of the king's affection. Jane felt this was a lost cause as the gossip at court concerned Henry, Anne and his desire for a divorce from Katherine.

"Do you think the king will be successful in his 'Great Matter'?" asked Lady Norris, sipping her wine, as they watched the dancers.

This was the term being used by the court to describe Henry's mania to annul what he saw as his unlawful and unholy marriage to the queen, in order to marry Anne.

"Will the queen have any choice but to capitulate? The king is the king; his word is law, surely?" said Lady Carew.

"Perhaps not," said Francis, passing Jane a platter of fruit and dropping a grape into her mouth, "remember, the queen has many influential relatives, including the Holy Roman Emperor, Charles V. She is his aunt and Charles could make things very difficult for the king."

"Is it true," Sir Henry Norris asked, "that the king plans to use Leviticus, chapter 20, verse 21, as his religious argument in order to secure the annulment of his marriage to Queen Katherine? *'If a man takes his brother's wife, it is impurity … they shall be childless'*."

"It seems a loose defence," said Jane, "as it can be contradicted by chapter 25, verse 5 of the Book of Deuteronomy, which states *'the widow of the dead man shall not be married outside the family, her husband's brother shall take her as his wife*'. Anyway, they're not childless, they have the Princess Mary."

"You're quite right," agreed Francis, "but the king requires a son. He is claiming the word 'childless' in the Leviticus quote refers to having no male heir…"

"Remember the older priests believe a king with no children is a judgement from God that his rule is illegitimate," interrupted Nicholas Carew. "By stating 'no children' but meaning 'no son', the king is suggesting his marriage has not been blessed by God and is, therefore, not valid."

"But he has a son," said Francis and nodded towards a woman at the centre of the dancing group. "Bessie Blount and Henry have Henry Fitzroy and the king has acknowledged him. When Henry created the boy as Duke of Richmond and Somerset three years ago, he made him the highest ranking noble in the country. At the same time, Fitzroy was created Captain of the Town and Castle of Berwick on Tweed and Keeper of the City and Castle of Carlisle."

"Which," said Nicholas, "has been an office held by the heir apparent ever since the time of King Richard II."

"Don't forget Fitzroy was also created as Lord High Admiral, replacing Thomas Howard, Duke of Norfolk," added Henry Norris, "and Norfolk was also pushed aside to create a space for Fitzroy in the Order of the Garter. Fitzroy is Warden General of the Scottish Marshes, a post Henry held when he was a child, and the king has made him the head of the reinstated Council of the North, which puts him in charge of the northern part of the country. Yet, the boy is nine years old. If the king is not proposing Fitzroy as a potential heir, I'm a jackanape."

"My brother, Edward, was Fitzroy's Master of Horse when he took over his new home, Sheriff Hutton, a few years ago," added Jane. "He said the house was run like a miniature version of the court with Fitzroy as the rowdy central point. Edward suggested there were times when Fitzroy was encouraged to run wild by his companions."

"It sounds rather like Henry when he was a boy," laughed Francis.

"Henry Fitzroy might have been ennobled to be the foremost duke of the realm but he remains illegitimate," said Lady Carew. "Despite the king's obvious devotion to the boy, there is no getting around the fact he is Bessie Blount's son and not the queen's. It's the same with Thomas Stukeley."

"Thomas?" gasped Jane, glancing over at their smiling hosts who were now in the centre of the dancers. "Joan and Hugh's son?"

"The rumour is, he isn't Hugh's but the king's. He may only be eight years old but the likeness to Henry as a youngster is quite marked."

"The same holds for Mary Boleyn's son, Henry Carey," said Lady Norris. "The king can't even acknowledge him, as he fears to admit to a relationship with Mary would make things even more complicated in his pursuit of Anne."

"Why would that worry the king?" said Jane, accepting another goblet of wine from Francis.

"If Henry has slept with Anne's sister and they have had children, it creates a family bond between the king and Anne. It could be considered that they are too closely related and this would make any marriage between them unlawful," said Nicholas.

"I would have thought someone as devout as yourself would have known such intricacies in the ways of the church, Jane," remarked Lady Norris, her eyes twinkling.

Jane rolled her eyes. "Is it my fault I have a talent for recitation? It doesn't mean I enjoy the turgid religious passages the queen adores. Ever since my idiot brother, Edward, told the queen I was devout, she has been trying to train me to be a nun."

"Rumour has it that you have the habit already," murmured Lady Carew.

"Who told you that?" Jane said.

Lady Carew grinned at her brother, Francis, who lounged at Jane's side, his hand never far from her own.

"You are supposed to be a gentleman, sir," Jane said, shooting him a look of mock fury.

"Whoever spread such a slanderous rumour?" he replied as the group laughed. "I shall damn them to hell."

Sipping her wine, with what she hoped was haughty dignity, Jane was unsure if she was angry or amused that Francis had given away her favourite disguise. When she was younger she had learned that the night-time devotionals of Matins, Lauds and Prime services that ran respectively at 2.30am, 5am and 7.30am, were the perfect cover for her to escape from the strict parameters of her parents' house to have adventures of her own. None of her family knew about her nun's habit, the perfect disguise when she wished to have moonlight trysts with her secret lover. No one would question a nun, especially if she appeared to be on her way to prayer.

The first time she had arrived dressed in her habit, Francis had been startled until she had removed it to reveal her usual gown below.

"You are the least devout nun I have ever met," he had laughed, drawing her into his arms and kissing her.

Yet among the sophisticated teasing of her friends, the jests felt warm, inclusive, welcoming her into their exclusive circle, as though they were congratulating her on her dangerous behaviour. Jane looked at Francis from under her eyelashes and she saw approval in his expression. Settling back, she allowed herself to relax, to enjoy this moment and not worry about potential scandals. If they came, well, she would weather them with the same quiet poise displayed by her father.

"Is this the reason why Sir Thomas and Lady Elizabeth have removed Anne from court and returned to Hever Castle?" asked Jane. "To protect her from the king while he tries to secure his divorce?"

"Such a thought can't be dismissed," said Lady Norris. "Although, it's a shame this has happened. Anne was happy with the match her father had suggested."

"The marriage to James Butler, son of Piers Butler, the Earl of Ormond?" asked Jane.

"Yes, Sir Thomas Boleyn was in contention for the earldom, through his maternal line, but it went to Piers Butler instead," explained Francis. "A number of years ago, it was suggested Anne and James should marry, uniting the lines. It would mean Thomas would miss out on the title but his grandsons would inherit."

"And Anne agreed?"

"It was one of the main reasons she came home from France at the end of 1521."

"But that was ages ago," Jane exclaimed. "Why aren't they married?"

"Politics," sighed Lady Norris. "Cardinal Wolsey became involved, as did Sir Thomas Boleyn and Piers Butler. After several years of wrangling, Anne and James were the only two people who were continuing to push for a marriage settlement because during those interim years, they fell in love."

"But she is now in love with the king?" asked Jane, who had been unaware of a connection between Anne and James Butler.

"Is she in love with the king, though?" asked Lady Carew, and Jane saw Francis, Henry Norris and Nicholas Carew exchange an uncomfortable look.

"Whatever Anne's true feelings, it was her father who ruined the betrothment agreement," said Francis. "Annoyed at losing out on the earldom, he spoke to the king in order to try and claim the Ormond title behind Piers Butler's back. Butler was furious and in retaliation he halted the marriage plans. There are rumours James is to marry Lady Joan Fitzgerald instead. I suspect the king may have told Butler to remove his son from Anne's orbit. The king has never enjoyed competition."

Jane sipped her wine. The intricacies of family trees had never interested her. These were things that could not be changed and, as such, she had never bothered to think about them. Her mother, Margery, and her elder brother, Edward, were always available to provide any information about family history. When they were younger, she and her brother, Tommy, would pretend to fall asleep when her mother recited their family connections. Edward, her other brother Henry and her younger sisters, Elizabeth and Dorothy, had usually paid attention.

The fire crackled. Outside the rain fell on a cold moonless night, while the room was vibrant with the colour and noise of the party, spinning and dividing as the younger courtiers whirled to the music, enjoying their youth and beauty, their wealth and power, each day a new adventure as they traversed behind the king in his dance of arrogant power and complete control. Never doubting their place in the world, assured the sun would rise and with it, new revels would begin.

With a cheer, the music reached a crescendo and the dancers swirled to a halt. The musicians bowed, taking a break while food was served. The crowd surged around the refreshments as pages hurried to bring food to those seated, offering trays of pies and sweetmeats. Jane selected a number of small tarts stuffed with her favourite shredded quail.

As they ate, a lilting voice said, "Elizabeth, my dear, may Gilbert and I join you?"

"Bessie, it would be a delight," said Lady Carew, springing to her feet and indicating for one of the servants to bring more chairs. "It's wonderful to see you at court."

Introductions were made and, as they ate, Jane tried not to stare at Bessie Blount, the legendary beauty who had been the king's mistress for many years. When her son, Henry Fitzroy, had been born in 1519 at St Laurence Priory in Essex, Jane's mother had been scandalised, wondering whether Bessie would be thrown from court in disgrace. The priory was known as Jericho and was notorious for hiding the illegitimate offspring of the nobility. Cardinal Wolsey himself was rumoured to have arranged for his two illegitimate children to be born there. Instead of banishment, the king acknowledged Bessie's child, a healthy son, and, in due course, arranged a good marriage for Bessie. The rumours that her eldest daughter was also the king's child were met with silence, followed by one of Bessie's dimpled smiles.

"We divide our time between court, our seat in Lincolnshire, my parents in Shropshire and the varying castles belonging to my son, Henry," said Bessie. "It is a busy life but we enjoy it."

Jane listened as the other women chatted idly, discussing the other courtiers. Placing her empty plate to one side, Jane washed her hands in a silver bowl provided by one of the many servants who circulated before reaching again for her brimming goblet. Francis winked at her and she smiled back. The wine was heavy and rich, the food was sumptuous and she was beginning to feel intoxicated with the evening.

The music struck up again and Jane stretched her legs under her skirts, wondering if it would be forward if she were to ask Francis to dance. However, before she could move, Bessie turned to her and smiled. "How are you enjoying court, Jane?"

"Very well, thank you," Jane replied, awestruck by Bessie's interest. The reports of her beauty were true, even in her late twenties and having borne three children, Bessie radiated youth, vitality and determination.

As though on a pre-agreed cue, Nicholas stood, his movement echoed by Francis, Gilbert and Henry, before beginning a discussion about the upcoming joust, diverting attention away from the women.

Bessie leaned forward and asked in a low voice, "Which way does your preference lie, Jane?"

"My preference?"

"Queen Katherine or your cousin, Anne?"

"With Anne," Jane replied, her response immediate, "she's a lot more fun."

Bessie laughed. "She is also intelligent, fierce and loyal," she said. "A good friend."

Jane stared at her in surprise. In her naivety she had thought Anne and Bessie would be rivals but it appeared she had misjudged the situation. "Where do your loyalties lie?" she asked in return, looking at the gathered women.

"With Anne," replied Lady Carew, and Lady Norris nodded.

A chill ran down Jane's spine as she remembered a conversation with her elder brother, Edward, the previous week.

"The court is in a state of warfare," he had said as they had walked along the river. "Battle lines are being drawn and we must have a care where we place our loyalties. There are great plans afoot and as Anne Boleyn is family, we must align with her but our strategy at present is not to show our true colours."

"You're not on the battlefield now, Edward," she had said.

"Don't be naïve, Jane. The queen's rooms are as much a theatre of war as France when I was fighting alongside the Duke of Suffolk. Skirmishes are taking place and plans are being drawn. Sir Thomas Boleyn and his brother-in-law, the Duke of Norfolk, are working behind the scenes to ensure victory and, as part of the extended family, we will all be expected to play our parts, even you, when the time comes. Our family will endure longer than your position as a maid of honour in the queen's court and it is to family and blood we must hold firm. For the present, we must appear to remain neutral but if things swing in Anne's favour it may advance all our social positions when we remind the king that we are her kin, too."

Jane had dismissed this discussion as her brother's overaction. Yet, it was undeniable that the swirling factions within the queen's court were intensifying. Over the past months, it had become apparent that Henry's infatuation with Anne was increasing rather than diminishing and subtle shifts had begun to take place among Katherine's women. Those who had been with her since the early days and were loyal to the queen and her daughter, Princess Mary, were excluding women whom they believed were close to Anne Boleyn. In response, Anne was making it clear she was choosing to associate with those from whom she would one day select her alternative court.

Bessie's silken, unnerving tone was making Jane's skin tingle and she was unsure where the conversation was heading. Unease began to creep through her.

"It is good to hear we are of one accord," said Bessie. "I believe Queen Katherine holds you in high regard, Jane?"

"Yes, Lady Tailboys," she said.

"Then we have something to ask you; a favour which will be of great service to your cousin Anne and the country."

"What?"

"We need a spy in Queen Katherine's employ," said Lady Norris, "someone she trusts."

"Your brother laid the groundwork by assuring the queen of your devoutness before you arrived from Wulfhall," continued Bessie. "He spent months telling her how your real calling was to be a nun but your parents would not allow it. From the moment of your arrival, the queen has been disposed to like you and your path shall continue this way if you are willing to become our eyes and ears."

Jane stared at the three women in disbelief, wondering if this was a joke, but from the rigid stance of Francis, Sir Gilbert, Sir Henry and Sir Nicholas who stood around the women like a shield, she realised their lively conversation was a mask to allow these requests to be made.

"You wish me to spy on the queen?" Jane clarified. Although she had spoken the words, they did not seem real.

"Yes," replied Lady Carew.

"But I've never done anything like this before; how will I know what to do?"

"We'll advise you," replied Bessie, "as will Francis. He has undertaken many an espionage trip on behalf of the king. You and he are friends and often seen in each other's company, no one will be suspicious if you spend more time together."

Jane stared around, wondering if this was a joke but the serious faces gazing back at her suggested otherwise. "Why me?"

"You are young, unknown, untried and, as far as the queen is aware, innocent."

"This is preposterous…" Jane began, her temper rising, but Lady Norris spoke across her.

"Did you not realise this was the reason you were brought here?" Her voice was full of apology. "To help us win this war?"

"No, I…"

"We needed a new face, a member of the family but distantly connected. Francis suggested you would be an ideal choice."

Jane threw a look of fury at Francis. There were many reasons he had cited that she should come to court, this had never been among them. "Why do you need a spy?"

"It is imperative we are aware of all that transpires in Katherine's court," said Bessie. "If your cousin is to continue with the king, we must do all we can to ensure she remains in his favour. We know his mood can change like quicksilver."

Jane stared at Bessie, wondering why she would embroil herself in such dangerous games on behalf of another woman. "Why though? Why would you help Anne to secure the throne?"

"The throne? This is no longer about making Anne queen," said Bessie and Jane felt a thrill of fear shiver down her spine. "Although, if this is necessary, then this shall come to pass. There is, however, another plan about which Anne and I have corresponded. We believe the king is no longer the man he was when he was young. I have known him well for many years and my fear is that he is showing signs of madness."

"What…?" began Jane, but Lady Norris held up her hand for Jane to desist, allowing Bessie to continue.

"His desire to annul his marriage, his endless overspending on his lavish lifestyle, as well as the money wasted on ludicrous wars with Scotland and France are bringing the country to ruin. One of my relatives, William Blount, Baron Mountjoy is Master of the Mint, he suggests that in order to try and refill the royal coffers the king plans to debase the currency."

"What are you talking about?" asked Jane, panic gripping her.

"To do this would mean a reduction in the amount of gold and silver used in the coins; they would be replaced with cheaper base metals, such as copper," Bessie explained. "The aim of the policy is to increase revenue for the Crown at the cost of the population through savings in currency production. If less bullion is required to mint new coins, the king will be able to claim the excess bullion for himself. He would become wealthy, while our own coins would be worth less. It could plunge the country into chaos."

"This is treason," whispered Jane. "Even speaking of these things is…"

"We are aware of the dangers," said Lady Norris.

"Anne and I believe there is an alternative, one which will enable her to escape the marriage to the king," said Bessie.

"Escape? What is this?"

The women exchanged a complicit glance before Bessie continued, "Mary Boleyn was told to bed the king, to amuse him, but the path decreed for Anne is to become queen and beget a Howard heir to the throne." Bessie's voice hardened with every word. "She has no desire to be queen, despite what is said. This is the work of her uncle, the Duke of Norfolk. When I wrote to Anne, I suspected my gentle enquiries would be met with hostility, yet she replied suggesting my proposals were a lifeline. She lives in terror, you see, Jane, she is no longer sure how much longer she can pretend."

"Pretend? What do you mean?"

"To love the king," Bessie whispered. "At first, when her father and uncle asked her to catch his eye, she explained how it seemed amusing. Back then her father was arranging a marriage for Anne to James Butler, the Earl of Ormond. Anne expected to enjoy a few weeks of flirtation with the king before leaving for Ireland. She did not expect the plans to change."

Francis's words from earlier swirled around Jane's head, dancing through her mind as though they were embroidered on her closed eyelids. Anne was in love with another, she did not want to marry the king. Her actions were being driven by — what? Jane wondered — fear? As her uncle the powerful Thomas Howard, Duke of Norfolk pushed her towards Henry with impunity. Anything for a Howard heir, any sacrifice was worth it, as long as he achieved his ends. Jane opened her eyes, unsure whether she dared to ask the question but knowing it could not remain in her thoughts forever.

"Who do you propose?" asked Jane.

"My son,' Bessie said. "With the right people around him, he will make a fine king."

Jane stared at Bessie as though she were the one afflicted by madness. For Fitzroy to claim the crown, there would have to be an empty throne. "How would you remove the king?" asked Jane, her voice tremulous.

"There are plans cooking as we speak," said Lady Carew. "If you are willing to help Bessie, to help Anne, the next time you see her, ensure you are wearing a five-pointed star, then she will know we have spoken."

"This is impossible," whispered Jane, terrified at what was being asked of her.

"Is it?" asked Bessie. "My inspiration comes from Margaret Beaufort."

"The king's grandmother?" asked Jane and Bessie gave a sharp nod.

"She was ambitious for Henry's father. She schemed and planned, eventually finding a way to give him the opportunity to fight for the throne. He won; he sired the Tudor dynasty. My son's claim to the throne is stronger than that of the old king, he cannot fail."

"And this is what you intend?" asked Jane. "For Fitzroy to become king."

"Yes. When it became apparent the king was unhappy with the queen and was willing to put her aside for Anne, I saw an opportunity for my son. If the king's marriage to the queen is not valid, then the Princess Mary is illegitimate and, despite being three years younger, Fitzroy has the advantage of being an acknowledged son. His claim to the throne is as strong as Mary's, stronger even, because he is a boy. Anne is willing to help. Are you?"

"What if the queen suspects me?" Jane exclaimed, fear mingling with the shock of such an unexpected endeavour.

"There is no reason why she should. She trusts you and you have also been able to befriend Princess Mary."

Stupefied, Jane tried to marshal counterarguments but she could think of none as she stared into the serious faces of the other women. After several moments of strained silence, she said, "I can try."

"This is all we ask," replied Bessie, squeezing her hand. "Any snippets of information, no matter how trivial, could help."

As though a signal had been given, the four men laughed and turned back to the women. Francis put out his hand to Jane, indicating they should dance and, in a daze, she allowed him to lead her towards the crowd in the centre of the room.

Despite the bright lights and wild atmosphere, Jane felt as though the evening had taken a darker turn.

CHAPTER THREE

"Have you seen this? It's the new prophecies from the Holy Maid of Kent."

Jane took the crumpled, ink-smudged pamphlet from Audrey.

"She's speaking today," said Jane, "not far from here. Shall we go and see what all the fuss is about?"

Jane smoothed out the page, reading the latest predictions and praises of Elizabeth Barton, the prophetess known as the Holy Maid of Kent. Barton's rise to fame had begun a few years earlier, when as a poor servant to Thomas Cobb, a man of middling wealth and influence in Aldington in Kent, an illness had caused her to fall into trances. Barton claimed to have been visited by the Virgin Mary who gave her tours of both heaven and hell. Since then, her fame had grown irresistibly. Men of learning, such as John Fisher, Bishop of Rochester and a strong supporter of Queen Katherine were beginning to take notice of Barton and her revelations. News of her prophesies had even reached Cardinal Thomas Wolsey, one of the king's highest religious advisors and, through him, the king. Rumours at court suggested both men were watching Barton with interest.

"It's not far from where we're going," said Audrey.

"She's been making a number of prophesies about the king and queen," said Jane, torn between wanting to see the famous prophetess but convinced the woman was a fraud. "She suggests the Sweat is a punishment to the king from God. If he turns away from Anne and returns to Katherine, not only will the illness vanish, but they will have a son."

"Do you think she might be correct?"

"No," replied Jane, folding the pamphlet and sliding it into the leather bag that hung from the belt at her waist. "I think she's talking nonsense. However, I do wonder if the queen might be interested. She's been following Elizabeth Barton's progress and is impressed with the woman's piety. Perhaps we should go, then I can tell the queen about her. On several occasions, Queen Katherine has mentioned trying to persuade Elizabeth Barton to leave St Sepulchre in Canterbury and become her spiritual advisor."

"I overheard Sir Francis saying he heard Cardinal Wolsey trying to persuade the king to grant her an audience," said Audrey.

"Yes, he mentioned it, but Francis believes the Holy Maid will have a long wait," murmured Jane, "especially while she blames the king for causing the Sweat. He's unlikely to look upon her with any great favour."

The past weeks had seen reports of the growing wave of deaths from the virulent illness known as the Sweat or the Sweating Sickness. A savage illness that could kill a person within hours. Every day messengers arrived with new and frightening details of the spread of the infection but it had yet to make itself felt in the palaces of Henry's glittering court. As such, there was an ambivalence towards it; many courtiers felt they were untouchable, they were too rich, too beautiful, too important to be afflicted by such an ailment.

Walking in the bright spring sunshine, the blue sky brilliant over the jagged roofline of London, Jane, Audrey and their accompanying page wandered through the streets gazing into shops and pausing at stalls to inspect the wares. While she was aware of the sickness sweeping across the country, Jane, like many of the other courtiers was confident this illness would pass them by, leaving them untouched. Refusing to believe she could be susceptible, she was instead enjoying the thrill of having her own money to spend on anything she chose.

Although her parents had always provided an allowance, they would check how this was being spent. For the first time in her life, Jane had money she had earned. Being a lady-in-waiting for the queen came with a stipend and, even after the deductions she needed to make and debts she had to pay, Jane was left with a small sum. Her objective today was to buy paper and ink, followed by lace from the drapers and to visit the apothecary for supplies of willow bark and camomile. Every month she suffered severe cramps and she found these the most effective way of soothing her pain. The majority of their purchases had been made and the page was weighed down with parcels, his frown of boredom deepening with every step. Jane paused at a sweetmeat stand; purchasing a bag of honey and cinnamon tarts, she offered one to Audrey, then passed one to the page, who stammered his thanks. Jane ate one as they wandered through the teeming streets.

She had been at court for over a year and, as requested by Bessie Blount and her associates, Jane had worked hard to ensure the continued trust of the queen and Princess Mary despite her blood-link to Anne Boleyn. Her acts of piety and quietness, so at odds with her true nature, had been successful and both the queen and princess viewed Jane as part of their inner circle. As the battle between Katherine and Anne raged through the corridors of power, causing turmoil and unease, Jane listened, smiled, sank into the shadows, learning the cunning art of the courtier with every passing day. Delivering information to Lady Carew and Lady Norris at regular intervals, she reported on the queen's mood and her views on the events.

Despite the king's protestations that his marriage to Katherine was not legal because of her previous marriage to Henry's older brother, Arthur, the queen maintained she had been a virgin when she had married Henry. Even though Jane listened with care in case Katherine's story ever changed, the queen never wavered, insisting her marriage to Henry was legal.

To Jane, her reports, which comprised unimportant everyday details, seemed trivial but Francis assured her when these were accumulated with their other information, they became the basis of intelligence used to strengthen Anne's position. Jane could not understand why Anne continued with the charade of being in love with Henry when really, she was working on behalf of Bessie and her plan to make Fitzroy king.

"It is better you don't know," Francis had said one evening when Jane had raised this enigma. "When the time is right, I will explain, I promise. Please, my love, trust me."

Jane agreed, deciding to let the responsibility for the plot fall on other shoulders. However, she did notice her intelligence was being used. One afternoon, Queen Katherine mused how it irritated Henry when she commented on the skills of other men at the joust, showing too much knowledge of the sport. It was a small point but during the next tournament, Jane heard Anne asking the king to explain the scoring system, pretending she did not understand, causing the king to puff up with male pride. It took all Jane's self-control not to laugh, especially when Anne walked past and winked at her. A few weeks later, the appointment of a new chamber in the palace for Anne, overlooking the tiltyard — a prime spot with easy access to the king's rooms — proved these small details mattered.

The spring sunshine warmed Jane's face as they strolled through the streets. It was a dream to be outside after hours stuck in the queen's gloomy rooms reading dull passages from the Bible. In a few hours, she would be meeting Francis and Gilbert, Baron Tailboys of Kyme, Bessie's husband to update them. A private house had been rented and she was relieved as a strange event had occurred that morning, which she felt they should consider.

Before her trip with Audrey, Jane had been with the queen and as ever, Katherine had requested Jane should read.

"Your voice is soft and bell-like," the queen had sighed, "it is like an angel reading the word of God."

Yet, the passage selected had sent a cold shiver run down Jane's spine.

"Perhaps you could recite the story of the brave woman, Rahab, from the book of Joshua," the queen had suggested. "The woman who saved the spies in order to further the word of the Lord."

"Spies, Your Majesty?" she had asked, trying to keep the sharp sting of nervousness from her voice. "This is not a story of which I am aware."

Wondering if the queen had heard rumours and was testing for her reaction, she forced her face into a gentle smile, but Katherine's expression was guileless. Nevertheless, Jane began the passage with trepidation. As the tale unfolded and Rahab and her family were saved, Jane realised this story led to the tale about defending the walls of Jericho. Another shiver ran down Jane's spine and she decided to report the incident to Francis.

It was well-known among the courtiers that the name Jericho was a crude reference to the manor of St Laurence Priory in Blackmore, Essex. Rumours abounded that this manor was where Henry met his mistresses, a place of hedonism and lewd behaviour. Jane read until the end, wondering what message the queen was trying to portray. Was it a warning? Or, merely, a passage the queen found informative? Either way, Jane was relieved to finish and flee the oppressive atmosphere of the queen's chambers.

"Here's the apothecary," she said, smelling the pungent herbs and unguents long before they reached the doorway.

Inside, it was dark but clean. The floor was freshly swept and the shelves were free of dust. Rows of preprepared simples and remedies jostled for position, offering cures and beauty treatments in abundance. The apothecary's wife smiled at the two women, exchanging pleasantries, before Jane asked about willow bark and camomile. As their transactions were made, Jane opened the leather bag hanging from her waist and withdrew her coins, before passing over a small, sealed note.

"For your husband," she said as the woman took it. "From Lady Margaret Blount, she is unwell today and requested I collect the remedies she ordered."

Hurrying through the curtain that separated the shop from the work room and living space to the rear, Jane and Audrey amused themselves perusing the many wares on sale.

"Is it Lady Margaret's foot that ails her?" asked Audrey.

"Yes, she was in a great deal of pain this morning," replied Jane. "It seemed a small thing to agree to collect her order."

Margaret Blount, known to all as Meg, was the younger sister of Bessie Blount and was known for her skill with herbs. It was Meg who had suggested the willow bark to Jane. When Meg had asked Jane to collect her order, she had been delighted to help. Meg had been born with a defect in her legs causing her right foot to turn inwards. The misshapen bone was often painful but Meg worked hard to try and minimise her disability, even learning to dance. However, there were times when she found it difficult to walk long distances.

Jane hummed to herself as she wandered around the shop, glancing at the preparations available, wondering whether to buy a small pot of the perfumed lotion offering soft hands. Audrey waited near the door where she could watch the page Francis had provided to accompany them.

"He won't run away with our purchases," she laughed, watching Audrey's suspicious gaze.

A movement behind her attracted Jane's attention and the apothecary hovered in the archway between the shop and the private space to the rear. He was in his middle years and Jane thought he had probably been handsome when he was younger but the grey at his temples and the lines around his eyes blurred his looks.

"Good day, Madam," he said, his London accent broad. "Are you a friend of Lady Margaret's?"

"Yes," replied Jane. "I am Jane Seymour, a lady of Queen Katherine's court, is there a problem with the order?"

The apothecary's brown eyes searched her face, then he gave a nod and disappeared behind the curtain. There was a whispered discussion and the apothecary's wife returned holding a parcel.

"Will you be returning to the palace?" she asked.

"In a short while," replied Jane, irritated at the strange behaviour of the apothecary and his wife.

In response, the woman wrapped another layer of paper around the parcel and placed it in a canvas bag. "The contents are delicate," she explained. "These wrappings will protect them. Please ensure you take great care or they will be of no use to Lady Margaret."

Jane took the parcel, her eyes narrowing in annoyance. "It does not behove you to speak to me in such a manner," said Jane. "However, I shall ensure the content is intact when it reaches Lady Margaret." Turning with as much hauteur as she could muster, Jane led Audrey outside.

"What was wrong with them?" said Audrey.

"No idea," replied Jane. "They're very protective over their wares, anyone would think I planned to steal Meg's order."

The two young women made their way towards the gathering crowd. Trailing behind was the page carrying their purchases. Despite her irritation, Jane heeded the apothecary's word and held the parcel for Meg herself. As they approached the platform that had been erected for the Holy Maid of Kent, she was wondering whether to join the excitable throng when she saw Henry Norris.

"Sir Henry," she called and as she hoped, he hurried towards them.

"My dear Jane," he said, bowing. Jane and Audrey curtsied and the page shuffled his feet. "Are you here to see the Holy Maid?"

"Queen Katherine is interested in her work," Jane said. "As we were here, it seemed prudent to assess her piety for myself."

"There are none more pious than you, Mrs Seymour," he said, grinning, and Jane gave him a knowing look. "Come, I shall escort you to a safer position." Indicating for his servant to clear a space for them, he bent low and whispered, "Are you meeting Francis?"

"In an hour at Baron Tailboy's house."

"I shall accompany you."

Ten minutes later, Jane watched as the slight figure of Elizabeth Barton was led on stage by Archbishop Warham. Dressed in the black habit of the Benedictine nun, the woman stood in the centre of the stage. With her eyes closed, she waited, the calmness and serenity of her pose seeping through the rowdy crowd. As though a spell had been cast, the shouting and calling ceased as everyone focussed on the Holy Maid of Kent. When there was silence, she opened her eyes, pulling a sealed letter from her sleeves and waving it for the crowd to observe.

"This letter was written by Mary Magdalene," she announced and Jane heard a collective gasp of wonder. "She visited me last night and dictated a message of great importance. We must repent, we must worship in the true faith and banish Lutherans. As we talked, she told me how to stop the ships of two monks travelling to the exiled Bible maker, William Tyndale. I used her power to turn the ships around, to return the monks to our shores, to make them repent of their unwholesome desire to read the word of God for themselves. There is no need for the Lord's Bible to be written in English. The word of God is for holy men, not for the likes of you." She raised her arm, pointing at the nervous crowd. "Who are you to sully the name of the Lord with your rough tongues? Her most holy lady, Mary Magdalene, guided me as I instructed another monk to burn the English Bible. Yet, this was not all. In the darkness of the night, as I walked with Mary in the holy gardens of the Lord, she told me of a message for His Majesty, King Henry. Our wise sovereign, led astray by the forces of darkness, by witchcraft. Our most holy lady showed me a book containing all there has been and all that will be. I saw wonderful things and I saw terrible things. Do you know what I saw?"

A murmur rose from the crowd.

"I saw the king, reunited with the queen. I saw a boy, a prince, the future king of this land, a wise and benevolent ruler. So wise," she murmured, bringing her hands together as though in prayer. "And I saw the one they call the Dark Lady,

Anne Boleyn. She stood alone and in the shadowed darkness. I saw the true horror of her actions writ large. For, as I stand before you now, a lowly nun, guided by the Lord himself, I warn that if the king does not return to the beloved Queen Katherine, then the punishment will fall on Anne and she will lose her head…"

A roar of approval went up from the crowd, and as the Nones bell chimed above them, Henry Norris led Jane and Audrey away.

CHAPTER FOUR

"Why doesn't she give up and retreat with dignity? It's obvious to anyone with eyes in their head that the king is in love with Anne," Jane sighed as she and Francis drifted down the river on his private barge. "The queen wants to spend her life in prayer and the king is offering her the opportunity to devote herself to God."

It had been a week since Jane and Audrey had witnessed Elizabeth Barton preaching in the London street. The meeting with Francis and Gilbert Tailboys had been brief but they had suggested Katherine had asked Jane to read the passage to watch the reactions of the women.

"The queen is no fool," Gilbert Tailboys had stated, "she must have deduced there is a spy in her inner circle. The fact she asked you to read it, Jane, makes me think it is not you whom she suspects."

"How can you be sure?" she had asked.

"If the queen thought it was you, she would have asked someone else to read it in order to gauge your reaction; people often give themselves away by a guilty look or nervous response. I'd guess the queen thought you would be the best person to read aloud because you, my love, are above suspicion," said Francis.

Jane had been uncertain about this pronouncement and had determined to sink further into the shadows over the next few days. However, it had been impossible as the queen had sought her out at every opportunity to discuss the Holy Maid of Kent's prophecies. Jane found these interviews uncomfortable but did her best to placate the queen.

"And she said we would have a son, the king and I?" the queen had asked on every occasion they had discussed the sermon.

Jane would smile and nod, wishing she had never mentioned her encounter with Elizabeth Barton. It was a relief when she had escaped this evening to her clandestine meeting with Francis, claiming family business. He was her distant cousin, she had reasoned, as she hurried to the jetty where his barge awaited, the thrill of excitement making her feet fly, so it was not a complete untruth.

Laughing, he had helped her into the sumptuous barge and they had glided away. Their relationship had moved from friendship to an understanding of marriage, although, due to her mother's disapproval, they were yet to announce their feelings. Jane had no doubt it would not be long before she and Francis were able to persuade her parents and, if not, they had decided they would elope. As they drifted down the gentle waters of the Thames, their conversation turned, as ever, to the turmoil within the court.

"Katherine is queen, she will never give up her position or her royal status," Francis replied, feeding Jane a sip of cool wine from his goblet. "Despite her strong faith, Her Grace has always believed it was her calling to be Queen of England, the mother to the nation, to the next monarch and the anointed wife of the king. These are not things she will step away from. Remember, Jane, the king has done this many times during their marriage. There was Bessie Blount, before her there were Etiennette de la Raume, and afterwards, Jane Popincourt, Lady Hastings, Mary Boleyn and these are the ones we know about, no doubt there were others. The Queen has gritted her teeth and waited for Henry's passions to fade and, so far, they have all drifted away like mist on the water."

"Do you think he will tire of Anne?"

"As for that, I have no idea," he said.

"Do you doubt the king's feelings?"

"The king is a complex man," he sighed. "News has reached me that Lady Mary Berkeley, daughter of James Berkeley and Susan Fitzalan, the wife of Sir Thomas Perrot of Carew Castle in Pembrokeshire, is with child."

"What has this to do with Anne?"

"The rumour is that, despite having been married for a while, their youth meant they were not permitted to live together as man and wife, yet Mary is pregnant..."

"These things happen..." began Jane but Francis shook his head.

"You misunderstand, my dear, the whispers suggest the king is the father. He and Mary were seen to be enjoying time together during one of Anne's absences from court. When Mary told the king of her situation, Wolsey arranged for the couple to be shipped back to Pembrokeshire with a large pension in order to have the babe."

"Do you believe this gossip?"

"Yes, I do," he said. "It has been many months since Henry shared the queen's bed and as Anne will not allow him into hers, he was happy to take advantage of a willing and very pretty young lady like Mary Berkeley. However, I feel this dalliance will have no impact on his quest to have your cousin. When she heard the news, Anne would have felt relief and perhaps hoped the king might be tiring of her. We both know Anne would grant the king his freedom from their betrothal in an instance."

Jane did not reply, considering Francis's words. *There was a time*, she thought, *when this information would have shocked me.* Until her arrival at court, she had always believed that love meant you were true to one person. The king claimed to love Anne, yet he could sleep with another woman, probably women. These casual infidelities were rife throughout the court and, despite Francis's declared loyalty, she shuddered at the thought that he, too, satisfied himself elsewhere. Jane had been in love with Francis for as long as she could remember. He claimed to love her, yet he would betray their love by dalliances with other women. The concept was hurtful and confusing but, it was something upon which she chose not to dwell.

"The king and I have been friends for years and this infatuation is different," Francis said. "It is not because Anne refuses the allure of his bedchamber, Henry is not so base. He believes they have a connection written in the stars and, therefore, they are destined to create a great monarch to follow in his footsteps."

"Is this what drives him with such determination?" asked Jane, intrigued by this concept.

"Henry has always believed he was chosen to build a powerful dynasty, to bring the glory and power of Camelot back to England. Yet, in order to do this, he needs sons…"

"He has sons…" began Jane.

"Not born in wedlock," replied Francis, "and this is the difference. If Henry can persuade Katherine that their marriage, while made in good faith, was unlawful, this would not invalidate the Princess Mary's legitimacy, making a princess available for a dynastic foreign marriage; it would also make it possible for the king to marry Anne and have a legitimate son. Yet, while the queen claims her marriage to Prince Arthur was unconsummated, there is nothing to be done."

"But nobody believes her," Jane said. "She and Prince Arthur were married for several months before he died. I don't believe their marriage remained unconsummated."

"Nor does anyone else," said Francis, "but how do we prove it? We can't, so the stalemate continues."

Jane settled back into the comfortable crook of Francis's arm as the golden rays of the sun set fire to the sky. Moving closer together, their touch familiar, Jane closed her eyes, happy to be alone with him. Few knew of their clandestine liaison, a choice they had made together, fearing interference from many sides: her family, his family, the king, possibly even the queen or Anne. Yet, Jane knew he was her love. No matter what, she knew her future held Sir Francis Bryan. Allowing this thought to push away her concerns, she changed the subject.

"Have you seen the latest pamphlet from the Holy Maid of Kent?" she asked, as they drifted through the dappled light.

"The one designed to earn the approval of Cardinal Wolsey, suggesting he can save the king from himself?"

"Yes, I ensured it was left somewhere the queen could read it," she said. "Katherine is very keen to take Elizabeth into her household."

"Meanwhile, the king has suggested to Anne that the Holy Maid joins her court. Anne is uninterested, she believes the woman is a fraud."

Jane did not respond. Barton's claim to have seen Anne without a head had shocked them all. While Jane did not think there was anything in the Holy Maid's declarations, the rumours that followed her pronouncement had swept through London and the surrounding counties, suggesting Anne was a witch and had lured the king into loving her with help from the devil. This had placed Anne in a dangerous position and Henry had insisted she have her own guards in order to protect her from the wrath of the mob.

"If the king declares it, it must be so," sighed Francis, "then Anne will have to make the best of it."

"As she must make the best of her current situation."

"She will be queen," replied Francis. "Is this not what all women want?"

"No," said Jane with a derisive snort. "Women want to be loved, to feel safe and to live as they choose, but we are never given such consideration."

Francis stared at her in astonishment. "What do you mean?"

"Anne wanted to marry James, yet through the machinations of her uncle, the Duke of Norfolk and her father, Thomas Boleyn, she is being pushed towards the king who she doesn't love…"

"Marriage is rarely about love, my sweet," said Francis. "It is usually a political or business transaction. Anne will be queen, she will ennoble her entire family, us included…"

"Yet, she helps Bessie Blount with her dreams of placing Fitzroy on the throne," interrupted Jane in frustration. "We work and scheme at this plot, that plot, this idea, but what are they really? Smoke on the water. You men with your scheming and your posturing, you have these grand ideas, but it is we women who manifest them."

"You're right," agreed Francis, "but Anne is playing a wise game. She knows, if Henry can find a way to annul his marriage, her path to becoming queen consort is laid out before her. In order to keep him happy, she agrees with all he says, except for when she loses her temper, which is a regular occurrence. Yet, she is also aware that she might not have a child with the king. These things are not guaranteed and, even if she does produce an heir, it might be a girl."

"How shocking," gasped Jane in mock despair. Her clear blue eyes locked with his golden brown and she raised a perfect blonde eyebrow, making him laugh. "A girl. What a disaster."

"You terrible wench," he laughed.

"Who's the scandalous one here, Sir Francis?"

Pulling her into his arms, he kissed her. Jane's heart pounded. Nothing mattered as long as Francis was nearby. It had always been this way and spending more time together since her arrival at court, she was even angrier with her parents for refusing the match between them, which was proposed several years earlier. Jane had always suspected it was a punishment for siding with her father during his affair with Catherine Filliol. Whatever the reason, she no longer cared; despite her parents' disapproval, she and Francis had long since come to an arrangement of their own. When he released her, he stroked his finger across her cheek.

"Anne knows that if she doesn't produce a son, Henry will search elsewhere and this is why she supports Bessie Blount. Anne believes a coup from Bessie to sweep her son on to the throne could save her from a life of misery."

"But Fitzroy is nine years old, he can't rule alone."

"Think Jane, think who Bessie holds as her inspiration."

"Lady Margaret Beaufort, the king's grandmother."

"It took Margaret years to place her son on the throne. Bessie is prepared to fight for as long as it takes. Do you know what Norfolk threatened Anne with when she told him she didn't want to marry Henry?"

"I don't," admitted Jane.

"He warned her that if she didn't catch the king, he would send her to a remote convent and have her walled in as an anchorite nun."

"No," Jane was horrified.

An anchorite nun was bricked into a cell to live a life of complete devotion but it was a calling for only the most devout of souls. Jane could not imagine her lively cousin surviving such an ordeal.

"Which is why Anne plays the role of devoted sweetheart of the king," he said. "She views the alternative as too terrible to contemplate."

As darkness fell, they walked towards the gates of Greenwich Palace, unlacing their fingers with reluctance, but as they entered the gatehouse it was apparent that in their absence a crisis had arisen. Chamberlains shouted instructions, boxes were transported to waiting carriages and baggage trains, horses' hooves clattered on the cobbles, dogs barked and courtiers hurried to and fro, fear written on their faces.

"What has happened?" asked Francis, grabbing a page in Howard livery as he scooted past.

"It's the Sweat, sir, there are two women in the queen's chambers who have fallen sick. The queen has sent a messenger to the king and they plan to leave. The Duke of Richmond and Somerset has been moved from Pontefract Castle to a place of safety…"

Jane winced as Francis grabbed her hand and dragged her through the crowd.

"Go to the queen, Jane, see where she intends to travel, I shall attend to the king." Above them the clock in the tower chimed the hour. "Whatever happens, meet me in my rooms in two hours with your belongings…"

"Why?" gasped Jane, her hand smarting from his grip.

"We're leaving; we will travel to Hertford Castle, it is forty miles from here and we shall be safe from the noxious odours."

A thrill ran through her, replaced swiftly by fear, but there was no time to voice her apprehension.

"The queen…" Francis prompted.

Gathering her skirts, Jane hurried through the mêlée, crashing through the doors to the queen's apartments. Women swirled from room to room. Lady Dormer, the Countess of Essex and Lady Fitzwilliam were issuing instructions, each order tinged with hysteria.

"Jane, at last," gasped Lady Dormer, "we'd given you up for lost. Take these sleeves and wrap them in linen so they don't mark when they're packed. The king has sent word that he and the queen are to travel to safety this very evening."

"The king is travelling with the queen, not with…"

"May the Virgin be praised, perhaps our prayers have been answered and the king has returned to his true love, the queen."

Jane was startled. Where was the king's undying love for Anne? Confused by these events, she nevertheless did as instructed and helped to prepare the queen's trunks for the journey. An unfamiliar laugh filled the room and Jane looked up from the task she had been allotted to see the queen transformed. Katherine was in the doorway of her bedchamber, a cloak around her shoulders, her face was aglow with happiness, making her look years younger.

"Did we not pray for this?" she enthused to Lady Dormer. "As soon as there is serious danger, the king's sense has been restored and he has returned to my side as I knew he would. All will be well again. This altercation will be but a memory and, in due time, we shall have a son. Praise be to the Holy Maid of Kent who predicted such a happy event."

The clock struck. An hour had passed and glancing around, Jane noticed several women were excusing themselves, melting away to join loved ones, their faces anxious. Closing the lid and locking the trunk she had been packing, she gave the key to the Countess of Essex.

"I must leave," she murmured and before the Countess could respond, Jane curtseyed to the queen and hurried from the room, ignoring the calls begging her to return. Francis had told her what to do and she intended to follow his instructions.

As she threw open the door, Audrey looked up from the wooden travelling case she was loading with Jane's belongings.

"Jane, the palace is in uproar. I thought it wise to pack, where shall you go?"

"We are going to stay with Sir Francis Bryan," said Jane. "We are to meet him on the hour. Our bags will be collected by his servant."

"What a relief," Audrey said. "Thank you. I was scared to stay in the city."

Jane moved around the room, wrapping her Bible and poetry books in a shawl and adding them to the trunk, hoping neither of her brothers, Edward or Henry, would arrive and insist she return to Wulfhall until the danger had passed.

The darkness was thickening around them as Jane was helped into a litter by Francis.

"You and Audrey will be safer in here, the journey is long and it will be better if you can sleep," he assured her as he tucked a blanket across her legs.

"What news of Anne?" asked Jane.

"Travelling to Hever Castle in Kent with her family," he replied. "We must see how events unfold. Perhaps the king has decided to return to the queen but, as he commanded his second physician to accompany Anne, while his lead physician travels with him, I think it unwise to make predictions."

"The Sweat has no respect for common or royal blood," said Jane. "We must all pray for salvation."

Moving over to make room for him to join them, Francis shook his head. "I shall ride with my guards in case of trouble."

He gave her a broad smile and his eyes glittered overbright and hard as diamonds. The tense mood at the palace had acted upon Francis like a curse. An uncontrollable excitement emanated from him, a quicksilver mood which Jane had witnessed before and disliked. In moments such as these, she was aware that Francis could flip from elegant courtier to violent thug in the blink of an eye. She hoped they would meet no cut-throats on the road tonight as Francis would slit their throats. The thought of unnecessary violence was repellent. This simmering elemental side was a darkness on his soul with which she had not yet come to terms.

"I shall awake you when we approach," he assured her. "I have sent word of our arrival so the castle will be ready to entertain a lady of your importance."

With a rakish grin, he pulled the heavy leather-lined curtains closed and as Jane heard him shouting instructions, the litter lurched and they set off into the night.

With Audrey murmuring her Rosary into the darkness, Jane pulled the covers around her, wondering whether this escape from court would save their lives and what other dangers it might bring.

PART THREE: MARQUESS HOUSE, 2021

CHAPTER ONE

Perdita stared at the page in front of her in astonishment. Picking up the top few sheets from a huge pile of printouts beside her, which had been scanned with one of Mark's high-tech devices from *The Pentagram Manuscript*, she ran her finger down the paragraphs, her mind whirring. Ever since the discovery of the hidden archive three weeks earlier, she had been trying to decipher the meanings within the poems they had found. Each was five lines long and arranged in series of five stanzas with a row of five pentagram symbols separating them.

It was clear to Perdita that the poems were not simply interesting tales of knights and ladies. She had begun to try and decipher the hidden messages within the lines of poetry, writing her own marginalia. To her surprise, a story had begun to emerge of a woman who was part of the Tudor court at the time of the upheaval of the 'King's Great Matter' — Henry VIII's divorce from Katherine of Aragon and his marriage to Anne Boleyn.

Perdita was certain this manuscript had not been written by either of those women. They described themselves as someone who had been the mother of a son and, despite it seeming fantastical, one of the potential candidates that Perdita had added to her list was Jane Seymour, Henry's third wife, and mother of the future Edward VI. The facts didn't match up, though, because the woman narrating the manuscript appeared to be betrothed to Sir Francis Bryan and, according to historical records, Jane had been single when she caught the eye of the king in September 1535.

Rifling through her notes and flicking through various history books scattered around her office, Perdita searched for Sir Francis Bryan. Although she was aware of the courtier and diplomat, he was not someone whose life she knew in detail. Checking his parentage, she discovered he was the son of Thomas Bryan and Margaret Bourchier. She checked one of her many family trees.

Margaret Bourchier was the daughter of Elizabeth Tilney and Sir Humphrey Bourchier. A year after Sir Humphrey was killed at the Battle of Barnet on 14 April 1471, Margaret married Sir Thomas Howard, the future Earl of Surrey. Their family was vast and well-positioned and her daughter, Elizabeth Howard, went on to marry Thomas Boleyn and they became the parents of Anne.

"Margaret Bourchier and Elizabeth Howard were half-sisters through their mother," said Perdita aloud, staring at her ever-growing family tree. "This meant that Sir Francis Bryan and Anne Boleyn were cousins, or half-cousins, if there is such a thing."

For some reason, this fact unnerved Perdita. Reading through various biographies, things became more mystifying and, when there was a knock at the door ten minutes later and Cal wandered in, she was staring at her board of family trees with her face screwed up in confusion.

"What's up?" he asked, his arms full of cables.

"Historical knots," replied Perdita.

"Would you like to expound?" he offered. "I appreciate I don't have Kit's knowledge or Piper's analytical skills but I'm happy to listen if saying it out loud might help."

"Do you have time?" she asked, aware that Callum's team of security specialists was once again updating all the systems at Marquess House.

"I'm the boss; my time is my own," he said with a flourish, laying the cables across a chair and sitting down opposite Perdita.

"Good point," she laughed. "Have you heard from Piper?"

"Not for a while," he replied, putting his phone on the desk between them. "She said she'd text when she was leaving."

For the past few weeks, Piper had been coordinating the reorganisation of artworks from not only The Mary Fitzroy Heritage Centre but also Marquess House, having discovered some hidden gems at the Bath storage facility. Jenny, Mark, Perdita and Stephanie had been organising the removal of the hidden archive which now occupied an entire room in The Dairy and Piper had agreed to oversee the loading of the final pallet of boxes.

Callum gave Perdita an amused grin. "More importantly, have you heard from Kit?"

"No, but he'll be back soon," she said. "Are you going to tease him?"

"Of course," replied Callum. "It's my duty as his best friend, I can't let the beginning of his descent into middle-age go unmarked."

"His descent into middle-age?" exclaimed Perdita. "He's picking up a pair of reading glasses."

"It's where it starts," said Callum. "So, how can I be of assistance?"

"Do you know anything about Sir Francis Bryan?" she asked, as she walked over to the table in the corner of the office where she kept a kettle and began making them both a cup of tea.

"Hell's Vicar, wasn't that Sir Francis Bryan?" said Callum.

Perdita stared at Callum in surprise. "I believe that was one of the names he was known by," she said, putting the mugs on the table. "Thomas Cromwell christened him with that particular nomenclature. How did you know?"

"A-level history," said Callum. "I wrote an essay about him. Mum hoped either Elliot or I would follow her into the world of historical research and join her in the library, but it didn't really appeal to us. He became a pilot and I went into IT but we both got an A in our history A-levels."

"I'm impressed," said Perdita. "Funny how the man listed in one biography as being a diplomat, soldier, code breaker, man of letters, poet, rake and libertine stuck in your mind."

"He was one of the more interesting characters we studied," agreed Callum. "Has Sir Francis of the Darkness, as I liked to call him back then, made his unsavoury presence felt in your research?"

"Yes, and in connection with Jane Seymour, the pious third wife of Henry VIII."

"Now there are two names I would never have put together," he said.

"My thoughts exactly," replied Perdita. "It transpires that Francis and Jane were distant cousins and shared a great-grandmother, Elizabeth Cheney."

As Perdita pointed to a complicated family tree on the wall, Callum sipped his tea and considered the twisting lines.

"Go on," he said.

"Elizabeth Cheney married twice, first to Sir Frederick Tilney. They had a daughter, Elizabeth Tilney, who also married twice."

Callum ran his finger along one of the lines on the family tree. "She was Sir Francis Bryan's grandmother," he said.

"Correct; from Elizabeth Tilney's first marriage to Sir Humphrey Bourchier. She had three children, including Margaret Bourchier, who married Sir Thomas Bryan. They also had three children, including Sir Francis Bryan." Perdita pointed to the first section of the tree. "Then from Elizabeth Cheney's second marriage to Sir John Say she had three sons and four daughters, one of whom was Anne Say. Anne married Henry Wentworth and had six children. One of their daughters was Margery Wentworth, who married John Seymour and gave birth to ten children, one of whom was Jane Seymour."

Callum studied the family tree, tracing another line which led to Anne Boleyn. "Why the interest in Sir Francis Bryan?" he asked.

"Even though history remembers him as a wild friend of Henry VIII's, the story unravelling in the manuscript we found in Bath suggests he was actually in love with Jane Seymour, as she was with him."

"What? How is that possible?"

"Exactly what I'm trying to discover," said Perdita. "According to traditional records, Sir Francis Bryan married Philippa Spice, who was a widow. They had no children, then after she died, he married Lady Joan Fitzgerald, who was the widow of James Butler, 9th Earl of Ormond. She had seven sons from her first marriage and one son with Francis and when he died, Lady Joan married Gerald Fitzgerald, 15th Earl of Desmond, who was supposedly a great deal younger than her."

"Good for Joan."

"Quite! There is another thing though; in this transcript, there are suggestions that Anne Boleyn, far from being in love with Henry VIII, was actually in love with someone else…"

"Sir Henry Percy," interrupted Callum.

Perdita grinned. "He would have been my guess, or even the poet Thomas Wyatt, but according to this, Anne had been in love with James Butler, 9th Earl of Ormond all along. Her father, Thomas Boleyn, was one of the heirs to the earldom of Ormond but it went to a cousin, Piers Butler, father of James. It was suggested that Anne and James marry, so the title would skip Thomas, but his grandsons would inherit it. However, before that could be organised, the king fell in love with Anne and all other marriages were off the table."

"Then Francis married James's widow?" clarified Callum.

"Peculiar, isn't it?" said Perdita.

The door opened and Kit entered.

"All right mate, how did it go?" asked Callum. "Let's see them."

Perdita smiled as Kit pulled the case from his pocket and put on his tortoiseshell glasses. She knew Kit was self-conscious about the idea of wearing glasses. Piper, who had worn both glasses and contact lenses since her teens, had reassured him. "Glasses are very attractive," she had said, then in a stage-whisper when Callum had finished sniggering. "Perds loves a man in glasses."

"I hate to say this, mate, but they do suit you," said Callum with pretend ire.

"Even more gorgeous," said Perdita, reaching over to kiss him.

Kit tucked the glasses back in his pocket and, looking at the piles of books and papers, asked, "Have I missed a big historical reveal?"

"Not really," said Perdita, "more of an historical query about one of Henry VIII's friends, Sir Francis Bryan."

While Callum made more tea, Perdita talked Kit through her thoughts.

"I'm going to have to hurry Mark up with his tests on *The Pentagram Manuscript*. I need to get to the original because this transcript seems to be suggesting some very odd things going on when Henry VIII was trying to divorce Katherine of Aragon in order to marry Anne Boleyn. The oddest thing is Jane Seymour being in love with Sir Francis Bryan."

Gazing at the wall of family trees, Perdita accepted the fresh mug of tea from Callum. Settling back, enjoying the banter between her husband and his best friend, the background noise of Marquess House hummed around them and she felt content.

Callum's phone rang.

"Hello, Callum Black speaking," he said in his most business-like tone.

Perdita and Kit grinned at each other but their humour, along with the relaxed, comfortable mood changed in a heartbeat as Perdita watched Callum stiffen, the colour draining from his face. There was a crash as he dropped the mug, reaching out to Perdita and Kit, beckoning them forward as he flipped his phone to speaker, his hands shaking, his eyes wild with panic.

"Where is she?" he shouted.

Perdita's heart froze. "Piper?" she gasped.

Callum nodded as the calm voice of the police officer on the other end of the phone continued to speak.

"Mr Black, would you like me to ring Mrs Mackensie?"

"I'm here, too," said Perdita, her voice harsh, unrecognisable. "What's happened to my sister?"

"There was an accident on the motorway. Your sister has been airlifted to Morriston Hospital in Swansea. Are you able to get there?"

"Yes," said Perdita. "Is she alive?"

"She is in a very serious condition, but she is alive," came the woman's voice.

Kit took the phone, writing down the details, passing on his own and checking the hospital had all their numbers. "We'll leave now," he said, handing the phone back to Callum as he reached for the internal phone to call his parents.

Perdita did not hear him; she was in a void of fear. Her mother had been killed in a car accident when she and Piper had been seven years old. Could history be repeating itself? A sea of images of her sister danced before her eyes. Piper, her twin, part of her soul. The floor buckled under her feet as she struggled to catch her breath.

"Piper," she whimpered, her vision blurring, "not Piper."

And everything went dark.

"Perds, wake up."

Kit's voice floated through the blackness; she could feel a hand stroking hers and moments later, the room came into focus.

"Piper," she gasped, fighting to sit up, furious with herself for her reaction. Piper needed her and she was collapsing like a damsel in distress.

"Give yourself a moment," said Kit, who was sitting beside her, holding her hand. "Breathe, it was the shock."

"Where's Cal?" asked Perdita, fighting to stand up, grateful to feel Kit's hand steadying her as she swayed.

"Fetching our grab bags, Dad is organising a car to drive us to the hospital."

"Grab bags?"

For a moment she did not understand, then her mind caught up with the situation. After the danger they had found themselves in previously, it was agreed between Alistair, Perdita, Piper and Stephen Haberfield, the head of MI1 Elite division of the Secret Service, that a special task force would be set up to monitor the situation at Marquess House and to help protect them.

Haberfield's assistant, Gary Ashley, had been made head of this small force and by working with Alistair and Kit, had assured their intrusion was minimal but their support, should it be required, would be the maximum protection special forces could provide. Stephen Haberfield had also required Perdita, Piper, Kit and Callum, once it was revealed he was in a relationship with Piper, to have anti-kidnap training, as well as advanced defensive driving lessons.

"It's essential to have a grab bag prepared at all times," Gary had informed them, "making it possible for you to leave at a moment's notice."

As Perdita and Kit had once before had to run for their lives, Perdita understood the wisdom of this advice. The self-defence lessons involved in the anti-kidnap training, as well as how to behave should the situation ever arise, had unnerved them all, but they had understood the necessity. Once the shock of the tutorials were over, Perdita and Piper admitted to each other that they felt more able to cope should an unexpected event arise. When the four of them were taken to an airfield to be taught defensive driving techniques, Perdita and Piper had enjoyed the high adrenalin chases. Both were confident drivers but the tips on how to manoeuvre themselves out of threatening situations and how to behave during an accident or should one occur around them, forcing them off the road, made them realise how unprepared they had been.

After this, their cars were taken away by MI1 and fitted with trackers, bullet-proof glass, reinforced panels and other embellishments which Perdita hoped she would never have to use.

"Shame there's no ejector seat," Callum had said to Kit upon the cars' return.

"Or rocket launchers," Kit had added, and they had exchanged a disappointed look.

As a final flourish, Haberfield had sent a request to inject each of them with a tracking device smaller than a grain of rice.

"It won't be activated unless there is a situation of dire necessity. We're not interested in keeping track of your movements, this is a security measure we feel is necessary due to the current situation. Randolph Connors may have been apprehended and be incarcerated in a place where he can no longer hurt you but his son, Xavier, remains free. Until this situation changes, we must take every possible precaution." Randolph Connors was a dangerous adversary who wanted to claim Marquess House for his granddaughters, Ruby and Pearl. He and his son Xavier had already attempted to kill the twins once and now it seemed they were trying again.

The four were continuing to discuss this suggestion, as they all felt it was a step too far and infringed on their privacy.

The door to the office opened and Susan Mackensie flew in.

"Perdita, are you...?"

"I'm fine," Perdita snapped, before apologising. Irritation with herself, combined with fear for her sister was making her behave irrationally. "Is there any news on Piper?"

"You've only been out for a few minutes," Kit reassured her. "Grab your coat, we need to leave. I've called Jenny to tidy up in here."

"Thank you," she said, looping her handbag over her shoulder, then grabbing his hand and dragging him out of the door.

Callum was running down the vast staircase, followed by Larry Eve, head of the security staff, who was carrying bags for Perdita, Kit and Alistair. Callum had his, Piper's and Susan's.

"Who's driving?" Perdita asked as she followed them through the doors.

"None of us," replied Alistair as two large, black SUVs skidded to a halt and two men in black combats jumped out. "I activated the code given to me by Gary Ashley as I felt this was an emergency. None of us should be driving such a distance and with these vehicles, there are advantages."

Perdita did not need to ask, instead she climbed into the back of the car in which Larry had stowed her luggage. Kit followed but as Callum tried to join them, the driver stopped him.

"Sorry, sir, my orders are that you should ride separately."

"What?" Callum asked.

Perdita leapt back out. "Why can't he travel with us?" she demanded.

Susan diffused the situation. "Think, Perdita," she hissed. "For the same reason Haberfield is reluctant for you and Piper to travel together. Your sister has been in a car accident. We can't all be in the same vehicle."

Admonished, Perdita climbed back into the car.

Moments later, the two huge vehicles tore from the driveway and into the setting sun. Perdita took Kit's hand, staring out of the window but not seeing, her breath shallow as the cars sped through the country lanes. The moment they hit the main road the cars picked up speed and Perdita realised other vehicles were moving aside. Turning around to look through the heavily tinted windows she saw blue lights flashing through the grills of the car carrying Callum, Susan and Alistair.

Kit's arm slid around her and she leaned into him.

"What if she's…?"

"Don't think about it," he said. "When Cal spoke to the doctor, she was alive."

His word hung in the air and Perdita bit back a sob, instead turning her attention towards her twin, certain that if anything happened, she would know.

"This way," said Gary Ashley, half an hour later, greeting them at the entrance to the hospital. Perdita had never covered the 65-mile journey from St Ishmaels to Swansea in such a short time but she was grateful for the skills of the drivers and the police outriders who greeted them twenty minutes into their journey. "Piper is in a private wing. This is Dr Garrick; he came with me."

"How is my sister?" demanded Perdita, as they hurried into the lift.

Callum stood white-faced and trembling between Alistair and Susan, who appeared to be holding him up.

"She's been very lucky," said Dr Garrick. "Thanks to her defensive driving, she was able to avoid the brunt of the collision, but she has numerous cuts and bruises. We've given her a brain scan and there are no internal bleeds. She has a hairline fracture on her left wrist and two broken ribs. At present she's sedated in order to give her body time to recover from the shock."

The lift stopped and before the doors were properly open, Perdita was pushing her way out. Gary stepped forward to lead the way. Moments later, they were beside Piper. Perdita stared down at her sister's fiery red hair, a bright spot of colour against the white pillows and around her ashen face.

Callum sank into the chair beside her, taking Piper's hand, tears streaming down his face. "The baby?" he croaked to the doctor. "What about the baby?"

Perdita gripped Kit's arm in surprise.

"Are you Callum Black?" the doctor asked. Callum nodded. "I'm sorry, Sir, Mrs Davidson lost the child."

Perdita let out a sob and Callum crumpled.

CHAPTER TWO

"Perds, sorry to interrupt but Gary Ashley's arrived with information." Kit's voice was apologetic over the internal telephone system.

"I didn't think he was due until later," Perdita said, saving the document on her desktop and powering it down. "Has something else happened?"

"He won't say until you're here," said Kit.

"Which means they've discovered something."

"Yes, I thought the same thing."

"On my way," she said and hung up, hurrying out of the research centre and across the gardens to Marquess House.

Kit's office was in one of the older wings of Marquess House. Like her grandmother before her, Perdita's preferred workspace was in the research centre, which was built into the old coach house. A garden separated the research centre from Marquess House and Perdita enjoyed the feeling of leaving her home and 'going out to work' each day. Her additional office was in The Dairy, which was attached to the research centre by a glass walkway.

Kit and Alistair's offices were in the corridors surrounding the kitchen complex within the manor itself. The rooms had once been the domain of the bailiffs, groundsmen, housekeepers and butlers but they had long been renovated and modernised. Each was decorated in a unique style and the three Mackensies worked in adjoining offices. Alistair with the larger corner office, Susan in the room next to his and Kit on her other side. Kit's office was a similar size to Alistair's but with a sleeker, more modern appearance. While Alistair enjoyed the ambiance of old filing cabinets and overflowing bookcases, Kit's office was pristine, with a row of simple cupboards in a pale grey wood and bookcases arranged with meticulous care.

Stuart had followed Perdita's example and worked from the research centre. At first Perdita found it strange seeing her brother-in-law wandering around, particularly as there always seemed to be a young woman trailing behind him with hopeful eyes. Stuart's colouring was similar to his mother's with soft brown hair and wide brown eyes, a contrast to Kit and Alistair who both had the more Celtic colouring of dark hair with piercing blue eyes. Stuart's chiselled cheekbones, gym-honed physique and easy manner won hearts wherever he went and Kit had often said growing up in his older brother's shadow had not always been easy.

At present, Stuart was in London working on another deal for Jerusalem. After Piper's accident he had offered to stay but they had all insisted he go as this was a project he had been working on for months and it was near completion.

It was a week since Piper's accident and they were all unnerved that she had been so near to death, particularly as a car crash was the way Louisa had died. For the first 48 hours Perdita, Callum and Kit had remained at the hospital, keeping vigil around the clock, ensuring someone was always there as her medication was reduced, allowing her to wake up gradually. Painkillers kept the discomfort of the fracture in her wrist and broken ribs at bay, but Perdita could find no way to remove the pain from her sister's eyes when she heard about the loss of her baby.

"I'm sorry we didn't tell you," Piper had whispered to Perdita. "It was something of a miscalculation around the time of our birthdays. Callum and I discovered it a few weeks ago and, once we were over the shock, decided to be cautious. We'd planned to tell you the evening I came home from Bath. Had you guessed?"

"I wondered," Perdita had admitted, "when we first discovered the hidden archive and you wanted to move it to Marquess House, for 'later on' you said. There was a moment when your hand fluttered over your stomach and it made me curious."

Piper had given her a wan smile.

Later, Callum told Perdita and Kit that the doctor had assured them there was no reason why Piper would not be able to have children in the future. Since then, an investigation team from MI1 had been liaising with the traffic police to try and discover the cause of Piper's accident.

As Perdita approached Kit's office, she saw his assistant Cora leaving with a pile of files.

"Hi Perdita," Cora said with a cheery smile. "Kit asked me to move these from under Gary's prying eyes."

"What are they?" asked Perdita, intrigued.

"Files on MI1 personnel," Cora replied. "Alistair has acquired a substantial amount of information over the years and passed a great deal of it on to Kit. They felt these were safer away from the meeting in case their presence was misinterpreted."

Cora hurried away and Perdita wondered whether she knew about the contents of the folders. A momentary spasm of unease flitted across her mind, then she calmed herself. If there was anything to know, Kit would inform her, of this she was certain. Forcing a neutral expression to her face, she opened the door to Kit's office.

"Hello Gary," she said. Alistair, Susan and Kit were chatting to the tall man from MI1.

"Ma'am," said Gary leaping to his feet.

Perdita smiled. "There's no need, Gary," she said as he towered over her. "Please, sit down. Kit said you have information about Piper's accident?"

"Yes, Ma... sorry, Perdita, we have footage of the collision," Gary said, then lowering his voice, he asked, "Is Piper here?"

"Callum has gone to collect her; one of your drivers has taken him in one of your vehicles," Perdita replied. "He's going to call when they're on their way back. We're not expecting to hear from them for at least another hour."

"Good, because I'd like you and Kit to see this footage and decide how much you feel Piper should know. I spoke to her a few days ago and all she remembers is seeing two vehicles who appeared to be racing one another. She pulled over to avoid them and then nothing more." Gary paused. "Perhaps you should see it for yourselves."

He pulled his laptop from his briefcase and moved to the long table on one side of the room. Perdita, Kit, Alistair and Susan followed, seating themselves around the screen. Flipping it open, Gary selected a file and hesitated.

"I have to warn you, this is shocking," he said. "Although she doesn't remember, it was thanks to Piper's defensive driving skills and the reinforcements on her car that she survived."

Perdita felt sick and reached for Kit's hand under the table. Ever since her sister's accident she had been having nightmares about car crashes. Kit had admitted his nights were disturbed too. He was terrified about what could have happened to Piper but in his night terrors, it was Perdita driving the car. Perdita glanced at Susan and Alistair who were rigid and pale-faced. Reaching out with her other hand, she found Susan's and held it tight.

Gary activated the file and they sat in silence as they watched the two cars race down the motorway before careering across three lanes and flying off at a junction. The carriageways were relatively empty, with a few vans and one lorry which pulled off behind the speeding cars. As Gary had stated, Piper had moved to the inside lane, avoiding the swerving vehicles which both seemed to vanish into the distance. Piper changed lanes in order to allow vehicles to join at the approaching junction but as she reached the slip road the two speeding cars raced back on to the motorway. One pulled alongside her on the inside lane, while the other sped across three lanes and blocked her in on the other side. Piper accelerated but they matched her speed, there was nothing behind her and she slammed the brakes on, allowing the cars to shoot past her, but she was too far past the junction to be able to exit, instead she pulled back into the inside lane, behind the protection of a white van.

Moments later, the white van pulled over and then dropped back and tucked in behind Piper. By now she had caught up with the other two cars. Piper began to speed up in order to outdrive them, but before she could accelerate away, the van crashed into her from behind and one of the cars drove into her side.

Perdita watched as the two cars and the white van worked together to force Piper off the road. Every defensive driving trick they had been taught flowed through Perdita's mind and she knew her sister's temper would have risen and she would have fought these drivers with everything she had. Then there was a terrible screech of brakes and Piper's car caught on the bumper of the van. The car rolled over and over, landing on its roof, sending a shower of sparks across the road as it skidded into the barrier in the middle of the motorway. The two cars and the van swerved around Piper and sped away. Seconds later other vehicles had stopped and the sound of sirens could already be heard in the distance.

Gary stopped the recording and Perdita rushed from the room to the bathroom down the corridor where she vomited. Shaking and horrified, she closed her eyes, trying to analyse what she had seen and, as her brain worked through her disgust and panic, words formed in her mind. Her sister had been deliberately targeted. This was attempted murder. After rinsing her mouth out, Perdita unlocked the door to find Kit waiting outside. He opened his arms and she walked into them. She was not sure which of them was crying harder.

"Thank goodness she doesn't remember," said Perdita, when their sobs slowed down and they released their iron grip on each other. "We can't let her see that footage."

"I agree," said Kit. "It's shocking."

"Thank goodness for MI1. Without them we would never have had the vehicles or the skills to avoid this situation and I have no doubt that Piper would have died."

"But she didn't," said Kit, staring down into her storm-coloured eyes.

"No, she didn't, but whoever put her through this ordeal is going to pay."

Returning to Kit's office, Perdita hugged a red-eyed Susan before moving over to do the same to Alistair. His arms came around her in a fierce bear hug. To her surprise, their despair calmed her and she felt more in control than she had since the dreadful phone call that had shattered their sunny afternoon laughter and plunged them into yet another chapter of darkness and fear.

"Are you ready to continue?" asked Gary.

Perdita took her place at the long table. "Yes, we need as many details as you're able to share," she said.

"As you saw from the footage, a police vehicle was near your sister when her car rolled over. Piper had activated the panic button we'd fitted inside her car. The officers who arrived at the scene radioed for back up to try and apprehend the perpetrators. Unfortunately, all three vehicles were found abandoned not far from the next junction with no sign of the drivers."

"Have you traced the registration plates?" Perdita asked Gary.

"They were all false."

"Of course, but have you tracked them?"

"Yes, the three vehicles in the collision were all stolen. The van went missing two months ago from Croydon, while the cars are from Liverpool and Wrexham. Through the chassis numbers we've managed to locate the real owners, none of whom were involved."

"Is there any information you can share about the possible identities of the drivers?" asked Perdita.

"We've managed to lift DNA from all three vehicles. Having eliminated the original owners, we were left with three other DNA traces. Running them through our databases we found three direct matches. These men have since been apprehended and arrested. They are in a secure centre being questioned."

"Are they linked to Xavier and Randolph Connors?" asked Perdita.

There was a ripple of fury from the Mackensies. Perdita knew they, too, had suspected Xavier's involvement from the moment they had heard about Piper's accident.

"Yes, all three men have at some point been employed by either Xavier or Randolph. This was no accident," said Gary, confirming Perdita's earlier suspicions.

"How?" demanded Alistair and even Perdita winced at the cold anger in his voice. "Randolph is in a secure prison and there is an arrest warrant for Xavier should he enter the country."

"He doesn't need to be in the county to coordinate an attack," said Gary. "At present, I have a team trying to find a link between Xavier Connors and the assault on Piper. We'll be searching the CCTV feed from the storage facility in Bath, as well as other facilities where the Marquess House collection is housed. Whether Xavier is watching Perdita and Piper as individuals or if he has any building connected to the manor and its archive under surveillance, we intend to discover his source. He may have people inside these organisations giving him information. Perdita, is there anything in these facilities that Xavier desires?"

Perdita thought hard but this was not her area of expertise. "Piper is the one who has been going through the collection; she would know if there was anything valuable, but most of these facilities house the overspill and unused parts of the collection."

"What about *The Pentagram Manuscript*?" asked Kit.

"It's possible," agreed Perdita, "but we didn't know it existed until a few weeks ago, no one did, so I'm not sure he could have been searching for it specifically."

"Unless another source knew about it?" suggested Gary.

"Who though?" asked Perdita. "The manuscript is very old and so it has monetary value but Mark and I are unsure whether it holds secrets, other than those of the usual Tudor variety."

"But Mary hid it?"

"Yes, for reasons we are continuing to ascertain," replied Perdita.

Gary held her gaze for a moment, then pulled an envelope from his briefcase. "There is also this, which arrived this morning."

"It's addressed to me," said Kit in surprise.

"We X-rayed it and checked for poison, nerve agents, bombs — the usual things — it's a letter and a document, which is rather disturbing."

Kit pulled out several pieces of heavy white paper. An ornate scrolling logo of a crown and two phoenixes filled the top and extravagant handwriting in blue-black ink filled the page. Perdita watched as Kit's face transformed into an angry snarl.

"How dare he?" He threw the letter down on the table.

Perdita snatched it up to read and she felt her own face transforming with anger and fear.

"Xavier Connors is demanding we legally declare his twin daughters, Ruby and Pearl, as Perdita and Piper's heirs to Marquess House," said Kit. "He wants us to state Ruby and Pearl will remain their heirs even if either Perdita or Piper were to have a daughter to carry on the female line. He states that as his daughters would be older than any offspring of either of you, their claim should take precedence."

Alistair's eyes narrowed. "The letter is signed from Xavier and his wife, Amber," he said. "It's preposterous."

"Is this legal?" asked Gary.

"The entail doesn't work like that," said Kit. "At present, technically, Ruby and Pearl would be Perdita and Piper's heirs but the moment either twin has a daughter, they are shunted further away from the inheritance. The line of inheritance follows the direct bloodline through the female heirs, first Perdita's daughters as she is the eldest, then Piper's, then if neither Perdita nor Piper have a daughter, it would look further afield, but Ruby and Pearl do not have nearly as strong a claim as Xavier believes."

"Which is why he's trying to force us to sign a document stating we will capitulate to his insane demands," said Perdita. "Considering what we've watched this morning, the timing of this letter is no coincidence. It's a threat. He's suggesting that if we don't sign his stupid document, there will be more attempts on our lives."

Gary placed a printout on the table. At the top were several pictures of an expensively groomed woman with long honey-coloured hair, wide, dark eyes, a smooth suntan and designer clothes. Perdita thought there was a harshness about her expression that detracted from her otherwise attractive features.

"Amber Connors *née* Prust, heir to a the Prust shipping and oil fortune," Gary said. "The darling of the glossy magazines and tabloids when she was younger, there was general surprise when she accepted Xavier Connors's marriage proposal as she had been about to marry Thomas Child, the publishing magnate. Xavier appeared from nowhere and swept her away. Two years later, she gave birth to Ruby and Pearl."

Gary placed more images in front of them: one of Xavier and Amber's wedding, where neither bride nor groom looked as though they wanted to be in attendance, followed by a series of images of them in various far-flung locations, on board yachts and at glittering parties. Another showed Amber and Xavier on a magazine cover each holding a baby, followed by further images of the two girls as they grew up.

"How old are Ruby and Pearl?" asked Kit.

"They were three years old earlier this year," replied Gary. "They were born in 2018."

The significance of this date overwhelmed Perdita. This was the same year Mary Fitzroy had been murdered by an assassin hired by Randolph. Understanding flooded Perdita. Until now, she had never fully connected the reason why Randolph had chosen the time he did to eliminate her grandmother but finally she understood and it tallied with the many conversations Alistair had been forced to have at the time with Randolph's legal team. Randolph had been convinced by Mary's act of distancing herself from Perdita and Piper for all those years, that under the terms of the Marquess House entail, Ruby and Pearl would inherit.

"Is this why he murdered Granny? To make way for his granddaughters?" asked Perdita.

"Sadly, I believe that was the case," said Alistair. "The girls were three months old when your grandmother died."

Perdita stood up, adrenaline pumping around her body, unable to remain in her seat. "And now?"

"The entail stipulates that Marquess House must be inherited through the female line," said Alistair. "As Kit explained, should anything happen to both you and Piper, Ruby and Pearl would, at present, be the next female heirs. However, if either you or Piper were to have a daughter, then Ruby or Pearl would no longer have a claim…"

"Unless something happened to the child," said Perdita, her voice harsh. "If Piper or I have a daughter, Randolph would target her alongside us."

Silence greeted this statement and Perdita turned to look at Kit who was white-faced with shock. Anger ran through her; the past year had been the most peaceful she and Piper had enjoyed at Marquess House and this serenity was not something she was prepared to give up to a bully like Xavier Connors.

A shudder ran down her spine as Randolph's voice floated from the past, from the dreadful moment when Perdita had feared for all their lives, "*I want your status…*" Was that what Xavier craved too? The house, their claim? Or was it revenge for them having his father arrested?

Walking over to the window and staring blindly out at the summer's day, Perdita tried to calm her thoughts.

Behind her, Alistair and Gary were poring over several pages of what looked like a legal document while Susan searched the bookcase, pulling out an old leather ledger and placing it on the desk, opening it at the page containing the details of the entail. Kit had returned to his desk and was searching through a multitude of files. Perdita swallowed hard, her nails digging into her arms as she brought her anger under control. Moving to the table, she stared down at the legal minutiae of the entail. Although she knew this was stored in Kit's office, she had never read it and she was surprised to see it dated back to 1535.

"I'd always liked the fact the house was passed down through the women but what if Piper and I can't have children?" she said, dragging her eyes away from the page. "Or we have sons? Do we have to become breeding machines in order to fulfil the criteria of laws created hundreds of years before we were born? It seems nothing much has changed since the house was first built centuries ago."

An uneasy silence followed her words.

"It is the intention of MI1 Elite that you won't have to worry about the question of inheritance for many years to come," said Gary. "Your sister is safe, as are you. The house and those who live here continue to be protected by The Milford Haven

143

Treaty." The treaty was an ancient document that created a sovereign state within Marquess House, making the sisters immune from arrest or harm by the Secret Service while they were living there. "The intelligence we have discovered today will help us to secure Xavier Connors and with luck, once Piper is fully recovered, your lives can go back to normal."

Perdita looked at Gary and smiled. "Thank you for the reassurance, Gary."

Susan moved forward and closed the ledger, replacing it on the shelf before tidying the paperwork on Kit's desk, her actions indicating an end to the meeting. "Piper and Callum will be back soon," she said. "Perhaps these revelations can wait until tomorrow. Will you be staying for dinner, Gary?"

Gary was already replacing his belongings in his briefcase. "Thank you, Susan, but no, I have to get home."

Perdita and Kit said their goodbyes and allowed Alistair and Susan to escort Gary out, leaving them alone in Kit's office. He closed the door and they sat on the black leather sofa in one corner, staring at each other.

"Everything feels crazy again," Perdita said, "like it was before Randolph was arrested and charged. I'd hoped we were past this fear and uncertainty."

"We should be," replied Kit, "but Xavier is stirring things up. Try not to worry though, Perds, Gary was SAS, he's tough and he's thorough; he won't let Xavier succeed."

The sun was setting, throwing golden-red light into the room, flaring behind Kit's head like fire.

"Have you thought any more about having a family?" Kit's voice was gentle but there was a catch in his voice, a timbre of emotion Perdita had not expected.

"It's never far from my mind, even more so since Piper's accident."

Whether he sensed her reticence, she did not know but as he reached for her hand he said, "I know we talked about it before we were married but we're still young; there's no rush to have children."

Perdita gazed into his blue eyes and realised the time had come to be honest. He was her husband and she could share anything with him, her wildest dreams and her darkest fears.

"Perhaps there is an urgency to have children," she said. "What happened to Piper was deliberate. What if Xavier had succeeded and Piper had died? I would have become his sole target and if he managed to dispose of me, his daughters would inherit the entire estate. Xavier is as insane as his father; they have a fixation on taking this house and our titles." Her eyes were wide with a combination of indignation and fear.

"Nothing else is going to happen to you or Piper."

"A week ago, Piper was inches away from death on the motorway. Granny Mary was murdered in this house. Mum was killed in a car accident caused by MI1. Our family tree is littered with women who have died young due to unexpected accidents. What if it's me next?"

Real fear was coursing through Perdita; the reality of their family tree was not something she could ignore. Ever since she had discovered it in the library a few years earlier, Perdita had taken it upon herself to discover what had happened to her ancestors and the results had proved unnerving. Kit stared at her in confusion as this was not information she had shared with anyone, not even Piper. Instead, she had drawn these discoveries deep inside her, hiding them in the dark place in her mind where her blackest memories dwelled, ignoring them, unwilling to face their sinister meaning.

"What do you mean?" asked Kit. "What accidents? Remember, Mary was 86…"

"But she was murdered by a woman hired by Randolph," said Perdita. "I've been checking the family tree. Granny Mary and her sister Cecily both only managed to produce one living child each. Their mother, Eleanor Fitzroy, died in childbirth. Eleanor's mother, Margaret, died in a riding accident. Margaret's mother, Lettice, was the exception, living into her eighties but her twin sister, Seraphina, died of tuberculosis and before them, Honor Fitzpatrick choked to death on a fishbone…"

"Enough, Perds, enough," said Kit. "None of those deaths were murders. MI1 is alert to Xavier and the new danger he poses. The security around Marquess House will be increased. You and Piper are not in any danger, not now. Besides, there is no reason why we should struggle to have children."

"Before we were married, we agreed we would wait for the right time," said Perdita, and Kit nodded. "Perhaps this is the right time."

"Perds, you mustn't let Xavier's behaviour force you into making a decision you might regret," said Kit, concern in his voice.

"You think I'd regret having our children?"

"No, that isn't what I meant. To have a family is a huge step in life, it's a big change in our relationship too, and I want you to be sure this is the right time."

"Your life will change too, Kit."

"Of course, but you're the one who will bear the brunt of this decision, not me. Don't let Xavier force us into making a decision through necessity rather than because we're ready."

Perdita stared into his open honest face, the seriousness of his blue eyes making her heart race. From the moment she had accepted Kit's proposal of marriage she had never doubted her decision and his words about their future — her future — made her realise how lucky she was to have found him.

"Piper and I will be thirty-two on our next birthday," she replied, her voice low and thoughtful, sounding like an older version of herself, a Perdita she had not yet met. "You and I have been married two years. Ever since Piper told me about the baby, I've been thinking about things and today has given me clarity. There will always be another research project, another piece of Marquess House that needs repairing, updating or developing, it will never end. Perhaps this was the push I needed to give serious consideration to my personal life rather than my career. Xavier may think he holds us to ransom but he doesn't. Piper and I are young, fit and healthy, as far as we know there is no reason why we wouldn't conceive. Piper already has, even if there was a tragic ending."

"Are you saying that you want to try for a baby?" asked Kit, and Perdita could hear the delight and excitement in his voice.

"Yes," she said, aware her concerns and fears about such a huge change were transforming into the thrill of excitement and hope.

They stared at each other, and Perdita felt as though the world had shifted, their lives had changed, moved to another stage, a more intimate understanding. Kit seemed unable to speak.

"If you change your mind, then that's fine too…" he began but Perdita shook her head.

"I won't," she said. "I want to start a family and it has nothing to do with Xavier Connors." She leaned forward to kiss Kit. When they parted, Perdita grinned. "Wow, that was big grown-up stuff," she said, relieved her voice sounded more like herself again.

"Very big and grown-up," Kit agreed. "Shall we have a glass of wine?"

"We probably need one," she laughed, excitement bubbling up inside her, determined good things would come from this disaster.

CHAPTER THREE

"Perdita Elizabeth Woodville Rivers will you leave me alone before I scream?" exclaimed Piper as Perdita burst through the doorway.

Piper was sitting on the floor of the sunny living room they shared surrounded by catalogues and photographs of paintings. The room was situated between their two suites of rooms and had once belonged to their grandmother. The twins had decided to incorporate it as common space for them all to use. It also gave them access to the bedrooms should they have friends to stay or need more rooms. There was humour in Piper's tone as she looked up at Perdita.

"You didn't answer your phone," Perdita said, her voice somewhere between apology, concern and accusation.

Piper pointed to where her phone was charging on the other side of the room. "I didn't get there in time and as you didn't leave a message, I guessed it wasn't important."

"Not important? You were nearly killed; it's very important to me that you're well and happy. When you don't answer, I worry."

Piper levered herself to her feet, wincing as she jarred her ribs before walking across the room and hugging Perdita. "I love you for being so protective but truly, Perds, I'm fine," she said.

"I know," said Perdita, squeezing her gently in return, "but I thought I'd lost you. It's going to take a while. When I think what could have happened…"

"But it didn't," said Piper, disentangling herself and returning to her position on a cushion on the floor. "The men have been arrested and, with luck, MI1 will catch up with Xavier very soon."

Despite concern from Perdita, Kit, Alistair and Susan, Piper had insisted on seeing the footage of her accident. Her face had been stony throughout, but she watched in its entirety. Callum, however, had to leave, unable to face the true horror of what Piper had experienced. Perdita had never doubted Piper's strength and she realised what a powerful force her sister had become over the years.

"Perds, come and sit with me," Piper said, pulling another cushion from the squashy sofa. "Please believe me, I'm fine and if that changes, you'll be the first to know."

"Promise?"

"Promise," said Piper and they touched the palms of their left hands together, their secret sign since they were children. "I'm sad, of course," Piper conceded, "but I refuse to let Xavier have any more of an impact on our lives. My wrist will heal, my ribs will repair themselves and Cal and I will have another child. Let's put this behind us and move on. If you want to be useful, you can help me go through this list of paintings and help me decide on the new exhibition in the Victorian wing of the Heritage Centre. Unless, of course, you're about to reveal another Tudor mystery, then I'd hate to delay you."

"No Tudor mysteries to reveal yet. Although, I'm waiting for Mark to call. He said there was an anomaly he was investigating in the manuscript."

"An anomaly?"

"Stephanie spotted a discrepancy in ink tones and as she wrote her thesis on steganography…"

"What's steganography?" interrupted Piper.

"It's the practice of concealing a message within another message or physical object, and focusses on ensuring the message is undetectable. Cryptography is the art of protecting the contents of the message alone, rather than the entire content, which is steganography. Stephanie has helped Mark to upgrade his equipment and introduced a new state-of-the-art scanner which can capture colour nuances of non-photographic materials such as papyri, parchment, vellum and fabric. Apparently, this level of light can highlight hidden messages, which is what Stephanie and Mark have decided to check."

"Do you mean it detects invisible ink?" asked Piper, intrigued.

"Yes, it's a gentler process and faster too than the old days when Mark used to heat things with a lightbulb or use ultraviolet light. His method could take hours and there was always the potential of damaging the pages. The downside of the ultraviolet light was it inability to detect the entire colour spectrum. This method can reveal high resolution images of entire pages of hidden writing within minutes."

"Do you think *The Pentagram Manuscript* might hold more secrets?"

Perdita shrugged. "Mark has said this is a trial procedure and might not produce any useable results."

"Or," Piper added, "there might be nothing there to discover."

"True. Anyway, I'm supposed to be doing dull paperwork for Kit concerning the research centre," continued Perdita, "but if I say I'm looking after you, he might take pity and do it for me."

"You know he won't," Piper laughed. "Paperwork is the one thing you always bicker about. I won't tell if you don't. We can hide up here."

Perdita gazed at the many printouts on the floor, their colours a rainbow of imagination and inspiration from across the centuries but Piper's words had snagged her conscience. It was rare for the two of them to be alone and a sharp wave of nostalgia washed through her as she remembered the hours they would spend together when they were growing up.

"Are you and Cal trying for another baby?" Perdita asked, aware Piper had dropped this revelation in among a series of other less important comments. A habit of hers when she was unsure whether she was ready to discuss an issue. Perdita was never fooled by this tactic.

"Yes," Piper replied. "While we didn't plan the first pregnancy, we talked about it when I came home and we decided we wanted a child. It has nothing to do with Xavier and everything to do with us." Piper hesitated, then leaning closer to Perdita so their shoulders were touching, a gesture leftover from their childhoods, she whispered, "Cal's asked me to marry him."

Perdita yelped in excitement. "And?"

"I've said yes but he wants to tell his mum before we tell everyone here. I said you had to know and he's going to tell Kit later."

"Pipes, this is wonderful news," said Perdita, gently hugging her sister. "Do you know when?"

"Not sure yet, but soon. When Mark's finished playing in the chapel, I expect. We can't use it while it's covered in dust sheets. You'll be Maid of Honour and give me away, like I did for you?"

"Of course," Perdita replied.

"Cal's going to ask Kit and Elliot to be his best men," Piper said.

"This is wonderful news, Pipes."

"And what about you and Kit?"

"What about us?"

"There's something different about you, it's a good different, but there's a change."

Perdita grinned, she and Piper had never been able to keep secrets from each other, it was the beauty of being a twin. "We're trying for a baby, too," she said. "We've been thinking about it for a while and with what happened to you, it made us rethink. As Socrates said: 'Enjoy yourself, it's later than you think…'"

"Although I prefer the Herb Magidson version of the song," teased Piper. "It has a better rhythm."

They clasped hands and understanding flowed between them. Although they both had partners who loved them, they knew that whatever happened, they would always have each other and their loyalty would lie with each other first and forever. Smiling, they turned their attention to the array of information spread across the floor.

"These are astonishing, Pipes," said Perdita.

"Startling, aren't they?" Piper replied. "Not all of them are ours; there are a few more famous images here that are in galleries around the world for reference but there are a number of 'lost' paintings from famous artists within our lists. I have no idea why they've been languishing in the storage facility. Perhaps Granny didn't like them; art is a very personal thing."

"Is that a Delaroche?" asked Perdita, pointing to a printout of a romanticised image of a young woman in a nun's habit.

"Yes, a lesser-known painting, but we own the original."

"Who is it meant to be? Is there a title?"

Piper checked her notes. "Elizabeth Barton, the Holy Maid of Kent, although like a lot of his paintings, there are a number of factually incorrect embellishments..."

"Elizabeth Barton? Are you sure?"

Piper showed Perdita the catalogue and Perdita stared at it in surprise.

"Is she important?" Piper asked.

"She was and her name has cropped up in *The Pentagram Manuscript*. Elizabeth Barton, the Holy Maid of Kent is another woman who has been obscured despite at one point being viewed as one of the most influential women of the sixteenth century."

"Really?" said Piper, leaning forward to examine the printout in front of them.

A pale-faced woman with wide blue eyes stared out of the black habit and white wimple of a Benedictine nun. Around her was a gathering of small children, all holding white flowers while golden light streamed through a gothic arched window giving the nun an ethereal glow. Scallop shells were scattered around her feet and in one corner hovered a Tudor rose and to Perdita's surprise a pentagram with each of the five points blossoming with a blood-red rose.

"Scallop shells," murmured Perdita.

"They're the emblem of St James the Great of Compostela," said Piper. "According to Dutch philosopher Desiderius Erasmus they were adopted by him because the shore of the abundant sea abounds in them. They have multiple meanings though, they're the emblem of the pilgrimage to St James's shrine on the Camino de Santiago. They're also a symbol of the divine feminine, as well as a Christian symbol for baptism."

"Erasmus," said Perdita, her mind beginning to make connections. "He was a close friend of Anne Boleyn's father, Thomas. I wonder if this is relevant…"

"To what?"

"The strange new version of events I'm beginning to think is being described in *The Pentagram Manuscript*. When Elizabeth Barton was at the height of her fame and influence both of Henry's queens tried to woo her to their side. Katherine of Aragon was intrigued by her, while Anne Boleyn offered her a place in her court as her spiritual advisor. Even men like Thomas More, Cardinal Wolsey and Thomas Cromwell gave her prophesies credence. The scallop shell could be a reference to Katherine of Aragon with her Spanish descent and Catholicism."

"But this woman was a nun, wouldn't it be a reference to her own religion?"

"Not necessarily," said Perdita, "before her rise to fame, Elizabeth was from a poor background. She was a servant when she fell ill and began having visions of the Virgin Mary. Her tales were in the style of Julian of Norwich's *Revelations of Divine Love*. Julian of Norwich had been an anchorite nun, walled into a room in a church, where she wrote about the visions of heaven she had experienced during a severe illness. In these revelations she spoke to Jesus. The most famous quotation from her is: 'All shall be well, and all shall be well and all manner of things shall be well'. She's cited as being the first female author to publish a book in English."

"Do you think Barton had read this woman's work and copied it?" asked Piper.

"No, Barton was probably illiterate, and the texts of Julian of Norwich weren't widely known about until the 1670s. This isn't to say she wasn't being coached by someone who was aware of them though."

"Cardinal Wolsey, Thomas More or one of the other influential men who began to promote her?" asked Piper.

"It's possible," said Perdita. "She was a young girl, alone in the world and here she was displaying possible signs of prophecy, it's no wonder people began to take notice. Nothing is known of Elizabeth Barton's parents. Barton's biographer suggests that her name indicates her heritage might be from people who made a living on church lands. In the Middle Ages, the manager of church plots was known as a *bertonarius*, which was truncated to Barton for a surname.

"Elizabeth lived in the Manor of Aldington in Kent which belonged to the Archbishop of Canterbury and had done since the eleventh century. For more than a hundred years before that it had belonged to the Benedictine monastery of Christ Church, Canterbury. When Elizabeth had her first trance, she was working in the household of a the *bertonarius* of Aldington, Thomas Cobb, a reasonably wealthy and influential man in Kent."

"Interesting," said Piper.

"Her fame began to grow as her prophecies began to hint at an outcome to Henry VIII's divorce from Katherine of Aragon. The mysticism around her was encouraged and eventually she made various predictions suggesting Henry should return to Katherine and they would have a son. Her concluding statement was to announce he would die within months if he married Anne."

"Which he didn't," said Piper.

"No, but Elizabeth Barton did; she was executed."

"Where were all her influential friends then?" said Piper bitterly.

"The moment she began threatening the king, her power waned and when her predictions failed, she was arrested. She confessed that she had been encouraged and coached by senior clerics and men in power."

"I bet none of them paid the price of the executioner's axe though," said Piper.

"Of course not," replied Perdita. "The thing that intrigues me is that she is another female character who has been virtually erased from history. In trying to trace her roots, it reminded me of Aphra Behn. A woman who challenged the status quo but whose origins have been lost."

"What do you mean?"

"Aphra Behn was born as Eaffrey Johnson before re-emerging as Aphra Behn when she was in her twenties; even though there are no records of her marriage to Mr Behn. She went on to become an influential writer before her name was forgotten for centuries. Elizabeth Barton is similar. During a politically turbulent period of English history, she was an influential voice, yet today, very few people know about her. I wonder if The Scribe removed her from the story or whether after her execution, those who had believed her distanced themselves from her and in the furore of Anne Boleyn's execution a few years later, Elizabeth Barton was natural wastage, forgotten and buried as an embarrassing episode."

"It's possible," agreed Piper. "We do have to stop trying to see conspiracy theories in every historical anomaly. As you say, some people disappear because it isn't possible to remember everyone."

"When Elizabeth Barton cropped up in some of the comments in the marginalia of *The Pentagram Manuscript* I wondered if she was supposed to be one of the women on the quest but as she became a nun, she wouldn't have been searching for blessings for a son."

"She might have been one of the people offering blessings," suggested Piper.

"Exactly, but I haven't found anything yet that links her. She died in 1534 after Anne and Henry had married." Perdita gazed at the innocent eyes of the young woman in the image. "What did you mean about embellishments in the painting, Pipes?"

Piper pulled a well-known Paul Delaroche image in front of them, his depiction of Lady Jane Grey's execution. At the centre of the canvas, Jane, blindfolded and dressed in white, fumbles for the execution block, while surrounded by weeping men and women.

Perdita raised an eyebrow. "This takes me back. Weren't we looking at this a few years ago when we were researching Arbella Stuart?"

"We were," agreed Piper, "but it's the best example there is for the changing face of history. This image was painted in 1833, over 250 years after Jane's execution. I suspect our Delaroche of Elizabeth Barton was a few years earlier, 1830, perhaps."

"There are fewer embellishments on the Barton image though," said Perdita as her expert eye gazed at the image of Jane. "The flowers are Victorian sentimentality and the Gothic window looks like a Victorian reproduction, it's too frilly to be Mediaeval."

"Whereas the painting of Lady Jane Grey is pure imagination," said Piper.

"One historian suggested the only realistic detail was the straw strewn on the floor," said Perdita. "It's recorded in numerous sources that Jane wore head to foot black, the dress styles in this image are incorrect, too, and the pathos of the event is more in keeping with the scenes from the French Revolution which had ended thirty years before this painting was created. Did you know this image is responsible for the texts on Lady Jane's execution being altered?"

"By whom?" asked Piper, in surprise.

"In 1852, the respected Victorian antiquarian, John Gough Nichols, published a revised version of the execution of Lady Jane Grey including descriptions taken from the Delaroche painting. He embellished and invented, giving the over-dramatized and incorrect version often now considered to be fact. Other, unaltered eyewitness accounts of Jane's execution state she was calm and stoic, her women wept but she was steadfast to the end."

"The Barton image seems relatively unscathed in comparison," said Piper. "Although, the pentagram is strange. It's more in keeping with Mediaeval imagery than Victorian."

"Am I right in thinking Delaroche was responsible for a great deal of Tudor imagery?" said Perdita.

Piper pointed to a large book beside her sister and Perdita dragged it towards them, her eyes lighting up when she saw it was a book of Delaroche prints.

"The Victorians were very fond of creating Tudor pictures, the trouble is, they did so in their own image," said Piper, flicking through the glossy images. "This one is hugely famous; it's entitled The Children of Edward and is of the princes in the Tower of London. This is Oliver Cromwell before the coffin of Charles I and this is the Death of Elizabeth I. There are numerous other Victorian images though: The Escape of Mary, Queen of Scots by C. Cooke; Pierre de Bocosel de Chatelard playing the lute to Mary, Queen of Scots by Andrew Duncan, which was painted in 1830, to name a few, but there are many more and they are all over-sentimentalised and incorrect. The clothes and hairstyles are often wrong, as are the settings. They resemble Victorian rooms rather than Tudor. One of the most famous images from history which is embellished is The Two Princes in the Tower by John Everett Millais. The setting and the styles are dubious yet many people believe this is an accurate portrayal."

A chill ran down Perdita's spine; there were so many links between the Victorians and the Tudors. Two eras where women had held the sway of power. The Victorians had been one of the first generations who had taken time to catalogue the past, to create their place in the passing of time and in doing so, they had brought the Tudors to life, filing, cataloguing and writing about these sparkling kings and queens from centuries past, romantic, untouchable, yet created in their own Victorian image.

"Of course," gasped Perdita, "why did I not see it before."

"What?" asked Piper. "I recognise that look, you've made a connection."

"We know a playwright was involved in the rewriting of history — Aphra Behn," said Perdita and Piper nodded, "and she helped The Scribe to leave behind versions of the six wives of Henry VIII. A few hundred years later, male Victorian scholars used this version of events to extrapolate their views of the six infamous queens. Yet, all these representations of the women were incomplete because Aphra and The Scribe were hiding as much as they were revealing. As such, the information left behind caused the Victorians to portray the wives as six caricatures, rather than as real people."

"What do you mean?" asked Piper.

"Katherine of Aragon was the first wife, wise, calm, beatific but who was unable to fulfil her wifely duty of providing an heir. Therefore, the easily led king was seduced by the evil second wife, Anne Boleyn, the social climbing, grasping, middle-class woman who would stop at nothing to achieve her own ends. However, in her scheming she brought about her own doom and destruction, when she was replaced by the paragon of virtue who was Jane Seymour. Jane, who was practically described as the Virgin Mary, made the ultimate sacrifice, as any good upstanding woman should, when she died giving birth to a son. Remember, in both Tudor and Victorian times, sons were more important…"

"Except in our family," said Piper and Perdita grinned.

"Next came Anne of Cleves, a foreigner — how shocking — as far as the Victorians were concerned. Yet even this is an echo because at this point Victoria was on the throne and had German blood, perhaps the casting aside of the German princess was what many Victorian males wished to do to their queen. Anne was sensible, she took her divorce quietly, allowing her husband to be seduced by the flighty teenager and good-time girl, Catherine Howard. Again, her naughtiness was punished in the harshest way but would have been seen as a just reward for her supposed lewd behaviour by the Victorians. Then, finally, Henry is saved by the respectable widow, Katheryn Parr."

"My goodness, Perds, you're right," said Piper. "No wonder the art gives romanticised versions of Tudor events. Do you think it was intentional?"

"I think the scholars were working within very narrow parameters," said Perdita. "Women have never been treated well by history and Henry's wives have been reduced to caricatures, then blamed for Henry's worst faults when it was the king who was the beating heart of all the disasters and violence which befell his wives."

Perdita's phone buzzed. "Hi Mark, any news?"

His voice was breathless, excited. "Perds, we've found something astonishing."

"We're on our way."

Ten minutes later, Perdita and Piper hurried into The Dairy. Mark's excitement was palpable.

"Look at this," he gasped, dragging Perdita into his laboratory and towards his workbench where the manuscript reclined on a broad cushion, the pages held open by padded weights.

Stephanie was staring at a large monitor. "Hi," she called. "You're in for a real treat."

"One of the things Steph and I found strange was the layout of each page," Mark began without preamble. "Here, here, here and here are gaps. Compare this with an image from *The Devonshire Manuscript*," he flashed an image on the screen in front of them. "There are four stanzas per page, limited marginalia and a gap between each stanza, a pattern which follows through the majority of the document. The first obvious difference with *The Pentagram Manuscript* is the fact it is far more ornate. Each chapter begins with an illuminated letter and there are illustrations throughout, giving it the feel of a Book of Hours. The other thing which confused me were the large blank gaps between stanzas. Paper and vellum were expensive products which is why they're usually crammed full of writing."

"Is it a design or artistic affectation?" asked Piper.

"My first thought, too, Pipes," agreed Mark. "I wondered if this was a status thing, showing money was no object, whoever commissioned this was so rich they could afford to leave blank spaces. Then I noticed a number of these spaces seemed to be framed with very light decorations of a combination of Tudor roses and our old friend the pentagram. It's very faint but if you look at this enlargement, you can make it out."

Again, he flashed an image on the screen and Perdita stared at it. The detail was simple, but Mark was correct: it was as though a faint frame had been drawn around the space. Perdita turned away from the screen and stared at him in wonder. Such was his excitement, he was shaking.

"Calm down, Mark," laughed Perdita but her own anticipation was rising at what he was about to reveal. "What have you found?"

He turned back to the first full page of text. "Look…" he pointed to the screen where Stephanie flicked up a digital image of the page.

"Writing," Perdita gasped. "Hidden writing between the lines of poetry. The scanner detected the invisible ink."

"Yes," beamed Mark, "and look at what it says."

"This is a true tale. The weak men believe we are unable to tell our story, yet I, Jane In Anger, shall show we women have our own power and together, we will topple the king and recreate this England for ourselves. Jane In Anger…" whispered Perdita.

"Jane In Anger," murmured Perdita to herself. "Jane In Anger, Jane Anger, no it can't be…" Perdita turned to Mark, her eyes shining. "The woman who owned this manuscript, do you think it was the same person behind the Jane Anger treatise?" she said, her own enthusiasm matching Mark's.

"There is a possibility…" began Mark before Piper interrupted.

"Explain, please," she said.

"Of course, sorry, Pipes," said Perdita. "In 1589, a treatise was printed by a writer signing herself, Jane Anger. It was entitled *Her Protection for Women* and was a poem citing the many reasons why women were superior to men, challenging the misogyny of the Tudor court."

Piper stared at her in surprise. "I've never heard of it," she said.

"Neither had I until recently," admitted Perdita. "It doesn't pop up very often unless you're looking for it. It was published in 1589 when Elizabeth I was on the throne, well, it seemed as though she remained on the throne," Perdita corrected herself, "even though it's possible it was written earlier."

"Could you imagine publishing anything this dangerous during Henry's reign, especially as he was showing increasing signs of madness?" said Piper in awe.

"Or even under the humourless Edward VI?" added Mark, who was beaming.

"Who was Jane Anger?" asked Piper.

"Historians have long debated her identity. A number have suggested the treatise was written by a man using a female pseudonym..." Perdita said as Mark shook his head in despair and Piper scoffed. "Others have suggested there were a number of women living with the name Jane Anger in the correct period but none seem probable and the name Anger might actually be a bastardisation of Anjou, which could broaden the potential spectrum of possible candidates. Yet, there is no proof anywhere corroborating the true identity of Jane Anger."

"But Perds, you said the tale you've been unravelling so far through the poems has centred on Jane Seymour," said Piper. "Could she have been Jane Anger?"

"It's not something we can rule out," said Perdita but she was cautious about making guesses until she understood more. "The sentence that intrigues me is the one about toppling the king and recreating England. There was never a challenge on

Henry VIII's throne, yet this manuscript was dated to the 1530s." Perdita stared at the words, browned with age, a secret within the pages of this extraordinary document. "Do you think there are hidden messages on every page?" she asked, excitement coursing through her as she wondered what else was lurking in the shadows of the book. Was a second story written alongside the one in view?

"With your permission, we'd like to scan all the pages as we believe there could be hidden messages throughout. It won't damage the manuscript, I promise," said Mark.

"Do whatever needs to be done," said Perdita. "Whatever secrets are waiting, we must ensure they are revealed."

PART FOUR: ENGLAND, 1531

CHAPTER ONE

"We have been summoned back to court."

Jane Seymour looked up from the accounts book and pulled a face of discontentment. "Must we go?" she asked.

"The queen has most specifically asked for the 'bell-like reading voice and devout study of my dear lady, Jane Seymour'," quoted Francis from the parchment in his hand.

"How tiresome," Jane sighed.

"Your cousin, Anne, has also questioned when I shall release you from my castle."

Jane laughed and from the corner of the room, a chuckle and gurgle drew both her and Francis's eyes. A wet nurse lifted the sturdy baby boy from his elaborate cradle and with a curtsey to the child's parents, left the room to feed their son.

"And what of Jasper?" asked Jane, leaning back in her chair, while Francis came to perch on the edge of the desk beside her.

"He will remain here with his nurse," replied Francis. "The court is no place for a child."

"I no longer wish it to be a place for me either," said Jane. "We're happy here, we're free from all the petty restrictions and I have no desire to become embroiled in the dangerous dance of the Boleyns."

Francis raised an eyebrow, but he looked amused. "Your eldest brother, Edward, might have other ideas," he said.

Jane frowned. "What's he done now?"

"He is determined to make a name for himself at court and is trying to catch the eye of the king in order to improve his prospects," said Francis.

"Isn't it enough he was made Fitzroy's Master of Horse? He's at Sheriff Hutton and learning the matters of court at the Council of the North with all manner of other rising stars: the elder Boleyn brothers; William Parr, brother of our friend, Catherine and various other wild stallions."

"Times change, my dear, and while you have been ruling our kingdom here like a queen, Fitzroy has been recalled from the North with his riotous entourage. Your brother, Edward, among them," said Francis. "The last I saw of your brother he was fawning over the king."

"I have no desire to watch while Edward and his social climbing wife, Anne Stanhope, insinuate their way into the nobility," Jane said, finishing the final row of figures with a flourish. "Neither do I wish for him to embroil me in his petty plans. Why can't we tell them the truth? Then I will be able to remain here…"

"Because you will be in disgrace, as will I," Francis said. "This is not the time to risk our favour with the king and queen, as you are well aware. As the king's friend and in his employ, I must retain his favour. While you, lovely Mistress Seymour, are sought after by both Queen Katherine and your cousin, Anne. What charm have you cast over the women of the court that they vie for your attention?"

"Nothing. The queen thinks I am as devout as a nun because it is easy for me to quote sections of the Bible verbatim. While Anne wishes me to continue in my role as spy while she and Bessie spin their plot. They are welcome to the court, His Majesty and their intrigues. I am done with these childish games. Please let me stay here." She fluttered her eyelashes at Francis, her head on one side, a coquettish smile on her lips.

"Stop with your seductive wiles, woman," laughed Francis, and Jane giggled. "There are more important issues to discuss. Your father has written to me again."

"Does he suggest I return to court and stop pestering you?" she asked.

"Not in so many words but he is concerned about the amount of time you're spending at Hertford Castle. Let us not forget, my love, I am known to be a debauched liar, ruffian and flirt. Once again, he has thanked me for keeping you safe from the Sweat but he has suggested it is time to discuss a marriage for you and asked if I would be able to aid him in this quest."

"With whom does he propose I would be a good match?" asked Jane, narrowing her eyes.

"Lord William Dormer."

A frown played across her face, drawing her pale eyebrows together over her light blue eyes. While not classically pretty like her younger sister, Elizabeth, Jane's appeal was more understated and subtle, created by the intelligence in her eyes and the confidence of her poise. During her years at court, where she watched from the shadows hiding behind a veil of demure piety, it was her self-possession that had shone through, making her impossible to ignore, drawing glances of admiration from both men and women.

"Lord William Dormer is in love with Lady Mary Sidney," said Jane. "The entire court is aware of this tryst. I imagine Mary Sidney's mother, Lady Anne, will hurry them up the aisle the moment the rumour reaches them that my father is interested. Ever since Father's affair, William's mother, Lady Jane Dormer has believed we Seymours are scandalous."

As Jane said the final word, she could not help but grin. Her father's affair, so long ago it no longer caused pain to herself, was a story of renown and she enjoyed being washed by its notoriety. It was a relief to have this edge to her persona as she was bored with the pious mask she had been forced to adopt while spying on Queen Katherine.

"Perhaps I should inform Lady Sidney there is nothing to fear because a marriage between you and William Dormer would be impossible. You have a husband and he is a jealous scoundrel who will share you with no other," said Francis, taking her hand and kissing it.

Jane gazed at him, her heart fluttering, as it always did when he touched her. "How long do you think it would be before my parents tried to annul our marriage if we told them?" she asked.

"Once they know about Jasper, they'll have no choice but to give us their blessing."

Jane did not reply. Her marriage to Francis was clandestine, his servants were some of the few who were aware of their union. When she had given birth to their son, Jasper, they had been sworn to secrecy but as Francis continued to bring her up to date on the news at court, Jane was aware her idyll in Hertford Castle was coming to an end.

Staring up at her husband, Jane knew her reluctance to return to the glittering, dangerous court was written on her face. The past few years had been the happiest of her life and she was unwilling to abandon her contentment in order to be drawn into the bitter morality play unravelling between Henry, Katherine and Anne. From the moment of her arrival at Hertford Castle, after their midnight flight from Greenwich, Francis's servants had looked upon her as the lady of the house and she had enjoyed this rise in status. Years of training from her mother were lying dormant in her mind and, within a week of her arrival, she was running the castle as though she had lived there for years.

In those frightening times, as the Sweat swept the land, killing thousands, Jane had helped Francis to secure resources for the castle and the surrounding villages, ensuring a plentiful supply of food, medicines and fresh well water, readying the castle for isolation in order to keep the Sweat at bay. Jane was happy to discover she and Francis worked well together, providing shelter and help for many of Francis's tenants.

However, within a few weeks, letters had arrived from her parents with desperate news. Her younger brother, Anthony, and sister, Margery were both dead from the Sweat. Jane's heart had broken for the two strong, funny children whose futures had been stolen. Days later, the death of Sir William Carey, husband of her cousin, Mary Boleyn, reached them, followed by the shock that Anne Boleyn and her father, Thomas, both languished at Hever Castle with the Sweat. Henry was travelling with Katherine and their enormous entourage in a bid to outrun the illness and Jane wondered if the King's Great Matter would be solved in the most tragic and desperate manner. As she had wiped away her tears, she was aware of Francis, the lines on his face deepened by grief and fear.

"Marry me," he had said.

"What?" she had gasped, thinking she had misheard him, her mind adrift with the appalling losses to her family.

"I mean it, Jane," he said and his one eye, handsome and serious, had focused on her, the embroidery on the patch which matched his doublet glittering in the firelight, as though casting a spell over her. "Marry me," he had repeated. "There is a chapel here and my chaplain could wed us this very day."

"Why would you suggest this?" Jane had asked, bemused. "We have discussed it but you have warned caution. You claim you must inform the king in order to avoid his wrath. Your excuse remains that you have no wish to upset him as Charles Brandon did when he married without permission. There is also the issue of my parents…"

There was no doubt in Jane's heart about the intensity of her love for him, they had been lovers for years — but to marry without her parents' permission would cause a furore. Sir John and Lady Margery Seymour had already turned down a match with Francis, stating their blood connection. Jane knew this was an excuse rather than a valid reason, as the link between them was very distant. The truth was that neither of her parents trusted Francis, knowing the tales of his fast living, his wild antics with the king and the other young men from the court. It frustrated Jane that her parents continued to believe these old stories, refusing to acknowledge the change in Francis, preferring to always believe the worst.

Despite this snub, Francis had remained loyal to the Seymour family, using his influence to smooth the path for her three brothers to find good positions at court and had been instrumental in obtaining her place there, too.

"The Sweat is stealing lives. Death stalks this land, harvesting souls each day, he laughs as he reaps his seeds, including two of your siblings. What if it were you or me next?"

"But Francis…"

"Jane Seymour, love of my life, please do me the honour of marrying me." He was on one knee in front of her.

Jane had dreamed of this moment for years, of hearing those words from him, but she had not anticipated it would be under these dreadful circumstances. Gazing down into his adored face, his expression imploring, steeped in love, sense fled her mind, to be replaced by passion, wilfulness and the knowledge he was correct. It could be her tomorrow or, worse, him. Without conscious thought, she nodded.

"Yes, Francis, I will marry you," she had said, her voice catching in her throat.

Francis had leapt up, sweeping her into his arms and spinning her around.

"My parents will be furious," she had whispered, her voice awestruck at her own audacity. "We must allow the turmoil of this terrible illness to calm before we tell them our wonderful news."

"Wise words, my love."

Bending over her hand, he had kissed it, then with a smile, departed, leaving her excited, confused and defiant. They had married a few days later and Jasper had followed nine months later. A second child, a daughter, had been born but to the heartbreak of her parents, had lived less than a day.

To the astonishment of all, both Anne and her father, Thomas Boleyn, survived the Sweat's clawing fingers and the illness released its grip on the land. With the nobles returning to Henry's court and the king taking up residence at Whitehall, Henry continued to pursue his Great Matter. Francis claimed that Henry saw Anne's survival of the disease which had killed so many as a sign from God that a union between them would be blessed. Henry had abandoned Katherine upon their return to the capital, ignoring her and refusing to speak to her unless it was unavoidable. Instead, his days were spent courting Anne while chasing the theologians and law makers for a way to release him from his tainted marriage to his brother's widow.

For the past few months, Francis had been dividing his time between Hertford Castle and his duties for the king. Jane had wondered when her parents would demand her return to court but as they were busy with their own lives and her remaining siblings — three brothers and two sisters — they had not yet insisted, instead writing to Francis each month, begging to let them know if her presence was a nuisance. None suspected the true relationship between them.

"When must we return?" asked Jane with reluctance.

"By the end of the month," Francis said. "Audrey may accompany you, but it is wiser to leave Jasper here. He is safe and settled."

Jane watched as Francis began to pick at the corner of the embroidered cushion by his side, a sure sign he was agitated. "What else has happened, my love?" she asked.

"The court is a dangerous place and will remain so while Henry continues to woo Anne," he said. "There are rumours of poisonings, murders, and the list of executions grows daily. Last week, the chef Richard Roose was boiled to death — the new punishment for poisoners — after being accused of trying to murder Sir Thomas More while he enjoyed dinner with John Fisher, the Bishop of Rochester."

"Francis, what an awful way to die. How could the king behave in such a barbaric manner?"

"His lust for revenge grows each day," said Francis. "It is disturbing. However, the most interesting development is connected to Henry Fitzroy. At present, the boy and his entourage remain at The More in Hertfordshire, not far from here, but he will soon relocate to Windsor Castle in order to complete his education. The rumours are that the king will then try to persuade the queen to take over The More as her home, leaving the court free for himself and Anne."

"Queen Katherine will never agree to it," said Jane.

"Where the king is concerned," sighed Francis, "she may have no choice."

"And you would like me to re-join Queen Katherine's court?"

"It would be useful, particularly as there is a whisper Bessie Blount intends to return to London."

"Why? She hates court."

"As a respectable widow, her prospects are improved if she is a courtier. Gilbert died a year ago and Bessie realises if she does not wed soon, her status will erode. She may be the mother of a potential heir but he has not yet been declared in law. All eyes are on Anne to see whether she can succeed where Katherine has failed and deliver a son. Anne has offered Bessie a place in her court but we will need you in Katherine's to keep us abreast of the situation."

"Very well," Jane sighed. "If Katherine is persuaded to come to The More, I shall remain with her as it will be easy for me to visit Jasper but if the king prepares to send her elsewhere, you must find a way to release me, even if we have to tell people we are married."

CHAPTER TWO

Jane breathed in the heady scent of spices, woodsmoke and the exotic perfume anointing the pulse points of the prowling courtiers as they vied for the king's attention. Candles guttered, throwing grotesque shadows across the walls as people jostled for position, determined to be seen as the most loyal, goading people to deploy a sharp elbow or swift tap on the ankle to move a rival aside. Watching with a smile on her lips, Jane felt reborn.

It had taken every ounce of her persuasion to convince Francis that before she returned to Katherine's court, he should allow her to join him at Windsor for a few days.

"We don't know when we'll see each other again," she had pouted, allowing her creamy shift to slip from her shoulder while her hair tumbled forward in a wave of curls.

"You're a witch," Francis had groaned, pulling her into his arms. "I can refuse you nothing when you look at me in such a manner. I shall grant you five days, but there are conditions."

"Which are?"

"Even though I shall entertain you and Audrey in my rooms, where you'll also sleep under my continued protection, you must promise to dine with your parents and your elder brother."

"Why?"

"This will give you a reason to be at Windsor, otherwise you may find Cromwell will send you to the queen where she waits at Hampton Court Palace and we'll be denied the excitement of bedding each other under your parents' noses."

Jane had laughed and agreed. Upon arrival, she had been surprised at the size and sumptuousness of Francis's rooms. "These are wonderful," she had exclaimed, running her fingers over the polished wood and expensive tapestries. "You are a man of status, Sir Francis."

"Indeed, Mistress Seymour, I am a close friend of the king," he teased, using her maiden name.

Her laughter had covered her surprise at how far Francis had risen since she had last been at court. The evening spent with her parents had been pleasant. Her mother and father had been delighted to see her and there was genuine pleasure in their greeting. Her brother, Edward and his new wife, Anne Stanhope, had been more reticent but the family feud had been kept at bay and when they had left, Jane was glad Francis had insisted on the reunion.

"Thank you," she had whispered as he wrapped his arms around her later that night.

"My aim is always to make you happy," he replied.

Although Jane had returned to court with reluctance, now the deed was done, she was surprised to find how much she had missed the hustle and bustle. She felt her soul was reawakening as she strolled the busy corridors of Windsor Castle. Friends, family and acquaintances greeted her with delight and she was pressed into many games of cards, invited to watch the practises in the lists and to lead dances. The colour and energy of the court swept her through the days, even though Henry and Anne were yet to make an entrance.

"Tomorrow, my love," Francis assured her, "and an entertainment has been arranged by the king. He and Brandon have been working on it."

Jane's heart sank. It would no doubt be a contrived masque about courtly love where men wooed docile and compliant women, who agreed to their every demand. The masque would have no thought for a woman's true feelings. Such a demure and pliant persona was the one she would be adopting again, but she was keen to put it off for as long as possible.

As the day progressed, the court watched as Henry and Anne swept into the castle, bringing glamour and laughter, a swathe of their favourites making up the glittering entourage. Disappearing to their chambers, the sense of anticipation grew as the courtiers waited for the spectacle created by the king and his best friend. Throughout the banquet which preceded it, the atmosphere took on an other-worldly intensity until Jane felt she had stepped into the pages of an Arthurian legend, where knights went on quests, fighting dragons, monsters and creatures of the deep, while women were rescued from towers or cast spells over suitors. Finally, they were summoned to the Great Hall.

The huge doors were thrown open and to the sound of silver trumpets, Henry led Anne inside, displaying her like a prize as he spun her into the seat by his side. His own vast padded throne was raised high on a platform, dominating proceedings. Anne laughed, smiling at Henry with adoration but Jane noticed the trembling of her hands and the moments where she thought no one was watching when her smile would drop and a mask of misery would flicker across her face.

"My friends," called the king, standing and clapping his hands to silence the excited chatter, "tonight, I celebrate the future with a dance created by myself and my dear friend, Charles." He waved towards the Duke of Suffolk who bowed to the eager, sycophantic applause.

The king gave two more sharp claps and the musicians began to play a lively tune. Behind Henry and Anne, two doors opened and a troupe of masked dancers entered, leaping and jumping, light as air as they sprang and twirled. Clad in Tudor green and draped in shimmering strips of cloth of silver and gold, they resembled sprites and faeries. Another door opened admitting more dancers, this time children. Jane watched transfixed as the sprites swirled around picking up the smaller dancers who laughed and giggled as they waved their hands and fingers in time to the music.

The lithesome creatures at the centre of the spectacle were young, she realised, ranging in age from fifteen or sixteen down to those who Jane guessed were a similar age to Jasper and were perhaps three or four years old. The children formed serried ranks and began to dance a more traditional pavane, the sinuous costumes giving them an ethereal air. With a swift run of notes the music changed and as it did, a swirl of women entered and surrounded the youngsters, and when they stepped away a few moments later, the children were transformed. Around their shoulders were heavily jewelled cloaks and the strange masks had been removed.

A collective gasp ran around the courtiers and the women who had joined the dance floor began a spirited almain. Princess Mary led it, her face screwed up in fury, and beside her was Lady Margaret Douglas, a proxy for Mary's mother, Katherine of Aragon. Beside them danced Henry Fitzroy with Bessie Blount. On Bessie's other side was her daughter, Elizabeth Tailboys. Next was Lady Jane Stukeley and her son, Thomas, neither of whom seemed comfortable and whose movements were stilted and reluctant. With a flamboyant toss of her head, Mary Boleyn, accompanied by Kathryn and Henry Carey danced a complicated reel before stepping aside for Lady Mary Berkeley, her son, John and Joanna Dingley, sister of Jane's maid, Audrey. Trying her best to throw her head with the same sophistication as Mary Boleyn, Joanna led her pretty toddling daughter, Ethelreda, in a dance with three-year-old John Perrot.

Jane jumped as a hand rested on her shoulder.

"What do you make of this?" asked Francis, his voice cold. "All the king's bastards and their mothers in a dance. Queen Katherine refused to take part and it was a last moment decision for the Princess Mary to join the throng. She agreed on the condition that Margaret would dance beside her."

"The king did this?" Jane whispered in horror. "It is humiliating for the women who are dancing and devastating for Anne."

"What do you think he means by it?"

"He is mad. That is what it means."

Jane dragged her eyes from the festivities on the dance floor to watch the king. His eyes were hooded and he watched the dancers with a look of cruel satisfaction. Against her will she looked at Anne, who was white-faced and transfixed, all trace of her former laughter draining away with the colour in her face.

"We must leave," she said to Francis, her own excitement and joy at being back at court disappearing as the dance reached its dramatic end.

"We can't," he whispered.

As the music faded away and the clapping petered out, a strange hush fell over the room as Henry levered himself to his feet.

"My children," he declared, and the gathered offspring of the king bowed and curtseyed, some with aplomb and arrogance like Fitzroy, while Princess Mary refused to move, remaining rigid. Elizabeth Tailboys, Kathryn and Henry Carey, and Thomas Stukeley gave the smooth obeisances of trainee courtiers while Ethelreda and John looked bewildered, giggling from nerves. "And their mothers," he continued, his eyes hard specks of obsidian in his flushed, excited face, as the women made their bows. "Yet now, a new era has begun in the legend of my reign. As I free this land from the tyranny of the Roman church, as I recreate God in the image of an English king, I take to my troth a true English rose and from her, I will have sons, strong sons who will take this land, my England, my Wales, land of my forefathers to become more powerful than the Spanish, the French and the Italians put together. I will reign supreme and they will beg me for mercy. Each of my offspring will be sent forth in a pact of a marriage and the foreign princes will tremble at my name."

With a jubilant roar, he clapped his hands together and the musicians began to play. Henry led an ashen Anne onto the dance floor and as the women ushered away the children, the assembled courtiers flooded to join their sovereign, unsure what to make of his pronouncement.

"Come, my love," said Francis, "let us leave. The king will not notice our absence now he is dancing."

Jane realised they were among others who were fading away under cover of the spinning dancers. Senior courtiers, loyal Catholics, men who had guided and advised Henry since he ascended the throne a few days before his eighteenth birthday. Ahead Sir Nicholas and Lady Elizabeth Carew, were accompanied by a recently bereaved Sir Henry Norris. His wife, Mary, had died a few weeks earlier but rather than being permitted to mourn, Norris had been ordered to court by the king.

"My lords, ladies, perhaps a drink in my rooms," said Francis and with murmurs of agreement, they hurried down the corridors.

Upon arrival, Jane organised refreshments and when the servants had retreated, she watched as Francis tried to take control of his thoughts.

"Have you spoken to Alphonso and Louis Blount?" asked Francis.

Nicholas Carew shook his head. "Not yet, they are working with Baron Mountjoy to raise funds for Bessie's plan but with the debasement of the currency taking place, Cromwell is becoming suspicious. He is convinced bullion is being syphoned off..."

"Which it is," interrupted Henry Norris. "Mountjoy might be Master of the Mint but Cromwell is like a terrier after a rat. There is no hole he will leave unexplored; we must have a care."

Jane stared from Francis to Nicholas Carew to Henry Norris, not understanding this exchange but alarmed by the sour voices and tense expressions.

Lady Carew caught Jane's glance and moved to sit beside her. "These are troubled times," she whispered. "Much has changed since you were last at court. The king overspends, the coffers are empty and he orders Cromwell to replenish his finances. Debasing the currency will cause huge financial hardship, yet the king is greedy and even the gold Cromwell provides is not enough. While the king uses the excuse of the tyranny of the Roman church for stopping his divorce, his real gripe is with the wealth of the monasteries."

"What do you mean?" asked Jane.

"The king wants a son, hence his plan to marry Anne, but his real objective has always been to find a way to break with Rome in order to plunder the wealth of the Catholic church."

"Does he not love her?"

"The king loves only himself, there is no room for another, but he is intrigued by Anne. He wants an English son to follow him, one whose allegiance is to England alone. He sees Katherine's Spanish heritage as a threat. He would like to destroy her and Princess Mary, but even he is aware of the furore this would cause. Instead, he humiliates and harangues them."

Jane felt bile rising in her throat. Anne was in love with James Butler. Katherine of Aragon was in love with the king and Henry was only in love with power. Encouraged by the Duke of Norfolk, Henry had selected an English girl to be his queen. If Mary Boleyn had not been married, perhaps she would have been in Anne's place, but Anne was the next best option: Mary had provided a son and daughter, if Anne, her sister, did the same then the Tudor dynasty was secure.

"Why do you think Anne is so eager to support Bessie in her quest for Fitzroy?" whispered Lady Carew. "It is the only way we will be able to free ourselves from the rule of a tyrant."

CHAPTER THREE

"Aunt Eliza, what a wonderful surprise," exclaimed Jane, sinking into an obeisance in front of Lady Elizabeth Boleyn, the Countess of Wiltshire.

A slender woman with a pearl-encrusted French hood, Lady Elizabeth Boleyn was elegant, calm and, like her daughter Mary, considered a classic beauty with blonde hair and blue eyes. Anne's dark hair and eyes followed her father's side, although Lady Boleyn's aristocratic cheekbones were evident in the faces of both her daughters. Her absence the previous evening had been noted by many but when asked, her husband, Sir Thomas, had said his wife was unwell. As Jane stood, she noticed the pallor of Lady Boleyn's face and the tiredness in her eyes. Perhaps the story had been true and Lady Boleyn had been suffering from an ague, rather than avoiding the humiliating dance prepared by the king, as many of the gossips had implied.

"Jane, my dear, it's a delight to have you returned to us at court. Whatever can you have been doing to amuse yourself at Hertford Castle all this time?" Lady Boleyn asked.

"The hunting is excellent," replied Jane. "Sir Francis has come to rely upon me to run his dwellings, he is so busy with all the extra duties required of him by the king."

Outside, a herald announced Anne Boleyn and a moment later she swept into the room followed by four women and three men. Jane sank in an obeisance but found Lady Boleyn lifting her back to her feet.

"There is no time," she declared. "You are leaving soon, Jane, and we have much to explain before you return to Queen Katherine."

Jane stared around in surprise. Anne seated herself beside her mother, and Mary Boleyn, Lady Jane Stukeley, Lady Mary Berkeley and Bessie Blount waited while the three young men arranged chairs for them. As the women seated themselves, the tallest of the three men glanced at Jane, giving her a grin.

"Cousin Jane," he said and bowed.

"Thomas Boleyn," she replied, bobbing a curtsey. "Court life seems to suit you."

Behind him stood Anne's other brothers, Henry — known to all as Hal — and the youngest of the family, George. The three Boleyn brothers were legendary among the younger set at court: dashing, dark-haired, dark-eyed, proficient at the joust and in the sword, fearless hunters and hard riders, showing no fear; they were admired by all, including the king. Thomas was the eldest, next came Hal, and then the youngest, George. While George, who as a youngster had suffered from colds and a weak chest, had remained at home, the eldest boys, Thomas and Hal, had been sent to live in the households of Cardinal Wolsey and Thomas Howard, Duke of Norfolk, respectively.

"Cousin Jane, how is it keeping house for that old rogue Sir Francis?" asked Hal with an exaggerated wink, causing Jane to blush.

"He's a true gentleman," she replied.

"Sir Francis? Perhaps there is an imposter pretending to be him," laughed Thomas. "How are Harry and Tommy?"

"My brothers are well," said Jane, smiling as she thought of her own family. "Harry is keeper of Taunton Castle and he and Barbara are expecting another child."

"And Tommy?"

"Running riot somewhere."

"Edward sends his regards," said Thomas, adopting a pompous expression.

"Thomas, stop it," demurred his mother. "You know Edward is a serious young man who wishes to become a great man at court."

Anne gave a derisive snort. Jane was aware her eldest brother, Edward, and Anne often clashed.

"Cousin Edward might need to develop a sense of humour before Henry gives him a position close to the crown. He's so sanctimonious. Apologies, Jane," said Hal.

"No offence taken; my eldest brother's special talent is offending people."

"Enough," said Anne, bringing the conversation to an abrupt halt, her dark eyes flashing. "As Mother stated, Jane will be leaving within the hour to join Queen Katherine and she must know the truth."

A ripple of apprehension went through Jane as silence descended and all eyes turned to Anne. When the invitation had arrived to visit Lady Elizabeth Boleyn before her departure, she had thought it was a routine call to a member of her extended family; she had not imagined they would be joined by Anne or the array of women seated before her.

"Alphonso, Louis and Meg, my brothers and sister, send their apologies but they are unable to join us," said Bessie Blount. "My brothers are with our cousin, Mountjoy, learning the skills of the diplomat, specifically the organisation of the Royal Mint, while Meg feels unwell after the revels of last night. She is most sad, Jane, as she wished to thank you for all the kind letters you have sent over the past year."

Jane was about to respond, saying she too regretted not having seen Meg as they had become friends during Jane's previous sojourn at court but Anne, once again, cut across the conversation.

"You will, no doubt, see Meg soon," said Anne, her eyes narrowed in irritation.

It was the first time she had looked directly at her and Jane was shocked at Anne's appearance. Underneath the layer of make-up, her pallor was cadaverous, her skin dull, with dark shadows like bruises under her eyes. Jane wondered whether Anne's illness had taken more of a toll on her health than she was prepared to admit or whether the endless torment of the court was to blame.

"There are plans afoot," said Anne. "After the debacle of last night, we are more determined than ever to offer the people of this country an alternative to the monster the king is becoming. Fitzroy has been recalled to court and will reside here at Windsor to complete his royal training. Bessie is betrothed to Edward Clinton, Earl of Lincoln, saving her from the possibility of King Henry deciding to marry her and legitimise Fitzroy. Next month, the king intends to leave the queen."

"Hasn't he already?" scoffed Mary Boleyn.

"Not officially," said Anne, "but we plan to ride out one day soon and the king will not return. Katherine and her court will be moved to an alternative home and they will never be together as man and wife again."

"Will you marry the king?" Jane was annoyed that her voice quavered as she spoke.

Anne bit her lip. "Yes," she replied. Jane saw the pain in her dull eyes, their usual sparkle faded to ashes. "He will have me; it is as though a demon is driving him. He once described me as faerie fire waiting to consume him with passion, but it is an act. It is why I lose my temper, why we bicker, there are times when I cannot bear to have him near me..."

To Jane's surprise, Mary Boleyn hurried to Anne's side, wiping away her tears.

When Anne had composed herself, she continued, "It will not be long before the king declares himself Head of the Church of England." The atmosphere in the room thickened. "Thomas Cranmer, who will soon be made Archbishop of Canterbury, has assured Henry that the Church of England is an autonomous province of the Catholic Church of which Henry holds both secular and spiritual supremacy. He is, after all, an anointed king, the representative of God on Earth. When Cranmer is officially created Archbishop, he will annul Henry's marriage to Katherine, declaring it was never legal."

"When will this be?" asked Jane.

"We don't know," replied Bessie. "Cromwell moves to split with Rome, enabling Cranmer to take over the highest position in the church, but these things take time. Cromwell is amassing clerks, calling them commissioners, to inspect the monasteries. If they are found to be lewd or have in any way offended the king, Cromwell will take an inventory before dissolving the monastery and claiming their wealth and land for the crown. Nobles are being asked to make bids for land they would like to buy, adding more money to Henry's coffers."

"People will never stand for it," said Jane Stukeley. "My husband is in a fury with the king."

"They will have no choice," said Mary Berkeley. "When the king wants something, he takes it."

The coldness in her voice made Jane wonder if the tales of Mary's affair with the king might be different if Mary were to relate events.

"However, we are not yet in a position to challenge the king," said Bessie. "This is why Anne must allow her romance with Henry to unfold. It is essential she becomes queen."

"Why?" asked Jane. "If you are planning a coup to replace the king, why does Anne need to be queen?"

"My son is too young to rule alone at present, therefore, we must delay," Bessie explained. "While a strong council would be created to help my son rule, it would not be ideal. Neither do we have the funds yet to march on the king. We must bide our time while my brothers gather money from the bullion at the mint with the help of my cousin Mountjoy. In the meantime, the declaration of a Protestant Archbishop will not satisfy many of the legitimacy of a marriage between Anne and Henry. It is essential Anne marries Henry and becomes with child."

"And if the wider world doesn't recognise the marriage?"

"Then the king has another illegitimate heir," said Anne.

"How will that help?" asked Jane.

"We are preparing the ground for a coup to place Fitzroy on the throne," said Bessie. "Yet, with Anne pregnant, it would appear there is the potential for a legitimate prince. On the surface, this would seem to ruin our plans, however, if there is doubt over Anne and Henry's marriage — which there will be — any child born to them could be claimed to be illegitimate. If it is a princess, then there is no threat but, with this framework in place, even a younger son of dubious legitimacy could be pushed further down the line of succession behind Fitzroy when the time is right for us to topple the king."

Jane felt her palms sweating but she realised it was not fear causing this reaction, it was excitement. "Why are you telling me this?" she asked.

"When Henry and I leave, Katherine will be moving to Wolsey's old home, The More in Hertfordshire," said Anne. "Are you prepared to travel with her, Jane?"

Relief flooded through her; Francis had been correct. While The More was no longer the luxurious manor it had been in Wolsey's day, it was close to Hertford Castle, close to her son. "Of course, it is the reason I was summoned to court," she said.

"Are you prepared to help us?" asked Bessie. "It may place you in danger."

For the briefest moment, Jane hesitated, then her resolve hardened. "I am willing," she said.

"If anything were to happen to the king," Anne continued, "Fitzroy would need a council to rule for him. He would choose those whom he trusts, those who have guided him so well while he has been the head of the Council of the North. My brothers are already making themselves invaluable to him. Your brother, alas, has his own agenda and, as such, we haven't believed it is safe to inform him of our plans. Are you still prepared to help us if it means working against your brother?"

Jane dismissed the concern in a heartbeat. "You have my loyalty, Anne. Edward has always put himself first and I would never trust him to consider my welfare above his own. He, alas, sees all his sisters as nothing more than assets to be used to further his ambitions."

"Rather like my elder brother, Norfolk," muttered Lady Boleyn. "However, this is our chance to influence events. As Lady Margaret Beaufort did before us when she managed to negotiate the throne for her son, Henry VII. Margaret Beaufort was descended from the illegitimate offspring of John of Gaunt, the third son of Edward III, and his mistress, Katherine Swynforde. After Gaunt married Katherine, the children were legitimised in 1407 by King Richard II and Pope Boniface IX but, initially, they were barred from inheriting the throne. However, things changed when the male line died out and the Lancastrians needed a male heir. This was how Henry's father, the old king, had a claim to the throne: through an illegitimate line from which his mother descended. Fitzroy's claim is far stronger, no one would doubt his place on the throne."

Throughout her life, Jane had been schooled to understand her destiny was not her own to choose, that her husband would be selected for her and she would live a life decreed by the men around her. Yet, here was a group of women asking her to become involved in political intrigue. It was a heady feeling and the idea tingled with danger, but had she not already taken her fate into her own hands by agreeing to her clandestine marriage to Francis? "What would you have me do?"

"You have experience of spying; we would like you to continue in this role while you are with the queen but when you are asked to leave, we would like you to coordinate our messages and collate them while we raise funds and put our plans into action. You are known for your memory, your quick wit and your intelligence, these are the very skills we require."

"You would trust me with such an important task?" Jane asked in awe.

"We agreed you were the best positioned person," said Mary Berkeley.

"Then I must ask for your trust in return, for I have a secret and I wouldn't like to endanger the plot if it's discovered." The women exchanged glances, as did the three Boleyn brothers. "I am married to Sir Francis Bryan and we have a son. Alas, our daughter died but we hope to have more children."

The look of incredulity on their faces proved to Jane that she and Francis had kept their secret well.

"You are married?" Mary Boleyn gasped. "But, Jane, this is wonderful news. You must allow the court to know, it will keep you safe."

"Safe?" asked Jane. "From what?"

"The men in our families are always looking for the next way to amuse the king. You are young, pretty and have an air of innocence. You would be an ideal substitute for his bed when, if everything goes to plan, I am with child," said Anne, "and I would not wish that on anyone. If you are married, then you are safe. It is for this reason you must not keep your marriage secret, you must make it known, no matter the consequences. It makes me shudder to think of the king's hands on another woman in my family but, if your father and your ambitious idiot of a brother decree it, you will have no choice but to do whatever they decide. Your marriage to Sir Francis could save you from ever being forced into my situation."

Jane stared at the women with incredulity and reached out to take Anne's hand. "I promise, I will never allow myself to be in this terrible position," Jane whispered as goosebumps rose on her arms.

CHAPTER FOUR

"Is it true?"

Jane came to an abrupt halt, startled to see Katherine of Aragon standing in the doorway of her bedchamber. The queen's face was tinged with yellow, the skin tightly drawn over her cheekbones, her white linen nightgown giving her an eerie, spectral appearance.

"Your Grace," said Jane bobbing a curtsey, "is what true?"

"Your cousin, The Concubine, today she is made Marquess of Pembroke. My husband, the king, raises her up so she is able to marry him."

To Jane's surprise, Katherine spat on the floor in disgust.

"Yes, Your Grace," said Jane, "it is true. The king is ennobling Anne in order to make her his queen."

"*I* am his queen," Katherine hissed. "I am Queen of England."

Jane did not respond. Katherine's protests were the backdrop to their days, her endless muttering, denying her separation from the king, refuting the consummation of her marriage to Prince Arthur, a litany of despair for a woman dying from anger, bitterness and disappointment.

"Is that letter from the court?" demanded Katherine, pointing to the sealed parchment in Jane's hands.

"No, Your Grace, it is from my cousin…"

"Pah." The queen turned away in disgust, disappearing inside her bedchamber, slamming the door behind her.

"My cousin, Lady Elizabeth Carew," Jane finished. She pulled a face before poking her tongue out at the unyielding wooden door and continued on her way. Katherine's moods were tiresome and Jane knew the queen had assumed the letter was from Anne but, if she had waited, she would have learned the truth and spared herself another dart of misery. Perhaps, thought Jane, she wants to be unhappy, then she can pray about it. "Being queen doesn't make you omniscient," she muttered to herself. "It does make you bad-tempered though."

Aware she should be with the other ladies, praying or sewing, two tasks of which she felt she had experienced enough to last a lifetime since being part of Katherine's household, Jane wondered if she would be able to slip away to her room unnoticed. Not wishing to draw attention to herself, she slowed her angry march, adopting a more cautious tread, creeping along the creaking wooden floorboards of the damp corridor, hoping she would not meet anyone as she hurried to her chamber to read the letter from Lady Carew.

The Carews were senior courtiers and, when she was not enjoying the glamour of Henry and Anne's world, Lady Carew would retire to her country estate of Beddington Hall in Surrey. Jane envied her cousin and her anger intensified as she considered her own clandestine marriage. At first, she had enjoyed the secrecy, the subterfuge, but loneliness was making her crave her husband's company.

It is time to reveal our union, she thought, as she walked on silent feet, *even if, at first, it does cause a furore*. As time passed, there would be forgiveness and she could enjoy life again. How she longed for laughter, dancing and hunting, instead of the drab routine of prayer, sewing and reading aloud from the Bible. Three weeks earlier, she had written to Francis asking to be relieved of her duties as a spy within the queen's household.

I miss you. I miss our laughter, our home and, most of all, our son. The More is a bleak place and I am dying of boredom here with the endless sniping and arguing of Katherine's other ladies. I long to ride, to hunt, to drink sweet wine with you again…

As Jane walked towards her chambers, her mind drifted to Anne as she imagined her preparing for the ceremony that would raise her to the higher echelons of the nobility. A letter from Lady Carew the previous month had described Anne's gown and the ermine-trimmed train, which would be carried by Mary Howard, the daughter of the Duke of Norfolk and another cousin. Jane wished she was there to witness the spectacle.

Suddenly, Eliza Darrell loomed through the shadows, startling her. "Guilty conscience, Mistress Semel?" asked Eliza with a wheezy titter.

Jane shot her a withering look. Semel was an old version of her family name and it was one she did not favour. Eliza had taken it upon herself to use the name whenever possible, accompanied by a sly leer, knowing it would irritate her.

"None whatsoever," sighed Jane. "I am distressed that you have prevented me from reading my letter from my cousin, Lady Carew. Did you want me or were you waiting in the shadows accosting anyone who happens to be passing?"

Jane knew she should guard her tongue and soften her tone, aware that Eliza Darrell was a confidante of Queen Katherine and would no doubt report this altercation with embellishments but she disliked the woman, knowing her to be disingenuous and self-serving.

"Lady Twyford sent me to find you," said Eliza, her snide manner replaced by one of offended hauteur. "You have a visitor waiting for you in the Great Chamber."

"Who?"

"Do I look like your servant?" snapped Eliza and, pushing past Jane, she barged her with her shoulder, causing Jane to stumble. Eliza marched away down the corridor, shooting a venomous look over her shoulder as she turned the corner and disappeared.

"Save me from these angry women," muttered Jane as she slid the letter in the leather pouch hanging from her belt before making her way to the Great Chamber.

Visitors were unusual at The More and she wondered who could have sought her out. Her father, perhaps, or one of her brothers; she doubted if any of her cousins or extended family would have dared showed their faces as they were known to be supporters of Anne and, therefore, sworn enemies of the household.

"There you are, Mistress Semel," said Blanche Twyford, hurrying to meet her as she approached the double doorway into the Great Chamber, her thin lips twisted with impatience. "You should have warned us you were expecting a visitor."

"As you are aware, Lady Twyford, this is a surprise. Who is here to see me?"

Jane felt no warmth towards either woman. Blanche was cold, dismissive of all who were not as pious as she, while Eliza Darrell was a gossip, yet Queen Katherine held both women in high regard.

"Your cousin," Blanche snapped. "Even though I have duties of my own, of great importance, I shall arrange to have refreshments sent."

"Thank you," replied Jane with a wide smile, knowing this would annoy Blanche even further. Hope suffused her as she pushed open the doors. A tall man waited, standing with his back to the fire, warming his legs. Turning as he heard the creak, Jane's breath caught in her throat. "Francis," she exclaimed and without a second thought ran into his arms. The relief at his presence, at feeling his touch, was overwhelming and to her surprise tears welled in her eyes.

"Jane, my love," he said, his voice soft and she could hear her own relief at being together again echoing through his murmurs. "I've come to take you home."

"Thank goodness," she said. "You have no idea what a miserable place this has become. When will we leave?"

"As soon as you are ready," he replied.

When they had first been forced to The More in November 1531, Katherine had arrived with an entourage of over two hundred people. However, as time passed many of her women had been ordered home by their families, particularly those who had decided to back the Boleyns as their way to powerful positions at court. As time passed, others had left, finding the remoteness of the house too bleak and more had been dismissed by the king as he and his henchman, Cromwell, whittled away Katherine's household.

At first, Jane had enjoyed the close proximity of The More to Hertford Castle and, under the continuing guise as housekeeper for Sir Francis Bryan, divided her time between the two properties. However, in the past few months, these visits had stopped as the queen had demanded her ladies remain with her. Jane was finding it tiresome, but she was also aware that it would not be long before her burgeoning pregnancy became impossible to hide. Francis was as yet unaware of this, and it was with delight that Jane realised she would be able to tell him in person.

"Praise be," she sighed. "What's prompted this?"

"Although she is as yet unaware, Katherine will be moving to Ampthill in Bedfordshire in the New Year and her attendants will be reduced further. It's time you were away from this house. You have done an exemplary job here, but it is over."

"Francis, what joyous news! The oppressive atmosphere of this house was taxing my nerves."

He pulled her into his arms and Jane felt the tension of the past months melt away. A footstep outside made them spring apart; Jane sank into an obeisance and adopted the demure and subservient tone which had served her so well during her time with Queen Katherine.

"The honour is mine, Sir Francis, but what sad news that I must leave my duties with the true queen…"

Blanche Twyford stood in the doorway, her narrow face alive with curiosity. Ushering forward the two reluctant page boys, who placed a jug of wine and savoury pies on the table at the side of the room, Jane was aware of Blanche's eyes flickering from herself to Francis and back again. The two boys scurried away, leaving Blanche hovering in the doorway.

"Arise, Mistress Seymour, there is no need to grovel before me. We are kin," said Francis, his tone imperious and impatient.

As Jane stood, Francis shot her an amused look, his one remaining eye sparkled with mischief at their charade. She turned the giggle that rose to her lips into a cough, earning her another look of disgust from Blanche.

"My apologies, Sir Francis, I was overcome…" she murmured, her eyes lowered as she tried to avoid giggling.

"My Lady Twyford," said Francis, turning away from Jane, "Mistress Seymour's parents have decreed that she must re-join them at their country home, Wulfhall in Wiltshire. Please call her maid, Audrey, and arrange for her belongings to be packed and sent on with all haste. When we have finished our repast, she will need her riding habit as we must travel to my castle in

Hertford before the sun sets. Audrey will travel with Mistress Seymour's belongings tomorrow."

Jane busied herself by the table, her back to Blanche, so the older woman would not see her broad smile. Lady Twyford would not dare question Francis and it was a delight to hear the sour-faced old woman being put in her place. Pouring wine into two goblets and putting a selection of small pies on a pewter serving platter, Jane did not turn around until she heard Blanche agree to Francis's instructions before slamming the door behind her.

"You're an old rogue," she laughed as she handed him the spiced wine.

"She enjoyed every minute of being bossed around," he grinned, slipping his arm around her waist and pulling her tight to him, kissing her deeply.

"I imagine she did; she's been a widow for many years."

"Probably killed him with one of her vicious looks."

"Francis, you're awful," laughed Jane, pushing him away. "We shall have to tell the queen I'm leaving."

"Yes, we shall, but the difference this time, my love, is we will be telling her. In the past, technically she gave her permission, now, alas, her power has been taken from her. While you change, I'll pay her a visit on behalf of the king."

"And it is true Anne has been created Marquess of Pembroke?"

"Yes, the ceremony is today,"

"Shall we return to court?" asked Jane. "If so, you must know, I am once again with child."

An incredulous smile spread across Francis's face. "My love, this is wonderful news, when is the babe to be born?"

"In the final days of winter," she replied.

"Then, my love, our way is clear. You must travel to another of my castles until the baby is born."

"But you said court..." Jane could feel her lip tremble as she bit back tears.

"When the child is born, we shall reveal all, until then my priority is to keep you safe. We have lost one infant, let us not lose another, and it would destroy me if anything were to happen to you."

"Won't I be needed?" she asked, disappointed that she would not be returning to court in triumph. "I have developed a code for myself, Anne, Bessie and the other women. I am their spymistress..."

"Silence," Francis hissed. "Hold your tongue on such matters." Jane was startled by his fierce tone and the unexpected pallor of his face. "These are matters of great danger," he continued. "Do not mention them until we are away from here."

"I'm sorry," she replied, furious with herself for dropping her guard. "If you are comfortable here, Sir Francis, I shall return to my rooms to dress for our departure."

Sweeping from the room, Jane felt her legs shaking. It had been foolish to mention the correspondence between Anne and Bessie, but being with Francis had felt safe and familiar. It could not happen again. She understood the dangers, even asking Francis about such things was treason. Bunching her skirts into her hand, Jane took the stairs two at a time, throwing off the demeanour of the demure wallflower which she had worn for so long, and instead allowing some of her own natural exuberance to flourish at last.

CHAPTER FIVE

"It is done then," said Jane, looking up from the scroll. "Anne and Henry are married."

Francis threw himself into the carved wooden chair by the fire, reaching down to stroke one of the three greyhounds who slept on soft, embroidered beds, their tails wagging drowsily. "A small ceremony with the Boleyns and a few close friends in attendance was held a month ago," he said. "Our cousin is Queen of England."

Jane's eye returned to the scroll as she considered its words. Anne Boleyn, her second cousin, was the highest-ranking woman in the country. This was a heady and unnerving thought. With her rising status over the years, her family had long felt the glow of power. Anne's father, Thomas, had been raised to be Earl of Wiltshire and Earl of Ormond. Her eldest brother was named Viscount Rochford while manors, land and positions aplenty had been bestowed upon the Boleyn family. Yet, there were details which bothered Jane, important and vital facts which could not be ignored.

Checking once again the pile of letters beside her, she pushed herself back from the table and considered the information. If her translations of the codes she had received from the wives of all the key players in Anne's rise to the crown were correct, then it was apparent many members of the court, particularly the Catholic courtiers who remained loyal to Katherine, believed the king remained married to the old queen, making his new marriage to Anne bigamous.

It was as the women had planned it two years earlier when they had sat in Lady Elizabeth Boleyn's rooms discussing the strange dance of children followed by Henry's desire to break from Rome and declare himself head of the Church of England. As Bessie had claimed, the king was in need of money and as he and Cromwell swept through the land with the same violent efficiency as the Sweat, they were destroying livelihoods as they dissolved the monasteries but unlike the pestilence, they were also gaining wealth. Jane knew from the coded letters she received that while some ruthless men were profiting alongside Henry, most were appalled by his decisions.

Her husband, Francis, had created the code and as he was an expert in ciphers, it was subtle and not easily discernible, and besides, Francis himself had explained to her that the letters between women were ignored. *Henry's codebreakers believe we are too stupid and our conversations too unimportant to be worth wasting time deciphering. Foolish men*, she thought, with a wry smile.

Even though she was living in a house which was considered safe, Jane had learned her lesson the day Francis had shouted at her at The More. Since then she had never dropped her guard or blurted out details of their plans. Walking to the fire where her three greyhounds slept, she threw on two logs, stoking the flames, causing them to flare up the chimney, before bending down beside her husband and whispering, her voice harsh and urgent, "Are the rumours true that Anne is with child?"

"You are wise, my dear wife," said Francis, nodding as he spoke. Understanding he would not say more until they were alone in their bedchamber, certain not to be overheard, she rose, taking her place on the other side of the hearth.

"Wise? Are you sure?" she asked. "I sit day after day working my way through the letters from Bessie Blount, Jane Stukeley, Anne, Mary Boleyn, Lady Mary Berkeley, my sisters-in-law: Anne Stanhope and Barbara Wolfe, as well as countless others, compiling the information to enable us to control events, yet I am stuck here, while you spend your time at court enjoying the entertainment. When are you going to tell everyone we are married? If you don't do it soon, my parents will begin suggesting more potential husbands. For goodness sake, Francis, we have two children, Jasper and Lois."

The subject was the cause of great strife between them and Jane used this to her advantage whenever possible. After first leaving The More and the household of Queen Katherine, Francis had taken Jane and their son to the far-flung Harlech Castle in North Wales, one of the many castles of which he was constable. While he had returned to court, Jane had given birth to their daughter, Lois. However, when a letter had arrived from her sister-in-law, Anne Stanhope, wife of her eldest brother, Edward, with news suggesting the continuing romance between Francis and Philippa Spice, after they had danced in a masque together, Jane began to wonder about her marriage.

As the weeks passed, with the continuing absence of Francis, Jane's loneliness, fury and despair had begun to build. Not long churched and with her husband continuing to claim that he could not yet leave court in order to meet his daughter, she wondered whether she had been a fool to agree to the terms of his marriage proposal and its continuing clandestine nature. After all this time, and with Anne now in a position of power, there was no need to continue the secrecy, yet he refused to allow her to return to court. Instead, she was hundreds of miles away, compiling documents and running his household, under the guise of his housekeeper.

With each passing day, resentment festered within Jane, stoking her fury to white-hot incandescent rage, so when Francis had arrived a few days after Anne Stanhope's letter, unaware of the news that had been delivered to Jane, her anger had broken over her husband like a malediction.

"Is this why you refuse to tell my parents we are married?" she had screamed, throwing the silver plate at him and causing the greyhounds to run whimpering from the room. "You regret our marriage and deny our children because you would prefer to dance with the merry widow as she simpers and flutters around?"

"No, my love," he had replied, ducking, his hands over his head as he tried to protect himself from the deluge of household items that were being thrown at him with force and malice. "We must keep up appearances, this is the plan…"

"May the Gods take the plan!" Jane had bellowed, launching a pitcher of wine at her husband's head with more intent than accuracy so it bounced off a nearby table and sprayed around the room.

"Jane, stop!" Francis had yelled, his voice somewhere between laughter and anger.

Jane, already feeling her own fury abating, had also felt her mouth twitch. "Admit that you're a loathsome cur!" she yelled, searching for another missile but in her moment of hesitation, he seized her, pinning her arms to her side and kissing her.

"I'm a loathsome cur," he said, before kissing her again.

Jane had squirmed, fighting to free herself from his iron grip but her anger was changing into the passion only Francis could rouse in her. "Admit I'm too good for you," she said, returning his kisses.

"You're much too good for me."

"On your knees and apologise."

"What? Really?"

With a devilish look in her eye, she had nodded and to her amusement he had taken a pace back, while continuing to hold her hands, and had lowered himself on to one knee.

"My lady, I am a cur of the lowest order, I do not deserve such as you to be my wife. Forgive me, my love. You are my one true heart."

Laughter had overtaken them both as she opened her arms to him but later that evening as they sat together in front of the fire, sated and happy, feeding each other wine and honey cakes, she had asked him again when they could return to court and reveal their marriage.

"This place is so isolated," she had sighed.

"My love," he had replied, reaching for her hand and pulling her on to his lap, "you know how dangerous it is at court. You are safer here and your work on our plans is essential."

"Yet, I am alone in a castle on the edge of a grey sea," she had whispered. "I want to come home, Francis. I'm bored and lonely."

Tears had welled in her eyes, which she had scrubbed away. She hated weepy women, but her frustrations were real. While she understood the danger their plans posed, she was confident there was a better place to hide her and their children.

"Would you be prepared to remain in Wales a little longer," he had asked, "if you were in a friendlier place?"

"Where did you have in mind?"

"A house, over one hundred miles from here but on a different piece of the Welsh coast and near people with whom you are familiar."

"Tell me, Francis."

"When you wrote to our cousin, Anne, without my knowledge…" She had opened her mouth to defend herself but he held up his hand to stop her, before continuing, "...she was saddened that you were in such a bleak castle and suggested an estate which came to her when she was invested as Marquess of Pembroke. It is in a village named St Ishmaels, once known as Llanismael. The bulk of the land was given to the church, but one portion was given by royal charter to Sir Stephen Perrot on the incident of his marriage in 1457 to the Lady Ann Tudor, half-sister of King Henry VI. On this acreage there is a manor, which was built around an existing sixth-century tower. For some years, the house fell into disrepair but was rebuilt a few years ago by Sir William Perrot, a descendant of Sir Stephen's. Sadly, due to William's gambling debts, the old king reclaimed the land which he believed was, by birthright, Tudor property."

"How will an estate in another part of Wales be any different to here?" she had asked as the wind howled, rattling the windows.

"The house is modern and warm; it's a manor, not a castle and there is a convent on the island, which will be perfect for the demure Jane Semel, who is practically a nun herself, if the old queen is to be believed."

Jane had laughed.

"Even better," continued Francis, "you will be near Mary Berkeley, now Mary Perrot who resides at Carew Castle." Jane gave Francis a curious glance. "And, should we have need of it, you are close to the coast to reach Ireland. This might be the safest place if things go awry with our plans."

She had stared into his handsome face, which for once was serious, showing his genuine concern. A manor rather than a castle, a nearby convent and court society. Jane had nodded and the necessary arrangements to move her and their two children from Harlech Castle to Marquess House were set in motion.

When she arrived, Marquess House was everything Francis had described, a comfortable manor built around an old sixth-century tower. Its many chimneys and fireplaces warmed the rooms and the large farm attached to the house provided bountiful food. A vast lake, which led down to the sea and dominated the grounds around the house, teemed with fish, while at its centre was the island convent of Llyn Cel.

At first, Jane had felt the presence of the convent would be intrusive, but the nuns were a small order, off the beaten track of the pilgrim trail to St Davids' cathedral, and she rarely encountered them. A passageway joined the chapel at Marquess House to the island and while the nun's observed the canonical hours of the church, Jane drifted there as and when the mood took her. To hear the nuns singing plainsong was soothing when her day had been fraught with the endless subterfuge which her husband continued to weave around her. The most interesting discovery for Jane, however, was the scriptorium.

"Is this usual in a convent?" she had asked the Mother Superior, Sister Adwenna, a few days after her arrival.

"Of course, my dear," the nun had replied, "it is not only men who wish to preserve the word of God. There are many women in the Bible whose tales must be told." Her blue eyes had twinkled and Jane had smiled.

"Do you take private commissions?" she asked.

"This is one of the ways we make our living," the nun replied, and Jane had outlined her plan.

Looking at the piles of paper on the large desk, Jane wondered if Francis would ever allow her to visit court. Despite his love for her, which she did not doubt, the words of the Boleyn brothers returned to her: Francis was a rogue. She had called him so herself but she could not understand why he was determined to keep her sequestered away. For a moment, her mind flickered towards the scandal caused by her father's affair. Was he ashamed to be connected to their family? With a shake of her head, she banished this idea; her father's indiscretion was old news, eclipsed by the ongoing scandals at court and, anyway, Francis would not care about such things.

As if to prove the removal of the stigma which had blighted her parents' rise at court, her brothers were doing well. Edward was now an Esquire of the Body to the king. He had been part of the king's train on a trip to France the previous year and was beginning to be given more responsibility; Thomas was younger, wilder and for a while had been part of Fitzroy's inner circle but, with Fitzroy in France, Thomas had begun to make himself useful to Francis who was ensuring small roles within the household were passed his way, helping him to earn his place as a courtier. Her third brother, Henry, had been appointed a sewer extraordinaire, a position which would bring him into regular contact with the king as it involved waiting at the king's table and was the first step in a career of a courtier.

Her parents were settled at Wulfhall and her sister, Elizabeth, was in Yorkshire with her husband, Sir Anthony Ughtred, while her other sister, Dorothy, had recently married Clement Smith and moved to Little Baddow in Essex. Jane knew Francis had helped to secure these positions for her brothers, as well as intervening in the negotiations of Dorothy's marriage settlement, which he would not have done if he was considering casting her aside. Yet, he was adamant she should remain at Marquess House.

Forcing herself to eschew such thoughts, Jane turned to the latest news she had received from court. The endless letters about the world of Anne and the king were bittersweet, easing the pain of her loneliness as she felt drawn into their glittering events. However, she did not forget the strange undercurrents and the feeling that the lives on show often held as much genuine emotion as the overblown masques and plays so beloved of the king. Everything was a masque, surface deep and with the potential to fall apart as easily as a stage set. In the past few weeks, news had reached her of the death of Sir Edward Burgh, leaving her friend, Katheryn Parr, a young widow. She wondered whether her family would push her into another union soon; everyone knew the Parrs were ambitious.

At least I am spared being used as a political bargaining tool, she thought.

More interestingly, news had reached her of a Bill written by Thomas Cromwell. The Act of Restraint in Appeals had been passed, making it law that any verdict concerning the king's marriage that was reached in an English court could not be challenged by Rome. Jane raised her eyebrows in derision as she read a note from Lady Carew explaining that within a few days of this Bill being passed, the English clergy had agreed that the king's marriage to Katherine of Aragon was not lawful and she would in future be styled as the Dowager Princess of Wales.

A certain sadness crept through Jane. Her time in the queen's service had not been unpleasant; there had been days of boredom but, for the majority of the time, the queen had treated her with kindness and consideration, despite her connection to Anne. Jane continued to believe that Katherine should have stepped down with dignity when she was offered the chance but, from one woman to another, Jane was disappointed for Katherine that her tenure as queen should end in such ignominy.

We are but pawns in the game played by men, she thought, and anger surged through her.

Doodling on a scrap of parchment in front of her she wrote 'Jane in Anger', embellishing it with flames, while she read the news concerning Fitzroy's extended stay at the French court. Whether the king was once again trying to secure a French princess for his illegitimate son, she did not know, but she had received an interesting letter from Jane Stukeley.

The Duke of Norfolk has made more plans in his attempt to place a Howard girl on the throne, she had written, *by proposing his daughter, young Mary Howard, as a bride for Henry Fitzroy.*

It was a logical development, thought Jane. No doubt the duke was concerned he might not retain control over Anne, who was after all, a Boleyn, even if by blood she was also a Howard. Pushing Mary forward to marry Fitzroy was a masterstroke. Should Fitzroy become king, then the duke would be father-in-law to the monarch and grandfather of a future heir.

"Wheels within wheels within wheels," murmured Jane, "these stories are supposed to bind us together, but will our ties remain firm or will they fray with time?"

Sorting out the piles of paper in front of her, she rolled several together and took them to the roaring fire, throwing them into its heart, watching while they withered to ash and rose into the chimney, their words lost forever. These letters were either too dull or too dangerous to remain in her possession. The remainder she would convert, as she had been doing for some time, into a manuscript, which was being illuminated by the Llyn Cel nuns.

The idea had come to Jane while she was awaiting the birth of her daughter, Lois, in the grim rooms of Harlech Castle. Her maid, Audrey, who had become a friend and companion, had been describing one of the illuminated pages she had once seen when visiting a church with her sister, Joanna Dingley.

"It was as though God himself had touched the page," she had whispered in an awed voice, "the images were so beautiful I hardly dared look at them…"

A book at which people were scared to look and which would be stored in a library away from prying eyes, Jane had thought. She had long since believed her work should be collated but the way in which to disguise it had eluded her until now. There was talk of the king's niece, Lady Margaret Douglas, having poetry writing competitions which they were intending to compile into a book. Jane had decided she would write down her discoveries in a similar manner. Having discovered a beautiful frieze on the ceiling of one of the tower rooms at Marquess House, depicting the legend of King Arthur and Camelot, Jane had decided she would hide the information she had gleaned within a similar tale, except she would write about women going on a quest.

No man will ever read a tale about women, she thought, *yet it will preserve our side of the story. Our tale and in between the lines, in invisible ink, I can leave messages. I can ask other women to write pages of their own and we can disguise it among the love poems of Anne's manuscript. Who would question silly lovestruck women writing poetry?*

Reaching for the stack of letters, Jane noticed one had a seal with a bull's head, her cousin Thomas Boleyn's cipher. He was in France with Henry Fitzroy and had been sending regular missives on the antics of the sixty-strong entourage who accompanied the illegitimate princeling. The letter was written in code and it took her over an hour to translate it.

King Francis I will be celebrating St George's Day in honour of Fitzroy. He's a member of the Order of the Garter to which the day is sacred. Perhaps King Francis is hoping this gesture will endear him to our gracious king and he might be offered an invitation to join the Order. After this, we will be heading to Marseille for the de Medici wedding. Hal and I shall soon be departing Fitzroy. We have been in correspondence with Alphonso and Louis Blount. Bessie and her new husband plan to continue with the parade we have oft discussed. There is much unrest among the Catholic factions who have been in discussion with Fitzroy.

Jane's breath caught in her throat. 'The parade' was the codeword which she always viewed with dread. Pushing the letter aside, she opened another. This from Meg Blount, whose passion was botany, particularly, herbs. As was tradition, the women of the house were all taught to make basic tinctures, simples and salves, as well as medicines to help their families, but Meg's interests were darker and, to the concern of her parents, she had begun to study poisons.

Her sister, Bessie, had explained, "Meg claims there are many poisons in nature. It's better to know and understand them and what cures them. If they are ingested by mistake, her knowledge could be invaluable."

While Jane agreed with this argument, she wondered if Meg's interests were innocent and for a moment her mind flew back to the day she had collected a vial for Meg from the apothecary and the woman who had been insistent that Jane carry it with care. She had assumed it was because the medicine was expensive or fragile and required to help Meg to ease the pain of her twisted foot but another thought occurred to her. Had the contents of the package been dangerous, and was this why the woman had been so reticent in handing it to Jane?

A knock on the door interrupted her troubling thoughts and Audrey entered.

"My Lady, there is a litter approaching, were you expecting visitors?" she asked.

"No," replied Jane, "is there any livery?"

"None that I recognise," Audrey replied.

Jane felt her heart flutter in concern. "Very well, we shall leave it to my steward, Jones, to discover who has surprised us and whether we shall choose to be at home."

CHAPTER SIX

Lady Mary Perrot stared around the room Jane used during the day. Large windows overlooked the gardens, while the enormous fire provided warmth and an impression of cosiness despite the high ceilings.

"Jane, this room is wonderful," she sighed. "It's so modern; every time I visit, my envy at your surroundings strikes me anew. The works on the Great Hall at Carew Castle continue as we attempt to bring it up to date but the rest is very old. It would be a delight to live in a home as comfortable as this manor."

Lady Perrot sank into a chair by the fire, staring at the flames, lost in thought while Jane watched her with interest. When she and Audrey had seen the unmarked litter approaching, Jane had feared the worst. Her nerves had not been calmed when it was revealed to be an unanticipated visit from Lady Mary Perrot, *née* Mary Berkeley, who lived fifteen miles away at Carew Castle.

Jane and Lady Perrot had corresponded over the years, their letters covering many topics and usually disguising a message either in code or written between the lines in invisible ink. When Jane had moved to Marquess House, they visited on a regular basis but Lady Perrot had never arrived unannounced in a carriage obscuring her livery. Jane liked the young woman who was enthusiastic about life and had a keen, sharp mind.

"Are you staying at Carew long this time?" asked Jane.

"My husband, Tommy, has declared it is his favourite place in the world and we shall stay for the foreseeable future," Lady Perrot said. Her voice was edged with tension.

"And how do you feel about being this far west?"

"It's the safest place for our son," she whispered, "especially as Tommy has explained there are moves to accelerate the parade."

Jane stared at Lady Perrot in astonishment as with these words the younger woman flipped back the edge of her sleeve to reveal a delicately embroidered five-pointed star.

"Are we alone? Can we talk safely?"

Jane swallowed the panic rising in her throat. Walking to the door, she peered outside into the great hall, but no one was lurking there and she knew the thickness of the walls would stop any eavesdropping. The chimney, however, opened on to the gallery of the floor above and she was nervous in case their words might be overheard by anyone near the flue.

"We shall move to the windows where the view is more pleasant and it is closer to the virginals, which I shall play to entertain us while we chatter," said Jane.

Seating herself at the instrument, which had been a recent present from Francis, Jane started playing scales as though warming up in preparation for a recital, although it was, in fact, an attempt to gain control over her trembling fingers. Lady Perrot joined Jane on the seat, poised to turn the pages of music on the rest above the keyboard.

"What has happened?" Jane asked, her heart beating with fear in case Francis or one of her brothers had been discovered in their subterfuge.

"It is the Boleyn and Blount boys," whispered Lady Perrot. "As you know, they have, until recently, been part of Fitzroy's household but a week ago, they left his employ under cover of darkness."

"Where have they gone? Do you know?"

"My husband claims they are heading to Ireland and the home of James Butler, Earl of Ormond, who is their distant cousin, but other rumours suggest they have remained in France and plan to travel overland to go into hiding in Venice."

"What?" Jane gasped as a terrible thought struck her. "Has the parade been discovered?"

"No," said Lady Perrot, placing a reassuring hand on Jane's arm. "It was an auspicious moment to leave because Meg Blount has been arrested."

"Meg has been arrested?" Jane was horrified.

"Yes, there has been a scandal which Queen Anne is trying to address. As you know, Meg makes tinctures for the queen — you know how talented Meg is with herbs — and it was claimed she left a bottle of poison in the chest with the medicine. No harm was done and Meg swears it was accidental but it was the king who discovered it and he went into a fury, demanding Meg be thrown in the Tower."

"But why would the Boleyns and Blounts have to leave France…?"

"Hal Boleyn and Meg have long had an agreement and it has been decided that it is safest for anyone connected with Meg to go into hiding."

Jane continued to play, her mind racing. These events must be very recent as no word had reached her through her correspondence with the women at court. "What are the charges against Meg?" she asked.

"The king believes Meg was trying to poison both himself and Anne," Lady Perrot replied. "In his fury, he has become convinced that Hal, Thomas, Louis and Alphonso — people all connected to Meg — are in a position to poison Fitzroy, too. The Blount boys have always shown an interest in alchemy and 'powders' — as the French call poisons — and it has come to light that Thomas and Hal have been in correspondence with the Venetian alchemists, the Council of Ten…"

"Who are also feared as sorcerers and assassins," Jane finished the sentence, understanding why the men might consider fleeing to the comparative safety of Ireland. "But why would Meg give Anne poison?"

"She claims the poison was brewed in order to kill vermin and should never have been included in the casket of medicines but neither the king nor Cromwell believe her."

"Poor Meg," said Jane. "How will she fare in the Tower?

Although she coped well with her disability, Meg was slight and prone to chest ailments. Jane imagined the Blounts would be paying for every possible comfort for her, but such a frightening ordeal would take its toll on Meg's health.

"Anne is doing her best to persuade the king it was a genuine mistake, and we think she is near to convincing him. If Anne is unsuccessful, then Bessie will plead for her sister. Despite everything, the king remains fond of Bessie, so we are hopeful Meg will soon be free."

"And the others?"

"Will remain in hiding as long as is necessary."

Jane moved on from scales to her repertoire of tunes, digesting the information. There were many layers of subterfuge taking place and while she had not known about a plot to poison the king, the bottle had not been placed there by mistake. Meg was meticulous and it would have been there for a reason. Quite what Anne's intentions had been, Jane shuddered to imagine.

"There is other news too," whispered Lady Perrot as she turned a page of music for Jane. "From Bessie."

"What now?" Jane asked, her fingers faltering with nerves as they fluttered over the keyboard.

"Mary Boleyn has left court and taken her children, and in particular her son, Henry Carey, away," Lady Perrot whispered.

Ever since Anne's marriage, there were those who suggested there was tension between the Boleyn sisters, rumours that while Anne was pregnant Henry was once again casting covetous eyes at Mary. From the letters from Anne's court, Jane knew this to be nonsense. It was poor Madge Shelton who had been shunted forward for the dubious honour of warming the king's bed while Anne was unavailable. The widowed Mary Boleyn remained with her sister as she was continuing to try and gain her widow's portion from the king. Until such time as her jointure was released, Mary and her children were financially vulnerable.

"Her son?" asked Jane, unsure why this was relevant.

"Think Jane," hissed Lady Perrot. "*His* son."

With a rush of understanding, Jane nodded. "The king's son," she said in a low voice.

"Exactly, but he is unacknowledged. Jane Stukeley has also retired to the family estates in Devon taking her third son, Thomas."

Jane understood: the children from the dance were being removed from the dangerous vicinity of their father.

"And my own son, John, of course," Lady Perrot said, her voice was low. She hesitated before continuing, "My liaison with the king was not by choice despite what you may have heard to the contrary."

Jane remembered Francis's flippant comments about Mary Berkeley being a comfort to the king when Katherine of Aragon was pregnant. Mary and her husband, Thomas Perrot, had both been wards of her uncle, Maurice, Lord Berkeley, when he had arranged their marriage, settling 500 marks on the couple.

"My husband was told to take me to the king's chamber," murmured Lady Perrot. "He and I are the same age and because we were young, it meant that while we were married, our union had not, at that point, been consummated. We had no idea what would be expected of me when I entered the king's chamber that night…" Her voice tailed away and Jane squeezed her hand. "There is no doubt he is the king's son but Cromwell will not allow Henry to acknowledge any of these boys," Lady Perrot continued. "The king strides around demanding a son when he already has four."

"Although none have been born in wedlock," sighed Jane. "No wonder he blamed poor Queen Katherine."

"Bessie suggested we remove all the boys from harm, and she has also withdrawn her daughter, Elizabeth Tailboys, who is also the king's; Mary Boleyn has done the same with Kathryn and Joanna Dingley, the sister of your maid, Audrey, has removed her daughter, Ethelreda, another of the illegitimate children of the king. It is feared that, in the light of Meg's arrest, should the parade be discovered, the king may take it upon himself to ensure there is no illegitimate Tudor blood to challenge his crown."

"He would never harm his own offspring," gasped Jane.

"It is not a risk we're prepared to take. He has cut a swathe through his Pole and Courtenay cousins who all have royal blood and, therefore, claims to the throne. We must hide the children in case he takes it into his head that they too might challenge his crown."

"This is madness," said Jane, the tune she was playing coming to an end. "If only I were at court, I would be able to help."

Lady Perrot stared at her aghast. "But you know why Sir Francis won't allow you to court?" she said, then put her hand over her mouth.

Jane gave her a shrewd look. "Do I?" she asked, her eyes narrowing. No doubt Francis was continuing to peddle the tale about her being his housekeeper.

"To keep you safe from the king," said Lady Perrot.

"From the king?" Jane said in bemusement.

"Queen Anne is with child," explained Lady Perrot, "which means the king must look elsewhere for entertainment."

"Norfolk has already flung another Howard girl into his bed," said Jane derisively. "Even the king can't want for more than one woman at a time…" Lady Perrot dropped her eyes. "What aren't you telling me?" demanded Jane.

"Your eldest brother, Edward, suggested you as a viable alternative to Madge, should the king tire of her while Anne is unavailable."

"Edward would never be so crass," Jane said.

"The chance of power can change anyone for the worst," said Lady Perrot. "Your brother has witnessed young George Boleyn strutting about court, enjoying the exalted position of brother to the queen and, while he knows this is impossible to achieve at present, he nevertheless craves this closeness to the king."

Nausea swept through Jane. She and Edward had always maintained a cordial relationship, even though her sense of humour meant she had more in common with her younger siblings, Tommy and Harry. They were close enough compared with the violence and control she had witnessed among some siblings but she thought Edward cared for and respected her enough not to suggest such an appalling liaison. Her appraisal of him had been incorrect and, it seemed, ambition was more important than family love. Perhaps this was his revenge after Jane sided with their father in the aftermath of the Catherine Filliol affair.

"Sir Francis was furious at the suggestion," continued Lady Perrot, "and we all thought he would strike your brother when your name was suggested. Sir Francis said he was glad to have taken you from the evil of the court and kept you safe and innocent in his employ. He declared you would return to court when you were safely wed which caused an outcry from your brother who told Sir Francis he would be the one to arrange your marriage. Edward claimed it was why he kept blocking your parents attempts to marry you to a good, honest fellow. With your other sisters already married, you are the only chance Edward has to win favour with the king."

"What did Sir Francis say to this?" asked Jane, wondering if she would vomit.

"He punched your brother in the face," said Lady Perrot. "There was quite a scandal, but the king forgave Sir Francis — you know what good friends they are. It is why my husband and I were sent to Carew. We needed to keep our son safe and also deliver this news to you. Sir Francis is aware we know about your marriage, and he trusted us to keep you safe."

Jane had stopped playing, in her dismay that her brother, Edward, would use her to gain political favour, treating her as little more than a whore in order to achieve his own ends. At last, she understood why Francis had refused to allow her to join him at court. It was not because he was seeing other women — the relationship with Philippa Spice was a front — it was to thwart Edward as he tried to negotiate Jane into the king's bed for his own personal gain.

"Lady Bryan, are you well?" asked Lady Perrot, her voice reaching Jane through a haze of anger and confusion.

"Your words have shocked me," Jane said, "but I shall recover. At least I understand the reasons why I am exiled."

"Sir Francis misses you every day, but he can't think of another way to keep you safe. Even if he announced your marriage, he doubts it will stop your ambitious brother."

Although it hurt Jane to admit it about her own sibling, she agreed with her husband. "Then we must focus on other matters," she said. "It appears there is unrest in the court. The king is making enemies and should his behaviour become untenable, we have a viable alternative. Will you stay tonight, Lady Perrot? The evening is drawing in and a storm is forecast."

"Thank you, Lady Bryan," she replied, then she hugged Jane. "You are far from court, and there is no reason why you should ever return. We will be safe here in Pembrokeshire."

"You're correct," said Jane, forcing back her swirling emotions. There would be time to examine them later, but for now, she must play the gracious hostess.

"Perhaps, I can meet your children," smiled Lady Perrot, her dimples showing, and Jane was reminded again of her youth. She was barely twenty-two and already involved in the dangerous intrigues of the court.

"Of course," said Jane, "and afterwards we shall dine. We shall speak no more of this in case we are overheard but I shall give you a letter to send for Sir Francis before you leave."

Turning away to call Audrey and organise Lady Perrot's accommodation for the night, Jane bit hard on her lip to stop tears of fury welling in her eyes. *Men*, she thought, as she breathed deeply to stop her shuddering breath, *one day, I shall have my revenge on them all.*

CHAPTER SEVEN

Anne had succeeded. Jane crumpled the letter in her hand and closed her eyes, trying to control the rising panic which seemed to be her constant companion. The child, a princess, named Elizabeth, for both her grandmothers was a disappointment to the king but a relief to Anne and the plotters of the parade. In his short letter, Francis claimed that the king had declared there was still time for them to have a son, yet despite the lavish christening, the atmosphere at court had changed. During their prolonged courtship and the King's Great Matter, Anne had promised him a son. In failing this, her first queenly task, she had proved herself fallible and vulnerable.

While riding across Bushy Park, the king vented his frustration to me, Francis had written. *He claims there will be a son soon but his enthusiasm for this liaison has waned. Cromwell is providing the king with vast amounts of gold from the dissolution of the monasteries. The king no longer feels it is necessary to be married to Anne, the switch to Protestantism is complete and his eye roves the court looking for the next comely maiden. Jane, my love, I implore you to remain at Marquess House for as long as possible...*

Moving away from the fire, Jane called Audrey, requesting her cloak. The air was crisp and Jane felt an overwhelming urge to be outside breathing in the golden light as it cast its glow over the reds, yellows and browns of autumn. Crunching along the paths of the knot garden, Jane considered the remainder of the letter.

The king has found Meg Blount guilty of treason, and she has been sentenced to death. According to the Poison Act, passed a few years ago, this will be to boil her alive. Anne is trying to intervene. Worse, Meg's brothers, Louis and Alphonso, have been arrested. They were caught in the grounds of the Tower, intending to free Meg. There are also arrest warrants for Hal and Thomas Boleyn, whom, despite Anne's best efforts, have been accused of conspiring with Meg and her brothers to murder the king. No one is sure why the king believes this, but the Boleyns have gone to ground. If they come to you, send them to Carew Castle where they are more easily hidden and where Thomas Perrot can arrange their passage to Ireland.

Every visitor, every hoof on the cobbles made Jane nervous. Even this far from London she felt the awful power of the increasingly tyrannical king. Yet, there was no need for Francis to pass on such a message, the Boleyn boys had already been and gone. After an overnight stay in a room above the stables, they had left at dawn to ride to Carew Castle, their usual swagger gone as they rode for their lives.

Jane paused, listening to the waves of Llyn Cel. A bell rang in the distance and she turned, walking over the muddy grass towards the chapel for Terce. Her years with Queen Katherine had taught her one thing, when she was anxious or angry, the serenity of the chapel calmed her nerves and this was what she needed. Slipping into the back as the nuns filed in from the passage joining the island to the chapel, Jane knelt on one of the beautifully embroidered hassocks and prayed. The familiar words of the Liturgy offered comfort, as did the smooth beads of her rosary as they slid through her fingers.

As the Latin words and the chanting of the nuns swirled around her, Jane forced herself to breathe slowly, allowing calm to suffuse her body. It was something she had watched her mother practise over the years, and she understood why. Her mother had held together their wayward family with a strength Jane was beginning to appreciate. The news of Anne's failure to deliver a son struck fear into Jane's heart: this meant

Bessie would push ahead with the plans. Sweet Bessie Blount who would flutter her lashes over her enormous blue eyes and pretend not to understand the complicated discussions of the men around her, yet she had absorbed the political cunning of a diplomat during her years at court. With her inspiration drawn from Lady Margaret Beaufort, who had won the throne for her son, Henry Tudor, Bessie knew where her future lay. A long game to gain a throne, this was Bessie's intent.

And we are all caught up in this plan, thought Jane.

Letters had continued to flood to Jane, but it was Bessie's notes which were the most dangerous. *The parade must take place soon. The Lady is in danger and there are the rumours the king might replace her, declaring their marriage to be unlawful, too. No more women must die in this insane search for an heir when there are numerous sons from whom he could choose. A veritable battalion of Tudor boys.*

Closing her eyes to allow the calming repetitiveness of the service to wash over her, Jane wondered whether this endless scheming would ever reach a conclusion. It had been years now, first raising Anne up, before this new dilemma of securing her throne until Fitzroy was old enough to take the monarchy from his father. The boy was only fourteen years old, as yet too young to head an army successfully.

Returning to her desk an hour later, in a more peaceful frame of mind thanks to the service, Jane continued to work through the letters from the women surrounding Anne. Among the trivial tales of the manuscript of love poems Anne was encouraging her lively court to write was the news that the Duke of Norfolk had persuaded the king to agree to the marriage of his daughter, Mary Howard, to Henry Fitzroy. Despite their ages — both aged 14 — the marriage would take place within the next few months. After the ceremony, Mary would return to court where she was a favourite of her cousin,

Queen Anne, and Fitzroy would continue to move between his various palaces under the tutelage of the great men of the day who were training him in the art of government.

"This is madness," sighed Jane, pushing the piles of paper away. "We are dancing with the devil and, sooner or later, he will change the steps without us knowing and we will all face the executioner's axe."

Once again, her mind flickered towards the Blounts and she shuddered. Meg Blount was no fool; if there had been poison concealed within the medicines Anne had requested then it was no mistake. Suddenly, it hit Jane. Of course, Anne had planned to poison the king. She was the closest person to him, both physically and emotionally, and sprinkling a few drops of deadly nightshade into his wine would be the action of a moment. Had that been Anne's plan? A moment of desperation when she felt she could no longer bear the strain of pretending to be in love with the man who held all their lives in the balance? If so, it was the action of a desperate woman.

They were in a dangerous situation and Jane could not see a way through the peril surrounding the throne.

PART FIVE: MARQUESS HOUSE, 2021

CHAPTER ONE

Perdita stepped into London's Bourchier Street, a conduit through to Wardour Street, and stopped, fishing a silver card from her handbag which she held to a glossy dark blue door, letting herself inside.

"Good evening, Perdita," said the woman behind the reception desk. "Was your day at the Tower of London successful?"

"Yes, thank you," Perdita replied. "Are there any messages?"

"Yes, Nicola said she would meet you at 7.30pm as planned in the library for drinks. She's booked a table in the dining room for 8pm."

"Thank you, Nina," said Perdita, and, taking her passkey, ran up the carpeted stairs to her private bedroom at Nympha.

The previous summer, Susan Mackensie had invited Perdita and Piper to her and Alistair's suite one evening for a drink. Somewhat bemused, the twins had accepted, wondering if Susan was planning a surprise for Kit or Alistair and needed their help.

"Oh no," Susan had laughed, when Perdita and Piper had admitted their bafflement and a possible cause. "It's because I want to give you these. Meg and I decided it should be in private."

Handing them a stiff silver envelope each with their full names and aristocratic titles engraved on them in swirling calligraphy, Perdita and Piper had exchanged an amused look before opening them and pulling out a thick cardboard invitation: *You are officially invited to join NYMPHA, a private members club for women.*

"Meg and I are both members, as were your mother and grandmother. The reason we haven't been able to give you these invitations before is because, despite you being hereditary members through Mary and Louisa, we were waiting for two places to become available. There is a waiting list, you see."

"What does it entail?" asked Piper. Perdita could see her sister was unimpressed. She disliked exclusivity and Perdita wondered if she might refuse the offer.

"It's a private members club for women, as the invitation states. *Nympha* is Latin for mermaid."

"Mermaid?" said Perdita and examined the card in more detail. Tilting it for the light to shine upon the card, she recognised the swimming image etched around the edge. It was similar to the mermaid who swam around the walls of Marquess House.

"Why have you never mentioned this before?" asked Piper, narrowing her eyes.

"I've wanted to tell you about our club since you moved here. You were eligible to join from the age of eighteen but, obviously, there were complications. Then life became rather hectic and there never seemed to be a right moment. As I said, the places which had been held for you on your eighteenth birthdays were filled by two other hereditary members after Mary explained you would not be taking them at that moment. Yesterday, I received notification that two places had become available and was asked to formally invite you to join."

"What does being a member involve?" asked Perdita.

"Nothing onerous," replied Susan. "There are social events, various committees, although they're not compulsory, and a selection of very pleasant properties around the world where you may stay. It's like the rather drab club Alistair has been a member of since he was twenty-one and which Stuart is a member. A place has become available there in the past few weeks and this will be offered to Kit.

"There's no hurry to give an answer," Susan continued, "but it is an interesting place for networking and, obviously, everything is confidential. If you become members, there are various charters to sign promising secrecy and anonymity."

Perdita and Piper had returned to Piper's rooms and read through the information Susan had given them.

"I like the idea of women working together," said Perdita. "Supporting each other and offering help."

"True," agreed Piper, "but it's a bit…" She groped for the right word, "snobbish?"

"Perhaps, but there are loads of private clubs. I suggest we join and, after a year, reassess. We can always leave if it's too prissy."

Agreeing this would be a sensible course of action, the twins had accepted, signing the many decrees and charters before each received a silver brooch in the shape of a mermaid. Intrigued again by the similarity to their own mermaid, Perdita had tried to research the history of the club to see if there were any links to Marquess House but each line of enquiry petered out to nothing. Suspicious of this lack of information, Perdita discussed it with Susan.

"There's an archive in the London house, which is the headquarters of Nympha," Susan had explained. "The Ladies of the Sea, as the senior members are known, are very protective of their history and, over the years, have acquired and stored any information pertaining to the history of the club and its origins. As a member, you will be allowed access to these rare documents. I know Mary used them, especially when she was writing her earlier books."

Perdita and Piper had visited the club house in Bourchier Street in Soho, London on two occasions and had agreed it was a pleasant place with interesting women and not in the least snobbish.

"If Mum and Granny were members, I think it's probably a good thing for us to be involved with it too," Piper had said when they were driving home to Pembrokeshire the following day.

"I agree," said Perdita, "and they have a huge archive which I can access."

"Oh no," Piper had groaned in mock despair, "what have I agreed to."

Letting herself into her bedroom, Perdita dropped her computer bag and handbag on to the bed before kicking off her shoes and flicking on the electric kettle. The Nympha archive had been one of the reasons for her trip to London and she had discovered a number of interesting documents, although none directly connected to her current research. However, while she was in the capital, Perdita had also arranged visits to the National Archives and the British Library, but it had been her day at the Tower of London that had been unnerving. The discoveries in the ancient records, each note she had made, every twist and turn of the documents had given her more conviction that the theory she was forming was true.

"True but dangerous," she mused aloud as she made a cup of tea.

Yet, she could not see how the many threads connected into a cohesive whole. She wondered if her meeting this evening with Nicola Weaver, a curator at the Royal College of Arms and a genealogist would illuminate a path through the many ideas racing around her mind and whether they would prove her hypothesis was a product of her vivid imagination or a viable alternative version of history.

Her phone buzzed with an incoming video call. "Hey Pipes," she said, "how are the party preparations? I'm sorry to have abandoned you."

"Perds, for the last time, you haven't abandoned me. The engagement party preparations were complete before you left. I was actually ringing to see how your research went today at the Tower of London? Do we own the Tower? I lose track…" Piper finished airily and Perdita laughed.

When she had first contacted Nicola Weaver with the request for help through the Nympha network, Perdita had been dismayed that the only days Nicola had been able to meet her were in the week before Piper and Callum's engagement party.

"Go," Piper had said. "You'll be away for five days; we can cope without you."

"Promise you don't mind."

"Go to London," Piper and Callum had ordered.

"Did you find what you were looking for?" asked Piper, bringing Perdita back to the present.

"Actually, Pipes, I found other things and it's made me nervous."

"Why?"

"The story in *The Pentagram Manuscript* is fascinating but it's not what I expected. I thought it would be an Arthurian tale of great deeds with plenty of Tudor moralising and a final happy ending of strong, healthy princes being born."

"But…?"

"It's letters and events telling the story of Jane Seymour."

"From your expression, I'd guess this is a new version of a familiar tale?" suggested Piper.

"Yes, a story so unexpected it's almost unbelievable but, when combined with the gaps in Jane's biographies and the facts I've discovered this week, it's beginning to feel like our previous discoveries all over again — a viable alternative to the current historical record which fills in the gaps. This is history written by the women as they were experiencing it and influencing events as much as they were able. In fact, I'm beginning to wonder if these women were the origins of the letter writers around Elizabeth I. Remember, Anne Boleyn was Elizabeth's mother…"

"But you said this was about Jane Seymour," interrupted Piper in confusion.

"It is about Jane, but she was at court during the final days of Katherine of Aragon's reign and during the transition to Anne Boleyn. These three women were inextricably linked in the Tudor court. All three women married Henry and all three gave him heirs who held the throne. Anne and Jane were ladies-in-waiting to Katherine of Aragon, then Jane was lady-in-waiting to Anne. Their lives were bound tightly together and the tale they're telling me is startling."

"Could it be true?" asked Piper, and Perdita noticed the nervous edge to her sister's voice.

"Yes, Pipes, I think it could and if Granny was aware of this tale, I think it might be the reason she locked the manuscript away. Pipes, sorry, I'm going to have to go. I'm meeting Nicola in half an hour and I want to have a shower. If she confirms my suspicions, I'll tell you everything next week, after the party."

"Promise?"

"Yes, promise."

Nicola Weaver was a small woman in her late forties with long ash-blonde hair falling in a perfect sheet down her back. Her brown eyes held caramel lights and from the moment they had first spoken a few weeks earlier, Perdita had liked her, admiring her wisdom, intellect and humour. Over drinks and dinner, they discussed many things, deciding they would wait until they were relaxing in the lounge afterwards before Nicola revealed her findings on the genealogical puzzle Perdita had asked her to investigate.

As they settled into a corner alcove with wide, comfortable armchairs and a long low table between them, Perdita poured coffee from the elegant white coffee set on the tray while Nicola pulled two bound documents from her bag, handing one to Perdita, while balancing the other on her lap.

"This was quite a challenge," she said in her soft Yorkshire accent.

"Yes, I thought it might be," replied Perdita. "It was the reason I asked you; my hope was that through your archives at the Royal College of Arms, you might have access to documents unavailable to genealogists without your contacts."

"You were right," said Nicola. "Although Sir Francis Bryan was never issued a coat of arms, he was a Member of Parliament, as well as a long-term courtier, so his name appears in many of our documents. As requested, I drew up his family tree and to my surprise, I discovered two more illegitimate children…"

"Two more children?" asked Perdita, her heart rate rising with excitement.

"Yes, Sir Francis was rumoured to be the father of Henry Spice, son of Philippa, who was thought to be his long-term mistress. However, there is a suggestion in some historical records that he married Philippa and they had no children; it's rather muddled, even within our records. In August 1548, he married Lady Joan Fitzgerald, widow of James Butler, 9th Earl of Ormond with whom he had a son. Joan already had seven sons and Sir Francis was thought to have another mistress during this marriage with whom he had a son but it seems, he had a daughter with this woman too."

"Were you able to discover her name?" asked Perdita, wondering if her theory was about to be corroborated by independent research.

"Have a look at page twenty-six of the document and tell me what you think," said Nicola, flicking through to the page. "The name is smudged but it looks like Joan or Joanna or even Jane. Whoever this woman was, I would surmise she might be the mysterious mistress. The children have rather unusual names: Jasper, who is, of course, a reference to the Tudor uncle of Henry VII, and Lois. It's a Biblical name, although not one that was used very often in the sixteenth century. It means 'most beautiful' in Greek, while in Hebrew it means 'better'. In the Bible, Lois was the grandmother of St Timothy who was the first Christian bishop of Ephesus. She is mentioned once and was thought to have been born into the Jewish faith before converting to Christianity."

"Did the Tudor Lois marry?" asked Perdita.

"Yes, and I've managed to construct her family tree to the present day. Jasper, however, died as a young man during Kett's rebellion, on 8 July 1549 when Edward VI was on the throne. There are few details but he was listed as being part of the forces sent with the Marquess of Northampton to suppress the rebels in Norwich, then there are details of a lavish funeral, paid for by the king. Rather surprisingly, he's buried in St Mary's Church, Great Bedwyn, which is the parish church of Wulfhall, home to the Seymour family. Sir John Seymour, father of Jane Seymour, Henry VIII's third queen, is buried there."

Perdita was elated. Nicola's research verified all she had read in *The Pentagram Manuscript*. "This is fascinating, Nicola, thank you," she said. "And Lois? You said you'd been able to trace her descendants to the present day?"

Nicola raised her eyebrows and sipped her coffee. "Indeed I have, and it's rather awkward." She gave a self-conscious laugh. "I'm on the Members' Committee and one of the more unpleasant tasks we must undertake is to reprimand members if they are in breach of our covenants." Perdita could not see how this was connected. "Throughout my years here, it has been convened once and that was, unfortunately, to expel a member."

"Expel a member?" said Perdita in surprise. "What had she done?"

"Revealed rather too much of our archive to her husband and father-in-law," Nicola looked uncomfortable. "Do you not know?"

"I have no idea what you're talking about," replied Perdita.

"The member we had to expel was Amber Connors, formerly Prust, who is, I believe, married to your second cousin, Xavier."

Perdita stared at Nicola in disbelief. "Amber Connors is descended from Lois, the illegitimate daughter of Sir Francis Bryan and…" she checked herself in time — "his unknown mistress?"

"If my research is correct, and I am certain of its validity. Amber claimed she had revealed information to Randolph and Xavier in error but it was a violation of our codes of conduct and we had no choice but to ask her to withdraw."

The letterhead with the phoenix flashed into Perdita's mind, did Amber know the identity of Lois's mother? Was this why she had used such an unusual motif for her letterhead or was it coincidence? And, if Amber knew, did Connors?

"What I am about to tell you is confidential,' Nicola continued. 'I don't like gossip, but it feels important to appraise you of the entire situation."

Perdita felt a flutter of nervousness but tried to keep her tone polite and calm. "Situation?"

"When I began my genealogical search on this particular family for you, I discovered two other people had previously commissioned the same search. The first was your grandmother but she halted the process before it was complete. I believe she became disillusioned with her work on the sixteenth century."

Perdita knew why. After the death of her mother, Louisa, her grandmother halted all her research into Tudor women. "And the second?" she prompted.

"Lady Marianne O'Rourke, who is, as you know, estranged from her husband, Randolph Connors. At present, she's living in Mauritius. The request was made six months before Xavier married Amber Prust. Marianne had a number of family trees commissioned including her own and discovered she was descended from Sir Francis Bryan's illegitimate son, Henry Spice. In order to see which other families this connected her to, she continued the research. Lois's tree was part of this commission and it crossed over with Amber Prust, as she was at that point."

"Thank you, Nicola, this is incredible."

"The research has been fascinating," said Nicola. "I hope it helps with whatever you're working on. You remind me so much of Mary. Not in looks but in your energy and your drive.

No doubt this will lead to a superb book; picking up where your grandmother left off."

"Perhaps," said Perdita. "Perhaps one day."

After discussing the findings for a few more minutes, Nicola said goodbye and left to catch the last tube home. As Perdita walked with Nicola to the door, the older woman paused.

"Do you see your cousin, Xavier?" she asked, and Perdita shook her head. "It's a shame what's happened. How one man can go through a fortune in the manner he has is staggering. Amber was in arrears to the club for over £20,000 when she was asked to leave. Please don't repeat this; as I said, I dislike gossip."

Perdita walked up to her bedroom at Nympha, her mind teeming with all she had learned, the historical and the personal. Was it possible that Xavier was on the brink of bankruptcy? It would explain why he was determined to try and steal her and Piper's inheritance if he had burned his way through the Connors' millions.

Pondering the historical connections, Perdita allowed her mind to roam free, making links, drifting through the ideas until sense began to emerge from chaos. Reaching for her laptop, she began typing furiously, throwing her ideas on the page, ready to be sorted into logical order when she had returned to Marquess House.

As she finished, Kit rang.

"Hey you," she said.

"Hey Perds, how was it? Any secrets?"

"Too many," she replied, suppressing a shiver. "I think I'm beginning to understand and, Kit, if I'm right, The Scribe rewrote history in even more ways than we realised."

CHAPTER TWO

Laughter drifted from the terrace through the house. Perdita stood beside Piper and gazed around at the crowd on the terrace. Deborah Black was laughing with Alistair and Susan, while Larry chatted to Cora and Stephanie in a milling crowd of Marquess House staff, though Perdita preferred to think of them as friends. Seeing how well both Cora and Stephanie had settled in made Perdita smile; it felt as though they had been part of the team for years.

"It's a shame Aunt Pamela couldn't be here," said Piper.

Earlier in the year, Perdita and Piper had paid for Lady Pamela and her husband, Brad, to go on a world cruise. The twins had arranged a spectacular trip as they hoped it would help her to recover from the shock of all that had happened at Marquess House.

"I miss her," said Perdita as Kit refilled their glasses.

"She'll be home soon," he said.

"Any more in that bottle?" came a male voice from behind them.

"Plenty. Here you are, Stu," said Kit, topping up his brother's drink before they were joined by their friend Edward Stone and Callum's older brother, Elliot.

"There are a lot of old faces here tonight," said Edward, staring around at the buzzing crowd.

A group of women nearby, including Briony Llewellyn, who ran the Louisa Woodville Animal Sanctuary on Home Farm, her friends Bathsheba Mundy and Eleanor Wilder, hauled Piper into their midst as they admired her diamond engagement ring, exuding laughter and love. Piper sparkled and

Perdita watched her sister with her heart bursting with happiness, delighted that after all the darkness her twin had suffered she was facing better days.

"It's summer and loads of people are visiting," replied Kit. "An engagement party is a great reason to bring everyone together."

Perdita felt Kit's arm slide around her waist and pull her close to him. Whenever there was a gathering of Kit and Callum's friends, she and Piper felt the same bittersweet loss. Although they had been welcomed with open arms and found friendships among the group of childhood friends, it saddened them to think of all they had missed during the years of estrangement from Mary and Marquess House.

"Are you going on Gabe's stag weekend in Cornwall?" Stuart asked Edward who grinned and nodded.

"Wouldn't miss it."

Bathsheba Mundy was marrying her rugby-player fiancé, Gabriel Wall, in early autumn and there were lavish stag and hen weekends planned. Bathsheba's hen weekend had taken place two weeks earlier but the stag party was a few weeks away.

"How are you feeling about Bathsheba Mundy finally getting married?" Elliot asked Stuart. "You always had a massive crush on her."

"It was never Bathsheba I fancied," said Stuart with a grin as he glanced over at the women. "My heart will survive."

"Is this because of the mystery lady…?"

Perdita squeezed Kit's hand and nodded towards the house. "I'm going to grab a jacket, back in a minute."

Perdita abandoned her nearly full glass on a table as she entered the Lady Isabel room through the wide-open French doors. Wondering whether to risk the listed Thomas Crapper

240

toilet Kit had mentioned the first day she had arrived at Marquess House and learned about her and Piper's inheritance, she decided against it, hurrying up to her own apartment where she grabbed a coat, brushed her hair, reapplied her make-up and wandered back downstairs. The party was in full swing and she was surprised at how much she was enjoying it. Shyer than Piper, Perdita often found large groups overwhelming but this evening, the happiness floating over the terrace was infectious.

The clang of the doorbell echoed through the great hall and Perdita grinned ready to welcome more guests.

"Gary," she exclaimed as the tall man from MI1 hurried through the door, but from the serious expression on his face, she knew he was not here for the party. "What's wrong?"

"Is Stuart here?" he asked, his tone clipped and nervous.

"Yes, he's on the terrace at Piper and Callum's engagement party."

Relief flooded Gary's face.

"What's happened?" asked Perdita in alarm.

"Could you text Kit, please, and ask him to meet us here? We've made a discovery and it involves Stuart…"

A moment later, Kit strode towards them across the great hall. "What's going on?" he asked, his voice sharp.

"I'm sorry to interrupt the party but this is urgent," said Gary. "Can you two disappear for half an hour? You have some files it's imperative we check as soon as possible."

"Yes, of course. I'll call Piper and let her know," said Perdita as Kit led the way across the hall and through the door into the Victorian wing and his office.

By the time Perdita had spoken to Piper, Larry had joined Kit and Gary in Kit's office. The three men were hunched over the monitor as Kit called up the files under Gary's guidance.

Perdita wondered what could be so urgent that Gary had arrived unannounced on a Saturday evening.

"These are the Hannah White files," said Kit, stepping back to allow Gary and Larry to scroll through them to the date Gary wanted to check.

"Hannah? What's happened?"

The twins had met Hannah White when they had bought a ruby ring from her, an item of jewellery that was essential to unlocking the dangerous secret hidden in the heart of Marquess House. They had discovered that Randolph Connors had also been closing in on Hannah and the ruby ring and so Alistair had been monitoring her movements ever since.

"It feels uncomfortable watching Hannah like this without her knowing," said Perdita.

"I know," said Kit, "but, remember, by monitoring Hannah, we'll also be in a position to save her life should it be necessary. Marquess House deletes the files every two months and MI1 doesn't have access to these files; it's why Gary's here this evening."

Gary remained silent through the exchange but as Kit finished speaking, he leaned forward and pointed to a file dated from two days earlier. "This might be the one," he said.

Larry picked up the mouse to move through the images. Perdita leaned forward to watch. Hannah was waiting in a smart London restaurant, checking her phone when the door opened and a tall, good-looking man arrived. He bent to kiss her on the cheek before joining her at the table. The body language of the two suggested they were an established couple.

"Xavier Connors," hissed Perdita, her eyes widening in anger. "How has he been allowed back into the country? Why didn't we know about this?"

When his father had been arrested, Xavier had been in India and an international arrest warrant had been issued. The twins had been assured that if he were to enter the UK under normal channels, he would be arrested.

"If Xavier is in the country," said Gary, "then it is a huge lapse by our department into which I shall be launching an investigation. If he's flown in on a private jet under an assumed name, it would explain why his arrival didn't light any red security flags. Xavier is a very wealthy man; money helps when you want to remain invisible. There's a possibility he's been in and out of the UK ever since his father was arrested, using false passports."

"Why would he take the risk though?" Perdita asked.

"He doesn't see it as a risk, he sees it as his right," said Kit. "From all the intelligence Dad and I have gathered, it seems Xavier Connors believes the British Secret Service is at fault for Randolph's arrest and his father has been wrongfully detained. His lawyers are working in Switzerland trying to prepare a case to have the charges against Randolph dropped."

"What?" Perdita stared at Kit in astonishment. "Why haven't you mentioned this to Piper and me?"

"Perds, there's nothing to mention," said Kit. "Don't you think if there was any hint of danger, you'd be the first to know? Lawyers, especially the top-flight team Xavier has employed in Zurich, work on cases like this all the time, but they rarely get to court."

Perdita was unsure how to respond. She trusted Kit and, as such, would have to rely on his judgement. Her uncertainty must have registered on her face because Kit continued, "These lawyers are pandering to the anger and the egos of the ultra-wealthy; making a show of challenging the legal status quo on their behalf. However, there is never a case to answer.

It gives the rich the chance to say they're more powerful than governments or conglomerates. These are vanity enterprises with no legal merit. Believe me, Perds, if I told you everything Dad's told me, you'd be amazed."

"Do I need to know?" she asked.

"No, think of it as white noise or background music," he explained, "if there's anything important, you and Piper will be told. Trust me, Perds, I'm not keeping secrets, it would be the same as you giving me every single detail of all your research. Most of it is information which is important in the greater scheme of the story you're uncovering but as isolated incidents they are not necessary to pass on. You know I'd never let anything happen to you or Piper."

Taking a deep breath, Perdita pushed these unnerving discoveries aside, trying to focus on the matter in hand. Larry was continuing to scroll through the footage, while Gary was setting up his own laptop.

"How did Hannah White become involved with Xavier Connors?" she said.

"We know Randolph had Hannah's details," said Gary.

"Which means Xavier would have access to them too," said Larry. "We know he can be charming when he wants something, which makes me suspect he's targeted Hannah. Despite what Randolph said, they have done anything but leave Hannah White alone."

Kit and Perdita exchanged a concerned look. A few years earlier, Xavier had groomed one of the Marquess House staff, persuading her to reveal secret information to him and his father.

"It's possible Xavier has convinced Hannah he's in love with her. There are many tales he could have spun to turn her against you and Piper," said Kit. "Perhaps he's suggested that when you bought the ruby ring from her, you were stealing his inheritance."

"It's possible," agreed Perdita. "Can he do anything?" she asked, hating to hear the tremor in her voice. "I mean really harm us, not his empty threats as he struts about pontificating?"

"Not that we've been able to ascertain but the trick with people like Xavier is never to underestimate them," said Gary. "The reason it was urgent to see you this evening was a piece of footage that was generated through our usual sweeps of London streets. We were tailing another suspect in the Southbank area when this was caught on a CCTV camera outside Stuart's apartment. It was a chance sighting but when it was sent to me this afternoon I realised we needed to check your footage. When none of you were answering your phones, I was concerned."

"Sorry," said Perdita. "We agreed to turn them off for the party."

Feeling sick at what they might be about to see, Perdita gripped Kit's hand.

Black and white images flickered across the screen. A tall man, unmistakeably Stuart Mackensie, opened the door to his exclusive apartment block. He was laughing and as his companion walked into shot both Perdita and Kit gasped. Stuart put his arm around her shoulders and they turned towards the Tate Modern.

"Hannah," said Perdita. "Stuart's mysterious new girlfriend is Hannah White."

"Who is having an affair with Xavier," said Kit, his voice hard. "She's honey-trapped Stu," he snapped. "No wonder she was resistant about meeting his family, especially when Stu took up my old apartment here."

Perdita stared at Kit's ashen face. "This is not Stu's fault," she said to Kit. "Xavier is up to his old tricks again."

Kit tapped Larry on the shoulder and he surrendered his position in front of the screen. For the next few moments, Kit's fingers were a blur, his face determined. "I've activated facial search recognition software," he said and within seconds there was a hit. "It's the day of Piper's accident."

Gathering around, they stared at the footage and Perdita struggled to contain the expletive that rose to her lips. Her eyes widened in rage as she stared at the image of Hannah White in reception at the storage facility in Bath. "How did she know?" she asked.

"I suspect Xavier and Hannah have been working together for a long time and Xavier knows a great deal about the Marquess House assets," said Larry. "His father has been obsessed with the estate for years and, if they are hoping Xavier's girls will inherit, then both men will have made it their business to search the public records for as full an inventory as possible."

"Why the storage facilities though?" asked Gary.

"Could they have been looking for *The Pentagram Manuscript*?" asked Kit. "It was in a room in the Bath facility marked as 'Mary Fitzroy — Private'."

"How would they know about it?" said Perdita. "We didn't know it was there. You, your dad and Jenny have worked with the archives for years and had no idea."

"Could they have had information from another source?" suggested Larry.

Perdita ran her hands through her hair in agitation and with reluctance said, "It's possible," causing all three men to stare at her in surprise. "When I was in London," she explained, "I discovered something about Amber Connors's ancestry which connects her to my research. It makes me wonder if her family has an archive that mentions it. I was also told Amber was expelled from a private members' club for revealing confidential information from its archive to Randolph and Xavier. I've searched the archive and at present have found no reference to *The Pentagram Manuscript* but it's not to say it isn't there somewhere. It's a large collection."

"Either option is possible," said Kit.

"Unless we can question Amber, we won't know," said Gary.

"There's something else, too," said Perdita. "It has been suggested to me by a reliable source that the Connors' fortune is running out. Before Mary's death, Randolph began buying archives and, if he couldn't persuade people to part with their paperwork, he would buy entire manors. In light of this, perhaps the material Amber passed to Randolph was the impetus for his obsession with buying other people's historical records. Randolph seems to have been searching for something and, I would guess, it was a document he believed would give him answers to the family mystery. He must have known the bulk of the paperwork was here at Marquess House but perhaps his information suggested there was another missing document. However, his endless expenditure has depleted his fortune and Xavier has never had the business acumen of his father, driving him to marry Amber Prust."

"You're saying he married her for her money?" asked Gary.

"I think so, although, there is a possibility he married her because of her family line."

"Perds, what are you talking about?" asked Kit.

"Xavier is trying to bolster his claim, our family claim, to power. What if he thought by marrying a woman who can trace her ancestry back to specific people in history, it would make his claim unassailable?"

"Are you going to explain?" asked Gary who was struggling to contain his frustration.

"Yes, when I've gathered my facts, I'll explain my theory and you'll be invited to join us Gary, but at the moment, we're in the middle of Piper and Callum's engagement party and I refuse to let the Connors family ruin it; they've done enough damage over the years," Perdita replied. "At the moment, our priorities must be Piper, Cal and, most importantly, Stuart," she and Kit exchanged a glance. "We must protect and support him because explaining the identity of his new girlfriend is going to be heart-breaking."

The three men gave her a curious look but did not challenge the finality in her tone. Perdita reached for Kit's hand and led him from the room. Her natural instinct was to protect those she loved but her decision to halt this distressing conversation was more than simply to save the party and comfort Stuart, she was aware her research would rip their lives apart and she needed time to prepare herself before she, once again, put those she loved through such trauma.

CHAPTER THREE

Here we are again, thought Perdita as she laid out notebooks, pens, pencils and the notes she had collated for reference. Jenny Procter ushered in a couple of her staff, pointing them towards the long table at the back of the room where they laid out refreshments. Alistair's beloved overhead projector was on its table in front of a screen, a pile of images beside it for Perdita to illustrate her revelations.

"Thank you so much for your help, Jen," she said, hugging the older woman as she passed by with a pile of printouts.

"You don't have to thank me, love," Jenny said. "The discovery and research of a new archive is a rare and privileged position; it's me who should be thanking you."

"Please don't underestimate how much your hard work has helped me to solve the multiple aspects of this puzzle," said Perdita. "Your discovery of the letter transcripts was like discovering a Tudor Rosetta Stone."

The reference to the ancient tablet that had helped linguist, Jean-François Champollion, to translate Ancient Egyptian hieroglyphics made Jenny laugh. "It's hardly in the same league," she said, "but I'm delighted we were able to help."

While Perdita had been concentrating on *The Pentagram Manuscript*, Jenny had organised a task force to catalogue the rest of the extensive archive. When she had discovered a cache of letters that had been transcribed into leather-bound ledgers by Perdita and Piper's ancestor, Lady Arabella Courtenay, *née* Talbot, even more anomalies had been revealed, each of which corresponded with the tale in *The Pentagram Manuscript*. Perdita had been delighted as this gave credence and provenance to the letter she had discovered when she had been searching the files Mary had left on Anne Boleyn which seemed to be a reference to Jane Seymour. This one letter had been mistakenly left behind when Mary had cleared out the archive and it fitted in with the letters in the ledgers.

Arabella Talbot had written the first history of Marquess House; a book Perdita had read during her own research into Catherine Howard and which she was in the process of updating. Through this work, Perdita had discovered Arabella viewed herself as an amateur historian and from one diary she had left behind had stated she was copying out 'letters of great age which are beginning to fade and crumble. It feels important they should be preserved for future generations of Marquess House owners to study', however, until they had discovered Mary's hidden archive, Perdita had been unable to source the letters referenced in these diaries.

When Jenny had begun cataloguing the archive, the beautifully written and well-preserved journals had been a revelation. Perdita's one reservation was whether or not Arabella had embellished any of the work but, at present, the letters dove-tailed with Perdita's own conclusions from the manuscript, as well as filling in many of the gaps. The original letters were yet to be discovered but as Jenny and her team were less than halfway through sorting the treasures within the archive, Perdita had to be content with the transcripts and trust to her ancestor's accuracy. In an ideal world, Perdita would have delayed revealing her findings until she had corroborated her theory but with the new situation around Hannah and Xavier, she was certain they had discovered a clue suggesting there was a missing archive and this had been the reason for Hannah being in reception at the Bath facility.

"Hannah has no connections with this area," Gary had informed Perdita a few days earlier. "We think she was snooping for Xavier. The manager remembers her because of her height. She was asking for pricing information as well as asking about secrets being hidden in forgotten rooms. It's a common theme, apparently, so the manager ignored it."

The door opened, admitting Kit and Piper, both carrying mugs.

"We were coming to help you set up," said Piper, "but we're too late." She settled into the chair to the right of where Perdita had placed her own belongings. Kit positioned himself on the left.

"How's Stuart?" asked Perdita.

"On his way," replied Kit. "He's coping."

A consultation with Alistair and Susan the day after the party had ended in Kit stating he would inform his brother of the situation. Upon revealing MI1's suspicions, then showing his brother the footage, Stuart's instinct had been anger and denial, stating his new girlfriend's name was Meredith Grey, not Hannah White. When Kit explained the reason why Marquess House had a file on Hannah White and showed him the footage of Hannah's lunch with Xavier, Stuart had taken control of himself and watched with calm resignation. By the time he'd finished watching it, he was determined to do all he could to help uncover her treachery.

Stuart had offered his help to Perdita and she discovered they worked well together. He was meticulous about research, a skill he had acquired from his years of buying and selling artefacts for Jerusalem and she found his insight useful, particularly when on occasions she felt as though she were caught in a never-ending spiral of questions.

The door opened again and Alistair, Susan, Stuart, Callum and Gary entered. Perdita nodded a greeting to Gary, wondering what her grandmother would say concerning this new and close liaison with MI1. *Times change*, Perdita told herself, *you're not betraying Granny or Mum by working with them. We need their help if we're to defeat the enemy within the family, Xavier Connors.*

"Morning everyone," said Perdita as Jenny took her place and the hum of conversation ceased. "Who would have expected us to be here again? As usual, ensure all electronic devices are powered down and off. We can't risk a security leak."

With reluctance, Gary pulled his phone from his pocket and powered it down, Stuart followed suit.

"As you're aware," said Perdita, "we're here because we've made some disturbing historical discoveries. With information from independent sources concerning Xavier Connors that has been verified by Kit and Alistair, we think the documents in Mary's hidden archive can be linked to Xavier's new attempt to inveigle his way into Marquess House, which he believes should belong to his daughters, Ruby and Pearl."

Perdita had flashed up photographs of Xavier, Amber and their daughters. Her heart broke a little as she saw the images of the two children grinning at the camera. They had been the catalyst for a campaign of violence and murder, yet they were innocent in their grandfather's and father's schemes.

"At present, I don't have all the answers," said Perdita, "but I have enough to create a workable hypothesis which will give us the information we require to keep ourselves and the people we care about safe. This meeting will also help us to consider our next moves in conjunction with the details MI1 has collated. This is the reason Gary Ashley is here."

All eyes turned towards the Secret Service man and a few surprised looks were exchanged. Gary raised his hand in greeting.

"Jenny and I have put together a basic crib sheet for you all, enabling you to have reference points and to give you historical perspective. I will give a very brief summary to begin but the finer points of the 'accepted' version of history is in your folder." Perdita glanced at her notes, then at Kit who smiled. Feeling reassured, she continued, "In Granny's secret archive we discovered *The Pentagram Manuscript*, a handwritten document, dated to 1536–37, with professional corner illuminations telling the story of five women on an Arthurian-style quest. As far as we're aware this is a unique occurrence from this era. Each poem is five lines long and there are five stanzas per page. Each illumination features the pentagram image from the title page as well as a Tudor rose." She flashed a selection of Tudor rose images on to the screen. "As you can see it is traditionally represented as a red and white rose with five green leaves."

"I'd never noticed that before," murmured Susan to Jenny.

"During this period in history five red dots were used as an emblem to represent the five wounds of Christ and was the sign of a rebellion known as the Pilgrimage of Grace," said Perdita. "Due to the unusual content focussed on five women, at first, I wondered if *The Pentagram Manuscript* was a fake, perhaps Victorian, but the endless references to the number five I keep finding during this era has given me more confidence in its authenticity and the fact these symbols are deliberate. This is supported by Granny's tests dating it to the correct period.

"Hidden within the poems is a code, which, when unravelled, tells the tale of Jane Seymour, third wife of Henry

VIII. Jane was the mother of Edward VI and was perceived to be the perfect gentle, unassuming Tudor wife for whom Henry grieved for two years before marrying Anne of Cleves. However, we all know this to be incorrect. The marriage gap was due to the unavailability of a bride rather than Henry's feelings, a fact which puts the 'most loved' part of the description of Jane into question. Add to this the fact that while Jane was toiling in labour at Hampton Court Palace with Prince Edward, Henry was living it up with friends a few miles away at his Esher residence and even after the birth of a son was eager to return to Esher, leaving Jane behind. Records inform us, she died two weeks after Edward's birth from an infection."

"Can we qualify for a history degree with all this knowledge?" asked Callum.

"Unfortunately, no, because if you told anyone about it in conjunction with the Marquess House discoveries, Gary would arrest you," replied Kit, and Gary laughed.

Perdita was pleased to see him relax. "Jane's parents were Margery Wentworth and Sir John Seymour. They lived at Wulfhall in Wiltshire and had six sons and four daughters, not all of whom survived into adulthood. John Seymour was known for allegedly having an affair with his daughter-in-law, Catherine Filliol, wife of his eldest son, Edward."

"Awkward," muttered Callum.

"Extremely, I'd imagine," Perdita grinned. "As a second wife, Edward Seymour married Anne Stanhope. Edward was ambitious and when his nephew, Edward VI, ascended the throne, age nine, on 28 January 1547, Uncle Edward became Lord Protector of England, technically king in all but name. Meanwhile, Jane's other brother, Thomas Seymour married Henry VIII's widow, Katheryn Parr, while also trying to groom the young Princess Elizabeth and win her hand in marriage. Thomas and Katheryn had one daughter, Mary Seymour, who disappears from the *traditional* records while she was a baby.

"Jane was nineteen when she first arrived at court," Perdita continued, "she was a lady-in-waiting for Katherine of Aragon, alongside her second cousins, Anne and Mary Boleyn. As the court ruptured into two factions, Jane remained with Katherine before vanishing from the records for four years. It's her whereabouts during these years combined with the real motivations behind Jane's absence which I believe are detailed in *The Pentagram Manuscript*. There is also an unexpected version of Anne Boleyn's story and how the women banded together during this period of fear and uncertainty.

"During the 1530s, Henry VIII was obsessed with two things: money and dynasty building. Due to lavish overspending and mismanagement, Henry's royal coffers were dangerously low. This led to debasement of the currency in order to gain extra bullion for the king, even while causing hardship to his subjects. Despite seeing his wealth increase, Henry wanted more and the debasement was followed by the spectacular idea of stripping the monasteries of their wealth and selling their land to the highest bidder. In order to assuage his conscience, this was all done in the name of God, leading to Henry declaring himself head of the Protestant church in order to achieve his other ambition: siring a legitimate heir."

"He was a charmer," said Piper, causing a ripple of laughter.

"Henry had been married to Katherine of Aragon since 1509, their union had produced one living child, Princess Mary. Despite this, Henry had numerous other children, including healthy sons, all of whom were illegitimate. With Bessie Blount, he had Henry Fitzroy, Duke of Richmond and Somerset, the only illegitimate child Henry VIII ever acknowledged and ennobled. Historians have suggested Bessie's daughter, Elizabeth, was also Henry's. Mary Boleyn had two children, Henry and Kathryn, both possible Tudors; Lady Jane Stukeley had a son, Thomas, who was thought to belong to the king; likewise Mary Berkeley, whose son John Perrot claimed Tudor parentage and Ethelreda Malt, daughter of Joanna Dingley a laundress at the palace.

"For now, the child we're going to concentrate on is Henry Fitzroy and his indomitable mother, Bessie Blount, as they are key to the story. Bessie was another courtier who was connected to a huge number of aristocratic families, even if she was from one of the junior branches. After giving birth to Fitzroy, she married twice, first to Baron Gilbert Tailboys of Kyme, with whom she had two sons, and secondly to Edward Clinton, Earl of Lincoln and they had three daughters. Throughout her life, she remained close to her eldest son and on cordial terms with the king.

"In June 1532, Loys de Heylwigen, a member of the household of the Holy Roman Emperor Charles V, wrote a letter to his sponsor suggesting that with Queen Katherine banished from court, Henry VIII was preparing to marry Bessie Blount and legitimise their son, Henry Fitzroy, in order to make him heir to the throne. This rumour was further enhanced when Henry went to see his son at Grafton and spend time with him enjoying the entertainments, including a bowling alley. Whether this was the plan or not, in July 1532 Bessie Blount scuppered it by marrying Edward Fiennes, Lord Clinton, defying any possible proposal from the king. Fitzroy, meanwhile, was being prepared to travel in Henry's train for the upcoming trip to France with forty attendants of his own. After this tour, Fitzroy remained in France, building connections and learning the art of kingship.

"Jane Seymour remains absent from the official records but I believe I've discovered the reason why and where she was living. Even more unexpected was the discovery that far from being the perfect Tudor bride, when Jane married Henry VIII, she was already married and the mother of two children."

"What?" exclaimed Jenny.

"According to this manuscript, Jane and Sir Francis Bryan, a friend of the king's, often referred to as the Vicar from Hell because of his antics, had been lovers for years. Francis arranged for her to come to court and, during a period of great difficulty when people were dying from the Tudor disease, the Sweat, they married in secret. This was the reason Jane was away from court. She was first at Hertford Castle, where Sir Francis was constable, then later in Harlech, another castle under Francis's control, before taking up residence here at Marquess House."

"No way," said Piper. "Jane Seymour has connections to this house?"

"Yes. In fact, I've been wondering if the Arthurian frieze in the Weeping Lady tower was the inspiration for the poems in the manuscript. There's a comment suggesting there was a scriptorium at the convent on Llyn Cel island and it was the nuns who created the corner illuminations. Although this is your area of expertise Pipes, I've noticed a few similar motifs."

"Let me have copies and I'll check them against my reconstructions of the ceiling and the carvings on the graves in the chapel to see if they're connected."

"Thank you," said Perdita, before resuming her revelations. "As we know, the manor was part of Anne Boleyn's dowry when she was created Marquess of Pembroke on 1 September 1532. In order to protect Jane, this house was made available by Anne for her use. There are comments in the marginalia suggesting Anne went one step further and bought this house, removing it from royal ownership. As it was so far from court, it must have slipped through the gaps as Thomas Cromwell never tried to requisition it."

"Why though?" asked Stuart. "Anne would have been in trouble if Jane was discovered and, also, why help a rival?"

"I think it was Anne's way of showing gratitude," replied Perdita. "At this stage, Jane was an insignificant member of the court and Anne's second cousin. The tale in the manuscript suggests it was Bessie along with several other women — Lady Elizabeth Carew, Lady Mary Norris, Lady Jane Stukeley and Anne Boleyn — who requested Jane to remain in Katherine of Aragon's household in order to spy for them while they hatched a plan to place Fitzroy on the throne instead of Henry VIII. Part of this plan included making Anne Boleyn queen. If the manuscript is to be believed, Jane was coordinating espionage for them and as thanks for Jane's help in spying on Queen Katherine, Anne offered her the property as somewhere to hide with her family as the court struggled with the uncertainty and danger of Henry's divorce."

"Is that why there are ceiling bosses of Anne Boleyn?" asked Kit.

"Probably," said Perdita, "although, my instinct tells me there might be more to it. I haven't yet found a definitive reason, but it doesn't mean I won't," she finished with a grin.

"Hang on though, Perds, if Jane was married to Sir Francis Bryan," said Callum, "how could she have married the king? Sir Francis was alive when Jane Seymour was queen."

"Jane and Francis kept their marriage a secret because her parents had already turned him down as a potential husband," explained Perdita. "Francis was wary about upsetting the king by marrying without permission and, every time a suitor was suggested for Jane, her brother, Edward, refused because he was hoping to push Jane forward as a potential mistress to the king if and when Anne Boleyn became queen and then, hopefully, pregnant. Edward's venality was another reason Francis wanted to keep Jane away from court, in order to protect her."

"But, if Jane's marriage to the king was bigamous, Edward VI, Henry's one legitimate prince, was actually illegitimate," said Kit.

Perdita nodded. "Yes, which means the only legitimate prince Henry VIII ever had was the one he didn't know existed: Catherine Howard's secret son, which we discovered previously. His two legitimate daughters were Princess Mary, the daughter of Katherine of Aragon and Anne's daughter, Elizabeth. Despite the legislation legitimising her, many historians have felt Queen Elizabeth I's birth-status is a grey area as far as legitimacy is concerned."

"At present, with the exception of Jane Seymour's rather unexpected marital status, things remain similar to the 'accepted' version of history," said Gary.

"You're right," said Perdita, looking from face to face, "but it's here things take an unusual turn. Once again, The Scribe has left a great deal of what was true within this story but there is a secret hidden in plain sight, and once you've seen it, it's very difficult to wipe away the possibility of an alternative perspective."

Perdita flashed a photograph up on to the screen, an enlarged section of the page of a manuscript. She read aloud: *"This is a true tale. The weak men believe we are unable to tell our story, yet I, Jane In Anger, shall show we women have our own power and together, we will topple the king and recreate this England for ourselves."*

"Topple a king?" said Callum.

"It took a great deal more research, not to mention, luck, before I could reconcile this reference but, having been through the letters discovered by Jenny, we have reached the conclusion this is a contemporary ascription to what became known as the Pilgrimage of Grace."

"But that was a march against Protestantism," said Gary, drawing looks of surprise. "The northern Catholics wanted the king to recognise their right to worship as they chose and to stop stripping the money and treasure from the monasteries."

"Exactly," said Perdita, "it culminated in the king inviting one of the leaders, Robert Aske, to court and promising to meet his demands before reneging on the agreement and executing Aske for high treason. To further hammer home the message, Henry ordered men from every town and village who took part to be hanged as a punishment."

"You're suggesting this didn't happen?" asked Kit.

"I'm suggesting it did but not in the way it's been remembered," said Perdita. "At the moment, I haven't read the entire manuscript so I don't have all the answers but the anomalies that I have discovered suggest vast sections of this story have been eradicated from history and Jane Seymour was at the heart of these rebellions."

"This is astonishing," said Alistair, "but why is this relevant? Edward VI died childless, so his legitimacy doesn't matter in the greater scheme of Tudor history."

"True," agreed Perdita, "but the trial and execution of Anne Boleyn, the Pilgrimage of Grace and the death of Henry Fitzroy all precede Jane's marriage to Henry and the story we have been told throughout history is very far from the truth."

"How so?" asked Susan.

"Anne was beheaded with five other people: her youngest brother, George Boleyn, Sir Francis Weston, Sir Henry Norris,

Mark Smeaton and William Brereton, who were accused of high treason for their alleged affairs with Anne Boleyn. These men were beheaded on 17 May 1536. History tells us that Anne should have been executed on 18 May 1536, but due to the French swordsman Henry had lovingly employed to despatch his second wife being held up by the tides, her execution was put back a day."

"Her youngest brother?" queried Piper. "George was her only brother."

"No, he wasn't," replied Perdita. "This was one of the things I wanted to check when I visited the Tower of London, to see the execution records. Anne Boleyn had two other brothers."

"What?" asked Susan in surprise.

"Thomas and Henry, known in Jane's letters as Thos and Hal," replied Perdita.

"But they died in infancy," said Jenny, then her eyes widened in understanding. "What do you think really happened to them?"

"I think they were executed at the Tower of London in response to a rebellion led by Henry Fitzroy, which was subsequently re-imagined by The Scribe as the Pilgrimage of Grace."

There was a tense silence following Perdita's pronouncement.

"When did Henry Fitzroy die?" asked Callum, his voice nervous.

"According to the records he succumbed to tuberculosis on 23 July 1536," said Perdita, "which is two months after Anne's execution, despite having been healthy and viewed in Parliament a week earlier, hence the many rumours over the years of his death being caused by poison rather than illness. However, the suggestion of foul play can't be ruled out especially when coupled with the king's reaction to the death of the boy he had been hinting he might name as his heir. When Fitzroy died, the king was furious, but rather than treating the boy like a potential prince, he commanded the Duke of Norfolk to remove the body under cover of darkness and bury it in a lead-lined coffin in the Howard crypt at Thetford Priory in Norfolk."

"What an extraordinary reaction," said Susan.

"This is all very interesting," said Piper, and Perdita understood her sister's brusqueness was from fear, "but how does it all connect?"

"This is why I have such admiration for The Scribe," said Perdita, placing another image on the screen. "She was an expert in misdirection. This is a copy of the list of executions that took place at the Tower of London."

Running a laser pen down the names she highlighted the famous royal executions, before resting the beam on another entry reading: *"Five unnamed persons, 15 June 1532, Tower Hill, Hanged, drawn and quartered. High treason — coining."*

There was a pause as the significance of another example of the number five appeared in the discussion.

"The dates are wrong…" interrupted Gary.

"Dates are easily changed," replied Piper.

"Why would the crime be changed?" asked Jenny.

"What if coining was the excuse, even if it wasn't the entire truth. It still carries the sentence of high treason but it makes it possible to remove the names without arousing suspicion," Perdita replied. "Workers caught coining at the mint wouldn't have had noble status, therefore, in Tudor eyes, they were unimportant, so they were unnamed. If the crime of coining was the reason Henry sent five more people to the block, it would be high treason but he and Cromwell would be able to disguise the truth."

"And you think this might be a contemporary alteration?" asked Gary.

"It's possible," replied Perdita. "Having seen the original records, the date of 1532 is spindly and pale, it could have been scraped away and changed."

"What year do you suspect?" asked Kit.

"1536, the same year as Anne Boleyn. It fits neatly between the significant deaths — Anne, George, Sir Henry Norris, Sir Francis Weston, William Brereton and Mark Smeaton in May and the unexpected death of Henry Fitzroy in July. What if the Pilgrimage of Grace was triggered by the events around Anne's execution but failed, resulting in five more executions?"

"Five?" asked Jenny but her question was overshadowed by Callum asking, "What's coining?"

"Coining can either be counterfeiting or what they called clipping coins, which meant trimming away the edges of the silver so the coin was smaller," responded Perdita. "If someone was working at the Royal Mint, which was within the Tower of London, then clipping a number of coins could prove extremely lucrative. At this point in history, the keeper of the royal mint was William Blount, 4th Baron Mountjoy, a distant cousin of Bessie's. There was already dissent among the nobles as Henry and Thomas Cromwell began the great debasement of coins in order to boost royal coffers while at the same time stripping the monasteries of their wealth. What better way for a potential army to fund itself than by having an insider at the Royal Mint who can shovel bullion your way, especially if the promise is a high-ranking position under a potential new king?"

"You're suggesting the two missing Boleyn boys and three other people were involved in raising funds for a rebellion and were caught and executed in June 1536?" confirmed Alistair.

"Yes, except it was two other people, Bessie Blount's brothers, while her sister, Meg, was executed for trying to poison the king: three more people who have also vanished from the official records."

A stunned silence greeted her words, then the internal phone at the centre of the table buzzed. Perdita answered it on speaker phone, there were strict instructions not to disturb them unless it was urgent.

"Perds, it's Mark," came a breathless voice. "We're in the chapel and, following your instructions, we're calling to let you know the ceiling boss is ready to be opened. Do you want us to wait?"

Perdita gazed around and made a decision. "No, Mark, could you open it and then send me the images? As you said, it'll probably be a plain stone ceiling boss."

"Wait on the phone while I do it…"

There were muffled voices, then a pause, before Mark's voice on the line was sharp, clear and tense. "It isn't a stone ceiling boss," he said. "You need to see this, Perds, you need to see this now."

CHAPTER FOUR

Mark was waiting in the porch when Perdita and the others arrived.

"We were in the middle of a meeting," Perdita explained, encompassing everyone in a sweeping gesture as Mark looked at them in surprise.

Dragging on protective suits, they followed Mark through the chapel. Perdita's heart was pounding. Was the interior of the ceiling boss a clue? And, if so, who had been responsible for its creation: The Scribe or someone else?

Mark hurried up the staircase on to the walkway erected near the ceiling. "There isn't room for everyone," he said. "Perdita and Piper will suffice, the rest of you will have to watch the screen." He pointed over to a monitor.

"Be careful, Perds," said Kit, squeezing her hand.

"I shall," she said, returning the gesture.

Hurrying up to join her sister and Mark, Perdita stared around in wonder. The cleaning and restoration teams had been painstakingly removing layers of dust to reveal the brilliance of the colours below. While the chapel was deep-cleaned once a year, it had never been done with such forensic precision and the difference was incredible.

"As you remember," said Mark, "we realised the supposed crack was actually an opening but years of being painted over had disguised it. The hinges, when we were able to examine them, are wooden, which makes them far older than we first imagined…"

"Do you have a date?" asked Piper.

"At a guess, I'd say sixteenth century but then the bulk of this part of the chapel is dated to then, so it isn't unexpected. The front part of the nave and the north transept are earlier, twelfth century, but there was major reconstruction in the early sixteenth century."

While Mark spoke, Perdita gazed at the ceiling boss which had been pushed shut again. For all his determined academia and thirst for facts above hypothesis and imagination, there was a certain theatrical flair in Mark and she knew he was enjoying his moment for a big reveal. Picking up a thin camera which looked like a pen, he called down to Stephanie, Jenny's new assistant. "Ready?"

"Yes," she called back, and Perdita caught a hint of amused exasperation.

"Perds, the images I sent you are nothing compared to the real thing. It is extraordinary," he whispered, then with gentle gloved fingers he prised the ceiling boss apart.

Perdita gasped in wonder as the pentagram was revealed in all its beauty. It was a replica of the image on the cover of the manuscript, glittering with hints of gold leaf, while bold reds, blues and greens shone in the light from Mark's camera pen. At the centre of the image was the tiny wooden figure of a blonde-haired woman wearing a crown and holding a swaddled baby. Hints of the Renaissance image of the Madonna and child, replicated a thousand times by artists over the centuries, were embodied within this serene figure. On the five points of the pentagram were initials: AB, MC, MB, EB, JP. Underneath each set of initials was a red circle surrounding a Tudor rose. Piper was taking pictures, zooming in on each section, Perdita simply stared.

"What do you think it means?" asked Mark.

"I think we might be looking to the answer to one of history's biggest mysteries," Perdita said.

"You do?" Mark's voice resonated with surprise.

"This research began because I wanted to trace Anne Boleyn, to discover why her image was the fourth ceiling boss. Even if the house had once been part of her dower, it's unusual for facial images of her to survive. Why would someone risk the wrath of Henry VIII by leaving an image of Anne? I wondered if The Scribe had added it later but, if this was the case, again it begged the question: why? The Scribe had been told to obscure the truth about Catherine Howard and while she had been told to denigrate the Tudors in order to show the Stuarts in a better light, the story of Anne Boleyn and Henry's marriage has always been the centrepiece.

"For a king to execute his wife was shocking, it rocked Europe and made the other powerful monarchs of the day wary of trusting Henry. In fact, it was so appalling, no one doubted its validity. In Catherine Howard's case we discovered things weren't as they seemed but it's my firm belief Anne Boleyn was executed. The reason I say this with confidence is because she was accompanied by four women, known as the Four Maids, yet their names have been removed from history, there has never been any hint as to their identity."

"And you think this reveals it?" asked Piper, looking bemused.

"Yes, I think this shows something extraordinary."

"What does it mean, Perds?" called Kit from down below where they were gathered around the monitor.

"At a guess, and this will need further study, I think the central image is Jane Seymour holding the future Edward VI, and I think the initials refer to all the women who gave Henry sons: Elizabeth Blount, Jane Pollard — who became Jane

Stukeley after marriage, Mary Berkeley and I would suggest, Mary Carey, better known as Mary Boleyn."

"Sons?" said Jenny. "Anne Boleyn didn't have a living son."

"Actually, Jen, I think she did," said Perdita, "and we are the only people in possession of records that can prove it."

"Perdita, you'll have to explain your statement," said Gary.

Perdita gazed up at the ceiling boss, wishing she had asked everyone to remain in the meeting room. The revelation of this image after centuries in the dark felt sacred, as had the moment when she and Kit had discovered Catherine Howard's grave, yet she was surrounded by people and in the middle of an explanation. Sending silent apologies to the images of the women in the boss, she whispered to Mark, "I have a few things to finish, then I'll meet you back here."

Hurrying down the stairs, she guided everyone to the back of the chapel. "The ceiling boss answers many questions," she said, "including the definitive proof that Anne Boleyn's second pregnancy went to term and she delivered a prince. There is one historian who believes the baby was stillborn and this was the reason for her downfall, while other historians describe it as a miscarriage, implying the baby was born before term. The Tudor priest and polemicist, Nicholas Sanders, wrote that Anne's son was born with hideous deformities which were the sign of her being a witch. However, he was writing many years after events, with no corroboration. We already own one document suggesting Anne's son survived."

"Was this the baby Anne was carrying when Henry fell from his horse?" asked Susan.

Perdita shrugged. "Again, the theory of Henry VIII falling and knocking himself unconscious for several hours, is one we have to question…"

"But this is key point in Tudor history, thousands of words and hundreds of books have been written on the subject," said Jenny.

"Yet, the tale comes from Rodolfo Pio da Carpi, Bishop of Faenza, the Papal nuncio in Paris, who throughout history has been the source of a great deal of historical gossip. From the records we have, there is no suggestion he was in England when the accident took place and, rather strangely, there is no corroborating evidence from any observers or witnesses in England concerning Henry's alleged dramatic fall. A similar rumour begun by Pio was the suggestion Anne Boleyn was not pregnant at this time but faked a miscarriage, however, we have corroboration in *The Catherine Howard Codex* that Anne did have a son and he died..." Perdita broke off, her mind whirring with the possibilities, desperate to examine the ceiling boss and learn its secrets, as well as to have time to finish the manuscript and discover its final truths.

"I think we've done enough for today," said Kit, his tone authoritative. "Mark's revelation could change things and we need to regroup and understand its significance before we continue."

"Of course," said Alistair, who was looking at Perdita with concern. "We shall await your email for a date and time to reconvene."

"Before you go," said Perdita, "I do need to update you on Jane Seymour and where she was in the run-up to the birth of Anne's child or, as recorded in the accepted version of history, a second miscarriage. Either eventuality leads to a catalyst in British history: the moment the king decided to legally murder his wife."

"Where was Jane Seymour at this point?" asked Piper.

"She was at Marquess House," said Perdita. "She spent several years here with her children, Jasper and Lois, providing a safe house for those wishing to travel to Ireland in order to escape Henry VIII's increasingly erratic reign. Her husband, Sir Francis Bryan, made the journey many times too but it all changed in 1535, when Jane was recalled to court. Anne had suffered her first miscarriage and her marriage to the king was in jeopardy. Katherine of Aragon was ill and not expected to survive. The feeling of fear and unease at court would have been overwhelming."

"And this was when Henry VIII noticed Jane Seymour?" asked Stuart.

"This is certainly where Jane flares on to the pages of history," said Perdita. "The accepted version of history tells us that Henry watched her dancing one night at court and then a few months later, during a summer progress, he and Anne stayed at Wulfhall as guests of Jane's parents. Jane, as the eldest daughter, was there helping to entertain the king and this was when he fell in love with her demure blonde looks and her ladylike manner."

"When was this?" asked Susan.

"October 1535."

"Which means Anne would have been pregnant with the son who we think was born in April 1536," said Susan.

"Yes, and when a queen is pregnant, there are opportunities for ambitious men to push their female relatives into the king's bed."

"Do you think this happened to Jane?" asked Piper.

"Yes," Perdita replied, "the trouble was, Jane was already married but this information was known only to a select few, none of whom dared tell the king."

There were murmurs of thanks as the meeting ended and Perdita waited for Alistair, Susan, Jenny, Gary and Stuart to leave. Piper had returned to the walkway with Mark and was taking a series of images, Callum wandered over the join them. Perdita and Kit remained in the pew, watching the gentle activity of the restorers.

"What do you think happened, Perds, and why is it important?"

"I have two more sections of the manuscript to finish," she said, "which I hope will explain how Jane Seymour became queen because this version of events is even more tangled than those we've already unravelled. Life must have been terrifying in Henry VIII's court, especially if you were a woman."

"Can I help you at all?" asked Kit.

She leaned her head on his shoulder, a wave of exhaustion overwhelming her. "If I send you some information, could you check it for me, please? You have access to far more records than me."

"Of course," he replied. "What will you do?"

"Finish the transcript, check the manuscript and discover what really happened to Jane Seymour. There is something strange here and my heart tells me there was no happy ending for anyone this time."

PART SIX: LONDON, 1536

CHAPTER ONE

The room danced with twilight and flames, shadows sprang across heavy tapestries, teasing the smooth planes of faces into cadaverous masks as the labouring queen groaned in pain.

Jane sponged Anne's forehead. "Not long now," Jane assured her. "Let's move you to the birthing chair."

Anne closed her eyes and Jane remembered her own experiences of childbirth: riding the wave of pain, praying it would end, wondering if each crescendo would carry away her life. As her cousin's fingers released their crushing grip on Jane's hand, Elizabeth Boleyn came forward.

"We must move her; she is very close."

Manhandling her cousin on to the birthing chair, Jane stood behind Anne, continuing to grip her cousin's hand. With the last of her energy, Anne screamed and in a gush of blood and mucus, her son was born.

His wail filled the air. The women beamed at each other. Elizabeth Boleyn hurried forward to hug her daughter. "It's a boy, my love," she whispered, wiping the tears and sweat from Anne's face. "You have delivered a fine prince."

"Tell him," Anne gasped, her eyes rolling back in her head. "Tell him I have fulfilled my promise." Then she went limp.

"Jane, help us," gasped Elizabeth Boleyn, as the women surged around Anne's lifeless form, returning her to the bed.

Jane stared down at the queen, transfixed. Anne's eyelids fluttered. She was alive but she was bleeding. Two midwives stepped forward, staunching the flow, while the baby was taken away and washed. Having been in many a delivery room, Jane made herself busy, tidying away the debris, rolling up the bloodstained sheets, leaving room around the bed for the most skilled of the women in attendance. A moment later, Elizabeth Wood, Anne's aunt by marriage, pushed a scroll into Jane's hand.

"Deliver this to your brother or, if you are able, the king," she whispered. "It is the news of the birth."

"To my brother?" asked Jane in confusion, wondering why this should not be given to Anne's father.

"Your brother is high in the king's favour; he will be more happily received. Hurry, Jane, this is no time for your weeping and wailing."

Elizabeth Wood was not well liked in the court, known for her spite and lack of humour. She was a woman Jane tried to avoid. Despite the anger flaring within her, Jane bit her tongue, refusing to lose her composure over the malevolent sideswipe. The most important task was informing the king of his son and, while she was free from the birthing chamber, she would be able to send news to Bessie, Lady Clinton. Whether this child would help or hinder her growing plans, Jane was unsure.

Slipping out of the fug of the queen's chamber, Jane was relieved to be away from the metallic smell of blood, the cloying smell of sweat and the unpleasant odour of the herbs which were being used to revive the queen. The image of Anne's inert form played on her mind as she hurried down the corridor to the locked double doors where a guard waited.

"Let me pass," she called, knocking, her fist making the softest of noises against the heavy panelling. A key turned in the lock and the familiar face of Thomas Cromwell peered at her as she wondered whether her cousin would survive the next few hours. Anne had been struggling for three days and she was exhausted.

"Mistress Semel," he sneered, "they have sent you to appease the king. Does this mean the news is bad? Another daughter, perhaps?"

"My message is to be given to my brother or the king, himself," Jane replied but there was no heat in her voice. She had no particular feelings about Cromwell. He was a courtier doing his best to make his way. Her circumstances were similar.

"I shall accompany you," said Cromwell, falling into step beside her. "Your brother is with the king."

Walking beside Cromwell, Jane shuddered at the thought of Edward's recent closeness to the king and wondered what had changed within the relationship to bring about this new-found friendship. Edward Seymour had been at court for many years and her impression had always been that, thanks to his sanctimonious attitude, he had made more enemies than friends. Ambitious, self-serving and ruthless, Edward Seymour was neither popular nor liked but viewed with suspicion. Yet, somehow, since Jane's family had entertained the king at Wulfhall the previous September during the summer progress, Edward had become a welcome member of the monarch's inner circle, replacing George Boleyn as the king's shadow.

A shiver ran down Jane's spine wondering what promises Edward had made to the king and how much of his exalted position was bound up with her and the endless meetings she was forced to endure with Henry. She could not even turn to Francis for help, as he remained abroad at the king's behest, smoothing over George Boleyn's most recent diplomatic disaster.

Cromwell led the way past the guards, knocking on the door of the inner chamber.

"Enter," roared the king.

Jane shook out her skirts, hoping she did not look too dishevelled after her days in the birthing chamber and followed Cromwell into the king's private rooms. Her brother Edward looked up in surprise from the game of chess he had been playing with the king, while an ashen-faced Thomas Boleyn started from his chair, coming to an abrupt halt when he saw Cromwell's leering grin. Henry Norris, William Brereton, Richard Page and Thomas Wyatt paused in their game of cards, while the musician, young Mark Smeaton, stopped in his soft playing of the lute, plunging the room into a tense silence.

"Sire, Mistress Seymour brings news of the queen," said Cromwell, bowing low. Jane dropped into a deep obeisance.

"The baby? It is born?" said the king, hurrying towards Jane and raising her up. His eyes bored into hers with an uncomfortable intensity, his fingers stroking her wrist as he raised her from the floor.

"Yes, Your Majesty," she said and handed him the scroll, which he threw aside.

"You tell me," he insisted, his brown eyes wide with anticipation.

"A boy…"

"Does he live?" The king's voice was sharp, eager.

"Yes, as does the queen."

Jane waited for the explosion of joy but instead the king's face twisted into a furious grimace. "And so, at the last, when I have seen the truth, I am thwarted," he muttered. "Once again, she halts my progress."

Throwing a confused look at her brother, not understanding the king's statement, Jane saw Edward's angry face with its narrowed eyes and lipless scowl. Revulsion trickled through her as the men exchanged glances of irritation. Turning to Thomas Boleyn, she saw he had returned to his seat, his fists clenched, knuckles whitened. He alone allowed the hint of a smile to play across his lips, relief flooding his handsome face. The king dropped her hand, striding up and down the room, his face red with fury and Jane felt sympathy and fear for Anne, even now lying in a sweat-soaked bed fighting for her life. A life the king held in the balance.

"Speak to no one of the events in the birthing chamber," said the king, breaking the tense silence. He spoke to the room at large but with an emphasis on Cromwell. "Until I have seen the child for myself, there will be no announcement. I do not believe she is capable of this task. Edward, escort your sister to her rooms, she must play no more part in this petty game."

Bemused, Jane wanted to protest, to assure the king that Anne had delivered a healthy child but as she opened her mouth to speak, Edward shook his head. Allowing her brother to slip his hand under her elbow, she let him guide her away.

"Come, Jane," he whispered, throwing a glance at the king who smiled, dismissing Edward.

"Until later, Mistress Seymour," the king called as Edward propelled her through the door. "We shall continue with our discussions of the scriptures."

Jane stifled her sigh. The scriptures were not discussed; Henry delivered his views and she was expected to smile, her eyes wide with incredulity at his supposed wisdom, agreeing with his every word, even though in her heart she wanted to shout at him and argue at his stupidity and misinterpretation of the verses. Years of experience learned from watching Anne trying to reason with a man who felt he had no equal had, however, taught her silence was the safest course of action.

"What's happening?" she whispered to Edward as he hurried her to her rooms, appointed a few weeks earlier, nearer to the king's.

"The king no longer wishes to be married to Anne but he doesn't know how to rid himself of a second troublesome wife."

"But Anne has delivered a son…"

"Don't be naïve, Jane," he hissed. "This is the one occasion the king didn't wish for a healthy birth."

"This is insanity," Jane replied. "He has a legitimate son."

"For how long?" asked Edward.

Jane felt sick as the implications of these words permeated her tired mind.

"This is our moment," Edward hissed, his usually pale face pink with excitement. "Ever since the king danced with you in the autumn at Wulfhall he has spoken of little else except your sweetness, kind heart and gentle soul. This situation holds power beyond our wildest dreams. We are stepping nearer to the king each day and with this…"

"Your career prospers," finished Jane with a sneer.

"Yes, but so does yours. You will no longer be the pitiful, plain Miss Seymour who wilts on the edge of court like a faded flower. There was a time when the position of royal mistress would have allowed you great power before securing a good marriage, as Bessie Blount has demonstrated, but with the king tired of the queen, if we hold our nerve, we might be able to aim higher."

"And Mary Boleyn, Jane Pollard, Mary Berkeley and Joanna Dingley?" she questioned. "Not to mention the countless others…"

"Necessary distractions," dismissed Edward, causing Jane's fury to notch up a level.

"These are women with feelings, hopes, dreams, who have been used by the king and left to raise his unwanted children…"

"Jane, put this womanish stupidity aside. The king has shown you a great honour by singling you out for special attention. Think what this could do for the entire family and do not allow selfishness on your part to ruin our rise to the upper echelons of the nobility."

After Edward left, Jane threw herself on to her bed, wondering if it would be possible for her to don her nun's habit and slip unnoticed from court. Francis had left her plenty of money meaning it would be easy for her and Audrey to travel to Marquess House where they could hide in the convent on Llyn Cel island. The house was so remote she doubted the king and Cromwell even knew of its existence. Edward's words, while no surprise, had disgusted her. He, like many other Tudor men, believed women to be lesser creatures, to have no control over their feelings and this injustice glowed within her like faerie fire; white hot and destructive.

When the summons from Anne to attend her at court had arrived eight months earlier, Jane had discovered a place of unease and quicksilver changes. She had been shocked to see the alteration in her cousin. Where once her pale skin and dark eyes had twinkled with mischief and a certain malicious glee, Anne's complexion had become blotchy, her gaze when she met Jane's, fearful.

"Jane," she had whispered, hugging her, "thank you."

Unsure what warranted these thanks, Jane had squeezed Anne back.

"Is this why you wrote to me?" she asked.

Anne had nodded. "If I am surrounded by women, I might be safer," she had replied.

"Safer…?" Jane had begun but the arrival of Jane Boleyn, wife of George Boleyn, brought the conversation to an abrupt halt.

Over the next few weeks, Jane had settled into her role as a senior member of the queen's bedchamber. Yet, the light-hearted joy which had once categorised Anne's court had been replaced by a taut, forced gaiety covering an underlying current of fear. Anne's laughter, once natural and joyous, was brittle with anxiety. Whenever the king was near, her first reaction was to flinch. Where once Jane had watched Anne and Henry verbally spar, their wit and cruelty bristling with sexual tension, the words passing between them had become bitter and accusatory, laced with frustration and terror.

For Jane though, life had taken a strange turn when a banquet thrown by the king for the Admiral of France caused further upheaval. While dancing with Francis, the king had beckoned her husband to his side, requesting her name. To Jane's horror, the king had insisted on dancing with her. Jane had been surprised at the king's gentleness and courtesy as he had taken her hand and led her to the centre of the room. Glimpsing Anne's horrified face as the king twirled her around, Jane was unsure how to feel. With the full force of his charm focussed on her, Jane could understand why so many women succumbed to his entreaties. The row with Francis that had followed had ended with her husband making her promise to tell him about any communication the king tried to have with her.

"This is why I wanted to keep you safe at Marquess House," Francis had exclaimed. "The king likes any new face; he will obsess over you and you must be careful."

"But he is married to Anne…" she had protested.

"And he was married to Queen Katherine when he met Anne," Francis had retorted.

A few days later, a family argument had escalated resulting in her brother Edward, supported by Anne, desiring that Jane be pushed forward into Henry's arms, while Francis and his brother-in-law, Nicholas Carew, had argued bitterly against such treachery.

"Is this why you demanded that Jane return to court?" Francis had yelled at Anne, his eyes narrowed while her lips flattened into a scowl.

"No, I invited her here because I missed her wise counsel but if the king likes her, it is better to appease rather than antagonise him."

Jane, who for so long had yearned to return to the glittering court, went to bed that evening longing for the calm of Marquess House and the sweet smiles of her children. The breach caused by the argument continued to fester. Francis struggled to speak to Anne, appalled by what he saw as her treachery in using Jane, when they had worked so hard to elevate Anne. Nicholas Carew narrowed his eyes whenever he was in the queen's company, turning away in disgust when Anne tried to repair the damage. Jane understood and remained loyal to Anne but Francis and Nicholas would not soften, refusing to speak to her. Jane and Francis, however, discussed the issue and again she begged him to inform the king of their marriage, but before they could agree on a strategy, the king sent Francis to Italy on a diplomatic mission.

As the months progressed Jane found herself infected with the culture of whispers, of the dazzling façade suggesting all was well while subterfuge and despair raged beneath the jewels, masques and flirting. Anne would pace her bedchamber whispering about Henry's affairs with first the woman known by court gossip as The Imperial Lady but whom Jane knew to be Joan Ashley, followed by Madge Shelton, who went to the king's bed with as much willingness as a pig to slaughter. Yet, the men of her family, encouraged by the king, refused to listen to Madge's protests. While Jane listened to Madge sobbing into the arms of her best friend, Lady Margaret Douglas, she wondered how much of Madge's predicament had been caused because Francis had refused to allow Jane to be flung into the king's bed.

Each day, Anne presided over her favourite pastime of writing courtly love poems, organised by Lady Douglas, Lady Howard and Madge Shelton, while Jane gathered information which she, Elizabeth Carew, Lady Stukeley and Lady Berkeley wove into poems, hiding secret messages and code in a second manuscript. This book of poems was the one Jane had begun during her tenure at Marquess House, for which she had requested the nuns create detailed illuminations. Each page contained five poems of five lines each, representing the five wounds of Christ, the five-pointed star and pentagram that Bessie Blount had chosen for her symbol so those working towards her plan to replace the king with young Fitzroy would recognise each other.

A knock on the door brought her from her reverie. Audrey's footsteps, her voice and the unbroken tones of one of the many pages who ran around the palace delivering messages. There was a tentative knock on her bedchamber door.

"Come in, Audrey," she called.

"A message for you, my lady," Audrey said, handing her the small scroll of parchment, sealed with the arms of England.

The women exchanged a concerned look.

"It is from the king," Jane sighed. "Quick, sit beside me, as we used to when we were girls."

Audrey hesitated but Jane shuffled over and with a grin, Audrey settled beside her.

"Do you remember how we would do this in the evenings when we were with Queen Katherine?" said Jane, her voice soft with nostalgia. "Poor Katherine, she died in Kimbolton Castle in Cambridgeshire, a miserable and lonely place. After her years of love and devotion to the king and this country, she deserved better."

"She was always kind to me," said Audrey. "Your cousin, Anne, is a good woman too. The birth of a prince will mend the sadness between the king and queen, won't it?"

The faint trace of hope in Audrey's voice made Jane wince. "It depends upon the contents of this scroll," she sighed. "The king has taken a fancy to me; it's the reason Francis has been so angry."

"I had heard the rumours, my la…"

"Jane, please, Audrey. We've been friends for so many years, when it's us, please call me by my name."

"I had heard rumours, Jane," Audrey murmured, "but I hoped they were mistaken."

"Shall we see what the king requests?"

Knowing this would be a summons, Jane placed the scroll on her lap, sliding her thumbnail under the seal. Cracking it in half, she watched as the tiny image of the broken arms fell to the floor, a shaft of late afternoon sunlight making it shimmer like a drop of blood. "He desires a meeting with him in the cloisters this evening. Another sermon on the sins of the flesh, no doubt."

Audrey stifled a giggle.

"When will this end?" sighed Jane. "The king has an heir; he can't be seen to depose the queen who delivered the prince."

"What does Sir Francis counsel?" asked Audrey, reading the scroll as Jane passed it to her.

"He is sure this will pass and instructs us to hold our nerve. Francis claims the king always runs to madness by the end of the darkness of winter. He claims that as spring arrives, the king's senses will clear and the world will realign. Especially since the death of Queen Katherine. There is only one living queen now. The mother of the heir to the throne."

"But many don't recognise their marriage. To the Spanish and French, this child has less right to the throne than..." whispered Audrey but Jane silenced her with a shake of her head.

"If I write to Bessie, will you see the letter is delivered?" Jane asked. "She must be told about the birth of the prince."

"And the queen?"

"Anne was alive when I left the birthing chamber, we must hope she survives."

An hour later, with her cloak around her shoulders, Jane walked with Audrey towards the cloisters, where Charles Brandon, the Duke of Suffolk loitered in the shadows.

"The king waits inside the chapel, he has requested a private audience," he said, opening the door. "Your maid and I will remain here. She will be safe in my company."

Even though she and the king had spent numerous evenings together, Jane had never been alone with him. Her brother or another member of Henry's inner circle, usually Cromwell, had always lurked in the shadows. Jane swallowed hard but reasoned, they were in a chapel, the king would never defile a holy space. At least, she hoped he would not.

"My Lady," the king's voice reached her through the shadows of the flickering candles. "You have responded to my request, as I hoped you would."

Jane stifled a scream as the enormous frame of the king loomed towards her out of the darkness.

"My love, do not be afraid," he said and smiled.

For a moment, Jane saw the twinkling prince of old, the man who was a friend to his courtiers, a champion of all that was good and holy, before disappointment and his creeping tyranny and madness had begun to weave its web around him.

"I'm not afraid," she replied, placing her hand on the arm he proffered and she was speaking the truth. In the beautiful chapel at Whitehall Palace, she knew no harm would befall her.

"My sweet Jane," Henry said, and Jane smiled, aware this was the expected response. "As you must know, for some months now, my heart has been divided. There is the queen, whom I love and has delivered me of a robust and handsome prince, whom we have named William after the most bold and dashing conqueror. Yet, my heart pines for you. I long for you when I am alone at night. For the softness of your hand in mine, your wise counsel and the beauty of your smile."

Jane dropped her eyes, demure, overwhelmed, while in reality, her heart beat fast in fear.

"I spoke to your brother about a suitable gift for you, a purse of money, perhaps, but he suggested this would be improper as you are yet unwed and a maiden."

"My lord, I should have no choice but to refuse such a gift," she said. "Unless you were to offer it as a dowry to my husband on the day I were to marry. However, there would never be one so noble, handsome or courageous as yourself, Your Majesty."

"You are too kind, Mistress Seymour." The king laughed in a self-depreciating way before his tone changed. "Are you betrothed? Your brother insists no offer of marriage has been made, which I find hard to understand, you are a true angel of beauty. Any man would be proud to marry you."

"There are no betrothals and have never been," whispered Jane, aware she was lying in a holy place, wondering if she would be struck down for her sin.

"Sir Francis Bryan...?" The king left the name hanging in the air.

"An old family friend who has been my chaperone in order to protect my modesty," she replied.

Despite the wild rumours concerning Francis and Henry's antics when they had been young, the king did not question her words. "Francis made the same claim," he said, relief apparent in the softening of his face and the twinkle in his eye. "However, there are rumours abounding and despite the unspoken nature of our love, you must remember, I am king and, at present, I am married."

"Indeed, Sire," she said, "to my cousin, Anne, who has given you a prince."

The sunshine which had flooded his face fled, his eyes narrowing in annoyance. "She claims it is mine," he snarled. "Yet, as king, I wield the power of life and death. Do not despair my love, our time will be soon. Our love will be accepted and exalted by all. You do not have to wait much longer for our desire to be made manifest." He reached inside his doublet and withdrew an ornate locket on a heavy chain. "This is for you, my love," he said, placing it in Jane's hand and wrapping her fingers around it. "Wear it when you are at court and I will know your heart is mine."

Before Jane could answer, the king had kissed her hand and vanished into the gloom of the chapel. Heart beating in fear, she opened the locket. Inside was a miniature of the king and the words: "Bound to Obey and Serve". Bile rose in her stomach as she ran to the door and threw it open. Audrey waited alone.

"What's happened?" she asked as Jane linked arms and hurried back to the privacy of her rooms.

"The king means to murder Anne," Jane whispered.

"Are you sure?"

"Yes, and worse, I think he intends to kill the young prince, too."

CHAPTER TWO

"Anne is to be churched," announced Bessie Blount as she entered the lavish apartments belonging to the queen. "This should be her moment of triumph but she fears for her life."

"Does the king continue to cast doubt over the prince's parentage?" asked Lady Stukeley, who stood beside Jane arranging vases of spring flowers to welcome the queen back.

"He changes his view from hour to hour, in one moment praising Anne for giving him his heart's desire, in the next accusing her of being a bawd who would taint the Tudor line."

"These men are repulsive," said Jane.

Lady Stukeley gave a derisive snort. Gathering the discarded stalks and leaves, she left the room. "I shall see you are not disturbed," she murmured to Bessie as she closed the door.

Jane and Bessie waited a moment, listening as Lady Stukeley's footsteps retreated before moving together, sorting the tangled embroidery silks piled on a side table.

"Charles Brandon has been tasked with organising a joust," said Bessie. "While most assume this is to celebrate the birth of an heir, the men snigger like schoolboys, suggesting Henry's true motive is to celebrate the death of Katherine."

"How dare they show such disrespect?" snarled Jane. "Queen Katherine was a princess of Spain, a queen of royal blood. A woman who achieved more in her life than any of these idiots."

"You're right, it's appalling," agreed Bessie. "This is why we must change things. Our plans have been brought forward and we intend to march within weeks. The king has become unpredictable. I fear the balance of his mind is upset. He behaves like a spoiled child who no longer understands the difference between right and wrong. All that matters is his will, his desire, but he suffers from monstrous cruelty, from a lack of empathy, believing he and he alone feels, that no one else has the same level of emotion. He is king, he can bend the law and the Privy Council to his will. Especially while he has Thomas Cromwell skulking in the shadows, fulfilling his darkest imaginings."

Jane saw her own incandescent rage reflected in Bessie's eyes. "And your son will be different?" she asked before she could stop herself.

"My son will have me to guide him, as I will have my council of women. This is where Lady Margaret Beaufort lost her edge. While she was skilful enough to place her son on the throne, upon achieving her dearest ambition, she tried to rule through him, to be the power behind the king, the true monarch, but she was alone. No one, man or woman, can work in isolation. We must have those around us whom we can trust. Lady Margaret was cast aside by the men of the Privy Chamber because she did not think to surround herself with women who would have been able to advise her and keep her son on the path of righteousness. When my son is king, there will be two councils, the one made of men who pontificate in government while we women shall sit in the shadows and ensure sense prevails."

Jane gave a derisive laugh. "You believe this is possible?"

"I know it. However, until that happy day we have work to do. The information you have collected over the years has been a godsend. We have used it to prepare for battle. In Lincolnshire, we have gathered loyal troops. These are supported by good men in Yorkshire, Lancashire, Northumbria and Cumberland where my son impressed them while he headed the Council of the North. He learned the ways of these men and came to understand them. We would correspond about making them our allies. We have friends in Scotland, too. My son and his cousin, James V, have an accord. Should it be necessary, the Scottish king will support my son in his claim. As will the League of Cognac…"

"But the king refused to sign it," interrupted Jane.

"The king refused but they approached Fitzroy and he was offered a pension from their endeavours."

"This war is over now; it was fought between the Hapsburgs and the Sforza families."

"You're astute, my dear," said Bessie, "but we have spent years building links with the important families in Spain, Italy, Savoy and France. Many felt Henry's actions were those of a coward, yet my son was seen to have the makings of a great warrior and a wise ruler. Thanks to guidance from the Boleyn boys and my own brothers, this is a reputation which has grown during his sojourn at the French court. We can count on the support of many of these families, should they be required."

"Bessie, this is high treason," whispered Jane.

"Of this, we are aware, but what wouldn't a mother do for a son? As Lady Beaufort won a throne for her son, Henry VII, whose claim was born through her blood and its illegitimate claim to the throne. My child is an acknowledged son of a king and I am able to trace my lineage to Edward III. His claim is stronger and my will is as implacable as that lady's."

"Bessie, you ask a great deal," said Jane. "Ever since I have arrived at court, I have been ordered to spy, to cheat, to haunt the shadows, bury my true nature and all for what? Being told I must deny my husband and children and fill my cousin Anne's place in the king's bed while I wait for a rebellion? What about my wishes? You are following your desires? Why shouldn't I?"

"And what do you desire?"

"Freedom."

Bessie placed the last skein of silk into its protective cotton pouch and shook out her skirts. "As do we all, Jane," she said, "and if Fitzroy is on the throne, I shall ensure freedom is what you are given as a reward for your efforts. You will be made a landowner in your own right; in fact, if you wish it, I shall ask him to gift you that manor in Pembrokeshire of which you are so fond, Marquess House. You will have wealth, status and your husband, I promise."

"And in return?"

"Should you be forced into the king's bed, you will continue the work Anne has begun."

"What?"

"The king can't be seen to die unexpectedly, he must be ailing, then his death will appear to be a natural consequence of a long illness. Each day, the queen delivers a drop of cuckoo-pint into his wine and the weakness has begun to show."

"This is a well-known plague remedy," said Jane, who had learned about herbs, tinctures and salves when she was younger at Wulfhall.

"Indeed," agreed Bessie, "but it has poisonous properties, too, and we have mixed it with hemlock and honey within the king's medicinal. Each day, he weakens, he is unable to heal and should an illness envelope him, the wise women assure us he will be carried away as though he were a mewling child."

"This is what Meg was discovered giving to Anne?" asked Jane.

"We were naïve, thinking the king would not question the remedies Anne had ordered. We should have known; he is endlessly in discussion with his physicians worrying about his health. Meg remains in the Tower but, one day, she will be free."

"And if I become the king's mistress, this will be my responsibility?"

"Yes, as it was Madge's before you. My husband, Eddie, and I shall be at court for a few weeks, I shall distract the king but it is possible you will be forced into his bed before the end of the month. Prepare yourself well, Jane, and if you are able to avoid becoming with child, then take whatever measures you see fit."

Bessie opened the doors, beckoning to the women who made up Anne's court.

Jane's mind was churning. She hurried to the writing desk, desperate to write, to clear her mind from the reams of words trying to fight their way free. Opening the polished wooden sides and folding out the leather sloping table, she unfurled the sheet of parchment and began to write.

"Jane In Anger," she muttered. "Anger will carry me through because all hope is lost."

Three days later, Jane realised life at court was about to fracture. Despite Anne's magnificent procession into banquet the previous evening the atmosphere was one of fear. Whispers and rumours ricocheted like demons through the rooms and, while Anne tried to rise above it, commanding music, dance and gaiety as the plans for the May Day joust abounded, a darkness stretched below every laugh, each song echoing like a death march in the feet of the dancers.

Jane watched from the shadows, enjoying her traditional position as shy, demure Miss Seymour, as the king's friends lounged in the queen's rooms. Anne's ladies sparkling as they entertained, flirting and giggling. Sir Henry Norris sat beside Anne and as Jane passed, she caught a snippet of conversation.

"I miss her," he whispered. "My wife, Mary, was everything to me and now I walk in dead man's shoes as I try to build a life without my beloved."

Lady Mary Norris had died two years earlier and Sir Henry had never recovered and, despite rumours of a betrothal to Madge Shelton, he had resisted. Anne squeezed his hand in an affectionate gesture. "When you are ready, you will know…" Jane heard her say as she walked to the group surrounding the handsome musician, Mark Smeaton.

In another corner a rowdy card game took place led by Thomas Wyatt, Robert Page, William Brereton and George Boleyn. The door opened and her brother, Edward, was announced. Bowing towards the queen, he spoke to her, awaiting her smiling response before searching the crowd. Jane watched, not moving until he finally found her. To her surprise, he held her cloak over his arm. Hurrying towards her, he swung it around her shoulders, bowing to Anne. As Jane curtseyed, Edward marched her from the room and along the quiet corridors in the direction of Jane's rooms.

"What has happened?" she asked. "Is it mother or father?"

"No, I have an urgent message from the king," he replied, and Jane felt her face flush with anger and embarrassment. "He insists you move house before the joust. There are plans afoot of which he wishes you to remain innocent. He will have you leave this evening…"

"What?" Jane spluttered. "He has no right to send me away…"

"He has every right; he is king and, whether you wish to admit it or not, he has been courting you for months. You are the only person refusing to see what is happening."

Jane felt sick. She was aware but had hoped by ignoring it, the king would return to Anne and take pride in his new son. "Where is he sending me?" she asked, fear swooping through her.

"To Beddington Hall, the country house of our cousin, Nicholas Carew. You are to remain there while…" Her brother stopped speaking, a guilty flush sweeping his thin face as though he had revealed too much.

"While…?" she prompted. "What's happening, Edward?"

"While plans are put into place allowing Father and I to arrange your marriage terms with Cromwell."

The words gripped her like a prison sentence. "Marriage? To whom? I have been informed of no such agreement."

"Who do you think?" Edward snapped, his arm gripping hers with such force she whimpered. "Your maid is packing; you will leave court this evening with an escort of the king's guard. Speak to no one, it's imperative you are gone from here."

They arrived at her door.

"I shall see you at Beddington Hall," he said and waited while Jane entered.

"What's happening?" asked Audrey as Jane stared around at the upheaval in her rooms.

A few hours ago, when she had left to accompany Anne and the other ladies for a walk in the gardens before returning to the queen's court, her rooms had been as she had left them. Looking around she saw her books had been packed, her desk cleared and through the open door to her bedchamber maids moved around, stripping her sheets, removing her curtains and packing her clothes.

"I was told to supervise the packing of your belongings but no one would tell me why," said Audrey.

"Have there been any letters?" Jane asked, not replying to Audrey's question.

"None," Audrey said. "Please, my lady, why are we packing with such haste?"

"Events have overtaken us," said Jane. "My brother has informed me it is the king's wish that I should move to stay with my cousins, Sir Nicholas and Lady Elizabeth Carew at Beddington Hall. We ride this evening; but you must not accompany me."

Jane marched through the chaos of the packing servants and into the bedchamber where she dismissed the three maids folding the bed curtains.

"You must leave," said Jane when she and Audrey were alone. "Take the manuscript, the letters, anything incriminating and hide it at Marquess House. I shall lend you a gown and give you money to enable you to travel more swiftly. If you are nobility, paths will be cleared, one of Francis's men will accompany you. When Francis returns from his diplomatic trip, he will arrange safe passage for you to Ireland to stay with Lady Joan Fitzgerald, wife of James Butler, Earl of Ormond. Take Jasper and Lois, they will be safe there until we can join you."

"But Jane…"

"I shall write to Bessie this evening," Jane continued. "There is no time to lose; the king runs mad and we must act before it's too late."

"Too late for whom?"

"For us all."

CHAPTER THREE

Running footsteps echoed along the corridor. Jane threw her sewing aside and leapt to her feet, her heart pounding. Lizzie Carew crashed through the doors.

"The prince is dead," she gasped and Jane felt the world tilt.

"How?" she demanded.

"No one is certain," replied Lizzie. "Bessie has been told that the king and queen were in the nursery with the prince. The babe was crying and the king held him, comforting him, then Anne screamed and Henry Norris, William Brereton, George Boleyn and Sir Francis Weston who were in the outer rooms ran to her aid. The king had placed the prince in his lavish golden cot but he was no longer breathing. It has been claimed by the royal physicians the child was victim of a fit."

"No," hissed Jane. "The king murdered him…"

"Jane, have a care," Lizzie ran to her, gripping Jane's arm, forcing her to stop.

"And Anne?"

"She is broken, her mental state near collapse. Anne's moment of triumph and safety has vanished like a will-o'-the-wisp."

Biting hard on her lip to stop the hot, angry tears that were welling in her eyes, Jane turned away. This was the news she had been dreading since her arrival at Beddington Hall. With the child gone, the king could move with brutal swiftness to clear the path of his much-despised second wife but Jane was struggling to comprehend the violence meted out by the king.

"There was no funeral," Lizzie continued, "the king ordered the child to be buried in the Tower of London. No one but Cromwell knows the exact position of the grave."

"Lizzie, this is shocking," gulped Jane. "What happens next?"

"The May Day joust is to go ahead as planned; the king claims it is a tribute to the prince."

Appalled, Jane turned away, trying to compose herself. Henry was insane, his son was dead and Jane had no doubt it was by the king's own hand. He was wooing her as though he were a single man while plotting the removal of his queen and his greed was plunging the country into a financial disaster.

"Norris spent the night searching for a Catholic priest who would be willing to take his confession, even though it's illegal," Lizzie whispered. "He refuses to speak about what he saw but he is desperate to leave court, however, the king refuses to grant permission. He said Norris can leave after the joust."

In a moment of clarity, Jane understood. "He will arrest Norris at the joust," she said.

"You could be right," replied Lizzie. "Sir Thomas Audley, the Lord Chancellor and Thomas Cromwell have set up two commissions of oyer and terminer in the counties of Middlesex and Kent. The Duke of Norfolk has been appointed to one and Sir Thomas Boleyn, the other."

"Who are they for?" Jane had gasped, aware from conversations in the past with Francis that this legal paperwork was usually created after an arrest as it provided the framework to begin an investigation and prosecution of a serious criminal offence, the most serious of which was treason.

"No one knows," Lizzie had whispered.

Jane wondered if Anne had suspected her life and that of her son were in jeopardy as the day before Jane's sudden departure from court, the queen had broken down, weeping, begging Jane to take care of her daughter, Elizabeth, who was under the care of Lady Margaret Bryan, Jane's mother-in-law.

"Whatever happens to me," Anne had whispered, "watch over Elizabeth. She is my legacy and she will be a great queen, I have seen her power in a dream."

"Anne, you'll be able to watch over her yourself," Jane had tried to reassure her.

"No, Jane, my days are short. The Holy Maid of Kent prophesied that the king would meet disaster if he divorced Katherine of Aragon. Did you know that in her book of prophecy there is an image that shows Henry, Katherine and me?"

"Of course it does," said Jane. "She was an old fraud. Her entire success was based around you, Katherine and the king. It doesn't mean any of it was true and she's been dead for two years."

"The picture of me was missing its head," whispered Anne, continuing as though Jane had never spoken. "I saw the same image of myself in the dream which raised my daughter, Elizabeth, up high. Promise me, Jane. If you become queen in my stead, care for Elizabeth and her sister, Mary. The king has pushed her away, too, blaming me for his cruelty towards her but this is untrue. You must do better than me. You must bring the sisters together and, if you have a son, beware the king."

Anne's words hung heavy on Jane's heart. *Beware the king.* This was not advice she could heed because the king was overwhelming her life. Her days at Beddington were busy with planning a lavish wedding chest. Each gown, pair of sleeves, delivery of jewels clutched Jane's heart with fear. While those around her believed she was nervous of taking on a public role, Jane's terror ran deeper. She was married to Sir Francis Bryan, they had two children and yet, she was being presented to the king as an innocent maiden. To marry him was to commit bigamy, a serious crime and, as such, any children she might bear the king — even though such a thought made her shudder — would be illegitimate.

"All we can do is wait," she said, reaching out to Lizzie, "and pray." It was then she noticed the embroidered five-pointed star on her friend's shoulder.

"There are few members of the court who do not wear Bessie's symbol," said Lizzie, touching the five red points. "Unrest abounds, the king is running mad and Fitzroy is seen as the solution. Hold your nerve, my dear, all is not finished."

Three days later, Jane received the news that Mark Smeaton had been arrested and admitted to adultery with Queen Anne. The May Day joust took place and while the nobility glittered and entertained, a letter from Lady Stukeley assured Jane the atmosphere was strained and brittle. When the king left with Henry Norris, a wave of anger washed around the lists, especially when hours later, Sir Henry languished in the Tower of London accused of treason. The following day Anne was arrested, her crime was to have committed adultery with her brother, George Boleyn, and the courtiers Sir Henry Norris, Sir Francis Weston, William Brereton and the musician, Mark Smeaton. Also arrested were the poet Sir Thomas Wyatt and courtier, Sir Richard Page.

"There are rumours Sir Francis is to be brought home for questioning too," said Nicholas Carew to Jane as he broke the news.

Jane turned away, horrified. "What is to happen to them all?" she asked.

"At present they are being questioned and it is possible Thomas Wyatt and Richard Page will be released," said Nicholas. "However, word has reached me that the trials for Norris, Smeaton, Weston and Brereton have been set for the 12th of May."

"What about Anne and George?"

"It's unconfirmed but the Duke of Norfolk has been told to arrange another hearing on the 15th of May, although, the accused have not yet been named. However, as you are to return to London after this date it is likely this is the day Anne and George will be tried," continued Nicholas. "Your wedding to the king will be arranged after the outcome of Anne's trial."

"But she may be innocent," said Jane.

"Doubtful," replied Nicholas, his face grim, "and if such a miracle were to occur, Henry has ordered Cromwell to annul the marriage."

"On what grounds?"

"Does it matter? The king no longer wishes to be married to Anne and, despite the fact I often argued with her and knew how awkward she could be, I never dreamed it would come to this. What the king plans is not far away from murder."

Two weeks later, the day of Anne's trial dawned and Jane sat in her private solar in her house in Chelsea, praying. Even life as an anchorite nun, the punishment Anne had dreaded, would be better than execution. Anne was young, vibrant, her crime was her verve and beauty, which caused her to be dangled in front of the king by her ambitious relatives. If she had been given her own way, Anne would now be living in Ireland, the wife of James Butler, instead she was on trial for treason, when everyone knew she was innocent of the monstrous list of crimes accredited to her.

A few days earlier, the king had insisted Jane return to London, claiming he could not bear to be without her by his side. A house on the river at Chelsea had been prepared and Henry declared he wanted Jane to ride under the royal banner. It was Nicholas Carew who had dissuaded the love-drunk king.

"The people of London are unpredictable, Your Majesty," he had claimed. "Let us keep their new, demure queen a surprise which they will relish when you reveal her to their loving embrace."

"Why did you say we were better travelling anonymously?" Jane had asked as they had left Surrey the following day under Nicholas Carew's arms.

"When Anne was first arrested, many believed she deserved such punishment," Nicholas had explained, "but throughout her incarceration the king has publicly humiliated her, yet she has maintained her innocence, acting throughout her trial with dignity. Opinion has softened towards her, especially as the king is striding around beaming and laughing in a way he hasn't done for years. With Henry's constant disappearances to see you, his jaunts to Jericho with a variety of other young ladies, sympathy is growing for Anne. Henry is losing popularity, his subjects long ago realised he was a tyrant in the making, his behaviour towards the queen for whom he changed the country's religion and killed hundreds of people, is causing much unrest. There has been rioting in London, Coventry, Norfolk and the Cornish are in open rebellion."

"Will they accept me?" Jane had asked.

"You are very different and you are unknown, yet it behoves us to proceed with caution."

Lizzie Carew knocked on the door, bringing Jane back to the unease of the present. "For you," she said, handing Jane a letter, "from the king."

Dreading another love note featuring terrible poetry, Jane turned away from Lizzie to open it. The king's arrogant handwriting leapt from the page in schoolboy glee as he announced that she would 'hear of Anne's condemnation before 3pm'. It was 9am; her cousin's life was no longer even being counted in weeks, perhaps it would be days. If the king set a precedence with Anne, what would happen if she, Jane, upset him? Would her fate be as brutal as her cousin's?

Sickened, Jane crumpled the note in her hand, not even reading the six-line poem. It would be dreadful in its childish pomposity. The balled-up letter hovered over the fire, before Jane changed her mind, instead smoothing it open and reading its content. Word had reached her from Chapuys, the Spanish ambassador, that when Henry had dined with the Bishop of Castille a few days earlier, he had proudly shown the man his notebook of self-penned poems and ballads.

Not long ago, Anne and George had teased Henry about some of his dubious couplets, laughing at his inadequate grasp of rhyme and metre. While the king had smiled, he had clearly been insulted as Jane had heard one of the charges laid against Anne and George was the mocking of the king's person. Not wishing to antagonise him, she read the lines, memorising them so that she could whisper them to him as though they were works of art when he next visited.

"What is it?" asked Lizzie as Jane rose.

"I need some air," she said and strode from the room towards the stables.

She wanted to ride, to feel the wind in her hair, to breathe freely away from the stench of murder, away from the fact that these people, her family and friends, were being tried and executed because of her. The king might be the person organising the carnage but it was in order to marry her and their blood was as much on her hands as the king's. Anne's words returned to her, 'Beware the king'.

Bessie's urging that the king was no longer to be trusted, that they would all be safer if her son Fitzroy were to rule with the wise counsel of women from the shadows, returned like a whisper on the breeze as Jane hurried to the stables. When Bessie had suggested the slow poisoning of the king, Jane had been horrified, *but*, she thought, as the groom helped her into the saddle of one of Nicholas's finest mares, *where my hand might once have been reluctant to add death drop by drop to the king's wine, now it is eager, as perhaps Anne's had been before the poison was discovered and Meg was arrested. If this task passes to me, I will ensure I shall do all I can to remove this tyrant from the throne.*

Returning several hours later, exhausted but with a calm, focussed mind after the exertion, Jane was startled to see a horse she recognised being brushed by one of the assistant grooms. Hurrying to dismount, she did not concern herself with her dishevelled appearance, running up the stairs and through the labyrinth of corridors to the sumptuous parlours above. Throwing open the door to her day room it took every shred of her self-control not to shout his name and throw herself into his arms.

"Mistress Seymour," he exclaimed, "you're back at last."

"Sir Francis," she gasped, aware they were surrounded by Nicholas, Lizzie and several members of her staff. Unsure whom she could trust, who might be reporting to the king, she turned to Nicholas, her eyes blazing. "Sir Nicholas," she said, "Sir Francis and I have matters of great importance to discuss.

Private matters," she emphasised but Nicholas was already ushering everyone from the room.

"You won't be disturbed," he assured them.

The door shut and Francis gathered her into his arms.

"Jane, my love, we don't have long. I have been sent by the king to inform you that Anne and her brother, George, will be found guilty of treason. The outcome is a forgone conclusion but few are happy with this turn of events. Even those who didn't like Anne or George believe the king runs mad."

"Will anyone be able to stop him?" she asked.

"No, the verdict will stand, the Duke of Norfolk will see to it…"

"But he's their uncle," she exclaimed.

"And he is loyal to the king and himself, no one else matters."

"How are my aunt and uncle?"

"Broken. Elizabeth Boleyn has been ill for some months and this blow may weaken her beyond saving. As for Thomas, I think he is as lost in his mind as was his mother before him. He has left court, or perhaps been banished, no one is sure."

"Francis, this is awful," she murmured, unable to comprehend the horror laid out before her.

"There is more," he said, his face set with a grimace. "Henry intends to execute all those he has accused along with Anne. George, Henry Norris, William Brereton and Mark Smeaton are to be executed on the 17th of May. On the 19th of May, a French swordsman will execute Anne."

"He is going to murder the queen in order to marry me." Jane felt her knees sag and was grateful to Francis for catching her and guiding her to a nearby chair.

"He is going to murder them all," said Francis, his voice shaking.

"No," Jane clutched his hand, "this is true evil."

A wall of blood and death loomed before her. While it might not be of her making, the king's infatuation with her was the cause. As his plan unfurled itself into her understanding, she said, "But what of the others? None of them deserve to die. Why is William Brereton even on the list? How could he have a part in the queen's downfall when he is usually on the Welsh Marches."

"He has been causing Cromwell some difficulty," said Francis. "Cromwell has taken his chance to remove him."

"How are the other members of the Privy Council allowing this to happen?" she asked.

"Most people have a secret that could be exploited by Cromwell or the king, and while few believe these trials have been fair or the accusations true, fear is holding their tongues as silently as when God spoke to Ezekiel, striking him dumb."

"No one will defend Anne?" asked Jane.

Francis shook his head. "None, and Anne has issued an order this should be the case as she fears that any who try to aid her will be punished. Instead, she has told those who wish to avenge her death to support Bessie and Fitzroy, especially since the king has lavished his son with many of the titles he had once been bestowed upon George Boleyn."

"And what of me?" asked Jane, her fear being replaced by a calm, white fury. "Through the machinations of my brother, I am to be betrothed to the king the moment Anne is executed. My opinion has never been sought, I have been pushed from one scheme to another, denying our marriage, hiding our children and now you wish me to become queen in order to — what? Send me to the block too?"

"No, my love, you know your role, you are there to continue what Anne began. You must have the courage of the lion of

England. As queen, you are the closest person to the king. You must weaken him irreparably so that when the moment comes for him to ride into battle, he will lose to Fitzroy and peace will once again be brought to England."

"You're as mad as Henry," she hissed, pulling her hands away from Francis.

"Mad?" Francis said and Jane could see anger flaring in his eyes. "Mad to want to spare my wife? I hate every moment of seeing the king pawing you but if Bessie and Fitzroy are successful, we shall soon be together as man and wife, our love spoken at last. We must be brave for a few short weeks."

"When this is done," she said, "will you promise me that we can leave court and live away from the intrigue and plotting."

"I promise with all my heart," he said, pulling her into a passionate embrace. "We have one more day together before you must return and play the part of the virgin bride. Nicholas has sent your staff away."

Burning with anger, loathing and fear, Jane thought being tumbled into bed by Francis would be the last thing she wanted, but as he kissed her a recklessness overcame her and taking his hand, she led her husband to her bedchamber.

CHAPTER FOUR

"There are crowds in the streets, hundreds and hundreds of women," Lizzie Carew shouted as she rushed into Jane's bedchamber.

"Women?" gasped Jane, throwing back her bedcovers.

"With more arriving all the time," continued Lizzie. "They are protesting about Anne's arrest and sentencing."

"Is this the beginning?" Jane asked as she called in her maids to help her dress. "Bessie said she would use every weapon she could muster; this must be her doing."

Ever since Jane's arrival in London, the king had been treating their romance with anything but caution. Every evening he would board the royal barge and ride in procession with other brightly coloured boats containing musicians, fire-eaters, performers, turning each trip into a lover's pageant as he continued to woo Jane with passion and extravagance. Defying anyone to challenge his overwhelming happiness. Nicholas Carew's words, however, proved correct and Jane received endless reports that the loyalty of the Londoners was waning. Few cheered the king when he passed on his barge, instead their voices were raised in jeers, while women shouted names: adulterer, being one of the politest. Jane's ever-present sense of disquiet grew with each passing moment. The riot of women was not a surprise, their anger had been growing for days.

Before Lizzie could respond, there was a knock on the door and Jane's brother entered, bowing before her.

"What's happening, Edward?" she said.

"There are crowds blocking the streets. The king orders they are to be dispersed, in the meantime, you and the princesses are to board a barge and take refuge in the Tower of London. The boats will arrive in the next hour and we shall sail with the tide. Word has come from Lincoln that forty thousand men have gathered under the banner of the five wounds of Christ and are preparing to march on London."

Jane's eyes widened in delight.

"Fitzroy is leading the charge from Lincoln, while in Yorkshire, Robert Aske is heading to join him with more rebels," Edward continued. "The king plans to lead his own troops to stop the rebellion and he asked me to accompany him, requiring my advice after all my years as a soldier." Edward's excitement was palpable.

"And...?" Jane prompted.

"He is drawing up the legislation to make you regent in his absence. Jane, you will be the most powerful person in the country, you will be the monarch."

Edward hurried from the room and with a smile, Jane turned to Lizzie. "We shall avenge them all," she said, before calling to her women. "Quickly, we leave for the Tower of London with the tide."

Workmen were fortifying the Tower as Jane led the princesses, Mary and Elizabeth, into the courtyard. Both had been declared illegitimate and bore the titles The Lady Mary and The Lady Elizabeth but to Jane they were of royal blood and she insisted they were treated in this manner. Staring around in wonder, Jane could feel the tension, the energy of battle as soldiers marched past, men shouted, dogs barked and horses whinnied. Stonemasons and carpenters hammered re-enforcements, while on Tower Green another group prepared a scaffold. A wave of nausea enveloped her, followed by the smallest flicker of hope. If Fitzroy was marching and Londoners were rioting, would the king, weakened by weeks of subtle poison, be easier to overthrow? Jane wondered if they might yet save Anne. However, before she could walk towards her own apartments, a herald wearing royal livery appeared at her side.

"My lady, the king requires an audience," he said, bowing low.

"Lady Carew, please accompany me," she called to Lizzie.

As she entered the king's presence chamber, Jane stiffened. The atmosphere was tense and Henry sat on his vast chair, his face blotchy with anger, his fists clenched. The rot from the wound on his leg gave off an unpleasant stench that was not disguised despite the heavy perfumes with which he had been anointed, even the burning of sweet oils were ineffective. A fall from his horse had been the cause of the wound and despite many months of treatments from his trusted physicians, his flesh refused to heal. Jane hoped this was due to Anne's administering of slow poison, a task she herself now relished.

"Your Majesty," said Jane, sweeping a gracious curtsey before approaching the king, swallowing hard so as not to gag at the stench. "May I be of assistance?"

The king scowled. Beside him stood Cromwell, her brother, Edward, the dukes of Suffolk and Norfolk and Cromwell's assistant, Thomas Wriothesley.

"What do you know of this?" the king demanded and Jane felt a faint flutter of fear.

"My lord?" she said, as though confused by his question.

"These women," he continued, "you are a woman, why would they behave in such a manner?"

Before she could speak, the Duke of Norfolk gave a derisive snort. "These women are being controlled by their men," he snarled. "Women would never be able to organise such a rebellion. While we are worrying about them, your abomination of a son has declared himself King of Ireland and Wales, and is riding towards London at the head of an ever-growing army. Who are these women to question you, Your Majesty?"

Henry roared in displeasure and Jane flinched. "Women, always women! They are the bane of my life." Jane wondered if the king would strike her as he turned to her. "You must address these harpies," he snarled, his face in hers, red, sweating, his breath thick with wine. "Norfolk will accompany you. Go out to these women, tell them to go home, or things will be the worse for them. Have I not shown my nerves will not take impudence? Send them away, Jane. I have greater problems to deal with today."

The Duke of Norfolk opened his mouth to protest but Cromwell had already cut across him, blocking his path to the king, who was rifling through the papers strewn on the huge table at the centre of the room.

"Come, my lady," Norfolk muttered, steering Jane away.

Moments later, Jane found herself surrounded by guards being led towards the battlements of the White Tower and her apartments.

"You can't face this crowd," said Norfolk, his mouth a thin line of fury. "They will tear you limb from limb. The rage against the executions has been growing for weeks. London is a tinderbox ready to explode. Many are blaming you for Anne's death. You must remain inside and I will deal with this nonsense. Your task is to distract the king, I shall send him to you presently. Calm him, soothe him; we cannot afford for the king to lose control."

Jane's mind was whirring. The rebellion had begun. Fitzroy was leading an army towards London in order to challenge his father to the throne. Jane felt a thrill of excitement run through her. She knew how important it was to continue her part in the plan. Things would be so much easier for Fitzroy if the throne were already empty; the war could be avoided and the young duke could ride in triumph to his new kingdom.

Wondering how she would be able to finish her appointed task, Jane tried to focus her wilding thoughts, to focus. Reaching into her pocket for her banned rosary, she let the beads slither through her fingers. Praying to Mother Mary, she asked for an opportunity to present itself, to end the war, to aid Fitzroy and Bessie. If she were successful and cleared the throne, there would be no need for war, Jane could spare hundreds of lives.

Delighted by this thought, Jane was smiling when her herald opened the door to her apartments. However, the sight of her women, their faces shocked, some in tears, as they unpacked her trunks brought her back to the difficulties surrounding them. Many clutched Bibles and fear was etched across their faces. Jane gave an inward sigh and wondered how Queen Katherine would have behaved under such circumstances.

Smiling as warmly as she could manage, she glided to the centre of the room. "Ladies, you need have no fear, we are safe in this stronghold with the king. He consults with your wise husbands who are offering guidance and advice. Let us pray for a swift deliverance from these problems."

Indicating her chair to be brought to the middle of the chamber, Jane seated herself and began to recite the prayers she had memorised in order to impress Queen Katherine. Around her the women knelt or bowed their heads, while Jane forced her voice to gentleness, resisting the urge to race through them, aware there was little she could do except wait until she was alone with the king. Even thinking these words made her shiver in exquisite terror.

The day passed with agonising slowness. Outside, soldiers drilled in the courtyard, their shouts fierce, full of blood lust. Accompanying this was endless hammering and shouting, the background noise to the joint tasks of building both reinforcements and finishing the scaffold. Within the Tower, Jane waited for a summons to join the king. As she finished her evening meal, her brother arrived, beaming with excitement.

"The women have been dispersed but the king and Cromwell intend to show them the error of their ways," he grinned. "Tomorrow, Anne will be executed as a punishment for these harpies. It is only a day earlier, who will care?"

"I care," gasped Jane before she could stop herself.

Edward shot her a look of disgust. "Then you must stop caring and support the king because this is his intention. When he is a widower, Archbishop Cranmer will perform a quiet marriage ceremony. The king intends to leave within the week in order to crush the rebels, when you will become regent."

"And if he stays?"

"You will remain his loyal wife," snapped Edward. "Do not doubt the bravery of the king, he will ride out to meet Fitzroy and he will crush him to dust."

Jane stared at Edward transfixed. She had to warn Bessie.

"Don't think you can write to anyone," Edward hissed in her ear. "You're being watched. Have your women dress you and this evening you will entertain the king."

Jane walked into her bedchamber on stiff legs, her emotions numb. Anne's trial had been set for the 15th May. Jane's women tidied her hair, slid jewel-encrusted sleeves on to her arms and a heavy gable hood was placed over her hair. *Demure*, she thought, *a stark contrast to the racy French hoods associated with Anne.*

Jane stared at herself. Despite the old-fashioned hood, she could not deny she looked magnificent, better than ever before in her life. Had the circumstances been different, she would have revelled in the splendour of the jewels, the clothes, the sheer extravagance of being queen, but the price of these baubles and trinkets was too high and she would gladly dispense with them all.

As Jane took her place beside the king, she adopted a concerned and understanding expression as she listened to Henry vacillate between delight at being with Jane, and self-righteous posturing as he blamed the women of London for Anne's fate before dissolving into maudlin crocodile tears for his lost son. As she left, he kissed her hand.

"Tomorrow, my love," he whispered, "we shall be together at last."

If Jane had sat through a longer night, she could not remember it. Unable to send a message to her cousin, she instead took comfort in prayer, a habit she had adopted while serving Katherine of Aragon. The heavy pall of night lightened into grey and Jane prayed with her rosary as she watched the solemn procession follow its slow and inexorable path towards the scaffold. Anne was flanked by her sister, Mary Boleyn, Bessie Blount, Lady Berkeley and Lady Stukeley, all the women who had borne the king sons. As Anne praised the king in her final earthly speech, the women stood silent. Jane watched through streaming eyes, desperate to look away but forcing herself to pray as her cousin knelt in the straw and in the twinkling of a flash of steel, it was done. Anne's body tilted and slumped to one side, Mary Boleyn stifled a sob of horror and the queen of England was dead.

Four hours later, Jane stood beside Henry VIII and became his third wife.

CHAPTER FIVE

Jane stared down at her elaborate gown. Each item of clothing she wore shimmered in the spring sunshine. Jewels weighed heavy around her neck, rings glowed on her fingers and her feet were shod in the softest of leather and silk slippers, embroidered with pearls, golden and silver thread so they sparkled as she walked.

I am Queen Consort of England, she thought, staring at herself in the mirror. *The third wife of Henry VIII.*

Turning away from her glittering reflection, Jane pondered her rise in status. It was not of her doing but was the orders of the king, yet she still could not reconcile such a position with herself.

"I am Queen consort," she said aloud.

Whenever she entered a room, people bowed, reminding her of a colourful, bejewelled wheatfield in the breeze, each stalk rippling in penitence, yet fury rose in her at this subservience. Mere months ago, no one would have even glanced in her direction when she made her way through the viperous crowds of the court. *With such speed do things change*, she thought in contempt.

Henry Fitzroy continued to cut a swathe across the middle of England, each day pressing closer and closer to the capital where his father waited, his fury growing. Jane, beside the king, wondered how long her tenure as queen would endure. Hull had surrendered, its army joining Fitzroy as he made impassioned speeches, promising to allow men to worship as they saw fit, an end to heavy taxation, to peace with France, Spain and Italy. The streets reverberated with cheers for the handsome young prince and in York he was declared King of Ireland and Wales. Each day, the king declared, if it were not for his advisers who were determined to keep him a virtual prisoner in the Tower of London, he would ride to meet his ungrateful son in battle.

It was ten days since Anne's execution and each night when the king joined her in the bedchamber, Jane would close her eyes and pretend it was Francis's arms that encircled her, his mouth kissing her. It was the only way she could endure bedding the king. His bulk overwhelmed her, the rippling flesh going to flab since he no longer hunted and jousted with such enthusiasm. While he murmured endearments, she felt he was as detached from her as she was from him; she could be any female body, any of his mistresses. Jane often wondered if he called her 'Sweetheart' while in her bed so he would not have to worry about saying the wrong name aloud.

Continuing with her demure persona, she had been reluctant to remove her ornate shift on her wedding night for fear he might notice her body did not have the tautness of a maid. The king, delighted by this show of modesty had agreed, falling asleep as soon as he had grunted his way to a climax. The smear of blood on the sheets, discovered by her women the following morning, had come from Jane's toe, sliced open with a silver fruit knife while the king slept in order to perpetuate her myth of being a virgin bride.

Despite this, dark rumours had begun, which she hoped would not reach the ears of the king, or worse, Thomas Cromwell.

"Her body does not look like that of a maid," Dorothy Howard, Countess of Derby had muttered after the wedding night.

Meanwhile, the Spanish ambassador, Eustace Chapuys had been heard to comment that he doubted Jane could still be a virgin after spending so many years at the Henrician court. "These halls are too debauched and she has lived too long under the care of a single man."

The king would hear nothing against her and with his fascination remaining constant, Jane continued to play her role of a demure, devoted Tudor wife.

Yet, as the shock of her new position receded, the power of being queen appealed to Jane. Having always been on the edges of society, ignored as insignificant, commanded by her parents and her brothers, her life not her own but to be directed by others, the potency of her new authority was washing over her like the heat from a fire on an icy day. For the first time in her life she could demand loyalty, she could direct her own fate. The nobility clamoured for her attention, begging favours, requesting her to intercede with the king on their behalf, to give places to their daughters in her court. While women who had dismissed or insulted her now sycophantically laughed at her weakest jests, agreed with her most outlandish comments and it hardened Jane's heart.

Jane and her women were watched closely. Edward assured her this was for her safety; she was above suspicion as were her women. Her years of playing the part of demure wallflower who was no threat acted as a perfect blind when in reality, Jane was receiving regular updates from Bessie Blount.

"Continue with your task as planned. The King of Ireland and Wales is days away..." one coded letter had read and Jane had felt a thrill of fear as she threw it on the fire. Turning towards the door of her inner chamber, Jane had taken barely a step when it was flung open by her sister, Elizabeth, a widow, who had returned to court upon their eldest brother's wishes. Although close as children, their separation of years had made them cautious around each other and Jane understood that Bess's desire to help her was not due to sororal love but to advance herself to a spectacular second marriage. However, Bess was unimpressed by the suggestion of a match with Gregory Cromwell, the son of Sir Thomas Cromwell.

"The family must be together," Edward had snarled when he had insisted Bess be at Jane's side, "we must show that not all English nobles are as troublesome as the Boleyns."

Whereas once the families had worked together in order to place Anne on the throne, since her downfall, the Seymours had distanced themselves from the Howards and the Boleyns, no longer claiming kinship, denying all but the most distant of connections. Bess followed Jane and, as they entered the presence chamber, there was a flurry of activity as the women cast aside games, poetry and sewing in order to fall to the floor in an obeisance.

"Rise, rise," snapped Jane, "this is unnecessary."

The women returned to their seats and Jane settled in her ornately carved chair. It was situated nearest the fire and light shone through the stained-glass window, draping her in a rainbow of colour. Aware all eyes were upon her; Jane forced a smile.

"My ladies," she said, "as you are aware, we women must prove we can be pious, trustworthy and demure." She ignored Lizzie Carew who quickly turned a laugh into a cough. "As I wouldn't dream of questioning the king about his decisions, we must never vex or stress our lords." Glancing up, her eyes brimming with laughter, she continued, "After all, their tiny minds can only cope with one thing at a time and they are usually preoccupied with remembering to breathe."

Lizzie laughed, unable to resist and the women followed suit, some gleeful, others nervous or disgusted.

"Come ladies," said Jane, clapping her hands and summoning her minstrels. "Play us a happy refrain, let us lift the mood of this court."

Jane's demands were a cover for her true feelings. Inside she remained sick at heart at Anne's death but she knew if music and glee emanated from her rooms, the king would be unable to resist joining them and with the diversion of the laughing courtiers, she might be able to add another dose of poison to his wine. Striking up a lively tune, the room filled with the hum of chatter. The afternoon wore on, the music played, the women danced, laughter spilled into the corridors, as poetry was read, with Jane judging which pieces reached her standards; then a sound from the corridor caused Jane's heart to freeze. Boots marching, ringing on the stone floors, the official guard, halting outside the door.

As though doused by a curse, the warmth and joy vanished, Jane's heart pounded as she sat up, alert: was this how it had been when Anne had been arrested? An afternoon of levity interrupted by the harshest of accusations? The vial of poison nestling in its silken pouch hidden within the folds of her skirt seemed to glow. Was her reign to be so short? Had the king already discovered her involvement in the rebellion?

Her women all turned to her but before she could speak, her herald called, "His Majesty, the king."

Beaming, Henry strode into Jane's chambers like a colossus, a giant in ermine and velvet, dripping with jewels, his hat perched at a jaunty angle designed to disguise the spot where his hair was thinning and Jane breathed out in relief. With the king were his favourites, Charles Brandon, Nicholas Carew and to Jane's surprise, Francis.

"We heard laughter and dancing," announced the king, hurrying to her side, "we have come to join the fun."

"My love, this is a delight," called Jane, indicating for her musicians to continue playing, her cheeks flushing with embarrassment as the king took her hand.

"You are pleased to see me, sweetheart?" he whispered, misinterpreting her blush, before kissing her cheek, his hand sliding around her waist. She could feel the scorching looks of Francis.

"I have been unable to remove you from my mind," Henry whispered into her ear, pulling her closer, his hand sliding up her waist, resting below her breasts. "You are a surprise, my lady, I did not expect you to have such knowledge in the bedroom."

Jane's blush deepened.

"Come, my love, let us entertain our friends," said the king, taking a goblet of wine. "It has been a long time since I was able to enjoy such pleasures as an afternoon with my closest compatriots. Such a time it was when I was scared to enter the queen's chambers for fear of my former wife's sharp tongue."

As Jane sank back, Henry boomed out the many occasions when he and Anne had quarrelled, stating at the end of his monologue that, "I never made a wiser choice than to rid myself of that turbulent woman."

Around him were fractured laughs and uncomfortable noises, which the king interpreted as agreement. He turned to Charles Brandon and began discussing the merits of the swordsman over the axe, each word leaving Jane sickened. "I showed my devotion as husband though," he claimed. "I designed Anne's scaffold myself. Let us hope I never need to use it again. Whereas now, with this woman —" he tried to haul Jane on to his knee but her skirts caught around his chair and she stumbled — "this demure creature of unblemished virtue, there is no doubt of our union. I have no wives living. Our union will be blessed with a legitimate son, a prince of whom I can be proud, a sturdy youth who will continue my father's illustrious line of kings."

Panic rose in Jane's chest; the king might have no other living spouse but this was not something she could claim. If they were discovered, it would mean death for them all, her family included. Forcing a smile, she waved to her sister to organise more refreshments but before she could rise to issue instructions, a cannon boomed and an explosion shook the ground.

"What is this?" shouted the king, soldiers running into the room to surround him.

Jane and Lizzie exchanged a terrified glance. As Henry began issuing instructions, Francis whispered to Jane, "Fitzroy has arrived; the signal was the cannon, he has taken London."

Outside came the sound of cheering, of men shouting, women screaming and the metallic clatter of horses' hooves on cobbles.

"Sire, they have breached the Tower of London," shouted the Duke of Norfolk, running into the room. "Fitzroy has claimed the throne, he requests your abdication and has issued a warrant for your arrest."

"In whose name?" screamed Henry. "Bring this boy to me and I will show him who is king."

"He is supported by over twenty thousand men," returned Norfolk.

"I will meet this unnatural child in the throne room and he will rue the day he ever believed he was worthy of my father's crown, of my crown." With a roar, Henry marched from the room.

Jane waited in the stunned silence, her fingers playing with the bottle of poison.

CHAPTER SIX

The great hall at the Tower of London was long and narrow. The afternoon light shone through the leaded windows as dust motes drifted in the spring sunshine. King Henry VIII sat on his throne, the jewels in his crown radiating colour, a rainbow of power around his white and angry face. Beside him sat Jane, her hands folded into the skirts of her ornate cloth of gold gown, on her head was a gable hood encrusted with jewels which had once belonged to Katherine of Aragon. On her chest was pinned the brooch, depicting her devotion to Jesus but which gave a hint at her own initials. The golden 'B' pendant synonymous with Anne drifted through her mind, then away.

Around Henry were his loyal men: Thomas Cromwell, the dukes of Suffolk and Norfolk, Edward Seymour, Nicholas Carew and Francis Bryan. Jane, with Lizzie Carew and Bess by her side, kept her eyes lowered, while in her chest, her heart beat fast as though she had been hunting for hours. Behind her, she knew Francis and Nicholas were armed; they had assured her and Lizzie that the three women would be removed should the encounter turn violent. The king, she realised as they waited, had offered no such assurance.

"Where is the evil spawn of my loins?" muttered Henry.

A time had been arranged for this meeting and the king had arrived late, showing his contempt over this entire affair. Fitzroy had trumped him and was not yet in sight. Jane shifted, uncomfortable in the heavy gown, nervous of her plan, the one she had formulated herself and discussed with no one, the poison hidden in the lining of her sleeve. Too much blood had been spilled and Jane could bear no more, it was her intention to end this debacle. Her visit to the great hall, accompanied by Lizzie Carew, had, she claimed, been to familiarise herself with the room to help her endure this ordeal with graciousness.

"If I have seen the room beforehand, I shan't be overwhelmed," had been her reasoning when questioned by her brother.

Snorting with derision he had waved two guards to accompany them but when Jane had reached the hall, as queen, she had demanded it be cleared in order for her to enter alone. Flicking her eyes upwards with the tiniest movement, she saw the goblet. Golden, jewelled, the ostentatious drinking vessel of a king, relief flooded through her like a spring tide when she saw it remained where she had left it beside the decanter of wine. One mouthful, she thought, will be enough. Meg's advice from her rooms in the Wakefield Tower had ensured the dosage and the king was obsessive that no one but he ever drank from this goblet, this decanter.

"His Majesty, King Henry of Ireland and Wales," the herald's voice rang out in the silence and outside came marching footsteps.

The double doors were flung wide and a row of three guards marched in, their livery was white bearing the emblem of the five wounds of Christ encased in a star. Jane gulped back her fear as beside her she heard Henry growl in fury. Coming to a halt, the guards stepped aside to reveal five men. Henry Fitzroy was in front, with the brothers Thomas and Hal Boleyn behind him and at the rear, Fitzroy's uncles, Louis and Alphonso Blount. Jane's first thought on seeing Fitzroy was that he had inherited the best of their looks from both his parents. The youth had his father's height and auburn colouring but the shape of his face and eyes were Bessie's.

"Father," he said, acknowledging the king with a nod, "it is good to see you keeping well."

The king leaned back in his chair, giving a "humph" of disgust, attempting to give the impression of amused calm but Jane could see his knuckles whitening on the arms of his throne. "You are an ungrateful bastard," he hissed. "There are reports you have turned my people against me."

"The work was all your own, Father," responded Fitzroy. "I have done nothing but promise to undo the mistakes you have made, to show the country the Tudors can be trusted, to make our monarchy great again."

"Our monarchy..." muttered the king. Jane could feel his anger building, the pressure of his fury filling the room like thunder before a summer storm. "You are an unworthy and unnatural demon," he roared, "a cursed and evil creature from the depths of hell, a changeling masquerading as my son. You are not king of any part of my realm; you claim you come here today to arrest me..."

"With my force of twenty thousand men and the blessing of the people of London," interrupted Fitzroy, the arrogance and ignorant bravery of youth giving him confidence. "I arrest you and demand you stand down. Your time as king is over and to prove to you that I have power over you, over your dominion, over your very soul, I shall drink the king's wine from the king's goblet."

The action was symbolic but powerful and hugely insulting and, as the youth swaggered toward the decanter, Jane watched in transfixed horror. Pouring a healthy measure of Gascon wine into the goblet, Fitzroy raised it in a toast to his father before tossing it down his throat.

Shutting her eyes, Jane prayed, begging that the dosage was incorrect, that she had misinterpreted Meg's whispered instructions but within moments, it was clear something was amiss. Fitzroy clutched his stomach, a dreadful rattling echoed from his throat. Blood pooled in his eyes and he began to foam at the mouth, before collapsing in convulsions of agony on the ground. No one dared approach the dying boy.

The king stood, his eyes narrowed as he watched the youth writhe on the floor. "Arrest them all," he declared and strode from the room, leaving Jane, her ladies-in-waiting and Henry's inner circle to stare in horror.

CHAPTER SEVEN

"Gently, please," whispered Jane. Every movement hurt, her entire body ached from the birth of her son, Prince Edward, three days earlier.

The sofa on which Jane lay was placed with great solemnity in the antechamber. The king had planned the christening and, as tradition decreed, neither Jane nor Henry would attend, instead they would wait outside until the ceremony was complete.

Jane watched as the children and ministers of the King's chapel at Hampton Court processed two by two into the beautiful building with its blue and golden ceiling. Behind them came the abbots and bishops, the lords, the ambassadors, the lord chamberlains headed by Thomas Cromwell, the Lord Privy Seal. The Duke of Norfolk followed with the Archbishop of Canterbury, Thomas Cranmer; the Earl of Sussex, Lord Montague and, to Jane's despair, Thomas Boleyn, now a widower and with only one of his five children left alive, Mary Boleyn. His remaining sons, along with Bessie's brothers, Louis and Alphonso Blount, had been executed days after Fitzroy's death from the poison Jane had meant for King Henry. Meg Blount was beheaded the same day.

Bessie had retreated from court and, while the rebellion continued to rage, even without its leader, the king with help from the dukes of Norfolk and Suffolk and Jane's brother, Edward Seymour, now Viscount Beauchamp subdued the armies. Robert Aske was hanged, drawn and quartered for his part, while eleven people including Lord Hussey, Lord Darcy and Sir Francis Bigod were found guilty of high treason and executed as rebels, with over thirty monks, laymen and villagers being punished alongside them. Jane had watched in horror as Henry had sought his bloody revenge.

It was when she discovered she was pregnant, she realised there was nothing she could do but capitulate and try to embody the role of queen. Francis divided his time between court and Ireland, giving Jane news of their children as Jasper and Lois grew. Each day for Jane was a torment, yet she believed it was what she deserved for having ruined the rebellion with her selfish act.

The doors closed on the procession and a shadow fell across Jane. Her husband glared down at her.

"Our son," he said, gesturing towards the chapel, "Edward, Prince of Wales. You have done well, Jane."

"Thank you, Your Majesty," she said with a demure smile. "Let us hope we are soon able to provide him with a brother."

Henry settled himself on the vast chair opposite her and took his time selecting a cake from the platter beside him. "But, my dear, he has a brother, does he not?"

"What...?"

"And a sister."

Jane forced a laugh. "What nonsense is this, Henry?" she said and reached for the goblet of wine, taking several gulps to steady her nerves.

"Nonsense?" he asked, his eyes watching her with satisfaction. "Did you think I wouldn't discover your secret?"

"Secret?" she whispered.

"Your marriage to Sir Francis, your hidden children in Ireland?"

"No," she gasped.

"While I was a single man when we married, you were not a single woman and, therefore, my son, the future king, is illegitimate and this cannot be allowed."

"No one will ever know," she whispered. "The secret is ours…"

"There can be no risk of scandal and I can't be seen to execute another wife so soon after disposing of Anne. In the end, my dear, it seems she was the virtuous wife who provided my true heir while you were nothing better than a scheming strumpet."

"What are you going to do to me? To Francis?"

"To Francis, nothing. He is my friend and I forgive him for becoming ensnared by your devious wiles. Like me, he was dazzled by your charm, your spells and your witchcraft."

"How…?"

"Sir Nicholas Carew, he has long been under my gaze. Cromwell was suspicious of him and his wife, Lady Elizabeth, the sister of Sir Francis."

"What have you done to them?"

"To Lady Carew, nothing. Nicholas Carew, however, was involved in another plot to try and remove me from the throne, foolish man. It was discovered before he could cover his tracks but, under Cromwell's persuasion, he spilled many other secrets, including your trip to the great hall with his wife the day my ungrateful offspring tried to steal my throne. If he had stopped before revealing your clandestine marriage, this conversation would have had a different outcome. You would have been lauded as the saviour of my throne but, alas, this cannot be. Therefore, to ensure no other man must suffer your evil wiles and to keep my son, my angel, free from the malign force of his wicked mother and the potential taint of illegitimacy, I have followed your example, my dear."

He glanced towards the wine in her hand, a cruel cold smile on his face. "The thing is, my dear, I will always be able to find another wife." He leant forward and kissed her on the cheek. "Goodbye, Queen Jane," he said and laughing, he left her alone in the antechamber.

"Henry, no..." Jane gasped as the goblet slipped from her numb fingers. She slumped back against the cushions, the poison stealing through her veins.

PART SEVEN: MARQUESS HOUSE, 2021

CHAPTER ONE

"Henry poisoned Jane Seymour," Perdita said. "For centuries history has told us she died in childbirth, but the king murdered her in cold blood." She looked at the horrified faces of Piper, Kit and Callum. They were in Perdita and Kit's living room with Perdita's notes spread on the coffee table in front of them.

"He was a psychopath," said Piper.

"Yes, there's no doubt in my mind," agreed Perdita.

"What did he mean about Nicholas Carew?" asked Kit. "Did he try to overthrow the throne?"

"This was a surprise," admitted Perdita, "and I think The Scribe changed some dates. In 1538, there was an attempt to place Henry Courtenay, Marquess of Exeter on the throne in place of Henry VIII. It was known as the Exeter Conspiracy. Courtenay was Henry's first cousin through their mothers. The king's mother was Elizabeth of York and Courtenay's mother was her younger sister, Princess Catherine of York, making him a grandson of Edward IV. His claim to the throne was far weaker than Henry's but, nevertheless, there were some who supported him, including Sir Nicholas Carew."

"But, didn't Jane Seymour die in October 1537?" asked Callum.

"Yes," concurred Perdita, "but it wouldn't be hard to fudge the dates. It seems even after Bessie stepped back from the fray, the desire to try and overthrow Henry remained. Cromwell uncovered the plot and, bizarrely, one of the men who sat on the council to convict Carew was Sir Francis Bryan."

"It was all so entangled," said Piper, "but it seemed there was a desperation to remove Henry. No one ever succeeded though."

"Do you think Henry did murder his and Anne's son?" asked Callum, white-faced.

Perdita nodded.

"Did you notice the names of the men who were in the outer chambers and rushed in to help?" asked Kit.

"It was the five men executed alongside Anne," said Callum.

"And, including Anne, there were five women at the block," said Perdita. "Thanks to the manuscript and the ceiling boss in the Marquess House chapel, we finally know who they were: Bessie Blount, Mary Boleyn, Jane Stukeley and Mary Berkeley. They weren't able to save Anne but they were able to present a united front and be with her during the final moments."

"This was the blue touchpaper for Henry Fitzroy's coup," said Piper. "After years of watching the king becoming increasingly violent, as he plundered the monasteries and the Royal Mint, leaving the country on the brink of bankruptcy, it was no wonder the nobility were looking for an alternative monarch."

"There's something else, too," said Perdita, rummaging through her papers. "We've noticed before that there are echoes through time in The Scribe's version of history, and last night, I remembered another one. Throughout this search, the number five has been a symbolic key but there was another point in history where there was political unrest over five men."

"When?" asked Piper.

"In the run-up to the arrest of Charles I," Perdita replied. "The Five were the members of parliament: John Hampden, Arthur Haselrig, Denzil Holles, John Pym and William Strode.

Charles I entered Parliament with his militia in an attempt to arrest them. The men had been warned and disappeared. Eventually, the king backed down and left but it was the beginning of the slippery slope that led to the English Civil War and Charles I's execution. The State Opening of Parliament is a commemoration of the monarch trying to enter the Commons. Perhaps The Scribe was leaving clues again."

"What do you mean?" asked Piper.

"Five men in the seventeenth century were seen as figureheads for the beginning of civil unrest, the number five is prevalent throughout *The Pentagram Manuscript*, it has to be relevant. Do you remember the five unnamed people on the execution records?"

"It couldn't have been these men, though," said Callum. "They were hundreds of years apart."

"No, that wasn't what I meant," said Perdita. "When Fitzroy tried to arrest the king, he was accompanied by four men: Thomas and Hal Boleyn and his uncles, Louis and Alphonso Blount."

"You mentioned the older Boleyn brothers before, Perds," said Kit, "but there is no mention of Anne having two more brothers at court when she was queen."

"True, but two more brothers are mentioned in Anne's younger days," said Perdita. "Depending on which historian you read, Thomas Boleyn was the eldest child of Elizabeth and Thomas Boleyn and he either died as a baby or in his late teens. There are two memorial plaques to Henry and Thomas Boleyn. The one to Henry is at Hever Castle beside the elder Thomas Boleyn, while the other is at Penshurst Church in Kent but there is no date stating when he died; however, it does state this was the brother of Anne, second wife of Henry VIII."

"This is the 'accepted' version of history?" clarified Piper.

"Yes," said Perdita, "but, as so often happens, because of the gaps left by The Scribe, there is disagreement among historians about the plaques and even the dates these memorials were created. One historian claims these two plaques were small, therefore they must have been commemorating children. While another suggests a record exists at the Ashmolean Museum in Oxford stating that the younger Thomas died in 1520.

"Yet, if we believe the letter written by their father, the elder Thomas Boleyn, that he and his wife, Elizabeth Howard, had five children between their marriage in 1498 and 1505, in 1520, the eldest child could have been aged 21 if born in 1499, or as young as 15, for the later date. Taking Thomas Boleyn to be the eldest, the comment in the Ashmolean file might be a unique reference to a man who has otherwise been written from history…"

"But," interrupted Kit, "the period we're discussing is years later, when these missing children would have been in their late 20s, possibly early 30s, yet there are no other records of them. Both their sisters, Anne and Mary, were at court. One had been the mistress of the king, one was about to become queen and their brother, George, was Viscount Rochford and a well-known figure in the Henrician court. Wouldn't two members of a high-profile family have left more of a paper trail to be followed?"

He looked up at Perdita who kept her expression soft and open. There had been a time when Kit's desire to challenge her had made defiance rise like a phoenix, but this had passed and she welcomed his questions, understanding that he did not doubt her but was determined to ensure her reasoning was sound.

"You're right," agreed Perdita. "My suggestions are that either Cromwell destroyed the records or The Scribe was told to eliminate them. A task she appeared to follow, except for the one document at the Ashmolean. Perhaps it was human error, perhaps it was deliberate. The names of Mary, Anne and George Boleyn are writ large across Tudor history, they shine like suns in splendour and even their downfall is dramatic. Why would anyone choose to look in their shadows? Until, of course, a document which has been hidden for centuries emerges, claiming both Boleyn boys grew into adulthood and were part of Henry VIII's court. I do wonder if this was the point where Granny began to realise the true danger of her discovery."

"I agree," said Piper.

"In 1533, when Anne was pregnant with the future Elizabeth I, *The Pentagram Manuscript* states that the Boleyn boys, having been part of the alternate court of young Henry Fitzroy, flee. They spend a night in the stables here at Marquess House with Lady Bryan, who we know better as Jane Seymour, while on the run to Ireland."

"Here?" said Piper in surprise, and Perdita nodded.

"What prompted the sudden fall from grace?" asked Callum.

"The arrest of Meg Blount on suspicion of trying to poison the king," replied Perdita.

"What?" exclaimed Kit.

"Who was Meg Blount?" interjected Piper.

"She was the sister of Bessie Blount and in our version of events was said to have been betrothed to Hal Boleyn. Yet, she is another person who, according to traditional records, died in infancy, along with two of Bessie's brothers. However, according to *The Pentagram Manuscript*, the brothers were named Louis and Alphonso, and they grew into adulthood. Along with Thomas and Hal Boleyn, they were part of Henry Fitzroy's entourage and were very close to their nephew."

"For clarification, we have the two missing Boleyn brothers, who we think were part of Henry Fitzroy's entourage and we have three missing Blount siblings of Bessie?" said Kit.

"Correct," said Perdita, "five missing people, who I believe are the five unnamed victims of execution for coining I found listed in the records from the Tower of London."

"Explain, please, Perds," said Callum.

"Once again, there is a huge clue concerning the survival of the Blount siblings which is in plain sight if you examine the evidence. Bessie Blount's parents were Sir John Blount and Lady Katherine Pershall. According to the parliamentary website they had three sons and five daughters, however, an intriguing detail on their tomb suggests otherwise. They're buried at St John the Baptist Church in Kinlet and the tomb depicts five adult males and six young women."

"But surely they represent children who have died?" said Kit.

"That is the view taken by historians," agreed Perdita, "however, it's unusual for children who died young — either as babies or as children — to be depicted as adults. While I agree this is inconclusive it does go a small way to corroborating *The Pentagram Manuscript*."

"Wouldn't records have turned up somewhere naming one of these missing people?" said Callum.

"Not necessarily. The Blounts were a huge family with numerous branches. The repetition of names is vast; there are so many Johns, Margarets, Katherines, Annes, Walters, Henrys, so losing a few somewhere along the way wouldn't be difficult. The details of hundreds of Blounts have been lost through natural wastage — loss of paperwork through negligence, crumbling to dust, being eaten by mice, burned by future generations. Burying the names of a few members of an enormous family would be easy."

"Why though, Perds?" demanded Kit. "I understand why the Blounts would support their sister, but the Boleyns didn't have the same incentive. In fact, wouldn't they be opposed to the raising up of Fitzroy? They would want to see their sister and her offspring on the throne. Think of the elevated status to them if they were uncles to a future monarch. Wouldn't it be more probable that they were trying to depose rather than support Fitzroy? He was the biggest threat to Anne's children."

"Don't forget, Anne didn't want to marry Henry," said Perdita. "She had been told to flirt with him but she had assumed this would be short-lived before she left for Ireland to marry James Butler. Maybe her brothers were acting to protect their sister, trying to save her from being pushed into the arms of a man who scared her and on to a throne where she would be out of her depth? Wouldn't you and Stuart want to protect Megan?"

Kit gave her a surprised look. "Yes, I suppose…" he replied.

Perdita watched as Kit's face clouded over while he considered this new perspective.

"Are you suggesting that the Boleyn boys and their supporters were prepared to take on the old guard in order to place their new young king on the throne?" Piper asked.

Perdita nodded. "Why did Elizabeth I never name her successor? Because she knew the moment there was an alternative to her as queen, particularly if it was a man, she would never be safe again. Henry VIII was desperate for a legitimate son and in divorcing Katherine of Aragon and making Mary illegitimate, he made a huge error."

"Why?" asked Callum.

"Of his two acknowledged children at that point in time, Fitzroy went from having no entitlement to the throne to the strongest claim because an illegitimate son will always outrank an illegitimate daughter. When Henry elevated his son to a double dukedom, he made him the most powerful man in the country after the monarch. By doing this Henry VIII selected the perfect candidate for his throne. Henry was even drafting legislation to name his own heir, which the Privy Council assumed would be Fitzroy. If Thomas and Hal Boleyn were close to Fitzroy, having been part of his entourage for years, then why wouldn't they want to elevate him to the throne? At this point, Fitzroy was too young to rule alone, so if they were successful in making him king, he would need advisors, a Lord Protector to rule on his behalf. Don't you think the idea of being virtually king as the power behind the monarch would have appealed to them more?"

"It's persuasive," said Kit. "What about their sister though?"

"Anne would be free to marry again," interjected Piper. "Win, win."

"There is also an example of a Lord Protector a few years later — Edward Seymour, older brother of Jane," Perdita continued. "When Edward VI became king, Seymour emerged as the leader of the council who were selected to rule on the young king's behalf. While his policies were popular with the common folk, they angered many of the nobles. There were two rebellions during Edward Seymour's rule: the Prayer Book Rebellion and Kett's Rebellion, as well as war with Scotland, which caused further unrest. When you're in such a position of power, you attract the attention of ruthless men who want to steal what you command. Eventually, Seymour was removed and in February 1550, replaced by John Dudley, Earl of Warwick and father of Elizabeth I's favourite, Robert Dudley.

Seymour was beheaded two years later in January 1552 for felony — attempting to change the government — after trying to overthrow Dudley's rule."

A surprised silence greeted Perdita's words.

"And you believe the sequence of events was set in motion when Bessie's sister was arrested for attempted murder with poison?" asked Piper, who was the first to recover.

"I think it began the slippery slide towards potential civil war in the same way the attempted arrest of The Five Members did over one hundred years later," explained Perdita. "This is why the number five remains significant throughout."

"Why do you think it was the women pushing the action?" asked Kit. "I know Bessie was the power behind the plot but are you suggesting they physically fought alongside the men?"

"There's a weird entry in the records," said Perdita, pulling another piece of paper from the pile and showing the others. "Jane writes about it in the manuscript, but her dates don't tally with the version which is presented in the 'accepted' version of history. The fact this event appears in both versions of the past tells me it was real, but I would guess the date was altered by The Scribe. The official records tell us that in October 1531, a mob of seven to eight thousand women gathered in London in order to attack Anne, who was dining without the king. Abandoning her dinner, Anne fled. While nothing was ever done about the riot, it was reported that among the women were men in disguise. Historians have always suggested this riot was to avenge Katherine of Aragon whom they viewed as the wronged woman. However, there is a great deal wrong with this report."

"Such as?" asked Kit.

"Well, for a start," interjected Piper, "Eight thousand women don't gather by chance."

"Exactly, it's a huge number of people," agreed Perdita. "At this point, London contained approximately fifty thousand people. If half of those were women and eight thousand of them gathered, that's over 30 per cent of the female population of London, which is a lot of people to corral spontaneously."

"Especially if you factor in the age ranges," said Callum. "It does seem an unfeasibly large proportion of women. Even if they came from elsewhere, they would have to have been coordinated to arrive at the rallying point. This was organised."

"Which is why you can understand my suspicion of this riot not being aimed at Anne but as Jane describes in *The Pentagram Manuscript*, this riot is a protest *against* Anne's arrest and impending execution, rather than her marriage to the king. It was the first part of Bessie's war against Henry; this was the women laying the foundations for Fitzroy's coup. The other thing that intrigues me is it presents us with an echo from an earlier period of history."

"Echoes," murmured Kit, staring at the list of figures Perdita had been using as reference. "We've had these throughout our search, moments of history which do seem to have happened but not at the time or in the way it is presented as fact in the accepted version of history."

"And this echo has its roots in another woman, one who also dared to reach for power against the wishes of her male relatives," said Perdita.

"Who?" asked Piper.

"Empress Matilda."

Callum groaned and dropped his head in his hands, causing them all to laugh. "Who was Empress Matilda?" he said, his voice was muffled.

"Matilda was the daughter of Henry I of England," said Perdita, her mouth twitching into a smile at Callum's dramatics. "Her brother, William Adelin, should have been king, but he was killed in the *White Ship* disaster in 1120. Her father asked his nobles to swear an oath to support Matilda's claim to the throne after he had died. Obviously, they all swore but when Henry died in 1135, the nobles and the Church reneged on the deal and instead backed Stephen of Blois, who was Matilda's cousin, to become king. In 1139, Matilda crossed to England to try and claim her throne. She was supported by her half-brother, Richard of Gloucester and her uncle, King David I of Scotland. She captured Stephen during the Battle of Lincoln but, unfortunately, her attempt to be crowned at Westminster in 1141, ended in disaster.

"Troops loyal to King Stephen rose up against Matilda in June 1141 and she was forced to flee at a moment's notice. Historians often point out that she fled leaving her dinner on the table, another detail attributed to Anne fleeing the mob in London. Matilda managed to make her way to Oxford where things became increasingly grim. Her half-brother was captured and she agreed to a hostage swap with the king. However, once the king was free, rather than storm Oxford Castle, he decided to embark on a long siege. Matilda knew she couldn't win, so as the snow fell, legend says that with a handful of knights, she fled into the wintry weather, disguised in a white cloak and escaped via the River Isis past the troops at Abingdon-on-Thames before riding to the safety of Wallingford Castle."

"Did she ever become queen?" asked Callum.

"No, but her son became king; he was Henry II," said Perdita.

"Another woman who sacrificed everything in order to put her son on the throne," said Kit. "An echo of Margaret Beaufort and Bessie Blount."

"And, perhaps, Jane Seymour, whose son was a king," said Perdita.

"It's compelling, Perds," agreed Piper, checking her crib sheet from their earlier meeting, "but, according to accepted history, at this date, Fitzroy was dead."

"Rather like Catherine Howard," said Perdita and Piper's eyes glittered with comprehension. "Except, I don't think he was; I think the whole story of Henry Fitzroy has been changed in order to hide the fact he was not a forgotten prince who never had his moment of glory. Henry Fitzroy would have been seventeen when he led his rebel army to semi-victory. Henry VIII was seventeen when he became king. The symmetry is perfect."

"What about Bessie Blount?" asked Callum. "Was she executed?"

"No, which is what makes it so strange," said Perdita. "Unless it was similar to the plots centred around Elizabeth before she became queen."

"What do you mean, Perds?" asked Kit.

"When Mary ascended to the throne, her marriage to the Spanish king, Philip II, made her very unpopular, as did her return to staunch Catholicism and her introduction of the Inquisition in this country. Both the princess Elizabeth and her cousin, Edward Courtenay, were implicated in a plot to remove Mary from the throne and incarcerate her in the Tower of London. There were also rumours that Elizabeth and Courtenay planned to marry, which seeing as he was a great-grandson of Edward IV, as Elizabeth was a great-granddaughter, they had a combined claim to the throne which was extremely strong."

"What happened?" asked Callum.

"Despite strong insistence from the Spanish that both Elizabeth and Courtenay should be executed before Philip of Spain would marry Mary, there was not enough evidence to convict them. Like Bessie, they had never marched with the rebels and both were non-combatants throughout its duration. In the summer of 1554, Elizabeth was removed to house arrest with Sir Henry Bedingfield and Courtenay was exiled to Europe."

"Why do you think Mary resisted?" asked Piper.

"There was a time when Mary and Elizabeth had been close," said Perdita. "Remember, too, that Mary had given the order in February 1554 to execute Lady Jane Grey, the nine-day queen. Jane was a cousin and Mary agreed to her death because her Privy Council suggested that while she was still alive, Jane was a good rallying point for rebellions. Whether Mary believed this or not, Jane was executed.

"However, Mary couldn't be seen to execute Elizabeth, her half-sister and the heir presumptive to the crown, no matter what the crime. The sisters had grown up watching their father, Henry VIII, cutting a swathe through anyone he felt was a threat to his crown, particularly those of royal blood. Signing a death warrant must be difficult enough, but signing the death warrant of someone you care about must be impossible, unless you're insane."

A stunned silence greeted Perdita's words.

"It was endless, wasn't it?" said Piper. "These battles for the throne, these men who believed they should have the power to rule and anyone could be sacrificed to their goal."

"You can understand why the women created a support network of their own," said Perdita. "While their husbands, fathers, brothers, sons, cousins and uncles all jostled for power, often using the women as bargaining chips to gain titles and land in marriage, was it any wonder the women reached out to each other, not only for friendship and safety, but to create intrigues and plots of their own? They may have had limited opportunities for education but they weren't stupid; many of them were more politically astute than the men on the privy council."

"And this is how you think Bessie Blount managed to avoid detection?" asked Kit. "Despite being one of the driving forces behind this huge rebellion, she remained on the edges."

"Exactly," said Perdita, "and, in Tudor times, who would look at the women? In this case, it's precisely where they should have been looking to discover the power behind the plot."

"Who was blamed for the Pilgrimage of Grace?" asked Callum.

"Robert Aske, Thomas Darcy, Lord Darcy de Darcy, Sir Robert Constable and Sir Francis Bigod," replied Perdita. "History remembers it as a rebellion against the king's change from Catholicism to Protestantism. Finally, the emblem of those marching on the Pilgrimage of Grace was five spots of red on a white background to represent Christ's wounds, however, they were arranged in the shape of a pentagon, which is the star found at the heart of a pentagram."

"Perds, is this a leap too far?" asked Kit.

"I don't think so," she replied.

"But wouldn't The Scribe have changed it?" asked Piper.

"Why would she need too? Remember, she was writing over one hundred years later. If the court trials claimed Anne had committed adultery and that these were the men who were her lovers, this was scandalous enough to stay. The Scribe had been told to highlight the worst bits of the Tudors, to shine the light away from the Stuarts. What better way than to leave the scandal in plain sight. If other documents suggesting the truth had ever existed, they were all destroyed. This has been hidden for centuries, first in the vaults here, then in the storage facility by Granny Mary. This is probably the only true account of what really happened at that chaotic time."

There was a silence as Piper, Kit and Callum absorbed Perdita's revelation.

It was Callum who spoke first. "Perds, to clarify something, in the accepted version of history, Henry was supposed to go into two years of mourning for Jane?"

"Which we know was untrue," she replied. "Even the records left in the public domain show that within weeks of Jane's death, Cromwell was searching for a new bride. In light of what had happened by marrying two English commoners in a row, perhaps this was why Henry was persuaded into a diplomatic marriage with a crown princess or foreign duchess. I would suspect if Henry was exhibiting strange mood swings at this point, it was self-pity and the beginnings of his mental health issues rather than grief over losing Jane."

"In that case, how do you explain Henry having Jane buried at Windsor and being buried beside her?" asked Callum.

"Despite what happened, Jane remained the mother of Henry's son and heir," said Perdita. "Fitzroy was dead and none of his other sons had ever been acknowledged. Edward was Henry's one hope of continuing the dynasty. When the queen died, there were protocols to follow and it's likely the matter was taken out of his hands ensuring Jane's funeral went ahead as the law dictated."

"And Henry requesting to be buried beside her?" asked Piper.

"Time had passed, the king's memory was shattered and he possibly couldn't recall the details of events. She was the mother of the next king and it was Jane's elder brother, Sir Edward Seymour, who was named Lord Protector. What better way to seal the importance of his family than by insisting the king had wished to be buried beside Jane, his favourite wife?"

"It's plausible," said Kit, raking his fingers through his curly hair.

"The question is, why did Granny hide the manuscript?" asked Piper. "What made it more frightening than the things she discovered in *The Catherine Howard Codex*, which she left for us to find. Why did she go to such lengths to hide this document?"

"A question I keep returning to with each revelation," admitted Perdita. "For some reason, she didn't want us to discover this part of the story. I believe she thought it was too dangerous but I can't fully understand why."

"But, ultimately," said Callum, who was looking through the print-outs, "why does this matter? It's interesting but..."

"Imagine if you read about this in a newspaper, how would you feel?" Kit asked.

"Shocked but it probably wouldn't make that much difference to me."

"Are you sure? Wouldn't it make you question other things? Wouldn't you wonder why this story has suddenly changed after hundreds of years of it never altering, no matter what new documents surfaced or what new evidence was discovered in archaeological digs?"

"I suppose, when you put it like that, yes, it would make me begin to doubt things."

"This would be a world-wide story," continued Perdita, "a discovery that Henry VIII, the tyrant king, was even more cruel and psychotic than previously believed, that his son was illegitimate and his reign was actually quite unimportant. He won no major wars, he didn't father a dynasty, he was most famous for his love life. He may have been on the throne for thirty-eight years, but so was Henry VI, and he was famous for losing the throne to his cousin Edward IV in the Wars of the Roses. Richard II — twenty-two years; Edward III — fifty years. Henry VIII's reign was nothing extraordinary, yet he is the most famous king in our historical pantheon. The Tudors are the most researched and written about royal family. Even people who have no interest in history have heard of Henry VIII, thanks to the many versions of his life that have been on film and television. Discovering it was all a lie would cause havoc in world markets because, as we've said from the beginning, what else has been changed and how much of the past can we trust? It's the Orwellian nightmare of the Ministry of Truth all over again."

They stared at her in silence.

"Why though?" asked Kit eventually. "Why did The Scribe change it all?"

"She was under orders to write a damaging history of the Tudors," Perdita reminded him.

"Murdering two queens on the trot would have been pretty damaging," said Callum.

"Exactly, so why change it?" repeated Kit.

Pausing, Perdita allowed her mind to wander, trying to bring together all she had discovered about Jane Seymour's version of events. "I think The Scribe was leaving a clue," she said. "There were three heirs of Henry VIII who took the throne: Edward, Mary and Elizabeth. Lady Jane Grey was the daughter of Henry's sister. Of the three monarchs fathered by Henry, Mary was the one who can be claimed to be legitimate. Katherine and Henry remained married when he wed Anne

Boleyn, so despite all the legislation, technically, Elizabeth was illegitimate. From what we've learned from the Pentagram manuscript, Jane Seymour was married to Sir Francis Bryan when she was coerced into marriage with the king. Therefore, Edward VI was also illegitimate. All three were granted their rights to the throne by Henry's Act of Succession."

"Are you saying these people were never monarchs?" asked Kit.

"No, I'm saying The Scribe hid the key to the secret in plain sight all along."

"What do you mean?" asked Piper.

"Henry VIII did have three legitimate heirs, as well as possibly nine illegitimate heirs — including Elizabeth and Edward — but the bizarre thing is, Henry VIII was unaware of two of his legitimate children. One became a queen, while one stepped aside for his illegitimate half-sister. The Scribe created three supposedly legitimate heirs from the carnage of Henry's madness and placed it in front of everyone. Then, she left clues for later generations to uncover. Unfortunately, the powers that be eroded and destroyed as many documents as possible which proved the truth.

"Despite their best efforts though, not all the documents were discovered and this is why there is confusion. When an untampered piece of evidence appears, like *The Pentagram Manuscript*, it threatens everything. The Scribe told us Henry had three heirs who sat on his throne. She had no idea it would be centuries before the truth was discovered or that the names of Mary, Edward and Elizabeth would remain famous. Perhaps she felt she had left a huge clue in leaving suggestions of their illegitimacy, assuming that the real truth would have been long discovered."

"The real truth being…"

"Henry VIII was not the magnificent monarch we have been taught but was, in fact, a murderer who through sheer tyranny, placed his illegitimate children on the throne. No wonder the Stuarts felt their claim to the crown of England was stronger; they're all legitimately descended from Henry's elder sister, Margaret. They were a royal house with no doubt about their sovereignty and their right to rule."

"And The Scribe was working at the behest of the later Stuarts," confirmed Kit.

"Exactly," said Perdita. "The Scribe was supposed to denigrate Henry but rather than her words demonising him, he and his wives have become one of the most studied periods in history. He was king during the Renaissance. There were huge changes taking place across the globe and Henry rode that wave, even though he was nowhere near as important in the greater scheme of politics as he believed. However, the Victorians took him to their heart. Here was a powerful male monarch, the last of the truly great English kings.

"Remember, Victoria was seen as German by many of her subjects. Going back through the monarchy, Henry was actually the last homegrown British monarch. His mother was a princess, his father was descended from Welsh kings, his grandmother was descended from John of Gaunt and Edward III. While Victoria had a British father, his descent was more German than British and her mother was German. The proud Victorian male who was beginning to piece together our island history would no doubt have revelled in the excitement of the Tudor king. He was a colossus, striding across Great Britain, invading countries, albeit without much success, and taking on the might of Rome. He was the perfect antidote to the female German monarch who ruled for sixty years."

"I'd never thought about it like that before, Perds," said Kit.

"This is why there are so many contradictions. Thousands of contemporary documents were destroyed but it was impossible for MI1 and their predecessors to find and remove everything. Our archive is the most dangerous because Marquess House was at the centre of the story. It was the refuge for the women, and they left us with the real version of events."

CHAPTER TWO

Perdita and Piper lolled against the kitchen counter as they waited for the kettle to boil. A burst of laughter from Kit and Callum in the living room made them both smile.

"It's a relief to hear Kit laugh again," said Perdita as she made a pot of tea. "He's been under so much stress."

"The weekend away will be great for them both. It feels as though all any of us ever do is work," sighed Piper. "Is Kit going? I know he was hesitant after the upheaval with Stuart and Hannah."

Perdita poured milk into a jug and hesitated before speaking. "Stuart wasn't the real reason," she said, pushing the kitchen door closed to avoid being overheard. "You know Kit's scared of heights?" Piper nodded. "In the past, he was able to manage it but over the last year, it's been getting worse. After all we've been through, it's not surprising. Kit has always tried to be strong for me, pushing his own emotions aside but when Gabriel said there was a treetop assault course as part of the stag weekend, Kit vomited at the thought of it and that was when we realised he needed help. He's been having weekly counselling sessions and the counsellor thinks his exacerbated reaction to heights was a form of post-traumatic stress disorder. Thankfully, the counselling is helping and Kit's fears are subsiding."

"Poor Kit," said Piper. "Does anyone else know?"

"Stuart and now you. I think he might tell Cal but he's feeling much better and last night we went up on the scaffold in the chapel together so he could see the ceiling boss. He was shaking when we reached the gantry but it passed and he was able to stand beside me and look at the carving. It's a huge step forward. He's going to see how he feels for the assault course but at least the idea of it no longer makes him physically sick."

"Good for Kit. It takes guts to admit to having a problem, let alone fixing it," said Piper.

"How are you getting on with the comparisons of the illuminations in the manuscript with the images from the Weeping Lady Tower?" asked Perdita, changing the subject as she carried the tea tray into the living room.

Piper followed carrying the mugs. "Very interesting," she replied. She gestured to Kit and Callum, who were busy discussing their upcoming holiday. "When these two have gone tomorrow, why don't you come over to the studio and I can show you what I've found?"

"Shall we clear this or is there more?" said Kit, gesturing to all the paperwork.

"What else could there be?" asked Cal in surprise.

"I was wondering," said Kit, "if Jane died, who finished the manuscript? Hadn't Jane given it to her maid, Audrey, to return it to Marquess House? Do you know who wrote the final sections?"

"We have an answer," said Perdita, sorting through the print-outs on the table and extracting a copy of a letter. "This letter was written in 1539, two years after Jane died, and it was from Audrey to Sir Francis Bryan. He was staying at Marquess House and she was reporting on the children. It appears he was heading to London before being sent away on another diplomatic mission for Henry. Audrey suggested he complete Jane's work in the manuscript, then hide it until his children were old enough to discover what happened to their mother."

"Sir Francis Bryan wrote the final sections?" said Callum in astonishment.

"It would appear that was the case," said Perdita.

"What happened to Jane Seymour's children?" asked Kit.

Perdita felt her stomach clench. "I know some of it," she said.

"You sound reluctant," said Piper. "What have you been keeping to yourself in order to protect us?"

Perdita looked up into the fierce gaze of her sister and husband and the double effect of their glares made her laugh. "Busted," she said. "Yes, I did keep this to myself. When I went to London, I looked through a few pieces at the Nympha archive but it was also to discover the results of a family tree I commissioned."

"Whose?" asked Piper with narrowed eyes.

"Jasper and Lois Bryan," admitted Perdita. "Nicola Weaver, who is a curator at the Royal College of Arms and a genealogist, told me I was not the first person to request information on the illegitimate child of Sir Francis Bryan."

"Children?" corrected Callum.

"In the accepted version of history, Sir Francis Bryan is recorded as having an illegitimate son with an unnamed mistress, who, if you consider our discoveries, was probably Jane Seymour, and the child wasn't illegitimate. There is no record of a daughter in the accepted version though. However, there is also a debate suggesting he had another illegitimate son, Henry, with his mistress Philippa Spice."

"Who else commissioned the family tree?" asked Kit.

"Granny Mary and Lady Marianne O'Rourke," replied Perdita.

"What? Lady Marianne O'Rourke is Randolph Connors's wife and Xavier's mother," Kit exclaimed. "Why didn't you tell us this? It could be important."

"I'm sorry," said Perdita. "It was a few days later that we learned about Hannah and Xavier and this dropped down my list of priorities."

Kit swallowed hard and regained control of himself. "I'm sorry," he muttered. "I shouldn't have shouted."

"What happened to the children?" asked Piper.

"Jasper died as a young man during Kett's Rebellion," said Perdita. "This took place on 8 July 1549 when Edward VI was on the throne. He was listed as being part of the forces sent with the Marquess of Northampton to suppress the rebels in Norwich. He was killed during the battle and the king paid for a lavish funeral including a burial in St Mary's Church, Great Bedwyn, which is the parish church of Wulfhall, home to the Seymour family. Sir John Seymour, father of Jane Seymour is buried there, which makes me wonder if the king knew Jasper was his half-brother."

"Why?" asked Piper.

"It has echoes of the lavish funeral and grave Elizabeth I paid for when Henry Carey, Baron Hunsdon died. He was the son of Mary Boleyn and, therefore, was probably Elizabeth's half-brother. Perhaps the idea came from having seen how Edward treated his half-sibling."

"And Lois?" asked Kit.

"She married her stepbrother, Walter Butler, the fourth son of James Butler, 9th Earl of Ormond and Lady Joan Fitzgerald. Lois and Walter had a daughter, Jane, who married Hugh Prust, a wealthy landowner."

"Prust?" said Kit. "Surely not; the line would be incredibly long."

"Amber Prust, Xavier's wife, is descended in a direct line through the men of the Prust family to Lois Bryan. Lady Marianne O'Rourke discovered this six months before Xavier swept Amber off her feet and proposed. Marianne, meanwhile, is descended from Henry Spice, who is the illegitimate son of Sir Francis Bryan and Philippa Spice. When Marianne discovered this, she commissioned more family trees and this was when she discovered Amber's heritage," said Perdita.

"Did they know Jane Seymour was Lois's mother?" asked Piper.

"I don't know," admitted Perdita, "but from the fact that Amber and Xavier use a phoenix and a tower as their letterhead and Jane Seymour's badge when she married Henry was a crowned phoenix rising out of a tower with her motto 'Bound to Obey and Serve', perhaps they have their suspicions, even if they don't have the proof."

"Oh my God, Perds, this is what you were talking about the night of the engagement party," said Kit.

Perdita nodded.

"But Jane Seymour had no blood claim to the throne; if there had been any it would have come through Prince Edward and he died childless," said Kit.

"Xavier might believe otherwise," said Perdita. "Perhaps he thinks being in possession of a document that proves Jane Seymour and Henry VIII's marriage was bigamous would be enough to blackmail governments. The reason we've been allowed to uncover the secret is because of the non-publication agreement we have with MI1, otherwise we would have been arrested. Granny was terrified of this story, so scared that even after her death she left it hidden in a locked, unmarked room."

"*Does* this give Xavier any more leverage?" asked Piper.

Kit shook his head. "Dad and I have been studying the entail going right back to the original paperwork and all the alterations since. Despite what Xavier thinks, Ruby and Pearl's claim to Marquess House is far weaker than he believes. There are two of you with the potential of you both having children. There is also a clause, inserted in 1765, stating that in the event of the current incumbent of Marquess House being unable to have children or only producing male heirs, the incumbent has the legal right to nominate a female heir from elsewhere on the family tree or even from outside the family, if there is a strong enough case. It would be passed to executors of the estate and an independent legal advisor to decide if this person is appropriate."

"Do you think Xavier knows about this?"

"It's unlikely. Dad and I didn't realise this clause existed until we pulled out the original documentation. There has always been a direct female heir, so this has never been an issue."

"So you mean that even if neither of us has a daughter, we can nominate an heir?" asked Piper.

"Yes, and it wouldn't have to be Ruby or Pearl. You could look to your grandfather's or father's line and choose from there, or even decide to leave it to someone outside the family who you know will treat the house with the respect it deserves. However, it would mean a ton of legal paperwork and probably months of negotiations and agreements."

Perdita and Piper stared at each other in surprise.

"When did you discover this?" asked Perdita.

"A week ago," said Kit. "We've been preparing a proper report. Dad wanted to discuss it with you when we were sure of all the facts."

Startled by this revelation, Perdita shuffled the print-outs on the table together in a nervous gesture. As she opened her mouth to ask if this meant they were no longer under threat from Xavier, Piper spoke, her voice quiet: "Do we know where Xavier is at the moment, Kit?"

"He's in Switzerland, checking on his insane legal claim, while Hannah is at a flat in London rented in Xavier's name. Larry and his team are monitoring them, as are Gary and MI1."

An hour later, Piper and Callum returned to their own apartment. Perdita gathered her papers, placing them in a folder before locking them in the safe, while Kit stacked the dishwasher.

"I'll miss you," he said as they wandered through the apartment, flicking off lights on their way to bed.

"You're only going away for four days; we've lasted that long apart before." She smiled.

"It's because of the upheaval with Xavier," admitted Kit. "Part of me feels I should stay here as protection."

"We've got Cora. She's military trained, remember, and there's the whole security team. Not to mention MI1 Elite at the touch of a panic button."

Kit pulled her into his arms. "Be careful while I'm away," he said.

"You, too," she replied, disentangling herself and heading to the bathroom.

When she returned a few minutes later, Kit was in bed, his new reading glasses perched on his nose.

"Is that a pregnancy test kit?" he asked, nodding towards her dressing table where a paper chemist's bag crouched.

"Several," she replied.

"And...?"

"Maybe, but then, we thought the same last month and we were disappointed."

"Shall we take a test in the morning?"

"It might be too soon, let's do it when you're home from your weekend away."

Flicking off the light, she snuggled down under the covers. Kit slid down beside her.

"I love you," he said.

"I love you too," she replied.

CHAPTER THREE

"Pipes, this is magnificent," exclaimed Perdita as she stared at the enormous canvas in Piper's studio.

Swirls of colour drew her in as she stared at the Arthurian scene her sister had created. She and Piper had been discussing the painting for weeks, but Piper had refused to allow her to see it until now. Perdita gazed at the intricate replicas of the images from the Arthurian frieze on the ceiling in the tower at the centre of Marquess House. Piper had woven these together with classic Mediaeval iconography, while bold splashes of modern colour and abstract designs added her own unique style.

"I'm going to paint the Celtic patterns from *The Pentagram Manuscript* down here," said Piper, pointing to an unfinished border section, "which is a play on the pentagram design used throughout."

"Shall we hang it in the great hall when it's finished?" said Perdita.

Piper gave a self-depreciating laugh. "No," she said.

"Why not? It's incredible and we have nothing of yours on the walls. We have Dad's paintings, which Granny bought over the years, but nothing by you. We could put it in the Minstrel's Gallery where the battered old tapestry is hanging. Ever since you discovered it was a nineteenth century, machine created copy, it's irritated me. This would look stunning in its place."

"Perhaps," said Piper, and Perdita hid a grin. Piper was never satisfied with her work and it was rare for her to allow anything to be displayed.

Perdita continued to study the picture as Piper pulled a large box file from a pile in the corner.

"While you're here, Perds, there are some updates from Mark, and I wanted your opinion on a few things."

"Of course," said Perdita, whose attention had been caught by the image of the tower at the centre of the painting. A thought began to spool through her mind as she stared at it. Dragging her eyes away from the painting, she joined Piper at the vast table at the centre of the studio, staring down at the large photographs Piper was placing with care.

"These are the images from the Arthurian frieze and the corresponding etchings in the chapel," said Piper. "Do you notice anything?"

"The tower," Perdita said.

"What about it?" prompted Piper.

"Is it our tower?"

"I'd suggest it was too similar to be a coincidence. Not many towers have red tiles on the crenelations like ours and they're picked out with paint in all these images, those from the frieze and in the manuscript."

"There's a pentagram flag on the Arthurian frieze, too," Perdita said in astonishment as she studied the images in more detail. "I've never noticed it before."

"It's hardly surprising; the image is minute in the original."

Perdita opened her phone and pulled up an image of her own, which she laid on the table amidst the photographs. Piper studied it, understanding flooding her face.

"This was Jane Seymour's badge when she married Henry VIII," said Perdita, pointing to the unusual image of the crowned phoenix rising from fire atop a tower, with a red and white flower growing on either side shaded by the bird's outstretched wings. "Do you think it was inspired by our tower? This imagery is everywhere in connection with Jane."

"It's difficult to dismiss the idea when you consider Jane was at Marquess House for four years. She must have known the Arthurian ceiling very well," said Piper.

"It's not too much of a leap to think our tower was her inspiration for *The Pentagram Manuscript*. Remember, when she was recalled to London, her children remained here. Maybe it was her way of continuing the connection with them, keeping them in her heart. Every time she looked at the tower, she thought of Jasper and Lois."

"The scriptorium at Marquess House was commissioned to create the illumination," said Piper. "They would have used the area around them as inspiration, with two towers, ours and the one in the island, which was part of the original convent, it's almost given they were the basis of all these designs — the Arthurian ceiling, *The Pentagram Manuscript* and Jane's emblem."

"How much influence would the nuns have had over the images?"

"It would have been the artist's choice and whatever they thought suited the text," said Piper, "but this was a commission, which means Jane would have had input into the designs. However, I don't think the frieze was the entire inspiration, I think Jane's methodology was more subtle."

"What do you mean?" asked Perdita in surprise.

"I have a historical reveal," Piper grinned.

"It's fun, isn't it?" Perdita laughed. "Nothing beats a historical reveal."

"While I was planning the Arthurian painting, I reread Sir Thomas Malory's *Le Morte D'Arthur* and, as we're in Wales, it seemed right to check Geoffrey of Monmouth's version of the King Arthur tales, too. In the opening stanza of *The Pentagram*

Manuscript there's a reference to 'The lady, Morgan, so sweet, so kind'…"

"'Her death we now revenge with tears…','" continued Perdita.

"Did you know in his tale of the Arthurian legends, Geoffrey of Monmouth identifies Morgan Le Fay as also being known as Anna, the daughter of Igraine and Uther Pendragon?"

Perdita stared at Piper in astonishment. "Anna?" she gasped. "Do think this is a hidden reference to Anne Boleyn? A tribute to Anne hidden in plain sight in Jane's emblem?"

"It's possible."

"Oh Pipes, this is wonderful. If we had any doubts, this clarifies things."

"There's also this," said Piper, moving the Arthurian images aside and spreading out a series of photographs of the ceiling bosses from the chapel. "Mark's team sent these over this morning. Can you spot anything?"

Perdita grinned at Piper and began searching the pictures. Throughout the cleaning and restoration of the chapel, Piper and Mark had consulted on the imagery and iconography, delivering their findings to Perdita every week. The set of photographs were the most recent in the huge task of the detailed cataloguing of the decoration on the chapel ceiling. Perdita gazed down at the photographs; each was of the ceiling bosses of Anne Boleyn, ten were familiar and identical but one was smaller and the colours were darker, less vivid.

"This one is different," said Perdita.

"I thought so, too," said Piper. "Mark said this smaller one was in the corner of the chapel. It was impossible to see from the ground because there were two very ornate Green Man images either side. The Dairy has tested the paint and it's different from the other bosses, the lead in the paint dates this as being almost one hundred years older."

"Do you think this was the original ceiling boss?" said Perdita in excitement. "Perhaps this was what inspired The Scribe to create the others, to show these women were important. If this is older, it could have been commissioned by Jane Seymour, probably to stamp Anne's ownership on the house even though she never came here and to remember the bravery of her cousin who died under such violent circumstances."

"Or perhaps by Sir Francis Bryan to remember his wife and his cousin because this tiny ceiling boss was next to her," Piper said and placed another page in front of Perdita.

Perdita stared down at the photograph Piper had placed on the table and felt a lump form in her throat. "Jane Seymour," she whispered, staring at the serene face with its gable hood and hints of blonde hair. The colouring was identical to the tiny image in the central ceiling boss. She turned to Piper who had tears in her eyes.

"We brought them both home, Perds," Piper said and they squeezed each other's hands.

"All of them," agreed Perdita. "Jane, Anne and the courageous women who accompanied her to the block. We know their story and all they endured."

The internal phone buzzed.

"Hey Larry," Piper began then flicked him on to speaker phone, "Perds is here."

"You need to get over to the Lady Isabel Room," he said, a hint of panic in his voice.

"We're on our way. What's happened?" asked Perdita.

"You're never going to believe this but Amber Connors has arrived with Ruby and Pearl. She's in a terrible state and says she needs your help."

"Amber Connors?" Perdita exclaimed.

"Yes, and even stranger, she used Lady Pamela's safe word; it's the reason we let her inside."

"How did she have Lady Pamela's safe word?" asked Piper and Perdita shrugged, bemused.

Everyone at Marquess House, including close family or friends, had been issued with safe words. These were to ensure either the Marquess House security team or MI1 Elite knew when there was a genuine request for help. There were other code words which indicated they were being coerced or threatened, however, the word Larry repeated to Perdita was Pamela's. Exchanging a concerned look with Piper, they hurried to the great hall where they found Larry, Alistair and Cora in deep discussion.

"What's happening?" said Perdita.

"Susan's in the Lady Isabel room with Amber, Ruby and Pearl," said Larry. "We thought she would be the best person to calm Amber down, but she's adamant she won't speak to anyone but you two."

"And she gave you no clue as to what she wants?" confirmed Perdita.

"Nothing," Larry replied.

"We should proceed with caution, Perdita," said Alistair, saying aloud what she had been thinking. "This could be a ruse by Xavier to infiltrate Marquess House."

"While I agree we have to be cautious," Perdita said, "if she has Lady Pamela's safe word, she must have been in touch with her and Lady Pamela wouldn't have given up the word easily. Amber has her children with her and she has come to the one place which should have been anathema to her. How desperate must she be if we're the people she turns to for help? Let's see what she has to say and discuss things afterwards."

"What if she's the forward party and Xavier is somewhere nearby?" said Piper.

"Xavier flew into the UK last night, he joined Hannah White an hour ago," said Larry. "We have live images from Gary Ashley running in the comms room. They're having lunch at The Ivy."

"Let's do this then," said Perdita. She walked across the great hall, throwing open the door to the Lady Isabel room.

Two little girls were staring at the portrait of Lady Isabel Baynton. "Her dress is so pretty, like a princess..." one of them was saying, then stopped as she heard the door open. Seeing Perdita and Piper, the two children scooted across the room and clambered on the sofa, either side of their mother.

"Here are Perdita and Piper," said Susan. "I'll leave you together."

"Thank you," said Amber, her voice low, with a hint of an Irish accent. "You've been very kind." She seemed to mentally brace herself as she turned to face Perdita and Piper, her blue eyes wide with apprehension.

Perdita had expected to feel anger at this intrusion but her first reaction was sympathy. Behind the expensive hair, glossy nails and exquisite suit worn with Givenchy trainers, Amber Connors looked like a woman on the point of collapse. No amount of make-up could disguise the gauntness of her face and the black rings of despair under her eyes.

"My apologies for my unexpected arrival," Amber said. "I didn't know where else to go to keep the girls safe and Lady Pamela assured me of your kindness and that you would always offer us a haven. It was why she gave me her safe word, in case

I needed help."

Safe. The word echoed through Perdita's mind. Upon her arrival at Marquess House all those years ago, Alistair's use of the word 'safe' during their conversations had jarred with her. As the burden of Mary's legacy and the secret they were forced to uncover unfolded, Perdita realised Alistair's words were correct. Being at Marquess House was a safe place.

"How do you know Lady Pamela?" asked Piper.

"She's an old family friend," replied Amber but Perdita noticed she would not meet their eye and she wondered if Amber was protecting Pamela's true identity in case the twins did not know her story. Turning to Larry, Alistair, Susan and Cora who were hovering in the doorway, Perdita said, "Would you mind waiting outside while Piper and I speak to Amber, please? I think she might be a bit overwhelmed if we all stay."

"If you need me, shout," said Larry. "Cora can stay."

Piper nodded and Cora perched on a chair by the wall, while Larry shut the door. Perdita sat on the armchair opposite Amber, who slumped back on to the sofa where Ruby and Pearl climbed on her, seeking reassurance. Piper sat beside Perdita and for a moment, they stared at each other unable to disguise their mutual curiosity.

"Apologies for the crowd, but you've rather taken us by surprise. I'm Perdita and this is Piper."

Perdita kept her tone light and, in response, Amber attempted a smile as a greeting but her lip was trembling as she fought to hold back her tears. The two girls stared at them with curious eyes as Amber introduced them both.

"Are you the Big Twins?" asked Pearl.

Perdita was startled to see miniature replicas of her own unusual storm-coloured eyes peering up at her through a red-gold fringe.

"We are," said Piper. "Does that make you the Little Twins?"

Pearl giggled.

"I'm thirsty," said Ruby, leaning around her mother, and Perdita started again, her own eyes but coupled with chestnut hair.

"Ruby, don't be rude," said Amber.

"I'll take them to get a drink," said Cora.

Amber looked uncertain.

"They'll be safe, I promise," said Perdita,

With obvious reluctance, Amber nodded. "No fizzy drinks," she called as Cora took a twin each by the hand and led them out of the room. "I'm sorry," Amber said again, as the door shut behind her daughters. "I didn't know where else to bring them. I thought if they were here, they'd be protected by The Milford Haven Treaty."

"Why would they need to be?" asked Perdita in surprise.

"Xavier," Amber said. "He's insane and I'm unsure what he might do next. When he left this morning to go and meet his new girlfriend in London, I grabbed a few things, bundled the girls into the car and drove here. It's the one place he can't reach them."

"Why would he want to harm his own children?" said Piper. "They're his key to Marquess House."

"He believes he has enough evidence to access Marquess House even without the girls," Amber said, "and, it's…" She paused, tears spilling down her face — "it's all my fault."

"Your fault?" Perdita and Piper exchanged a bemused glance.

"Yes," Amber said, blowing her nose on a white handkerchief she pulled from her pocket. "My stupid fascination with the past. If I'd never told Xavier, he and

Randolph wouldn't have spent years searching, squandering a fortune…"

"Amber, what are you talking about?" asked Perdita.

Amber blew her nose again and with a considerable effort fought to control her emotions. "This might take a while," she said.

"We have as much time as you need," Perdita assured her. "Would you like a drink or something to eat? You look exhausted."

Piper pulled the cord and a few minutes later, Susan arrived with the tea trolley.

"We were on our way," Susan said, then turned to Amber. "The girls have said they love swimming and we have a pool here. Larry, our head of security and, Cora, who has military training, have offered to take them for a dip. Larry is a lifeguard, too, so they won't come to any harm. We have an array of swimming costumes."

"If it won't be a bother, they do need something to distract them," said Amber.

Susan left and when Perdita was satisfied Amber was not going to collapse from exhaustion or dehydration, she urged her to begin her tale. Her instincts told her this was important, beyond Xavier and his obsession with Marquess House. Perdita trusted Lady Pamela implicitly and if she had offered support to Amber, there was more to this visit than might have first appeared.

"Many years ago," began Amber, "my father employed an archivist to catalogue all the family papers. He and I are both interested in history and when the archivist found a letter between one of our ancestors, Lady Lois Bryan and a family retainer called Audrey, discussing Lois's mother, Jane, we were intrigued, especially as there was a reference to Marquess House."

Perdita and Piper stared at her in surprise.

"To Marquess House?" Perdita said.

"Yes, and because I was a member of Nympha, this was even more exciting as I knew your grandmother and that she lived at Marquess House. I was a huge fan of her books and when I met her at a social event at one of the Nympha houses, she was so kind, listening to me rattling on and on about family history. When I finally stopped for breath, she suggested we look through the Nympha archive together to see if there were any references to my ancestors. At this point, I hadn't mentioned the name, but it was not through deviousness, rather through enthusiasm and lack of experience."

"Did you and our grandmother discover anything?" asked Perdita.

"Mary was in the process of having various family trees researched and she was using the Nympha archives to supplement her own. As we went through her notes, she discovered one of these genealogical searches crossed over with mine and I eagerly told her about Lois Bryan and how she was connected to Marquess House through her mother, Jane, but I didn't know the identity of this woman as there were hundreds of Janes at the Tudor court. However, as soon as Mary heard the name, she became distressed. She explained that at around the time when her daughter died, she had found some information about this woman in a document called *The Pentagram Manuscript*. It revealed the identity of Lois's mother. Mary tried to laugh it off by saying she was unsure whether the contents were genuine. Her suggestion was I look into other parts of the family tree and leave Lois Bryan to history. I was devastated to have upset her and did as she suggested, but I asked if we could remain in touch."

"Did you?" asked Piper.

"No, because of what happened next," said Amber. "I was too embarrassed to contact Mary, especially after she had been so kind."

"What happened?" asked Perdita.

"Not long after my meeting with Mary, I became engaged to a man called Tommy Child. It wasn't arranged but there had always been a vague understanding between our families, then, out of nowhere, Xavier swooped in. He was dashing, funny, charismatic and I fell head over heels in love. When he proposed after a whirlwind romance, I said yes and thought we were set for the big happily ever after, but when we returned from our honeymoon and began to spend time with his parents, I realised he and his father were obsessed with Mary and Marquess House to the point of madness. In order to impress my new husband, I told him about my connection to Lois Bryan, who was connected to Marquess House. I even revealed my conversation with Mary and that she owned a document which would confirm the identity of Lois Bryan's heritage, the mysterious Jane.

"Xavier and Randolph became as obsessed with finding this document as they did with trying to discover whatever else they thought was hiding at Marquess House. They were convinced the two secrets were connected and if they could find the documentary proof, they'd be able to blackmail governments, or some such nonsense.

"Then two months after we married, I was at Nympha having lunch with my mother, crying because I'd realised what a mistake I'd made, when Marianne, Xavier's mother, arrived, and joined us uninvited. She was already quite drunk and ordered more champagne. She explained that her plan had worked better than she could ever have imagined. When my mother asked her to elucidate, Marianne told us through a genealogical search she had discovered she was descended from Henry Spice, the illegitimate son of Sir Francis Bryan and Philippa Spice. In order to discover who else this connected her to — she's a terrible snob and social climber — she discovered I was also descended from Sir Francis Bryan through Lois. As Sir Francis was loosely related to the Seymour family, you know, Jane Seymour, Henry VIII's third wife, Marianne figured this made them almost royal, hence the stupid letterhead with Jane Seymour's emblems. She decided if Xavier and I combined our bloodlines, it would help boost her social standing and might help in their eternal war against Mary. This was why she and Randolph had ordered Xavier to marry me. However, my revelation after the wedding about the missing manuscript and the way it had upset Mary led them to believe it must have been something to do with her family secret and Marianne had been correct to unite the bloodlines."

"They're all mad..." muttered Piper.

"Why didn't you leave?"

"I was pregnant," Amber replied. "Not with the girls. I had a son, but he died when he was three weeks old."

Perdita felt sick. "I'm so sorry. What happened?"

"Xavier was furious when I had a baby boy," Amber said, her hands shaking again. "He kept threatening to smother him but, sadly, Piers was a very poorly baby. His lungs hadn't formed properly and he was in intensive care his entire life. I was with him for every minute. Xavier saw him once and didn't attend his funeral. I wanted a divorce but Xavier refused. It was a nightmare. Every day I feared for my life. Xavier can exude charm when he wants to win people over but behind closed doors it's an endless battle of coercion, manipulation, bullying and threats. He would hit me but always in places that didn't show and when I refused to sleep with him, he raped me. It happened twice and the second time I fell pregnant with the girls. When they were born, he and his father became even more determined to take Marquess House. When you two inherited, I thought Randolph was going to have a stroke he was so angry.

"Every day I planned to leave but fear kept me there. Fear for the girls, fear because he threatened to have me locked away, declared an unfit mother, to poison me. Yet, on the surface we had what seemed a glorious jet-set lifestyle. I deliberately had myself barred from Nympha because I didn't want him to have access to the archives through me. By then, his mother had left his father in all but name and had moved to her home in Mauritius.

"Randolph and Xavier are on the verge of bankruptcy. They've squandered their entire fortune and while they hoped I'd bring my father's millions to the marriage, he was wary and made them sign an incredibly tough pre-nup. It's a good thing he did because the money he gifted us has nearly gone; spent on Randolph's archive."

"Could you tell us more about these?" asked Perdita, as she and Piper exchanged a startled look. It seemed the rumours Nicola Weaver had heard were true.

"He's been buying archives, documents, stately homes for years and when the collection outgrew his Shropshire estate, I suggested I oversee a storage facility. My father bought it in the names of Ruby and Pearl and, because Randolph and Xavier were so impressed with this and are such poor businessmen, they didn't realise that he had put a clause in the contract stating that all documents deposited become property of the archive and are owned in their entirety. My father and I run the company on behalf of Ruby and Pearl. It means we can stop Xavier from accessing or using any of the documents within it.

"When Xavier discovered this six months ago, he was furious. He broke my jaw. My father wanted to call the police but I was too scared. Instead, Xavier continued buying archives and during a search for a secure location to hide them, he discovered the Marquess House estate owns several storage facilities. Ever since, he's been trying to buy them because he's convinced one of them might house this missing document but he has neither the money nor the business acumen to pull off such a deal. Instead, he's been sending this new girlfriend to gather information, but I don't think they've discovered anything."

There was a pause. Perdita's brain was in overdrive. This was it, she realised, the reason her grandmother had hidden *The Pentagram Manuscript* and left no trace of it in any of the paperwork. Always a contentious document, Mary must have put it into storage with the rest of her Tudor archive, moving it to the secure off-site facility and destroying all record of its existence in her paperwork after learning of its connection to Amber, particularly when she married Xavier. The possibility of this document falling into the hands of Connors would have created even more danger for Mary and, in their turn, Perdita and Piper. At last, they had the truth. Perdita remembered what Alistair had told them, the storage facility in Bath was owned by the son of one of the former members of staff at Marquess House who had begun the business with a small loan from the Marquess House Trust. They would have been loyal to Mary and if she had wanted to create a hidden archive, even concealing it from Alistair, then Perdita did not doubt they would have helped facilitate her request.

"Thank you for sharing this with us, Amber," Piper said, and Perdita pulled herself out of her teeming thoughts, "but why have you come to us?"

"After Randolph was arrested, Lady Pamela contacted me via a mutual acquaintance. We've known each other for a long time through my father but she revealed something…"

Amber hesitated, looking at Perdita and Piper.

"Lady Pamela is family," said Perdita and relief washed over Amber's face.

"You know then? Her true identity?" Amber asked and Piper nodded. "This was why she approached me," Amber continued, "having seen what her son had become, she was concerned Xavier might be his father's son — which, sadly, he is — and she was worried for Ruby and Pearl. I managed to contact her when Xavier was away, it was a relief to hear her side of the story. When I said you would probably refuse me entry, she assured me that wouldn't be the case and gave me her safe word.

"In the past two weeks, Xavier's violence towards me has increased and last night, he threatened to kill me. He knows my father will never give him a decent divorce settlement, so he wants me out of the way in order to marry a rich widow who can continue to fund his obsession. I was terrified and when he roared off in his sports car this morning, I knew it was the best opportunity we'd ever have to escape and so I came to Marquess House."

"What do you want from us?" asked Perdita.

"If you could help us travel to safety, to my parents, then I would be willing to sign the archive over to you in its entirety. It's worth a fortune and there are some fascinating documents in it." Amber dropped her head into her hands; she was emotionally spent.

Perdita and Piper moved as one, sitting either side of Amber, hugging her tightly.

"You, Ruby and Pearl have a home here for as long as you need," said Perdita.

"Really?" gulped Amber through her tears. "Despite being the one who began this nightmare?"

"You didn't do anything wrong," said Piper, "and anyway, that's what the women of this family have done for centuries — worked together to protect themselves from unworthy and violent men."

The door was flung open and Ruby and Pearly erupted into the room followed by Cora and Larry, wet hair flying everywhere.

"Mummy, Mummy, they have a swimming pool full of mermaids and they have ponies and artists and a staircase with a banister you can slide down. Can we stay?"

Perdita looked at Piper, who nodded.

"Welcome home, girls," Perdita said as Ruby and Pearl began to squeal in delight.

CHAPTER FOUR

Perdita was watching television in their shared living space when Piper put her head around the door.

"Have you heard from Kit?" she asked.

"Not since lunchtime, why?"

"I thought they'd be back by now."

Perdita glanced at her watch. It was approaching 7pm and she could not understand why she was exhausted. Before she flopped on to the sofa she had decided it was due to the upheaval accompanying the unexpected arrival of Amber, Ruby and Pearl a few days earlier. Susan had settled them into a large suite of rooms in the Victorian wing and the girls were excited to be living in such a busy house.

While they were used to large homes, from what Perdita had gathered from their non-stop chatter, these were solemn places filled with silent staff and vast empty rooms. The girls were intrigued by the number of people who lived within the walls of Marquess House and they were fascinated with Perdita and Piper — the Big Twins. Ruby had discovered the artists' studios and was making herself known to them all, desperate to help anyone who would let her, while Pearl followed Jenny around like a lost lamb desperate to help "with papers and stuff", which amused Perdita and Piper immensely.

After the first good night's sleep in years, Amber had been more composed, agreeing to answer all Perdita and Piper questions about Xavier's plans but, to Perdita's frustration, Amber's knowledge was sketchy. "He never confided in me," she had explained.

Any information she was able to reveal was passed on to Gary, while Larry had contacted Kit and Callum, warning them to be aware of anything unusual.

Perdita had spoken to Lady Pamela who assured her Amber's distress was genuine.

"I'm sorry for breaking security protocols and giving her my safe word," she had said over the crackling ship-to-shore phone line. "Are you angry with me?"

Perdita and Piper had assured her they were relieved Pamela had sent Amber, Ruby and Pearl to Marquess House.

"We had to check her story though, you do understand, don't you?"

"Of course, my dears, I would expect nothing less of you, Mary would have done the same thing."

Perdita glanced at her watch as Piper curled up on the sofa beside her.

"It's nearly three hundred miles," Perdita said, trying to reassure her sister. "They were going to stop halfway to swap over."

"I tried ringing Cal but his phone went to voicemail," Piper said.

"Perhaps they were in an area with no service."

Perdita watched as Piper ran her hand through her hair, separating one strand, which she began to weave through her fingers, a nervous gesture left over from their teenage years.

"What's really the matter, Pipes?" Perdita asked, her voice gentle.

"You'll think I'm insane," Piper replied, and Perdita was startled to see tears in her sister's green eyes.

"Tell me," Perdita said. "Nothing you can say will ever make me think you're insane."

"Ever since I woke up this morning, I've had this feeling of dread here." Piper placed her hands on her solar plexus.

Perdita reached for her phone. Piper's words had sent a chill through her and her sudden need to speak to Kit, to hear his voice, was visceral. She wanted the reassurance that all was well and they were on their way home but as she hit his name, the phone clicked, then went straight to voicemail.

"Let's give it fifteen minutes," Perdita said, trying to push away the fear that was welling up inside her. "Sarah will be serving dinner. Come on, let's go downstairs. Maybe Alistair or Susan has heard from them."

Piper hesitated and Perdita thought her sister was going to refuse, then she gave a sharp nod and stood, her arms folded across her chest in an attitude of both protection and defence. Glancing again at the time, Perdita surreptitiously hit Kit's number. Voicemail.

It's seven o'clock and Kit had said they wouldn't be back before nine, she told herself, as she and Piper made their way downstairs, there was no reason to worry yet. Kit would call any moment and ask why she sounded worried, more concerned for her than himself. Sliding her phone into her back pocket, she followed Piper towards the dining room.

Every evening, Sarah and her team cooked dinner for whoever wanted to partake. The dining room was laid with round tables or, in the summer, when it was warm enough, tables on the veranda. It was a sociable way to spend the evening, although Perdita and Kit often disappeared to their apartment upstairs to cook. Piper, too, usually preferred the peace of her own space, so she and Callum could catch up on their day.

"Hello girls," said Sarah, as they entered the vast kitchens. "If you like, I can plate up some food for Kit and Callum? They'll be hungry when they get back."

This blast of unconcerned normality shook Perdita from the unexpected fears swamping her. Piper's confession had unnerved her and, while she did not doubt her sister's feeling of foreboding, she did not think it was time to worry. Not yet anyway, she told herself.

"Thanks Sarah," Perdita said, smiling, "that would be great. A stag weekend usually consists of liquid and junk food, so they'll probably be desperate for a decent meal."

The bright lights of the kitchen, the calls of greeting from the people who lived at Marquess House and the smiles from the researchers and artists were an antidote and Perdita noticed that even Piper had relaxed.

"Let's go into the dining room," Perdita said.

She led the way into the large square Victorian room. Sitting near the window were Alistair and Susan.

"Hello, you two," Perdita heard Piper say. "Would it be a terrible interruption if we joined you?"

"My dear, it would be a pleasure."

As Perdita sat beside Alistair, he smiled, "I shall fetch more glasses…" He began placing his own wine glass on the table but Perdita shook her head.

"Not for me, thanks," she said and smothered a smile as she saw Alistair and Susan exchange an excited glance.

"Me neither, thanks," said Piper and Susan raised her eyebrows, looking even more excited.

"Have you heard from the boys?" asked Alistair.

"Not this evening," replied Perdita. "There have been plenty of photos all over social media but I think they must be in a no service area because both their phones keep going to voicemail."

"What?" Alistair's voice was sharp.

Susan placed a placatory hand on his arm. "Kit and Cal are grown men," she reminded her husband. "We weren't expecting them back until at least nine and it's not quite seven-thirty yet."

"In which case," said Alistair, "they should be this side of the Severn Bridge, probably not far from Carmarthen where there would be good phone service."

Without another word, Alistair rang first Kit, then Callum. Perdita glanced over at Piper, whose face was flooded with relief that Alistair was taking charge.

"Curious," he said, placing his phone on the table, an action he usually abhorred. "There's no reason why both their phones would be uncharged as they can use the charge points in Kit's car."

"Do you think something could have happened to them?" asked Piper.

Alistair gave her a penetrating stare. "You clearly think there is something awry," he said. "Let's go to my office."

Susan stacked their plates and delivered them to Sarah, while Perdita, Piper and Alistair wove their way through the tables towards the side door which was a short cut to the back of the house where the offices were situated. After Alistair had seated himself behind his desk and flicked on his vast computer monitor Perdita sank into the chair opposite him, Piper waited by the window. Refusing to allow herself to panic, Perdita kept telling herself all was well.

"I can activate the tracking device in Kit's car from this terminal and we can work from there."

A moment later, Susan slipped into the office and after exchanging a glance with Perdita, joined Piper who was staring into the summer evening, her face rigid with fear. Alistair entered multiple passwords as Perdita watched him, waiting for an exclamation of relief but instead he remained silent, a crease between his eyes as he flipped through several screens. Rounding the desk, Perdita stood beside him, her eyes searching the information as it flashed before her.

"Where are they?" Piper's voice was stretched thin, older than Perdita had ever heard her twin sound. "They're not in Wales, are they?"

"No, my dear, Kit's car appears to be heading towards London."

"What?" gasped Perdita, leaning closer, following Alistair's finger as he traced it across the flashing pages.

"The green light is the tracker," he said. "It's heading towards the South Bank."

"Then let's call Gary," said Piper. "The MI6 building is in Vauxhall. I've no idea where MI1 is based but they can't be too far away."

Perdita had already pulled her phone from her pocket and punched in Gary Ashley's number. It did not ring but clicked through several exchanges, then a man's voice said, "This is Red-652, identify yourself, please."

"Purple-619," replied Perdita, delivering her unique security code.

"Perdita, what's happened?" said a familiar voice.

"Warren?" she gasped. "Where's Gary?"

"On leave. He's returning at midnight. Where are you? Are you safe?"

"Piper and I are at Marquess House. We're fine, but Kit and Callum are missing. They've been away for the weekend and should have been nearly home by now. Both their phones go to voicemail and the tracker on Kit's car shows it travelling towards south London."

"And there's no reason they would have detoured?"

"None whatsoever."

Perdita could hear the faint click of a keyboard.

"Remain at Marquess House, and leave this with me. Someone will update you on the secure line every half an hour." He hesitated, then spoke with a slight edge to his voice. "As Kit Mackensie's wife and, therefore, his next of kin, do I have your permission to activate the tracker in his arm?"

Swallowing hard, trying to control her shaking voice, Perdita said, "Yes, activate the tracker. Piper has authority to activate Cal's — would you like to speak to her?"

"For the sake of protocol, I must. Don't worry, Perds, we'll find them. Now, Piper, please, then keep this phone and the secure line clear."

Handing the phone to Piper who was beside her, Perdita heard her sister issue instructions before hanging up. Alistair and Susan were white-faced.

Suddenly, Perdita's knees began to tremble and the nightmarish image of Kit kneeling on the floor with a gun held to his head swam before her. Piper's hand was a vice-like grip on her arm, manoeuvring her into a chair.

"Breathe," Piper said. "Warren will find them."

Perdita was surprised at how calm Piper sounded. It was as though in a heartbeat, their emotions had changed places; as panic enveloped her, Piper became the voice of reason. Perdita's mind was blank, an hour ago she had been sprawled on her sofa watching television with nothing on her mind other than the secrets they had uncovered in *The Pentagram Manuscript* and the arrival of Amber, Ruby and Pearl. In the blink of an eye, her world had been turned upside down and, once again, the Connors family was at the heart of her devastation.

As the threats on their lives increased, Perdita had contacted MI1 Elite and given authorisation for the tiny, state-of-art trackers to be injected.

"These are being used on top-level members of the government, the royal family and other persons in need of protection," Gary had said. "It's a sophisticated tracker which is invisible to X-rays, scans and any kind of metal detector or airport security…"

"I'm not sure I want you tracking my every move," Piper had interrupted.

"We wouldn't," Gary had replied. "It's a precautionary measure which will only be activated in times of emergency, for example, if you are kidnapped or lost. The tracker will be triggered by the leader of your security detail and will transmit your coordinates, making you easier to locate. The device can only be activated by permission of your nominated next of kin. There will be a list of ten people who will have the authority to allow this to happen. When the crisis is over, the tracker will be deactivated."

Never in her wildest dreams had Perdita ever imagined the tiny device would have to be activated. Behind her, she could hear Piper's low voice explaining the details of the phone conversation with Warren, Susan holding her hand, while Alistair returned to his chair, his face ashen. Tapping into the secure line he called first Meg, then Stuart to ensure their safety.

"We're fine, Dad," Meg said, "but I'll let you know if anything changes."

Moments later, Stuart crashed through the door, his brown eyes the only pinpricks of colour in his alabaster face.

"What's happened?" he demanded. "Is it Kit? They were half an hour behind us."

"He and Cal are missing," said Alistair, bringing Stuart up to date on events.

Perdita felt as though she were underwater. Words did not reach her; all she could hear was the pounding of her heart as the reality of Kit's disappearance wound its way around her mind. His face swam before her, laughing, his blue eyes twinkling. The anger he had shown the first time they had met before his features transformed with a smile when he realised who was knocking on the door. His support throughout her quest to reveal the truth, his love reaching out to her, even when she was unsure whether to trust again and become involved, Kit never wavered in his loyalty. He was in danger again because of her and the torments of her family.

A burst of laughter outside the window in the courtyard brought her back to reality. Alistair's office where they all sat frozen was in a very public place within Marquess House, it was essential to wait somewhere secure, which could serve as a base of operation. As this thought filtered through her numb mind, it galvanised her into action. Standing up, her unexpected movement caused Piper to lurch towards her but Perdita shook back her hair and said in a voice as close to normal as she could muster, "We need to move to The Dairy. It's the source of the secure lines and there's more privacy than this office."

Alistair did not hesitate, he was on his feet, gathering files. "You're right, my dear," he said. "I don't think it's necessary to go to a Code Red yet but The Dairy is the secure hub."

Perdita reached for Piper's arm and together they led the way.

True to his word, half an hour to the minute since her first call, Warren rang on the secure line. By then, they were assembled in the boardroom in The Dairy. Perdita flipped Warren on to the large screen, confident no one but the people in the room could witness his update.

"We've worked out every route Kit and Callum could have taken from Padstow," said Warren, his face appearing to one side of the screen as a map filled the remainder. "His car last tripped an automatic number plate reading on the A30 when he pulled off at the Fivelanes exit heading towards Trevague…"

"That's where they were dropping one of their friends, Tim Buckstow. His parents live on the edge of the village," confirmed Perdita.

"After that, he vanishes," said Warren. "There are no more sightings of the car yet the tracker states that half an hour later it was back on the A30, heading towards the A303."

"Were the number plates changed?" asked Stuart.

"No car matching the description of Kit's was seen, with or without fake plates," replied Warren. "We believe it was loaded into a closed vehicle and transported away."

"And my son?" Alistair's voice was cold.

"His tracker and that of Callum Black show they are situated in Southwark, South London. A team is heading towards the building where they are being held, we are minutes away."

"Southwark?" said Piper in confusion. "Why take them there?"

"City Airport, perhaps," suggested Stuart.

Perdita felt her insides freeze. Before she could speak her phone buzzed. Warren on the line, snapped, "Who is it?"

"Unknown number," replied Perdita.

"Answer it on speakerphone," Warren commanded. "Silence from everyone else, please."

Placing her phone on the boardroom table, Perdita accepted the call.

"Hello?"

"Perdita, my dear, how wonderful to speak to you at last," said an unctuous voice.

"Who is this?" Perdita asked.

"It's your cousin, Xavier," the man replied, amusement rippling through his voice. "By now, you must have realised I have something of yours which is very dear to you."

"Where is Kit?" she demanded.

"Ah, young love," sighed Xavier, and Perdita had to use every ounce of her self-control not to scream at him in her fear for Kit. "Your husband is safe and well, as is Piper's fiancé, Callum. It's within your power to keep them both that way."

"Meaning?"

"Perdita, you and Piper know very well what I want. All you have to do is agree and your husband and his friend will be released. Make my daughters your heirs, then step aside to allow them to inherit."

Alistair and Warren were both shaking their heads.

"Xavier, you can't blackmail me over this; your request is preposterous," Perdita said. "You know the details of the Marquess House estate as well as we do. Let Kit and Callum go, then we can arrange a meeting of our legal teams…"

"A meeting of our legal teams? How quaint," Xavier said. All warmth had left his voice. "Give me what is mine or your husband dies."

"Your daughters are at Marquess House."

"Liar," laughed Xavier, the sound cold and terrifying. "My daughters are at home with my useless wife…"

"Amber is here, too," interrupted Perdita.

"We have his location…" hissed Warren. "Hang up. Now."

"You're…" began Xavier but Perdita had shut the call down. Behind her she could hear Warren issuing instructions.

"What's happening?" said Piper, her voice shrill.

"Xavier is five miles from Marquess House," replied Warren.

"What?" exclaimed Susan, her voice fearful. Perdita turned around in surprise, in all the years of knowing Susan, she had never once seen her crumble, but Xavier's proximity had shaken her. "Is he alone?"

"Unclear," replied Warren, who was continuing to issue instructions to teams behind him and, Perdita presumed, on the ground.

"Stu, fetch Amber, Ruby and Pearl," said Alistair, before he turned to Warren and explained in three terse sentences the events of the weekend.

Perdita called Larry. "Sorry to do this on your night off, Larry, but we have a situation," she said. "We need to go to Code Red, immediately. I'm with Piper, Susan and Alistair in The Dairy. Stuart has gone to fetch Amber and the girls. MI1 have traced Xavier to a location five miles away. Kit and Callum are being held hostage."

"Remain in The Dairy, we're setting up a secure perimeter. My team will ensure the safety of all Marquess House personnel. You are to remain in The Dairy. Repeat, remain in your secure location."

Perdita turned back to the screen and gasped. In the space of her phone call, Warren had split the screen and was showing the camera from the Hunter division who were working their way towards the location where Kit and Callum were being held.

"A helicopter will be patrolling the air space above Marquess House in the next two minutes," said Warren, "and there is a SWAT team ten minutes away. The kidnap was a distraction. Xavier is trying to finish what his father began; he wants the manor."

But Perdita's eyes had been drawn back to the screen and the blurred images from the helmet camera. Piper was beside her. They gripped each other tightly as the team of five men walked on silent feet along a shadowy but expensively carpeted corridor.

Piper let out a cry, which she stifled. Perdita felt tears streaming down her face. Beside her Susan and Alistair were clutching each other. Stuart had not returned. Perdita was relieved; she did not want Ruby or Pearl to witness this and she hoped he had taken them somewhere safe.

"We're going in," whispered the team leader and Perdita braced herself. *He's alive, he's alive, he's alive…* she repeated over and over again in her head. *He's alive, Kit's alive, Cal's alive…*

The door shattered and the five men roared into the apartment. "Clear!" shouted each member of the team in turn as they ran into the different rooms. "Clear! Clear!" Then: "Master bedroom, quick…"

"No," whimpered Perdita, unaware she had spoken until Susan and Alistair enveloped them.

Perdita gasped as the camera moved to the wide glass balcony where two inert figures lay face down, their hands and feet zip-tied together.

"Cal!" screamed Piper, and Perdita felt her sister trembling.

The black-clad MI1 officers lifted Kit and Callum, carrying them inside and laying them on the floor.

"Breathing but unconscious," said the team lead. "Medi back up, in here, now!"

"They're alive," gasped Perdita but as Kit was rolled over, she felt the world tilt; his lips were blue and his eyes half open to reveal slits of white. "What have they done to them?"

As the medical team raced into the apartment, Warren stopped the feed. "I'll keep you updated," he said. "Remember, they're alive and they're in the best hands. We need to worry about you and Xavier. I'm going to liaise with Larry Eve, but will you please remain in The Dairy."

The screen went blank.

Perdita turned to Piper. "They're alive," she said. "We must hang on to that; they're alive." Despite her words, the image of Kit's face danced before her eyes and she slumped into the nearest chair.

Above them, they heard the roar of the helicopter. One of the security personnel entered the room.

"Larry and his team are in place around Marquess House. We've put Amber and the girls in the small boardroom."

"And Amber?" asked Alistair. "Has she heard from Xavier?"

"Nothing. She's given me her phone so we can monitor any calls he might try to make."

"What does he want?" asked Susan. "He knows he has no claim on the house."

"Xavier and Randolph are penniless," said Perdita, her voice cold, "part of this is about money. The rest is about what he sees as his right to own this house through a superior claim."

"What superior claim?" asked Alistair, astonished.

"Many years ago, Xavier and Randolph discovered Mary was working on *The Pentagram Manuscript* and it linked Amber to this house. He believes her claim, combined with the blood link through his daughters, gives him a priority."

For the next fifteen minutes, Perdita explained the remainder of their discoveries. As she spoke, it calmed and distracted her, helping her to push away dark thoughts of what might be happening to Kit and Callum, the fear MI1 had been too late, the possibility of them dying. Dying because of her and Piper, and Xavier's insane obsession. Alistair and Susan listened in silence as she spoke, their eyes wide with surprise.

There was a buzz and Alistair leapt forward, accepting the call. Warren's face filled the screen. "We have Xavier Connors," he said. "Larry Eve apprehended him in the gardens of Marquess House. Xavier was carrying a firearm and was threatening to kill his wife, children, Perdita and Piper. He's been arrested and removed. The area is secure."

"Kit and Callum?" asked Perdita, reaching for Piper's hand.

Warren frowned, then pressed a button and the screen switched back to the apartment.

"Observations are normal," came a female voice, then the blurred image cleared revealing Kit and Callum wrapped in foil blankets, leaning against the bed, bleary eyed but alive.

"Kit!" screamed Perdita as Piper shouted, "Cal!"

Susan was sobbing and even Alistair had tears in his eyes.

The team leader removed his helmet cam and handed it to Kit and Callum. They heard him muttering and the two men gave a vague wave.

"Sorry love," said Kit, his voice slurred. "We're going to be a bit late home."

It was the early hours of the morning when Perdita, Kit, Piper and Callum were finally reunited. After being checked at a private MI1 facility and cleared as medically fit, Gary Ashley had arranged for cars to bring them home.

"They'd been drugged but it was a standard sleeping shot," he assured Perdita and Piper. "We've checked their bloods and there will be no long-term physical effects. Kit also wanted you to know he's no longer scared of heights."

"What?" Perdita asked, bemused.

"He and Cal were held on a glass balcony," replied Gary. "They were placed face down, so they appeared to be suspended in mid-air. Kit said by the time the drug had kicked in, he was no longer scared of the height. He was more scared about never seeing you again, Perdita."

At this point, Perdita excused herself, needing to be alone.

The clock showed 5am when the two black SUVs roared on to the gravel drive of Marquess House. Perdita and Piper led the charge as Kit and Callum were helped out. Piper threw herself at Callum, while Perdita pulled Kit into a fierce hug.

"I'm sorry," she said.

"Don't be ridiculous," Kit replied, kissing her.

"We love you so much," she said.

"We?" Kit replied, confused, and from her pocket Perdita pulled a slim white plastic tube, a positive blue cross showing in the little window.

"We love you," she whispered again and as realisation dawned on Kit's face, he picked her up and spun her around, tears streaming down both their faces.

"I love you both, too."

EPILOGUE

Laughter filled the air, followed by the gurgle of a baby.

"Shhh," giggled Perdita, leaning over to stroke her daughter's cheek where she lay in her father's arms, "you're being christened, this is the solemn part."

The vicar sprinkled water over the child's forehead. "Penelope Louisa Mackensie, I christen you in the name of…"

Perdita stared around at the packed chapel. Kit held their daughter, his blue eyes fierce with pride. Beside him stood the godparents: Sarah Eve, Piper, Callum and Stuart, while the pews were packed with friends and Mackensie relatives. Ruby and Pearl with Amber. Susan, Alistair, Meg, her husband Pablo and their son, Joseph, who was eager to watch his cousin have water poured all over her head.

As the ancient ceremony finished, Perdita stepped back to let Kit pass, carrying their daughter. A happy child with her mother's unusual eyes and hair as curly as her father.

"This way, Pipes," she murmured to her sister, easing her down the step from the font at the back of the beautiful Marquess House chapel.

When the restoration had been completed the previous year, Piper and Callum had married in a small but exquisite ceremony, after which, Piper announced what Perdita and Kit already knew, that she was pregnant too. A week away from giving birth, Piper's slender frame was vast. Perdita and Kit had said they would wait a few more weeks to hold the christening but Piper had insisted.

"Let Penny have her moment," Piper had insisted. "She shouldn't have a younger cousin upstaging her on such an important day."

With the service over, Perdita took her daughter from Kit and mingled with the crowd as it made its way back to the terrace for a champagne reception.

Everywhere she looked there were smiling faces. Stuart poured Briony Llewellyn a glass of champagne, the summer sunshine sparkling on her diamond engagement ring. After his romance with Hannah White had ended in disaster, Stuart and Briony had rekindled their childhood friendship to discover it had become something more. Briony would be the next bride walking up the aisle at the Marquess House chapel.

Megan and Pablo dodged out of the way as Ruby and Pearl dragged Joseph past, chattering at full volume as they explained they were off to explore the knot garden below the terrace. Larry and Cora walked the length of the balcony side by side, and Perdita felt they were patrolling, even though this was a social event.

Mark began to march towards Perdita but Stephanie held him back and Perdita wondered what email would be awaiting pertaining to a new discovery Mark had made when she returned to her desk on Monday.

"These people are all yours," Perdita whispered to her daughter, Penelope. "Every single one of them loves you, but no one loves you as much as me, Daddy, Auntie Piper and Uncle Callum." She turned towards the graveyard beside the chapel. "Over there are your grandparents and great-grandparents. It is because of Granny Mary and all the strong women before her that we have our beautiful home and these wonderful people in our lives."

It was a year since Xavier Connors had been arrested and sectioned under the Mental Health Act. Such was the level of his psychopathy, Perdita and Piper had been assured he was unlikely to ever be a free man again. Randolph Connors, meanwhile, had suffered a huge stroke in the private prison where he was being held. Unable to walk or speak, any threat he might once have posed was gone.

Perdita watched the happy crowd, peace and contentment in her heart. Her eyes flickered towards the lake but no arm broke the surface today.

"Here you are," said Kit, handing Perdita a brimming champagne flute. Piper and Callum followed, Piper rubbing her back and wincing.

Kit gave Piper a flute of fizzy water.

"One more week," she laughed. "One more week."

Callum topped up his own glass.

"A toast," said Kit. "To my beautiful wife and daughter, Perdita and Penelope. To my wonderful sister-in-law, Piper, my best friend, Callum, and my new niece, whom I hope to meet soon."

They clinked glasses.

"My turn," said Perdita, smiling up at Kit. "To my wonderful husband, my daughter, my sister and my brother-in-law but, most importantly, to Marquess House." She turned to face the sun-drenched building with its central tower and winding Tudor chimneys, its Victorian glasshouse and the magical grotto. In the distance was the lake, Llyn Cel, with its island full of ruins and secrets. Leaning back into Kit's embrace as he slipped his arm around her waist, she saw Callum take Piper's hand.

"And, to all the women who have paved the way," continued Perdita, "may you know your secrets are safe with us and may you forever rest in peace."

A NOTE TO THE READER

Dear Reader,

Thank you for taking the time to read *The Jane Seymour Conspiracy*. I hope you enjoyed joining Perdita as she revealed more historical mysteries hidden within Marquess House.

This is fiction but, once again, I have tried to use verifiable historical fact where possible.

Jane Seymour was a character I first wrote about in the original version of *The Catherine Howard Conspiracy* but the scenes were deleted; however, I kept them on file. When I first began researching this story, it was not intended to be a Marquess House book. It was not even meant to be about Jane Seymour. It was supposed to be about Elizabeth Boleyn, mother of Anne, Mary and George but, the more I researched, the more Jane Seymour pushed herself forward. When Perdita, Piper, Kit and Callum began pointing out discrepancies in history, I knew we were back to Marquess House.

The lives of Henry VIII's first three wives were woven together in a way that is rarely discussed. Both Anne and Jane were ladies-in-waiting to Katherine of Aragon. Jane was lady-in-waiting to Anne Boleyn. Jane and Anne were second cousins. All these women were in thrall to the king who held their lives in his hands. Each relationship may have begun with love but this did not last. In this story, I have tried to show how frightening it must have been, as a woman, to know you were often only a glance away from being forced into the king's bed.

Jane is an interesting figure to study. Often passed over for the more dramatic queens of Henry VIII, to me her depiction as the demure, shy wife has never tallied with the description of her behaviour – flirting with the king, accepting gifts, preparing her marriage chest while Anne was in the Tower of London, attempting to persuade Henry to return to Catholicism and trying to bring his two daughters, Mary and Elizabeth, back into Henry's lives. These are the actions of a woman who knows how to survive and has a strong streak of determination, not an inexperienced wallflower.

Discovering there were so many gaps in Jane's real story was a gift from history, enabling me to spin a conspiracy theory within it. I have kept to the facts for the vital parts of Jane's life: including her timed returns to court, the moment the king first noticed her and the fear of being told you are about to marry a man who is murdering his wife in order to honour his proposal. Her marriage to Sir Francis Bryan and the birth of two children is not substantiated anywhere except in my imagination.

For more information about Jane Seymour, I recommend: Elizabeth Norton, *Jane Seymour: Henry VIII's True Love*. For more information on the other women who populated the court and appear in support of all my female leads, I recommend: Kathy Lynn Emerson, *A Who's Who of Tudor Women*.

The Pilgrimage of Grace, the unexpected death of Henry Fitzroy two months after Anne Boleyn and the five unnamed people in the Tower of London execution records are all real. For more details on Henry Fitzroy, I recommend: Beverley A. Murphy, *Bastard Prince: Henry VIII's Lost Son*.

The information about Thomas and Henry Boleyn's grave markers is real as is the document I mentioned that is in the Ashmolean Museum in Oxford which references a Thomas Boleyn, although some historians suggest this was another

Thomas Boleyn and not Anne's missing brother. It is a very grey area. For more details, you can compare: Lauren Mackay, *Among The Wolves at Court, The Untold Story of Thomas and George Boleyn;* Alison Weir, *Mary Boleyn 'The Great and Infamous Whore'* and Elizabeth Norton, *The Boleyn Women.*

William Blount, 4th Baron Mountjoy was Master of the Royal Mint from 1509 to 1534. As a courtier he was never out of favour with Henry VIII, although I have exaggerated his closeness to Bessie Blount.

Elizabeth Barton, the Holy Maid of Kent, was an extraordinary woman, alas though, she was manipulated by powerful men who had their own agendas. Sadly, it was Elizabeth who paid the price. For more information: Alan Neame, *The Holy Maid of Kent: The Life of Elizabeth Barton 1506– 1534* and Elizabeth Norton, *The Lives of Tudor Women.*

The painting of Elizabeth Barton by Paul Delaroche does not exist. However, there is one entitled 'The Young Martyr', so I decided to improvise. All the other paintings listed in this scene are real.

The treatise – *Jane Anger: Her Protection for Woman* is a real book, published during the reign of Elizabeth I. As I state in the book, no one has been identified as the real Jane Anger. I appropriated it for my version of Jane Seymour.

The story of Anne Boleyn's fall is well-known and for a while this story was called *The Anne Boleyn Conspiracy*, but I realised the story needed to continue beyond her death, which was when Jane Seymour stepped centre stage.

The best book on Anne Boleyn is: Eric Ives, *The Life and Death of Anne Boleyn.* For information on her family, I recommend: Elizabeth Norton, *The Boleyn Women,* and Lauren Mackay, *Among the Wolves of Court: The Untold Story of Thomas and George Boleyn.*

Thank you to everyone who has helped with *The Jane Seymour Conspiracy*, particularly Sara Keane, my wonderful agent, and Amy, Caoimhe, Richard, Natalie, Matilda and Helen at Sapere Books. It has been a huge and thoroughly enjoyable task. Once again, any mistakes are mine. Please forgive me.

If you have enjoyed the novel and would like to leave a review on **Amazon** or **Goodreads**, I would be so grateful as reviews are very important to authors. I love hearing from readers, so if you would like to contact me, you can through **Twitter**. You can also follow my blog on **my website**.

Thanks again for reading *The Jane Seymour Conspiracy*.

Alexandra Walsh

www.alexandrawalsh.com

Sapere Books is an exciting new publisher of brilliant fiction and popular history.

To find out more about our latest releases and our monthly bargain books visit our website:
saperebooks.com

Made in the USA
Columbia, SC
11 December 2022

73465564R00220